PENGUIN CLASSICS

THE HOUSE OF THE DEAD

FYODOR MIKHAILOVICH DOSTOYEVSKY was born in Moscow in 1821, the second of a physician's seven children. When he left his private boarding school in Moscow he studied from 1838 to 1843 at the Military Engineering College in St Petersburg, graduating with officer's rank. His first story to be published, 'Poor Folk' (1846), was a great success. In 1849 he was arrested and sentenced to death for participating in the 'Petrashevsky circle'; he was reprieved at the last moment but sentenced to penal servitude, and until 1854 he lived in a convict prison at Omsk, Siberia. Out of this experience he wrote *The House of the Dead* (1860). In 1861 he began the review *Vremya* (*Time*) with his brother; in 1862 and 1863 he went abroad, where he strengthened his anti-European outlook, met Mlle Suslova, who was the model for many of his heroines, and gave way to his passion for gambling. In the following years he fell deeply in debt, but in 1867 he married Anna Grigoryevna Snitkina (his second wife), who helped to rescue him from his financial morass. They lived abroad for four years, then in 1873 he was invited to edit *Grazhdanin* (*The Citizen*), to which he contributed his *Diary of a Writer*. From 1876 the latter was issued separately and had a great circulation. In 1880 he delivered his famous address at the unveiling of Pushkin's memorial in Moscow; he died six months later in 1881. Most of his important works were written after 1864: *Notes from Underground* (1864), *Crime and Punishment* (1865–6), *The Gambler* (1866), *The Idiot* (1869), *The Devils* (1871) and *The Brothers Karamazov* (1880).

DAVID MCDUFF was born in 1945 and was educated at the University of Edinburgh. His publications comprise a large number of translations of foreign verse and prose, including poems by Joseph Brodsky and Tomas Venclova, as well as contemporary Scandinavian work; *Selected Poems* of Osip Mandelstam; *Complete Poems* of Edith Södergran; and *No I'm Not Afraid* by Irina Ratushinskaya. His first book of verse, *Words in Nature*, appeared in 1972. He has translated a number of nineteenth-century Russian prose works for the Penguin Classic series. These include Dostoyevsky's *The Brothers*

THE HOUSE OF THE DEAD

✳

FYODOR DOSTOYEVSKY

TRANSLATED WITH AN INTRODUCTION
BY DAVID MCDUFF

PENGUIN BOOKS

PENGUIN BOOKS

Published by the Penguin Group
Penguin Books Ltd, 27 Wrights Lane, London W8 5TZ, England
Penguin Books USA Inc., 375 Hudson Street, New York, New York 10014, USA
Penguin Books Australia Ltd, Ringwood, Victoria, Australia
Penguin Books Canada Ltd, 10 Alcorn Avenue, Toronto, Ontario, Canada M4V 3B2
Penguin Books (NZ) Ltd, 182–190 Wairau Road, Auckland 10, New Zealand

Penguin Books Ltd, Registered Offices: Harmondsworth, Middlesex, England

This annotated edition first published 1985
10

Copyright © David McDuff, 1985
All rights reserved

Printed in England by Clays Ltd, St Ives plc
Filmset in 9/11 Monophoto Times

CONTENTS

Notes

TRANSLATOR'S INTRODUCTION

On 23 January 1850, Dostoyevsky entered the prison fortress at Omsk, Western Siberia, to begin a four-year term of penal servitude for his part in the Petrashevist conspiracy. In 1854, some ten months after his release from prison, he wrote to his younger brother Andrey: '... I consider those four years as a time during which I was buried alive and shut up in a coffin. Just how horrible that time was I have not the strength to tell you ... it was an indescribable, unending agony, because each hour, each minute weighed upon my soul like a stone.'

In the prison Dostoyevsky's sufferings were compounded by the fact that, for at least the first year of his sentence, he found himself almost totally isolated. He was a 'nobleman', while nearly all the other convicts seemed to belong to the peasantry and the artisan classes. The full horror of his experience of prison is given vivid utterance in the first letter he wrote after his release. It was addressed to his brother Mikhail:

'I had got to know something of the convict population back in Tobolsk; here in Omsk I was to live for four years in close proximity to it. These men were coarse, irritable and malicious. Their hatred of the nobility knew no limits, and so they received us noblemen with hostility and a gleeful schadenfreude. If they had had half a chance they would have devoured us. Consider for yourself what sort of protection we had against them, when we had to live, drink, eat and sleep with them for several years, and when to complain was impossible, given the myriad variety of the insults and affronts to which we were exposed. "You're noblemen, iron noses, you nosed us to death. When you were a gentleman you used to make our lives a misery, now you're worse off than the lowest trash among us, you're our brother now": such was the refrain they repeated to me in chorus for four years on end. A hundred and fifty enemies never wearied of persecuting us; this was their amusement, their entertainment, their occupation, and the only thing that saved us from this misery was our equanimity, our moral superiority, which they could not help but comprehend and which they respected as a sign that we were not subservient to their will. They always acknowledged our superiority to them. They had no inkling of what our crime might have been. We ourselves never said anything about this, and so we had to put up with all the persecution and vindictiveness which they brought to their dealings with the nobility, and which were the very breath of life for them. Our living conditions were terrible. A military prison is much tougher than a civilian one. Throughout those four years I lived nowhere but within the confines of the prison, leaving it only in order to go to work. The work we had to do was physically arduous (although not always, however), and it would happen that I would grow exhausted in the rain, the wet, the sleet or, during winter, in the intolerable cold. I once spent four hours on special emergency work when the mercury in the thermometer had frozen and the temperature must have been forty below. I got frost-bite in one of my legs. We lived all of a heap, crowded together in one barrack. Imagine, if you will, this dilapidated old wooden building which had long ago been scheduled for demolition, and which was now quite unfit for use. In summer the airlessness inside was intolerable, likewise the cold in winter. All the floors had rotted through. The floor was covered in nigh on two inches of muck; it was easy to slip and fall. In winter the small windows were covered in hoar-frost, making it almost impossible to read for much of the day. The ice on the windowpanes was also nearly two inches thick. There were leaks in the roof, and a constant draught prevailed. We were packed in like herrings in a barrel. Only six logs were used to heat the stove; there was no warmth (the ice in the room barely melted at all), but terrible fumes – and this went on all winter. The convicts washed their linen in the barracks, and the whole of the small room would be fairly awash with water. There was no space to turn round in. From dusk to dawn no one could go outside to relieve himself, as the barracks were locked up; instead, a tub was placed in the passage, and the stink was intolerable. All the convicts stank like pigs, and they would say that they could not help behaving like pigs, that "man is only human". We slept on a bare plank bed, and were permitted one pillow. We had to cover ourselves with our short sheepskin coats, our legs sticking out all night uncovered. All night we shivered. There were fleas, lice and cockroaches by the bushel. In winter we wore our short coats, which were often of the most miserable quality and which hardly kept us warm at all, and our short-legged boots – for walking about in the snow and the sub-zero temperatures, if you please. For food we were given bread and a cabbage soup which contained a quarter of a pound of beef per man; but the beef was ready diced, and I never saw any of it. On holidays there was kasha with practically no vegetable oil in it at all. On fast days there were cabbage leaves and water and hardly anything else. I suffered terrible stomach trouble and was ill several times. You can judge for yourself whether it would have been possible to live without money; if I had had no money, I would certainly have died and no one, not one of those convicts, could have stood such a life. But each man worked at some trade or other, sold his merchandise and made a copeck or two. I lived on tea and the occasional piece of beef which I bought for myself, and this saved me. It was also forbidden to smoke, for men might have suffocated in such airless conditions. Smoking was done on the sly. I was often a patient in the hospital. Because my nerves were upset I suffered fits of epilepsy, but these were rare. I also have rheumatism in my legs. Apart from this, I feel quite well. Add to all these delights the almost total unavailability of books – what you got, you got on the sly – the continual animosity and quarrelling around you, the cursing, the shouting, the noise, the hubbub, always being under guard, never alone, and this for four years without a break, you will, I think, forgive me for saying that life was terrible.'

Dostoyevsky's involvement with Petrashevism has been seen in varying lights by different biographers and commentators: by some as an expression of youthful idealism, by others as a misconceived and self-destructive flirtation with radical politics. Some have even gone so far as to assume that Dostoyevsky was innocent of the charge of conspiracy that was brought against him. Yet his most important contribution to the Petrashevists' activities was by all accounts not to the relatively innocuous Petrashevist circle proper, with its eccentric, Fourierist leader and its endless debates on questions of Fourierist theory, but to one of its satellite groupings, the mysterious Palm-Durov circle. One of the charges on which Dostoyevsky was convicted was 'the attempt, along with others, to write works against the government and circulate them by means of a home lithograph'; although the attempt failed, it gave rise to another, much more serious conspiracy that included the setting-up of a secret printing press and a call for the violent overthrow of the monarchy. This conspiracy, which never came to the attention of the authorities, was organized by the revolutionary terrorist Nikolay Speshnyov under cover of the Palm-Durov circle of the group, and although there is no direct evidence to show that Dostoyevsky was one of the conspirators, it is probable that he knew about the plot and sympathized with its aims. His assertion in the *Diary of a Writer* for 1873 that 'I could never have become a *Nechayev*, but a *Nechayevist*, this I do not vouch; it is possible, I too could have become one ... in the days of my youth' should not be taken lightly. The nature of his relation to Speshnyov is shrouded in mystery. Yet one thing seems certain: at some point shortly before his arrest, Dostoyevsky had, at least temporarily, accepted many of Speshnyov's ideas, including the need for a violent overthrow of the ruling order. Many years later, Speshnyov was to emerge in fictional form as the hero of Dostoyevsky's novel *Devils*, in the person of Nikolay Vsevolodovich Stavrogin.

Before the catastrophe of his arrest and imprisonment, Dostoyevsky had been a writer of novels and short stories that took their subject-matter primarily from the dreams of individuals oppressed by a hostile social environment. He had concentrated on the depiction of unhealthy, morbid states of mind, fusing these with a vision of another, brighter but unattainable sphere. His heroes had been sovereigns in a world of fantasy, and he had shown how, as they soared in airy realms they lost touch with the earth and their personalities became increasingly unreal. In *The Landlady*, Ordynov's love for Katerina is a grotesque compound of uncontrolled emotion, delirium and physical reality – what begins as an ennobling impulse ends as delusion and sickness. The dreamer of *White Nights* attains his 'moment of bliss' in the love he feels for Nastenka, only to sink back once more within the dim, faded walls of his room at the conclusion of the tale. Above all, such dreaming is seen as an absurd arrogance – the ridiculous, eccentric dreamer imagines himself to be a mighty conqueror whose power is limitless. The political dreamer, too, must have occupied Dostoyevsky's thoughts in the months that preceded his arrest. 'It would truly be very difficult to explain many of his oddities,' he wrote in his deposition on the subject of Mikhail Petrashevsky. 'Often you would meet him in the street and ask him where he was going and on what errand, and he would give you some odd reply, describe some strange plan which he was just about to put into action; you would not know what to think, either about the plan or about Petrashevsky himself. He would sometimes make such a terrible fuss about some business which was really of no significance whatsoever that you would have thought his entire estate was at stake. On another occasion he might be hurrying off somewhere for half an hour to clinch some little matter, when in actual fact it would have taken two years to clinch the little matter in question. He was forever on the move, always busy with something ...' It is the dreamer's self-absorption, his pride, his vanity, his inability to take account of others and of practical reality that constitute his weakness. Later on in the deposition, Dostoyevsky describes the attitude of many of the members of the circle during the heated political debates that took place in it: '... personal vanity, too, comes to the aid of the speaker and eggs him on, as does his desire to please each and all; sometimes, for the sake of show, it makes the orator agree with an idea he does not share at all – he agrees with it in the hope that in return some sincerely cherished idea of his own will not be assailed. Finally, there is the self-regard that excites a man and makes him demand the floor repeatedly, so that he awaits impatiently the next such evening, when he will be able to refute his antagonists. In other words, for many (for very many, in my sincere opinion), these evenings, these speeches, these debates are about as serious an occupation as are cards, chess, and so forth, which also undeniably divert a man and which play in the same manner on the same whims and passions. I think that very many deceived and confused themselves at this game in Petrashevsky's house, mistaking the game for something that was serious.'

But while Petrashevsky and the 'antagonists' were one thing, Speshnyov and his 'activists' were quite another. Dr S. D. Yanovsky, who treated Dostoyevsky for epilepsy, wrote that between the end of 1848 and the time of his arrest some three months later, his patient 'grew rather melancholy, more irritable, more ready to take offence, to quarrel over the slightest matter, and very frequently complained of dizziness'. Yanovsky tried to set Dostoyevsky's mind at rest by telling him that there was no organic cause for these symptoms, and by suggesting that the depressed mood would probably soon disappear. To which Dostoyevsky retorted: 'No, it won't, it will torment me for a long time to come. I've borrowed money from Speshnyov (he named a sum of five hundred rubles) and now I am with *him* and am *his* . . . I'll never be able to repay a sum like that, and he'll never accept a repayment – that's the kind of man he is.' And several times Dostoyevsky repeated the sentence: 'Do you realize that from now on I have my own Mephistopheles?'

Quite clearly, Speshnyov was associated in Dostoyevsky's mind with a force of evil. Is it too much to suppose that this force was Speshnyov's political activism, with its concomitant atheism, terrorism and communism? Was the episode concerning the loan merely the trigger which set off an extended moral and spiritual crisis in the writer, one that was to last for several years, almost until the time of his release from prison? Whatever may have been the case, there can be little doubt that the rude and violent events that accompanied his arrest, trial, sentencing and imprisonment were not experienced by him simply as an awakening from dream to harsh reality, but also as a visitation from God – a God on whom he had come perilously close to turning his back – for having sinned against the Russian people and himself. After ten months of agonized waiting in the Peter and Paul Fortress, after being sentenced to death and being given a last-minute reprieve on the place of execution itself, he was sent for a term in hell.

Dostoyevsky began to plan his new novel, whose full title, literally translated, is *Notes from the House of the Dead*, while he was still in prison. Although for the most part he was deprived of the possibility of writing, during one of his hospital visits a certain Dr Troitsky allowed him to make notes. These jottings, together with remembered material added subsequently, form the *Siberian Note-book*, a series of 522 entries consisting of isolated phrases, catch-words and songs overheard in the convicts' day-to-day life. Each of these items was associated with a given situation, character or story. More than 200 of them were utilized by Dostoyevsky when he came to write his novel. Thus, for example, the scene in which the convicts first meet Isay Fomich (I, 9) is constructed out of one short phrase and two phrase-sequences (entries 91, 92 and 202), while the slanging-match between the two convicts (I, 2) is con-structed on the basis of one entry (90). The directness and un-doubted authenticity of all this material give *The House of the Dead* a freshness and spontaneity which are immediately evident, and which constitute an entirely new element in Dostoyevsky's writing of this period.

The writer's term in prison was followed by five years of com-pulsory military service in the Seventh Line Battalion in the West Siberian garrison town of Semipalatinsk. Although he began to write again during this period, completing the tale *Uncle's Dream* and the comic novel *The Village of Stepanchikovo* in preparation for his return to a literary career at the end of his deportation, it was not until 1859 that he began serious work on this book. It was conceived as a novel in two parts and was first published in serial form during 1860 in the newspaper *Russian World*. It met with a huge critical and popular success.

In order to understand the significance of the style and structure of the book, it is necessary to bear in mind that it was the result of a terrible mental, spiritual and physical ordeal. Once again we should recall the characterization of his imprisonment given by Dostoyevsky to his brother Andrey: '. . . I consider those four years as a time during which I was buried alive and shut up in a coffin'. During the years in Semipalatinsk, Dostoyevsky occasionally alluded to the notes he was making about his convict experiences. In 1856 he wrote to A. N. Maykov: 'At times when I have nothing else to do I write down some of my memories of penal servitude, the more interesting ones, that is. However, there is little that is purely personal in them.' In October 1859 he wrote to his brother Mikhail: 'These *Notes from the House of the Dead* have now assumed a

complete and definite plan in my head. This will be a short book
of some six or seven printed sheets. My personality will disappear
from view. These are the notes of an unknown; but I can vouch for
their interest.' The intensity of the suffering undergone by the writer
seems to have been such that he was unable to approach its recollection in personal terms. In order to write his memories down, he
had to construct a 'novel', with a fictitious narrator-hero, the
'unknown' referred to in the letter: the former convict Aleksandr
Petrovich Goryanchikov.

What can we decipher of Goryanchikov's personality? In many
respects, his character as outlined in the novel's introduction bears
many similarities to earlier creations of Dostoyevsky's fantasy: he
is pale, withdrawn, unsociable, with a reputation for eccentric
behaviour, and is even suspected of lunacy. His chief aim in life
seems to be 'to hide as far away as possible from the rest of the
world'. In his past lie the murder of his wife out of jealousy and the
nightmare years of his imprisonment and deportation. At nights a
light is to be seen burning in his windows. 'What was he doing
sitting up until dawn? Could he be writing? And if so, what?' The
publisher of the book gives an account of his discovery of Goryanchikov's scribblings: 'But here there was one fat, voluminous
exercise book, filled with microscopic handwriting and unfinished,
perhaps abandoned and forgotten by the author himself. This was
a description, albeit an incoherent one, of the ten years of penal
servitude which Aleksandr Petrovich had undergone. In places this
description was interrupted by another narrative, some strange,
terrible reminiscences scribbled down in irregular, convulsive handwriting, as if following some compulsion. I read these fragments
through several times and was almost persuaded they had been
written in a state of madness. But the notes on penal servitude –
"Scenes from the House of the Dead" as he calls them somewhere
in his manuscript – seemed to me not without interest.'

Much has been made of the documentary authenticity of the
novel, of its closeness to the actual conditions in the prison at
Omsk, as described by Dostoyevsky in the letter to his brother
Mikhail and as corroborated by independent accounts such as that
of Szymon Tokarzewski (*Siedem lat katorgi*, Warsaw, 1907). Of

course, it is undeniable that much of it is essentially autobio-graphical reminiscence, and that Dostoyevsky was relying on the documentary impact of the work as an important element in secur-ing large sales for it, sales which it most certainly achieved. As Konstantin Mochulsky has observed, the book has 'an unusually adept structure. The description of prison life and of the convicts' temperaments, the robbers' histories, the characteristics of indivi-dual criminals, the reflections regarding the psychology of crime, a picture of conditions in the gaol, journalism, philosophy and folklore – all this complex material is distributed freely, almost without order. Meanwhile all the details are calculated and the particulars subordinated to a general plan. The principle of com-position in the *Notes* is not static, but *dynamic*.' In the first part, the picture of the prison is built up very rapidly, yet the cyclical, rhythmic movement of its life is maintained, with chronological descriptions of the visit to the bath-house, the feast of Christmas, the stage show. In the second part, the chronological principle is abandoned, and the events of the subsequent years are sum-marized, although the overall impression is still one of intense vividness and authenticity.

Yet it would be a mistake to view the novel simply as a work of documentary realism. It is important to realize that the book also describes an inner crisis – a spiritual death and an awakening. Dostoyevsky is correct when he predicts that in the book his personality 'will disappear from view'. The tormented, eccentric Goryanchikov is all that the book contains by way of a character-ized central figure. Even this fictional 'I' suffers from an inner contradiction: while Goryanchikov is supposed to have been deported and imprisoned for murdering his wife, a remark Akim Akimych makes in the second chapter of Part One implies that Goryanchikov is a political prisoner, like Dostoyevsky himself. The point about the novel, however, is that it charts the reawakening of a man *without a personality*: it is the personalities of the convicts, men who create their own freedom even in captivity out of their own violence, vulgarity and cruel will to life, that dominate the work. Only gradually, under their influence, does the 'I' of the narrative, locked away in speechless suffering, 'shut up in a coffin', begin to respond to their vital stimulus. The letter to Mikhail quoted at the beginning of this introduction contains an important passage which seems to contradict the extreme negativity of Dostoyevsky's initial remarks about his fellow-convicts. It is a passage that has a profound relevance to the novel: 'Even in penal servitude, among thieves and bandits, in the course of four years I finally succeeded in discovering human beings. Can you believe it: among them there are deep, strong, magnificent characters, and how cheering it was to find the gold under the coarse surface. And not one, not two, but several. Some it is impossible not to respect, others are quite simply magnificent. I taught a young Circassian (who had been sent to prison for banditry) to read and write Russian. With what gratitude he enveloped me! Another convict wept when he said goodbye to me. I had given him some money – it was not much. But his gratitude was boundless. In the meanwhile, however, my own character deteriorated; I was off-hand, impatient with them. They respected the mental and spiritual condition I was in, and bore it all without a murmur. Apropos: How many popular types and characters I have brought with me out of penal servitude! I grew accustomed to them, and for this reason I think I know them pretty well. How many stories of vagrants and bandits and all that black, wretched existence. I have enough for whole volumes. What a wonderful people. My time has not been wasted. Even if I have not come to know Russia, I have come to know the Russian people better than many know it, perhaps.'

Like Goryanchikov, Rodion Romanovich Raskolnikov, the hero of *Crime and Punishment*, is convicted of a civil murder and is deported to Siberia, where he languishes in a penal colony. Like Goryanchikov, and like Dostoyevsky himself, he suffers the venom and malice of the other convicts because he is a 'nobleman', a 'gentleman'. But Raskolnikov is exposed to yet another form of torment:

> 'You're a gentleman,' they used to say to him. 'You shouldn't have gone murdering people with a hatchet; that's no occupation for a gentleman.'

During the second week in Lent his turn came to go to Mass with the other convicts in his barracks. He went to church and prayed with the others. He did not know how it happened, but one day a fight occurred: they fell upon him all together in a frenzy.

'You're an atheist!' they shouted. 'You don't believe in God! You ought to be killed!'*

We are told that even when Raskolnikov had been contemplating suicide, 'he had perhaps been dimly aware of the great lie in himself and his convictions'. Dostoyevsky continues: 'He did not understand that that vague feeling could be the precursor of the complete break in his future life, of his future resurrection, his new view of life'.†

There seems little doubt that for Dostoyevsky, the 'great lie', the crime against himself and against God that had lain at the root of his flirtation with radical politics and his ensnarement by his 'Mephistopheles', Speshnyov, was equivalent to, even worse than the crime of hatchet-murder. The crime was also an offence against the Russian people. The novel is to some extent an act of atonement. Not only does it contain the quasi-expressionistic portrait of Gazin, the psychopathic child murderer; in the figure of the Schismatic, the old man from the settlements at Starodubye, Dostoyevsky draws the first sketch in a line of portraits that includes such transfigured emanations of the Russian national and spiritual consciousness as Bishop Tikhon (*Devils*) and the elder Zosima (*Brothers Karamazov*).

At the end of the book, Goryanchikov describes his emotions as his fetters are removed:

The fetters fell to the ground. I picked them up. I wanted to hold them in my hand, to have a last look at them. Already I could hardly believe they had ever been on my legs at all.

'Well, God go with you!' said the convicts in voices that were curt, gruff, but somehow also pleased.

* Dostoyevsky, *Crime and Punishment*, tr. David Magarshack, Penguin Books, 1951, p. 554.
† ibid., p. 553.

Yes, God go with you! Freedom, a new life, resurrection from the dead ... What a glorious moment!

The 'glorious moment' is the one at which, with freedom, the divine gift of personality is restored to the hero. Without freedom, there can be no personality. This individual 'resurrection from the dead' is the beginning of a long road that leads from the 'new life' mentioned here, through the 'gradual regeneration' referred to in the final paragraph of *Crime and Punishment*, and the purgatory of *Devils*, to the confession of faith in a universal resurrection of mankind that concludes *Brothers Karamazov*.

PART ONE

✽

INTRODUCTION

In the remote regions of Siberia, amidst the steppes, mountains and impassable forests, one sometimes comes across little, plainly built wooden towns of one or often two thousand inhabitants, with two churches – one in the town itself, and the other in the cemetery outside – towns that are more like the good-sized villages of the Moscow district than they are like towns. They are generally very well provided with district police inspectors, assessors and all the other minor-ranking officials. In general, a government post in Siberia is an uncommonly snug one, in spite of the cold. People live simple lives, and are not prone to take a liberal view of things; their customs are old and fixed, and sanctioned by time. The officials, who it is fair to say fulfil the role of a Siberian aristocracy, are either native Siberians or migrants from Russia, mostly from St Petersburg or Moscow, attracted by high rates of pay, double travel allowances and alluring hopes for the future. Those of them who are adept at solving life's problems nearly always remain in Siberia and gladly put down roots there. Subsequently they bring forth sweet and abundant fruit. But others, of a frivolous turn of mind and not adept at solving life's problems, soon grow tired of Siberia and ask themselves wearily why they ever came here in the first place. Impatiently they put in their allotted term of service, three years, and as soon as it is over they instantly petition to be transferred and go home, abusing Siberia and pouring ridicule on it. They are wrong: it is possible to be supremely happy in Siberia, not only from a government service point of view, but from many others as well. The climate is an excellent one; there are a great many extremely rich and hospitable merchants; there are a great many exceedingly well-to-do native Siberians. The young ladies bloom like roses and are moral to the very limits of virtue. The wild game flies about the streets and comes to meet the hunter of its own accord. An inordinately large amount of champagne is drunk. The caviare is marvellous. In some localities the crops give a fifteen-fold yield ... Generally speaking, a promised land. All one needs is to know how to make use of it. In Siberia they know how to make use of it.

It was in one of these lively, self-satisfied little towns, one with the most endearing inhabitants, whose memory will remain imprinted on my heart forever, that I met Aleksandr Petrovich Goryanchikov, a settler[1] who had been a nobleman and landowner born in Russia, but who had subsequently been made a convict deportee of the second category for the murder of his wife and who, when the ten-year spell of hard labour accorded him by the law had been up, had gone to spend the rest of his days peacefully in the little town of K.[2] He was officially registered as an inhabitant of a rural district that lay near the town, but he lived in the town itself, since it was there that he was able to earn at least some kind of a living by giving lessons to children. In Siberian towns one often meets teachers who are convict settlers; they are not regarded as inferior. They are mostly teachers of French, a language so indispensable in life, and one of which without them no one in those remote regions of Siberia would have the slightest notion. I first met Aleksandr Petrovich in the house of Ivan Ivanych Gvozdikov, a worthy and hospitable official of the old kind, with five daughters of various ages who promised well for the future. Aleksandr Petrovich gave them lessons four times a week, taking thirty copecks for each lesson. His appearance interested me. He was an extremely pale and thin man, not yet old, about thirty-five, small and frail. He always dressed very neatly, in the European manner. If you were talking to him he would look at you very fixedly and attentively, listening to your every word with austere politeness, as if he were thinking it over, as if by your question you had set him some problem or were trying to elicit some secret from him, and he would eventually reply clearly and briefly, but weighing each word of his reply so carefully that you would suddenly feel embarrassed and be glad when the interview was at an end. I asked Ivan Ivanych about him at the time and learned that Goryanchikov led a life of irreproachable morality and that otherwise Ivan Ivanych would not have invited him to give lessons to his daughters; but that he was terribly unsociable and hid from everyone, was extremely learned, read a great deal, but spoke very little, and that in general it was rather hard to have any kind of conversation with him. That some people held he was a positive madman, though they did not really consider this an important defect, and that many of the town's respected citizens were ready to be kind to Aleksandr Petrovich in all sorts of ways, that he could even be useful, could write up petitions and the like. It was supposed that he must have respectable relatives in Russia, people who were perhaps not the least in the land, but it was known that from the time of his deportation onwards he had cut off all communication with them – in a word, he was his own worst enemy. What was more, everyone knew his story, knew that he had murdered his wife in the first year of his marriage, had murdered her out of jealousy and had given himself up to the authorities (a circumstance which greatly lightened his sentence). Such crimes are always regarded as misfortunes, and are looked upon with compassion. But in spite of all this, the strange man had stubbornly kept himself apart from everyone, appearing in public only to give lessons.

At first I did not pay him any particular attention, but gradually, for some reason unknown to me, he began to engage my interest. There was something mysterious about him. Not the slightest possibility existed of having a conversation with him. Of course, he always answered my questions, and even made it appear that he considered it his primary duty to do so; but in the wake of his answers I somehow found it hard to question him any further; what was more, after such conversations his face always wore a look of suffering and weary exhaustion. I remember walking back with him from Ivan Ivanych's one fine summer evening. I suddenly had the idea of asking him in for a minute to have a cigarette. I cannot describe the look of terror that seized his face; he lost all his presence of mind, began to mutter some incoherent words and suddenly, giving me a look of angry irritation, took to his heels in the opposite direction. I was quite taken by surprise. From that time onwards whenever he met me he would look at me with a kind of fear. But I was not to be put off; something drew me to him, and a month later, for no reason in particular, I called on Goryanchikov myself. This was no doubt a stupid and inconsiderate thing to do.

He had his lodgings on the furthest outskirts of the town in the home of an old woman of the petty bourgeoisie who had a consumptive daughter. This daughter had an illegitimate child, a pretty, merry little girl of about ten. Aleksandr Petrovich was sitting with her teaching her to read at the moment I went in. When he saw me he became so covered in confusion that one might have thought I had caught him in the enactment of some crime. He completely lost his head with embarrassment, leapt up from his chair and stared at me with wide-open eyes. Finally we sat down; he followed my every look intently, as though in each he suspected some special hidden meaning. I guessed that he was distrustful to the point of insanity. He looked at me with hatred, almost as good as putting to me the straight question: 'When are you going to go away?' I started to talk to him about our town and about the news that was current; he kept his silence, smiling angrily; it turned out that not only did he not know the most ordinary news of the town, news that was familiar to everyone, but he was not even interested in knowing it. Then I began to talk about our part of the country and its needs; he heard me in silence and looked me in the eyes so strangely that in the end I felt sorry I had ever started our conversation. However, I almost succeeded in winning him over with some new books and magazines; they were with me ready and to hand, had only just arrived by post, and I offered them to him with their pages still uncut. He cast a hungry look at them, but immediately changed his mind and declined the offer, making the excuse that he was too busy to read them. At last I took my leave of him, and as I went out I felt as though some intolerable weight had been lifted from my heart. I felt ashamed of myself: it now seemed to me an extremely stupid thing to have gone bothering a man who had made it his chief aim in life to hide as far away as possible from the rest of the world. But the deed was done. I remember that I noticed hardly any books in his room and that consequently it could not be true what people said about him, that he read a great deal. However, as I passed by his windows on a couple of occasions very late at night, I noticed a light in them. What was he doing sitting up until dawn? Could he be writing? And if so, what?

Circumstances led me away from our town for some three

months. Returning home after the onset of winter, I learned that Aleksandr Petrovich had died that autumn, died in solitude without even once calling a doctor to his side. He had already been almost forgotten in the town. His lodgings were empty. I at once made the acquaintance of his landlady, with the intention of finding out from her what it was her lodger had occupied his time with, and whether he had in fact been writing something. In exchange for a twenty-copeck piece she brought me a whole basketful of papers the dead man had left behind. The old woman confessed that she had already thrown away two of the exercise books. She was a sullen and taciturn old woman, from whom it was hard to elicit much sense. She could not tell me anything that was particularly new about her lodger. According to her, he had hardly ever done a thing, and for months on end had not opened a book or taken a pen in his hand; but he would walk up and down the room all night long, and he had sometimes talked to himself; he had been very fond of her little granddaughter, Katya, and had been very kind to her, especially after he had discovered that her name was Katya; on St Catherine's day he had always gone to have a requiem mass sung for someone. He had not been able to abide visitors; had left the house only in order to give lessons; had even looked on her, the old woman, with suspicion when once a week she had come to tidy up his room a little, and had hardly said a single word to her in all the three years he had lived there. I asked Katya if she remembered her teacher. She looked at me in silence, turned to the wall and began to cry. So even this man had been able to make someone love him.

I took his papers away and spent a whole day looking them over. Three quarters of these papers were trivial, insignificant scraps or contained handwriting exercises done by his pupils. But here there was one fairly fat, voluminous exercise book, filled with microscopic handwriting and unfinished, perhaps abandoned and forgotten by the author himself. This was a description, albeit an incoherent one, of the ten years of penal servitude which Aleksandr Petrovich had undergone. In places this description was interrupted by another narrative, some strange, terrible reminiscences scribbled down in irregular, convulsive handwriting, as if following some compulsion. I read these fragments through several times and was almost persuaded they had been written in a state of madness. But the notes on penal servitude – 'Scenes from the House of the Dead' as he calls them somewhere in his manuscript – seemed to me not without interest. This utterly new world, hitherto unknown, the strangeness of some of the facts, some of the particular observations on this lost tribe of men fascinated me, and I read some of what he had written about it with curiosity. It is, of course, possible that I am mistaken. As a sample I have excerpted two or three chapters to begin with; let the public be the judge ...

1

THE HOUSE OF THE DEAD

Our prison stood at the edge of the fortress, right next to the ramparts. You would sometimes take a look at God's world through the cracks in the fence: surely there must be something to be seen? – and all you would see would be a corner of sky and the high earthen ramparts, overgrown with weeds, and on the ramparts the sentries pacing up and down, day and night; and then you would think that whole years would go by, and you would still come to look through the cracks in the fence and would see the same ramparts, the same sentries and the same little corner of sky, not the sky that stood above the prison, but another, distant and free. Imagine a large courtyard, two hundred yards long and a hundred and fifty yards wide, completely enclosed all round by a high stockade in the form of an irregular hexagon, that is a fence of high posts (pales), driven vertically deep into the earth, wedged closely against one another in ribs, strengthened by cross-planks and sharpened on top: this was the outer enclosure of the prison. In one of the sides of the enclosure a sturdily constructed gate was set; this was always kept closed and was guarded by sentries at every hour of the day and night; it was opened on demand, in order to let men out to work. Beyond the gate was the bright world of freedom where people lived like everyone else. But to those on this side of the enclosure that world seemed like some unattainable fairyland. Here was our own world, unlike anything else; here were our own laws, our own dress, our own manners and customs, here was the house of the living dead, a life like none other upon earth, and people who were special, set apart. It is this special corner that I am setting out to describe.

As you enter the enclosure, you see several buildings inside it. On both sides of a broad inner courtyard stretch two long, single-storeyed buildings with wooden frames. These are the barracks. Here the convicts live, quartered according to the categories they belong to. Then, in the interior of the enclosure, there is another similar wooden-framed building: this is the kitchen, divided into two artels; further on there is another structure where cellars, granaries and storage sheds of various kinds are housed under one roof. The middle of the courtyard is empty and consists of a fairly large level parade ground. Here the convicts are formed into line, head-counts and roll-calls take place in the morning, at noon and in the evening, and sometimes at several other times of the day as well, depending on how suspicious the guards are and how quickly they can count. All around, between the buildings and the fence, a fairly large space is left. Here, along the rear of the buildings, some of the prisoners, the most unsociable and gloomy ones, like to walk in their non-working hours, concealed from the eyes of everyone, and think their own private thoughts. Meeting them in the course of these walks, I used to like to look into their sullen, branded faces and try to guess what they were thinking about. There was one convict whose favourite occupation in his free time was counting the pales of the fence. Of these there were about one and a half thousand, and he knew each of them individually, had counted each one. Each pale signified a day for him; every day he marked off one of them and in this way, from the number of pales that still remained to be counted, he could see how many days he still had to serve in the prison before his term of hard labour was up. He was sincerely glad whenever he finished a side of the hexagon. He had many years still to wait; but in prison there was time in which to learn patience. I once saw a convict who had been in prison for twenty years and was at last going out into freedom saying farewell to his companions. There were those who could remember when he had first entered the prison, young, carefree, never having given a thought either to his crime or to the punishment he had received. He was leaving prison a grey-haired old man, with a face that was sad and morose. He went the rounds of all six of our barracks in silence. As he entered each one, he prayed to the icons and then bowed to his companions deeply, from the waist, asking them to remember him with kindness. I also remember how a convict who had been a well-to-do Siberian peasant was summoned to the gate one evening. Six months earlier he had been given the news that his former wife had remarried, and he had been violently affected with grief. Now she herself had come to the prison, had asked to see him and had given him alms. They spoke together for a couple of minutes, both shed a few tears, and then took leave of one another forever. I saw his face when he returned to the barracks ... Yes, in this place you could learn patience.

When it got dark we were all taken back to the barracks, where we were locked up for the whole night. I always found it hard to come into our barrack from outside. It was a long, low unventilated room, dimly lit by tallow candles, with a heavy suffocating smell. I do not understand now how I managed to live in it for ten years. I had three boards of the plank bed to sleep on: that was all the space I had that was mine. On this plank bed some thirty men slept in our room alone. In winter the door was locked early; there were some four hours to wait before everyone was asleep. And until then there were noise, uproar, laughter, swearing, the sound of chains, soot and fumes, shaven heads, branded faces, ragged clothes, all that is accursed and dishonoured ... yes, man has great endurance! Man is a creature that can get used to anything, and I think that is the best definition of him.

In our prison there were about two hundred and fifty men – this figure was more or less constant. Some arrived, others finished their sentences and left, others died. And what a variety of men there was! I think that each province, each zone of Russia had its representative here. There were non-Russians as well, there were even some convicts from among the mountain tribesmen of the Caucasus. They were all divided according to the degree of their crime and consequently according to the number of years their sentence carried. I suppose there was no crime that did not have its representative here. The basic constituent of the prison population was civilian-category convict deportees (*ssyl'nokatorzhnyye*, or sil'no*katorzhnyye* – 'heavily punished convicts' – as the men themselves mispronounced it in all innocence). These were criminals who had been completely deprived of all the rights of their status, pieces cut from society, with faces that had been branded in eternal witness to their expulsion from it. They were sentenced to hard labour for terms of from eight to twelve years and were then sent to live as settlers here and there throughout the regions of

Siberia. There were also criminals of the military category; as is the custom in Russian military convict battalions, they were not deprived of the rights of their status. They were given short sentences; on the completion of these they were sent back where they had come from, to serve as soldiers in the Siberian line battalions. Many of them returned to prison almost immediately, after committing a second, serious offence, and this time their sentence would not be short, but one of twenty years. This category was known as 'habitual'. But the 'habituals' were still not completely deprived of all the rights of their status. Finally, there was one more category, a fairly numerous one, made up of the most serious criminals, soldiers for the most part. It was called the 'special category'. Criminals were sent here from all over Russia. They considered themselves prisoners for life and did not know the length of their sentences. By law they had to perform two or three times the normal number of prison duties. They were being kept in the prison pending the opening in Siberia of projects involving the heaviest penal labour. 'You're doing time, but we're in for life,' they used to say to the other inmates. I have heard that this category has since been abolished. What is more, the civilian category in our prison has also been abolished, and one general military convict battalion has been instituted. Of course, the prison authorities were also changed when these innovations were brought about. So I am describing bygone days, things that belong long ago in the past ...

This all happened long ago; it all seems to me like a dream now. I remember my arrival in the prison. It was in the evening, in December. It was already getting dark; men were returning from work; they were getting ready for roll-call. At length a mustachioed NCO opened the door for me into this strange house in which I was to spend so many years, to endure sensations of which I could not have had even an approximate conception, had I not experienced them in actuality. For example, I could never have conceived how terrible and agonizing it would be not once, not even for one minute of all the ten years of my imprisonment, to be alone. At work to be constantly under guard, in the barracks to be with two hundred other convicts and not once, never once to be alone! None the less, I had to get used to this, too, whether I liked it or not.

Here there were men who had committed unpremeditated murder and those for whom it was a profession; here too there were brigands and brigand chiefs. There were petty thieves and vagrants who had been convicted of burglary with breaking and entering. There were also those about whom it was difficult to decide why they had been sent here. All the same, each of them had his own story to tell, as vague and crushing as the hangover that follows a bout of heavy drinking. In general, they did not talk much about the past, did not like telling their stories, and evidently tried not to think about what lay behind them. I even knew murderers among them who were so cheerful, so completely lacking in concern about what they had done, that one could safely bet their consciences never bothered them. But there were also gloomy ones, who practically never said a word. In general it was rare for anyone to tell the story of his life, and curiosity was unfashionable, somehow not the done thing, not the custom. Perhaps on rare occasions someone might start talking out of idleness, and someone else would listen to him in gloom and indifference. No one could say anything that was a surprise here. 'We know how to read and write,' they would often say with a kind of strange satisfaction. I remember that once a brigand who was drunk (it was sometimes possible to get drunk in prison) began to describe how he had knifed to death a five-year-old boy, first enticing him with a toy, then taking him to an empty shed somewhere and murdering him. The whole barrack of convicts, who up till now had been laughing at his jokes, cried out as one man, and the brigand was compelled to be silent; the men had cried out not from indignation, but because you were *not allowed* to talk *about this kind of thing*, because it was *not done* to talk *about this kind of thing*. I will observe in passing that these men really did 'know how to read and write', and this not in any figurative sense but in a quite literal one. It is probable that over half of them were literate. In what other place where ordinary Russians are gathered together in large numbers would you be able to find a group of two hundred and fifty men, half of whom could read and write? I have since heard that someone has deduced from similar evidence that literacy is harmful to the common people. This is a mistake: causes of quite another kind are involved here, although it cannot be denied that literacy does develop the common people's self-sufficiency. But this is surely not a fault. Each category of convicts was distinguished by the clothes it wore: the jackets of some were half dark brown and half grey, as were their trousers – one leg grey, the other dark brown. Once, at work, a girl selling kalatches[3] came up to the convicts, looked at me for a long time and then suddenly burst out laughing. 'Well, isn't that the limit,' she cried. 'There wasn't enough grey cloth to go round, and there wasn't enough of the black stuff neither.' There were also those whose jackets were all of grey cloth, with only the sleeves made of dark brown The convicts' heads were also shaven in different ways: some had half their heads shaven lengthwise along their skulls, while others had them shaven crosswise.

You could discern at first glance one single glaring characteristic that was common to all this strange family: even the strongest, most original personalities who dominated the others without trying, even they attempted to fit in with the general tone of the prison. Generally speaking, all these men – with the exception of a few indefatigably cheerful souls whose good humour made them the object of general scorn – were sullen, curious, terribly vain, boastful, quick to take offence and preoccupied in the highest degree with good form. The ability not to be surprised by anything was considered the greatest virtue. They were all madly obsessed with the question of outward behaviour. But quite often the most arrogant manner would be replaced with the swiftness of lightning by the most craven one. There were a few genuinely strong individuals; they were straightforward and did not give themselves airs. But it was strange: some of these truly strong characters were vain to the utmost degree, almost to the point of insanity. In general vanity and outward appearance were what mattered first and foremost. The majority of these men were depraved and hopelessly corrupt. The scandals and gossip never ceased: this was a hell, a dark night of the soul. But no one dared to rebel against the endogenous and accepted rules of the prison; everyone submitted to them. There were violently unusual characters who submitted with difficulty and effort, but submit they did, nevertheless. To the prison came men who had gone too far, had overstepped the limit when they had been free, so that in the end it was as if their crimes had not been committed by them personally, as if they had committed them without knowing why, as if in some fever or daze; often out of vanity, raised in them to an extraordinary degree. But in our prison they were soon brought to heel, in spite of the fact that some of them, before they came here, had been the terror of whole villages and towns. Looking around him, the new convict soon realized that he had come to the wrong place: that there was no one here whom he could surprise, and imperceptibly he grew resigned and fitted in with the general tone. This general tone outwardly consisted of a certain special, personal dignity with which almost every inmate of the prison was imbued. As if the status of convict, of one on whom sentence has been passed, was a kind of rank, and an honourable one at that. Not a trace of shame or repentance! Yet there was, too, a kind of outward resignation, as it were an official one, a kind of calm reasoning: 'We're lost men,' they would say. 'We didn't know how to live our lives in freedom, so now we have to walk the green street⁴ and stand in line to be counted.' – 'We wouldn't listen to our fathers and mothers, so now we must listen to the skin of the drum instead.' – 'We didn't want to sew gold thread, so now we must break stones instead.' All this was said frequently, both in the form of moral exhortation and in the form of everyday proverbs and sayings, but never seriously. It was all just words. Hardly one of these men inwardly admitted his own lawlessness. If anyone who was not a convict tried to reproach one of them for his crime, berating him (although it is not in the Russian spirit to reproach a criminal), there would be no end to the oaths that would follow. And what masters of the oath they all were! They swore with finesse, with artistic skill. They had made a science of swearing; they tried to gain the upper hand not so much by means of the offensive word as they did through the offensive meaning, spirit, idea – and this in the most refined and venomous manner. Their constant quarrels developed this science among them even further. All these men worked under the threat of the stick, and were consequently idle and depraved: if they had not been depraved before they came to the prison, they became so here. They had all been gathered together here against their wills; they were all strangers to one another.

'The devil's worn out three pairs of shoes in order to get us all
into one bunch,' they would say of themselves; and so it was that
scandals, intrigues, old-womanish slander, envy, quarrelling and
malice were always to the fore in this burdensome, desperate life.
No old woman would have been capable of being so old-womanish
as some of these murderers were. I repeat, there were strong men
among them, characters who all their lives had been used to charging at obstacles and giving orders, who were hardened and fearless.
These men were automatically respected; they, for their part,
although very jealous of their reputations, tried in general not to
be a burden to others, avoided getting involved in empty exchanges
of curses, comported themselves with unusual dignity, were reasonable and nearly always obeyed the authorities – not out of any
principle of obedience, not out of a consciousness of duty, but as
if they had some kind of a contract, and recognized its mutual
advantages. None the less, these men were treated with caution. I
remember how one of these convicts, a man of fearless and determined character, well-known to the authorities for his brutal
tendencies, was once summoned to be flogged for some misdemeanour. It was a summer day, work was over. The field-officer,
who was in immediate and direct control of the prison, came in
person to the guardhouse, which was right by our gate, in order to
witness the punishment. This Major was a kind of fatal presence
for the convicts; he could reduce them to a state of trembling. He
was severe to the point of insanity, 'pounced on folk', as the
convicts said. Most of all they feared his penetrating, lynx-like
stare, from which nothing could be concealed. He could somehow
see without looking. When he came into the prison he already knew
what was happening at its far end. The prisoners called him 'Eight-
Eyes'. His system was a mistaken one. By his acts of vicious fury
he only increased the bitterness of men who were already bitter, and
had there not been stationed above him a superintendent, a man
of nobility and reason, who sometimes moderated his wild excesses,
he would have caused much trouble by his method of administration. I cannot understand why he did not come to a bad end; he
passed into retirement well and in good spirits, although he did
have to face court proceedings.

The prisoner turned pale when his name was called. Usually he lay down under the birch in silent determination, endured his punishment without a word and got to his feet again afterwards as fresh as ever, looking coolly and philosophically at the misfortune that had overtaken him. He was none the less always treated with caution. But on this occasion he considered himself for some reason to be in the right. He turned pale, and in secret from the guards managed to shove a sharp English cobblers' knife up his sleeve. Knives, and all other sharp instruments, were strictly forbidden in the prison. Searches were frequent, unexpected and no joking matter, punishments were severe; but since it is difficult to find something on a thief's person when he is particularly determined to hide it, and since knives and sharp instruments were a continuous necessity in the prison, they never disappeared entirely. Even if they were confiscated, new ones immediately took their place. The entire prison rushed to the fence and looked through the cracks with hearts that beat violently. Everyone knew that this time Petrov would refuse to lie down and be flogged, and that the Major was done for. But at the most decisive moment our Major got into his droshky and drove away, entrusting the execution of the punishment to another officer. 'God has spared him!' the convicts said afterwards. As far as Petrov was concerned, he endured his punishment with the greatest of calm. His anger evaporated with the Major's departure. A convict is obedient and submissive to a certain degree; but there is a limit beyond which one should not go. Incidentally, there is no phenomenon more curious than these strange outbursts of impatience and obstinacy. Often a man will suffer in patience for several years, resign himself, endure the most savage punishments, and then suddenly erupt over some trifle, some piece of nonsense, almost over nothing at all. In one view, he may be termed insane; and is indeed considered so by many.

I have already said that for a period of several years I saw among these people not the slightest trace of repentance, not one sign that their crime weighed heavily on their conscience, and that the majority of them consider themselves to be completely in the right. This is a fact. Of course, vanity, bad examples, foolhardiness and false shame are the causes of much of it. On the other hand, who

can say that he has fathomed the depths of these lost hearts and
has read in them that which is hidden from the whole world? It must
surely have been possible over so many years to have noticed
something, to have caught at least some feature of these hearts that
bore witness to an inner anguish, to suffering. But this was absent,
quite definitely absent. Yet, it seems that crime cannot be compre-
hended from points of view that are already given, and that its
philosophy is rather more difficult than is commonly supposed. Of
course prisons and the system of forced labour do not reform the
criminal; they only punish him and secure society against further
encroachments on its tranquillity. In the criminal, prison and the
most intense penal labour serve only to develop hatred, a thirst for
forbidden pleasures and a terrible flippancy. But I am firmly convinced that the famous system of solitary confinement[5] achieves
only a spurious, deceptive, external goal. It sucks the vital sap from
a man, enervates his soul, weakens it, intimidates it and then
presents the withered mummy, the semi-lunatic as a model of
reform and repentance. Of course the criminal, who has rebelled
against society, hates it and nearly always considers himself to be
in the right and it to be in the wrong. What is more, he has already
suffered its punishment, and he nearly always considers that this
has cleansed him and settled his account. It may be concluded from
this point of view that right is indeed on the side of the criminal.
But, leaving aside all partial positions, everyone will agree that
there are crimes which, ever since the world began, always and
everywhere, under all legal systems, have been indisputably considered as crimes, and will be considered so for as long as man is
man. Only in prison have I heard stories of the most terrible, the
most unnatural actions, the most monstrous slayings, told with the
most irrepressible, the most childishly merry laughter. One man
who had murdered his father stays particularly in my memory. He
was of noble origin, had worked in government service and had
been something of a prodigal son to his sixty-year-old father. His
behaviour had been thoroughly dissipated, he had become embroiled in debt. His father had tried to exert a restraining influence
on him, had tried to make him see reason; but the father had a
house and a farm, it was suspected he had money, and – his son

murdered him in order to get his hands on the inheritance. The crime was not discovered until a month later. The murderer had himself informed the police that his father had disappeared. He spent the whole of this month in the utmost debauchery. Finally, in his absence, the police discovered the body. In the farmyard, along the whole of its length, was a ditch for the draining of sewage, covered with planks. The body was found in this ditch. It was dressed and neatly arranged, the grey-haired head had been cut off and laid against the torso; under the head the murderer had placed a pillow. He had made no confession; had been stripped of his nobility and government service rank, and had been sentenced to twenty years' deportation and penal servitude. All the time I lived alongside him he was in the most excellent and cheerful frame of mind. He was an unbalanced, flippant man, unreasoning in the extreme, though by no means stupid. I never observed any particular signs of cruelty in him. The prisoners despised him, not for his crime, of which no mention was ever made, but for his silliness, for not knowing how to behave. Sometimes, in conversation, he would mention his father. Once, when he was talking to me about the healthy constitution that was hereditary in his family, he added: '*My parent* never complained of any illness to the end of his days.' Such brutal lack of feeling is, of course, outrageous. It is a unique phenomenon; here there is some constitutional defect, some physical and moral abnormality which science has not yet been able to explain, not simply a question of crime. It goes without saying that at first I did not believe he had committed this crime. But men from his town, who must have known all the details of his story, told me about the whole case. The facts were so clear that it was impossible not to believe them.

The convicts once heard him crying out at night in his sleep: 'Hold him, hold him! His head, cut off his head, his head!'

Nearly all the convicts talked and raved in their sleep at night. Oaths, underworld slang, knives and axes figured most prominently in their ravings. 'We're beaten men,' this used to say, 'we've had the insides beaten out of us, that's why we cry out at night.'

The forced public labour that took place in the fortress was not an occupation but an obligation: a convict completed his assignment or worked fixed hours and then went back to the prison. The work was looked upon with hatred. Without his own, private task, to which he was devoted with all his mind and all his care, a man could not live in prison. And how indeed could all those men, who were intelligent, had lived intensely and wanted to live, had been brought forcibly together here in one herd, forcibly uprooted from society and normal life, how could they have led a normal and regular life here of their own free will? Idleness alone would have developed in them criminal tendencies of which they had hitherto had no conception. Without work and without lawful, normal possessions a man cannot live, he grows depraved, turns into an animal. And for this reason every man in the prison had, as a consequence of a natural demand and an instinct for self-preservation, his own craft and occupation. The long summer days were almost entirely filled with prison labour; in the short nights there was hardly enough time to sleep properly. But in winter, according to regulations, the convicts had to be locked into the prison as soon as it started to get dark. What were they to do during the long, tedious hours of the winter evenings? And so in spite of an official ban, almost every barrack was transformed into an enormous workshop. Work itself was not forbidden; but it was strictly forbidden to possess any implements in the prison, and without these work was impossible. But men worked on the sly, and it seemed that in some cases the authorities did not bother to inquire too closely. Many of the convicts arrived in the prison knowing no trade at all, but they learned from others and subsequently left prison as good craftsmen. Here there were bootmakers, shoe-makers, tailors, carpenters, locksmiths, engravers and gilders. There was one Jew, Isay Bumshteyn, a jeweller who was also a moneylender. They all worked away and earned a few copecks. Orders for work were obtained from the town. Money is freedom in the form of coins, and so for a man who has been completely deprived of freedom it is ten times as dear. He is already half consoled by the mere sound of it jingling in his pocket, even though he may not be able to spend it. But money can be spent at any time and in any place, all the more so since forbidden fruit tastes twice as sweet. And it was even possible to get vodka in the prison. Pipes were most strictly forbidden, but all the men smoked them. Money and tobacco saved them from scurvy and other diseases. And work saved them from crime: without work the convicts would have eaten one another like spiders in a glass jar. In spite of this, both work and money were forbidden. Searches were quite often made at night, all forbidden items were confiscated, and no matter how carefully money was hidden, it was none the less sometimes found by the searchers. This is partly why it was not saved up, but soon spent on drink; and this is how there came to be vodka in the prison. After each search the offenders, in addition to being deprived of all their money and equipment, were usually severely flogged or beaten. But after each search the deficiencies were immediately made good, new equipment was brought into the prison and everything continued as before. The authorities were aware of this and the convicts did not complain about their punishment, even though this life they led resembled that of settlers on the slopes of Mount Vesuvius.

Those who did not have a skill made money by other methods. Some of these were quite original. Some men, for example, earned money by doing nothing but buying and selling secondhand goods, and sometimes personal effects were sold which it would never occur to anyone outside the walls of the prison to consider as articles for sale and purchase, or even to consider as articles at all. But the life of penal servitude was one of extreme poverty, and the convicts were men of great commercial resourcefulness. Every last scrap of cloth was prized and was used for some purpose or other. Because of the general poverty, money in the prison also possessed a value that was quite different from the value it had outside. Long and elaborate toil was remunerated with pennies. Some men practised successfully as moneylenders. Convicts who were too exhausted to work or had run out of money took their last possessions to the moneylender and received from him a few copper coins at an exorbitant rate of interest. If they did not redeem them in time, these possessions would be sold without pity or delay; moneylending was such a flourishing activity that even items of prison property which were subject to inspection were accepted as pledges, things like prison clothing, boots, shoes and the like – things that were necessary to every prisoner at every moment. But pledges like these involved another turn of events, one that was not really surprising: the man who had pledged the goods and received money for them would immediately, without further ado, go to the duty officer who was in immediate control of the prison, and report to him that public property had been pledged; the goods would be immediately confiscated back from the moneylender, without the higher authorities being informed of the matter. It is a curious fact that there were never any quarrels on this account: the moneylender would silently and sullenly hand over whatever he had to and would even make it appear as though he had been expecting something like this to happen all day. Perhaps he could not help admitting to himself that had he been in the borrower's place he would have done the same thing. And so if he sometimes did a bit of cursing after it was all over, it was without any malice, and merely to appease his conscience.

In general the convicts did a fearful amount of stealing from one another. They nearly all had their own locked boxes, in which they kept items of prison issue. This was permitted; but the boxes were no safeguard against theft. I think it may be imagined what skilful thieves we had among us. One prisoner, a man who was sincerely devoted to me (I say this without any exaggeration), stole my Bible, the only book we were permitted to have in the prison; he confessed to me the same day, not because he had repented for what he had done, but because he felt sorry for me when he saw me spend such a long time looking for it. There were men who peddled vodka and quickly grew rich. I will give a more detailed account of this trade elsewhere; it was rather remarkable. In the prison there were many convicts who had been sentenced for smuggling, and so it was not surprising that vodka was brought in, inspections and guards notwithstanding. Incidentally, smuggling is by its very nature something of a special crime. Can one believe, for example, that money and gain are of only secondary importance to a smuggler? And yet precisely this is the case. The smuggler works passionately, with a sense of vocation. He is something of a poet. He risks everything, faces terrible dangers, employs cunning, inventiveness, gets himself out of scrapes; sometimes he even acts according to some kind of inspiration. This passion is as strong as the passion for cards. In the prison I knew one convict who was outwardly of colossal proportions, but so gentle, quiet and resigned that it was impossible to imagine how he could ever have ended up in prison. He was so lacking in malice, so easy to get along with that during his entire stay in prison he never once quarrelled with anyone. But he came from the western frontier, had been sent to prison for smuggling and had of course not been able to restrain himself, but started to smuggle vodka into the prison. How many times he had been flogged for this, and how he feared the birch! And the trade in illicit vodka brought him only the most meagre returns. The only person who made any profit from the sale was the entrepreneur. The curious fellow loved his art for its own sake. He was as tearful as an old woman, and how many times after he had been flogged did he repent and swear never to smuggle again. He would sometimes master himself courageously for a whole month, but in the end he was always unable to hold out any longer ... It was thanks to characters such as him that there was no shortage of vodka in the prison.

Finally, there was one source of income which, although it did not make the convicts rich, was none the less constant and beneficial. This was alms. The upper class of our society has no conception of how our merchants, tradesmen and all our people care for the 'unfortunates'. Their alms are almost continuous and nearly always take the form of bread, bread rolls and kalatches, much less often that of money. Without these gifts, in many places the lives of the convicts, especially those who are awaiting trial and who are kept under a much stricter regime than are those on whom sentence has been passed, would be too hard. The gifts are religiously divided into even shares by the convicts. If there is not enough for everyone the loaves are cut into equal portions, sometimes into as many as six pieces, and each prisoner receives his piece without fail. I remember the first time I was given money. It was shortly after my arrival in the prison. I was returning from the morning's work alone with the guard. Towards me came a mother and her daughter, a little girl of about ten, as pretty as an angel. I had already seen them once before. The mother had been a soldier's wife and had been made a widow. Her husband, a young soldier, had been under arrest and had died in the convict ward of the hospital while I was ill there. His wife and daughter had come to say goodbye to him; both had cried terribly. When she saw me, the girl blushed and whispered something to her mother who immediately stopped, fished a quarter copeck out of her bag and gave it to her daughter. The little girl came rushing after me ... 'Here, "unfortunate", take a copeck in the name of Christ!'[6] she cried, running out ahead of me and pressing the coin into my hand. I took her quarter copeck, and the girl returned to her mother thoroughly satisfied. I kept that quarter copeck for a long time.

* 2 *

FIRST IMPRESSIONS (1)

The first month and indeed the whole of the early phase of my life in prison come vividly to my mind's eye now. The years of prison that followed are much fainter in my memory. Some of them seem to have withdrawn completely into the background, mingling together, and leaving one undiluted impression of heaviness, monotony and suffocation.

But everything I experienced in the first days of my penal servitude seems to me now as though it had only happened yesterday. And this is the way it is bound to be.

I distinctly remember that, from the first step I took in this life, what struck me was that there seemed to be nothing striking, unusual, or shall I say unexpected about it. All this had seemed to flit before me in my mind's eye when on the march to Siberia I had tried to guess what lay in store for me. But soon a whole host of the strangest surprises and most monstrous facts began to pull me up at almost every step. It was only later, after I had lived in the prison for quite a long time, that I was able fully to comprehend the exceptional and surprising nature of this existence, and I marvelled at it more and more. To tell the truth, this sense of wonderment stayed with me throughout the entire long term of my imprisonment; I was never able to shake it off.

The first impression I had upon entering prison was a most loathsome one; but in spite of this – how strange! – it seemed to me that life there was much easier than I had imagined on the journey. Although the convicts wore fetters, they walked freely about the whole prison, swore, sang songs, did their own private work, smoked pipes, even drank vodka (though only a very few did this), and at night some of them played cards. The work itself, for example, did not seem at all like the hard, *penal* labour it was supposed to be, and I realized only much later on that its hardness and *penal nature* consisted not so much in its being difficult or unalleviated as in its being *forced*, compulsory, done under the threat of the stick. It is probable that the peasant in freedom works incomparably harder and longer, sometimes even at night, especially in the summer; but he works on his own account, with a reasonable end in view, and this makes it far easier for him than for the convict with his work that is compulsory and quite without use to him. The thought once occurred to me that if one wanted to crush and destroy a man entirely, to mete out to him the most terrible punishment, one at which the most fearsome murderer would tremble, shrinking from it in advance, all one would have to do would be to make him do work that was completely and utterly devoid of usefulness and meaning. Even though the work convicts do at present is both tedious and lacking in interest, in itself, as work, it is reasonable enough: the convicts make bricks, dig the land, do plastering, construction; in this work there is a sense and a purpose. The prison labourer sometimes develops quite a liking for such work, wants to do it more skilfully, faster, better. But if, let us say, he were forced to pour water from one tub into another and back again, time after time, to pound sand, to carry a heap of soil from one spot to another and back again – I think that such a convict would hang himself within a few days or commit a thousand offences in order to die, to escape from such degradation, shame and torment. Of course, such a punishment would quickly become a torture, a form of revenge, and would be pointless, because it would achieve no reasonable purpose. But since there is an element of this kind of torture, pointlessness, degradation and shame in all forced labour, the work that convicts do is vastly more unpleasant than any work done in freedom, simply because it is forced.

I arrived in the prison in winter, however, and had as yet no idea of the work which was done in summer, and which was five times as hard. In winter the amount of prison work done in our fortress was generally small. The convicts went to the River Irtysh to break up old wooden government barges, they worked in the workshops, shovelled the snowdrifts away from the government buildings after blizzards, baked and pounded alabaster, and so forth. The winter days were short, the work was soon at an end, and all our men made an early return to the prison, where there was practically nothing for them to do unless they happened to have their own work. But perhaps only a third of the convicts had work of their own, the rest frittered their time away, loitered aimlessly around all the prison barracks, swore, carried on intrigues, scandals, got drunk if a little money came their way; at night they would gamble away their last shirt at cards, and all this out of boredom, idleness and having nothing else to do. I subsequently came to understand that in addition to deprivation of freedom, in addition to forced labour, there is in a convict's life one more torment, one that is almost more powerful than all the others. This is *forced communal existence*. Communal existence is, of course, to be found in other places; but to the prison come such men as not everyone would care to cohabit with, and I am certain that all the convicts experienced this torment, even though for the most part they were not conscious of it.

The food, too, struck me as sufficient, on the whole. The convicts assured me that this was not the case in the convict battalions of European Russia. Of this I cannot judge: I have not been there. What is more, many of the convicts were able to have their own food. Beef cost half a copeck a pound, in summer it was three copecks. But only those convicts who had a constant supply of money could arrange to have their own food; most of them ate what the prison provided. When they praised the food they had in mind only the bread, and expressed satisfaction that it was distributed to all the men in common, and not portioned out by weight. This latter idea horrified them: if the bread had been distributed by weight a third of the men would have gone hungry; distributed to the artel, there was enough for everyone. The bread we were given was particularly appetizing, and its fame was well established in the town. People ascribed its high quality to the construction of the prison ovens. The cabbage soup was very unprepossessing. It was cooked in a common cauldron, was slightly thickened with meal and, especially on weekdays, was thin and watery. The enormous quantity of cockroaches it contained horrified me. But the convicts gave this no attention whatsoever.

For the first three days I did not go to work; every new arrival received this treatment, and was allowed to rest after the journey. But on my second day I had to go out of the prison to have new fetters put on me. The fetters I had were not the regulation ones, but were the ringed kind, 'jinglers', as the convicts called them. They were worn outside one's clothes. The regulation prison fetters which were designed to be worn at work consisted not of rings, but of four iron rods, each of almost a finger's thickness, connected by three rings. They had to be worn under one's trousers. To the middle ring a strap was fastened, which in its turn was fastened to the belt one wore next to one's shirt.

I remember my first morning in the barrack. In the guardhouse by the prison gate a drum beat through the dawn, and some ten minutes later the duty sergeant began to unlock the barracks. Men began to wake up. By the dim light of a tallow candle, the kind that is bought six to a pound, the convicts got up, shaking with cold, from their communal plank bed. Most of them were silent and sullen with sleep. They yawned, stretched and furrowed their branded foreheads. Some crossed themselves, others were already beginning to quarrel. The stuffiness was appalling. The fresh winter air burst in at the door as soon as it was opened, and flowed in clouds of steam through the room. The convicts crowded round the water buckets; in turns they took the dipper, filling their mouths with water and washing their hands and faces in it. The water was brought in the night before by the *parashnik* (latrine orderly). In accordance with prison regulations, each barrack had one convict, elected by the artel, whose responsibility it was to look after the room. He was called the *parashnik*, and did not go to work. His job was to keep the room clean, to wash and scrub the plank bed and the floor, to bring in and take out the night pail and to supply fresh water in two buckets – one in the morning, for washing, and another in the evening, for drinking. Quarrels began immediately over the dipper, of which there was only one.

'Where do you think you're shoving your way to, brand-head?' snarled one tall, morose-looking convict, lean and swarthy, with strange protuberances on his shaven skull, as he jabbed his elbow into another man, fat and stocky, with a merry red face. 'Stop where you are!'

'What are you shouting for? You have to pay folks for stopping where they are in our parts, you know; why don't you just clear off yourself? Gawd, look at him standing there, stiff as a monument. Than means he's lacking in luckability, chums.'

The word 'luckability' produced a certain effect: many of the men laughed. This was all the genial fat man wanted. He was apparently the barrack's self-appointed jester. The tall prisoner looked at him with the most profound contempt.

'Fat sow!' he said, as if talking to himself. 'Look at him, stuffed with prison bread. Glad he's going to give birth to twelve little piglets in time for Christmas.'

At last the fat man grew angry.

'What kind of a bird are you, anyway?' he shouted suddenly, turning red in the face.

'Just a bird!'

'What kind?'

'This kind.'

'What kind's this kind?'

'Just this kind.'

'What kind?'

They both fixed their eyes on one another. The fat man waited for an answer, clenching his fists as though he meant to hurl himself straight into a fight. Indeed, I thought there was, in fact, going to be a fight. All this was new to me, and I watched with curiosity. But later on I realized that all such scenes were thoroughly harmless and practically never ended in fighting. All this was fairly typical, and was illustrative of the way men behaved in prison.

The tall convict stood calmly and majestically. He could feel that the prisoners were watching him and waiting to see if he would bring shame upon himself by his answer or not; that he had to sustain his position and prove that he really was a bird, and of what kind. He squinted at his adversary with inexpressible contempt, trying, in order to give the maximum offence, to look down on him over his shoulder, examining him as though he were an insect, and said, slowly and distinctly:

'King cockerel! . . .'

Meaning that he ruled the roost. A loud volley of laughter greeted the man's quick-witted response.

'You're no king cockerel, you're a villain!' the fat man roared, sensing he had been outdone on all fronts, and flying into a violent rage.

But as soon as the quarrel started to take a serious turn, the two men were immediately set upon by the others.

'What's all the noise about?' the whole roomful of convicts yelled at them.

'Why don't you fight with your fists instead of your throats?' shouted somebody from a corner.

'That'll be the day,' came a voice in reply. 'We're a fearless lot, we are; as long as we're seven to one . . .'

'They're a nice pair, aren't they! One of them's doing time for pinching a loaf of bread and the other's just a runaway who got caught.'

'All right, all right, that's enough out of you!' shouted the disabled veteran who lived in the barrack, supervising it, and sleeping in a corner on his own bunk.

'Water, lads! Vet'ran Petrovich has woken up! Water for Vet'ran Petrovich, our dear brother!'

'Brother? . . . I'm no brother of yours. We've not so much as drunk a ruble's worth of vodka together, and now it's brother,' growled the veteran, struggling into the sleeves of his greatcoat . . .

Preparations for roll-call were being made. It was beginning to get light; in the kitchen a dense and quite impenetrable crowd had gathered. The convicts in their sheepskin coats and bicoloured caps were thronging round the bread which one of the cooks was cutting up for them. The cooks were chosen by the artel, two to each kitchen. They had custody of the kitchen knife that was used to cut up bread and meat; each kitchen had one of these. The convicts were sitting in every corner and around the tables, dressed in their caps, sheepskin coats and belts, ready to go out to work instantly. In front of them stood wooden cups of kvas. They crumbled their bread into it and sipped the mixture. The noise and hubbub were intolerable; but some men were talking reasonably and quietly in the corners.

'Good appetite, old man Antonych, and good morning to you!' said a young convict, as he sat down beside one who was toothless and frowning.

'Well, good morning, if you mean it seriously,' said the old man without raising his eyes, trying to chew his bread with his toothless jaws.

'You know, Antonych, I thought you were dead, I really did.'

'No, you can die first, I'll follow on later . . .'

I sat down beside them. On my right two sedate convicts were holding a conversation, each evidently trying to preserve his dignity before the other.

'No one's going to steal anything from me,' one of them was saying. 'It's more likely I'll steal something from somebody else.'

'Well, keep your hands off my money or I'll give them a nasty burn.'

'Nasty burn, eh? Come off it, you're just an ordinary con like the rest of us; cons, that's what we are . . . she'll grab all your money without so much as a by-your-leave. That's how my last copeck went. She came here herself the other day. I didn't know where to take her. I tried Fedka the hangman, he used to have a house in the outskirts, bought it from Scab Solomon he did, the Jew that hanged himself . . .'

'I know him. He was one of the vodka sellers here three years ago, they used to call him Grishka Blackboozer. I know.'

'The hell you do; Blackboozer was somebody else.'

'No, he wasn't! A fat lot you know. I've got that many witnesses ...'

'Oh yes? Where are you going to get them from, and who do you think I am?'

'Who do I think you are? You, the one I used to beat the living daylights out of, no kidding, and you're asking who do I think you are?'

'Beat the living daylights out of, I like that. The man's not been born that could beat me in a fight; and them that's tried it are pushing up the daisies now.'

'Bender pox.'[7]

'I hope you get the Siberian blackrot.'

'I hope you end up talking to a Turkish sabre ...'

And the cursing continued.

'Here, here, here! What a racket!' came the cry from men all around. 'Couldn't live as free men, now they're glad they've got white bread to eat ...'

This quietened the two men down at once. Cursing and 'tongue-lashing' were allowed. They were in part an entertainment for the other prisoners. But fighting was not always allowed, and it was only in exceptional cases that two enemies would come to blows. Fighting was reported to the Major; searches would begin, the Major himself would arrive – in short, it would be no good for anyone, and for this reason fighting was not allowed. And indeed it was rather for the sake of entertainment and as a verbal exercise that the two enemies swore at one another. Not infrequently they would deceive themselves, they would begin in a terrible fevered frenzy, and you would think: in a minute they're going to throw themselves on one another; but not a bit of it: they would reach a certain point and then immediately part company. At first this was all a source of great surprise to me. I have purposely given here an example of the most common kind of prison conversation. At first I could not understand how they could swear for enjoyment, and find in this an amusement, a cherished exercise, a pastime. One must not, however, leave personal vanity out of account. The dialectician of the curse was held in great esteem. He was applauded almost like an actor.

On my first evening I had noticed that the men looked askance at me.

I had already caught one or two dirty looks. On the other hand, some of the convicts hung around me, suspecting I had brought money with me. They started at once to curry my favour: they began to instruct me in how I should wear my new fetters; they got me, in return for money, of course, a box with a lock, so that I could hide in it the items of prison property with which I had been issued and also what few of my own clothes I had been able to bring with me to the prison. On the following day they stole this box back from me and drank the proceeds from its sale. One of these men subsequently became my most devoted companion, although he never ceased to rob me at every convenient opportunity. He did this without the slightest embarrassment, almost unconsciously, as if following some compulsion, and it was impossible to get angry with him.

Among other things, they told me I ought to have my own supply of tea, and said it would be no bad thing if I were to have my own teapot as well; for the meanwhile they lent me someone else's teapot and recommended one of the cooks, who they said would cook for me whatever I wished for thirty copecks a month, if I wanted to eat separately and buy in my own provisions ... Of course, they borrowed money from me; on my first day alone each of them came to me three times asking me to lend him some.

In penal servitude former members of the nobility are generally taken a dim view of and are looked upon with ill will.

In spite of the fact that they have already been deprived of all their rights and are completely on a par with the other convicts, the men never accept them as their companions. This is not out of any conscious prejudice, but is simply so, a sincere and unconscious predisposition. They sincerely acknowledged us as noblemen, even though they liked to tease us about our fallen state.

'No, that's enough of that, stop! Pyotr was one of Moscow's shining hopes, now Pyotr is sitting making ropes,' and so on and so forth.

They looked with glee upon our sufferings, which we tried to hide from them. We had a particularly hard time at work because we were not as strong as they, and could not help them properly. There is nothing more difficult than to gain the confidence of the common people (especially these people) and to earn their love.

In the prison there were several men of noble origin. To start with, there were five Poles. I will speak of them separately later on. The convicts had a special dislike for the Poles, an even greater one than they had for those exiles who had been Russian noblemen. The Poles (I speak only of the political offenders) behaved with a sort of refined, insulting politeness towards them, were extremely uncommunicative and could in no way conceal from the convicts the revulsion they felt for them; the convicts, for their part, understood this very well and repaid them in their own coin.

It took me nearly two years of living in the prison before I won the favour of some of the convicts. But most of them came to like me in the end and acknowledged me as a 'good' man.

There were four Russian noblemen besides myself. One was a mean and villainous creature, horribly depraved, a spy and informer by trade. I had heard of him before I arrived in the prison and after the first few days I broke off all relations with him. The second was the parricide I have already mentioned. The third was Akim Akimych; I have seldom seen such an eccentric as this Akim Akimych. He has remained sharply imprinted upon my memory. He was tall, lean, slow-witted, practically illiterate, a born arguer and as punctilious as a German. The convicts used to laugh at him; but some of them were afraid to have anything to do with him because of his fault-finding, exacting and quarrelsome character. He got on familiar terms with them from the word go, showered them with abuse, even fought with them. He was phenomenally honest. If he observed an injustice he would immediately intervene, even though it might have nothing to do with him. He was naïve in the extreme: for example, when he quarrelled with the other convicts he sometimes upbraided them for being thieves, and he would seriously exhort them not to steal. He had served as a lieutenant in the Caucasus. We were friendly right from my first day in the prison, and he lost no time in telling me about his case. He had started out as a military cadet in an infantry regiment stationed in the Caucasus, had toiled away there for an age and had finally been promoted to the rank of officer and been sent as a senior commander to some fortress or other. The chieftain of one of the neighbouring peaceful tribes[8] had set fire to his fortress and had made a night attack on it; the attack had failed. Akim Akimych had been cunning and had not even given a semblance of knowing who the malefactor was. The incident had been laid on the doorstep of the hostile tribes, and a month later Akim Akimych had invited the chieftain along for a friendly chat. The chieftain had arrived, suspecting nothing. Akim Akimych had lined up his regiment; he had publicly accused and upbraided the chieftain, contending that it was shameful to set fire to fortresses. Right there on the spot he had delivered to him a most detailed reprimand concerning the way in which he should behave himself in future, and in conclusion had shot him; he had immediately reported the entire incident to the authorities. For all this he had been tried and sentenced to death, but his sentence had been commuted and he had been deported to the fortresses of Siberia to do forced labour for a period of twelve years. He fully admitted that he had acted wrongfully, and he told me that he had known this even before he had shot the chieftain, had known that the head of a peaceful tribe ought to be tried according to the law; but although he knew this, he was somehow unable really to admit that he was guilty.

'But I mean to say, the fellow set fire to my fortress, didn't he? What was I supposed to do, get down on my hands and knees to him and say thank you?' he would reply in the face of any objections.

However, in spite of the fact that the convicts laughed at Akim Akimych's eccentricity, they nevertheless respected him for his punctiliousness and his capability.

There was no trade that Akim Akimych did not know. He was a joiner, a cobbler, a shoemaker, a painter, a gilder, a locksmith and had learned all these skills in prison. He had taught himself all of them: one glance and he got the hang of it. He also made various boxes, baskets and children's toys and sold them in the town. In this way he made a little money and he would immediately spend it on extra shirts and underwear, a softer pillow or a folding mattress. He lived in the same barrack as myself, and he helped me in many ways during the first days of my imprisonment.

When they left the prison in order to go to work, the convicts were lined up in two rows in front of the guardhouse; in front of them and behind them stood ranks of guards with loaded rifles. There followed the appearance of an officer of the engineers, an NCO and several engineers of lower rank who supervised the work the convicts did. The NCO counted the convicts and sent them to work in parties where they were required.

Together with the others I set off for the engineering workshop. This was a low, stone building which stood in a large courtyard that was heaped up with piles of various materials. Here there was a blacksmith's forge, a locksmith's, a carpenter's, a paintroom, and so on. Akim Akimych came here and worked in the paintroom, boiled the linseed oil, made up the paints and grained tables and other items of furniture to make them look like walnut.

While I was waiting to have my new fetters put on I talked to Akim Akimych about my first impressions of the prison.

'No, they don't like noblemen,' he observed, 'especially the political ones, they'd like to sink their teeth into them. No wonder. To start with, you're a different sort of person from them, and then again they were all serfs or soldiers before. You can see for yourself that they'd find it hard to take a liking to you. Life's tough here, I can tell you. And in the Russian convict battalions it's even tougher. Some of the men here have come from those battalions, and they can't say enough that's good about our prison, it's as if they'd left hell and swapped it for paradise. It's not the work that's the trouble. They say that over there, in the first category, the authorities are not completely military, at least they behave differently from the authorities here. They say that over there the convicts are allowed to live in little houses of their own. I've never been there, but that's what they say. They don't have their heads shaved; they don't wear uniforms; though I must say I think it's a good thing we're made to wear uniforms and have our heads shaved; it's more orderly, and it looks better. Except they don't like it. Just look at that riff-raff! This one's a Kantonist,[9] that one's a Circassian, over there we have a Schismatic, and there's an Orthodox peasant who's left his family and his dear children behind; there's a Jew here, and there's a gipsy, heaven knows what that one is – and they've all got to get along with one another no matter what, they've got to agree with one another, eat out of the same bowl, sleep on the same plank bed. And there's no freedom at all: if you've got an extra bit of food you must eat it on the sly, hide every penny in your boots, and the world is nothing but prison and more prison ... You can't help getting some funny ideas in your head.'

But I already knew this. I particularly wanted to ask him about our Major. Akim Akimych made no secret of things, and I remember that the impression his words made on me was not an entirely pleasant one.

But I was destined to live for the next two years under his authority. Everything that Akim Akimych told me turned out to be perfectly true, with the difference that the impression made by reality is always more powerful than that made by a mere story. This man was frightening, because he had almost unlimited power over two hundred souls. In himself he was just a man of spite and impropriety, nothing more. He looked upon the convicts as his natural enemies, and this was his first and greatest mistake. He really did have some abilities; but everything about him, even that which was good in him, was somehow mangled and distorted. Ill-natured and lacking in self-control, he would sometimes even burst into the prison at night, and if he noticed a prisoner sleeping on his left side or on his back, he would have him flogged the next morning: 'Sleep on your right side like I told you to,' he would say. In the prison he was hated and feared like the plague. His face was crimson and malevolent. Everyone knew that he was completely in the hands of his personal attendant, Fedka. He cared most of all about his poodle, Trezorka, and almost went out of his mind with grief when Trezorka fell ill. It was said that he had sobbed over the dog as if it were his own son; he had dismissed one vet and, after his usual fashion, had almost come to blows with him. Hearing from Fedka that one of the convicts in the prison was a self-taught vet whose treatments were extremely effective, he immediately sent for him.

'Save my dog! I'll load you with money, just make Trezorka well again,' he shouted at the convict.

The man was a Siberian peasant, cunning, clever, really a very skilful vet, but a peasant through and through. 'I had a look at Trezorka,' he told the convicts afterwards, a long time after his visit to the Major, however, when the whole affair had been forgotten. 'I looked: the dog was lying on the sofa, on a white cushion; and then I saw that it had an inflammation, that all that was needed was to let a bit of blood and the beast would get well again. "Well, I don't rightly know," I said. And I thought to myself: "What if I don't bring it off, what if the beast dies?" "No, your honour," I said, "you've sent for me too late; if you'd asked me to come yesterday, or the day before, about that sort of time, I could have done something for the dog; but now I can't do anything . . ."'

So Trezorka died.

They told me the details of an attempt on the Major's life. In the prison there was a certain convict. He had already been with us for several years and was noted for his gentle behaviour. It was also observed that he hardly ever spoke to anyone. He was looked upon as some kind of a holy fool. He could read and write and for the whole of the past year he had read the Bible constantly, both by night and by day. When all the men had fallen asleep, he would get up at midnight, light a wax church candle, climb onto the stove, open the book and read until morning. One day he had gone to the duty sergeant and told him he did not want to go to work. They had reported the matter to the Major, who had flown into a rage and had instantly arrived at the gallop. The convict had hurled himself at him with a brick he had ready, but the blow had missed. The man had been seized, tried and flogged. All this had happened very swiftly. Three days later he had died in hospital. As he had lain dying, he had said that he intended no harm to anyone, but simply wanted to suffer. He was not, however, a member of any schismatic sect. He was remembered with respect in the prison.

At last they changed my fetters. While it was being done, several girls selling kalatches came into the workshop one after the other. Some of them were very young girls. They usually went selling kalatches until they were of age; the mothers baked, and they did the selling. When they were of age they kept on coming round the prison, but without kalatches; this was almost always the case. There were also some who were not young girls. The kalatches cost half a copeck apiece, and almost all the prisoners bought them.

I noticed one convict, a carpenter, who was already grey-haired, but of fresh complexion, flirting with the kalatch sellers. Before their arrival he had wound a red calico handkerchief around his neck. One fat and pock-marked woman put her tray down on his bench. They started a conversation.

'Why didn't you come here yesterday?' said the convict with a self-satisfied smile.

'What? I did, but there was no sign of you,' answered the woman, pertly.

'We were wanted at work, otherwise we'd definitely have been here ... Anyway, all your lot came to see me the day before yesterday.'

'Who was that?'

'Maryashka came here, and Khavroshka, and Chekundá, and Dvugroshovaya ...'

'What's all this?' I asked Akim Akimych. 'Is it true?'

'It does happen,' he replied, modestly lowering his eyes, for he was extremely chaste.

It did of course happen, but very rarely and involving the greatest of difficulties. In general it would be true to say that the men were more interested in where, for example, they could get hold of a drink than they were in such matters, in spite of all the natural irksomeness of the life they were being forced to lead. It was difficult to get women. You had to choose the time and the place, you had to come to an agreement, make an assignation, find a secluded place, something that was particularly difficult, win over the guards, which was even more difficult, and altogether to spend an enormous sum of money, relatively speaking. But in spite of all this I did sometimes later witness love scenes, too. I remember one day in summer there were three of us in some shed or other on the bank of the Irtysh, firing a kiln; the guards were being good-natured. At last two 'floozies', as the convicts called them, appeared.

'Well, where have you been all this time? Up at the Zverkovs', I'll bet,' was how they were greeted by the convict they had come to visit and who had been waiting for them for a long time.

'All this time? A magpie could sit on a pole longer than I was at their place,' the girl answered cheerfully.

This girl was the dirtiest I have ever seen. She was the one called Chekundá. With her had come Dvugroshovaya. She was beyond all description.

'I haven't seen you for ages,' continued the ladies' man, addrus- sing Dvugroshovaya. 'Got thinner, haven't you?'

'Maybe I have. I used to be that fat, but now it's like I'd swal- lowed a needle.'

'Still friendly with the soldiers, eh?'

'No, that's a lot of stories wicked tongues have told you; but anyway, what of it? Though he hasn't got a bean, I love my soldier lad.'

'You give up those soldier lads and love us instead, we've got money ...'

To complete the picture it is necessary to envisage this ladies' man, his head shaven, in fetters, wearing striped clothing and under guard.

I said goodbye to Akim Akimych and, learning that I might go back to the prison, I returned there accompanied by a guard. The convicts were already gathering. First to return were those prisoners who were on piecework. The only way to make a convict work hard was to put him on piecework. Sometimes the tasks assigned were enormous, but all the same they were completed twice as fast as they would have been if the men had been forced to work right up to the dinner drum. Once he had completed his task, the convict could go back to barracks without hindrance, and no one could stop him.

The convicts did not eat supper all together, but in the order 'first come, first served'; indeed, the kitchen would not have been able to hold all of us at once. I tried the soup, but being unaccustomed to it could not eat it and made some tea for myself instead. We sat down at the end of a table. I had a companion with me who like myself was from the nobility.

The convicts came and went. But there was a lot of room, they had not all come back yet. A group of five men had sat down apart from the others at a large table. The cook poured soup for them into two bowls and placed on the table a platter of fried fish. They were celebrating something, and were having their own food to eat. At us they looked askance.

'I've not been home, but I know it all,' one tall convict shouted, as he came into the kitchen and looked round at all who were present.

He was aged about fifty, lean and muscular. There was something shy and at the same time jovial about his face. Especially noticeable was his thick, sagging lower lip; it gave his face an extremely comical look.

'Well, had a good night's sleep? Not saying good morning, are we? Ah, our friends from Kursk,' he added, sitting down beside the men who were eating their own food. 'A hearty appetite to you! May I be your guest?'

'We're not from Kursk, chum.'

'Maybe it's Tobolsk, then?'

'We're not from Tobolsk, either. You're not going to get anything from us, chum. You go and find the rich peasant, ask him.'

'John Collywobble and Mary Belch have come to live in my belly today, brothers; and where does he live, this rich peasant?'

'Gazin over yonder's a rich peasant; you go and ask him.'

'Gazin's on a binge today, lads: he's drinking all he owns.'

'That's twenty silver rubles,' observed another.

'It pays to be a vodka seller.'

'So you're not going to offer me anything, then? Oh well, I'll just have to make do with the prison muck.'

'You go and ask those gents over there for some tea.'

'What gents, there's no gents here; they're just the same as we are now,' said one convict who was sitting in a corner, in a gloomy tone of voice. He had not said a word until now.

'I could use a cup of tea, but I don't like to ask: we have our pride, you know,' said the convict with the thick lower lip, looking at us good-naturedly.

'I'll make you some tea if you like,' I said, inviting the convict to be my guest. 'Would you like that?'

'Like it? How can I refuse?' He came over to the table.

'Look at him! At home he used to drink soup out of his shoe, but here he's discovered tea; he wants to have what his masters drink,' said the gloomy convict.

'Don't people drink tea here, then?' I asked him, but he did not deign to reply.

'Here they come with the kalatches. What about a kalatch as well?'

The kalatches were brought in. A young convict appeared with a whole bundle of them in his arms, and sold them around the prison. The baker woman allowed him to keep every tenth kalatch for himself; he was counting on that kalatch.

'Kalatches, kalatches!' he cried, as he came into the kitchen. 'Moscow kalatches, hot from the oven! I'd eat them myself but I need the money. Well, lads, there'll be one kalatch left over at the end. Which of you had a mother?'

This appeal to filial affection made everyone laugh, and several convicts bought kalatches from him.

'One thing, lads,' he said, 'Gazin's gone on the binge and he's heading for trouble, God help him. What a time to pick for it. What if Eight-Eyes shows up?'

'They'll hide him. Real drunk, is he?'

'And how! He's turned vicious, started grabbing hold of folk.'

'Well, that means it'll end in a fight . . .'

'Who are they talking about?' I asked the Pole who was sitting beside me.

'It's Gazin, one of the cons. He sells vodka here. As soon as he gets a bit of money for the stuff he drinks it all away. He gets mean and vicious; but he's quiet when he's sober; when he gets drunk it all comes out; he goes for people with a knife. Then they have to calm him down.'

'How do they do that?'

'About a dozen of the prisoners charge at him and start beating him until he's unconscious, they have to beat him half to death. Then they put him on the plank bed and cover him up with a sheepskin coat.'

'What if they were to kill him?'

'Anyone else and they would have killed him by now, but not Gazin. He's incredibly strong, stronger than anybody else in the prison, and he's got a constitution like an ox. The next morning he gets up as right as rain.'

I continued to question the Pole. 'Tell me, they also have their own food to eat, and I have my tea. But they look at me all the time as though they envied me my tea. What does that mean?'

'It's not the tea that bothers them,' replied the Pole. 'They don't like you because you're from the nobility and are different from them. Many of them would like to pick a quarrel with you. They would like nothing better than to insult you and humiliate you. You will meet with a lot more unpleasantness here. All our lives are very hard here. Ours are harder than the rest in every way. You will need all the detachment you are capable of in order to get used to it. You will meet again and again with unpleasantness and abuse because you drink tea and have your own food, even though very many of the men often eat their own food and some of them drink tea every day. It's all right for them to do it, but not for us.'

Having said this, he got up and left the table; a few minutes later, his words came true.

* 3 *

FIRST IMPRESSIONS (2)

M—cki, the Pole who had been talking to me, had no sooner left than Gazin burst into the kitchen, completely drunk.

The sight of this convict, drunk in broad daylight, on an ordinary weekday when everyone was compelled to go out to work, within close proximity of a strict commander who was liable to come into the prison at any moment, of a duty sergeant whose task it was to supervise the convicts and who never left the prison, of guards and veterans – in the close proximity, in short, of all this strictness, threw all the ideas I had begun to form about the convicts' daily lives into total disarray. And I had to live in the prison for a long time before I was able to explain to myself all the circumstances that were so mysterious to me in the early days of my imprisonment.

I have already said that the prisoners always had work of their own and that the desire for such work was quite natural given the conditions of prison life; that, as well as having this desire, the convicts were inordinately fond of money and prized it above all else, almost on a par with freedom, and that they felt consoled as long as they could hear it jingling in their pockets. On the other hand, a prisoner would be despondent, sad, restless and out of spirits if he did not have any, and then he would be ready to steal or commit any deed in order to get his hands on it. But, even though money was so precious in the prison, it never remained long with those who were lucky enough to possess it. For a start, it was difficult to keep it from being stolen or confiscated. If the Major found it during his sudden searches he confiscated it at once. Perhaps he spent it on improving the convicts' diet; at any rate it was to him that it was brought. But more often than not it was stolen: it was impossible to trust anyone. We subsequently discovered a method of keeping money in complete security. It was given for safekeeping to an Old Believer, an old man who had come to us from the settlements of former Vetka schismatics at Starodubye[10] ... I cannot help saying a few words about him here, even though I digress from my subject.

He was a little, grey-haired old man of about sixty. From the first time I set eyes on him he made a strong impression on me. He was so unlike the other convicts: there was something so calm and peaceful in his gaze that I remember I used to look with particular satisfaction at his clear, bright eyes, which were surrounded by fine, radiant wrinkles. I often used to talk to him, and in all my life I have seldom encountered such a good-hearted and kindly person. He had been sentenced for a very serious offence. Some converts had begun to appear among the Old Believers in Starodubye. The government had given these converts every encouragement, and had begun to exert every effort to gain the conversion of other dissenters. The old man, together with other fanatics, had decided to 'stand up for the faith', as he expressed it. Work had begun on the building of a Yedinover church,[11] and they had burnt it down.

As one of the instigators the old man had been sentenced to deportation and penal servitude. He had been a prosperous trades-man; he had left a wife and children at home; but he had gone into exile with fortitude, because in his blinded condition he had considered it a 'martyrdom for the faith'. After living for some time alongside him, one could not help wondering how this man, who was meek and gentle as a child, could ever have been an insurgent. I had several conversations with him on the subject of 'the faith'. He had relinquished none of his convictions; but there was never the slightest trace of rancour or hatred in his answers. And yet he had burned down a church, and did not deny it. Because of his convictions, he seemed to have considered his action and the 'martyrdom' he had endured for it as a noble cause. But no matter how closely I scrutinized him, studied him, I could never observe the slightest trace of pride or vanity in him. There were other Old Believers in the prison, mostly Siberians. They were men of great natural intelligence, wily peasants, passionate students and inter-preters of the Bible who could also be dry-as-dust pedants, formid-able dialecticians in their own way; men who were supercilious, arrogant, sly and intolerant in the extreme. The old man was quite different from them. As an interpreter of the Bible who was perhaps superior to them, he avoided arguments. He was very sociable by nature. He was cheerful, he laughed frequently – not the coarse, cynical laughter of the convicts, but one which was clear and quiet, one in which there was a great deal of childlike simplicity and which somehow went very well with his grey hair. I may be wrong, but it seems to me that it is possible to tell a man by his laugh,[12] and that if on first meeting you like the laugh of a person who is completely unknown to you, then you may confidently say that this is a good person. The old man had won the respect of the whole prison, but he was not in any way conceited about this. The convicts called him 'grandad' and never said anything that might hurt his feelings. I could understand in part the influence he must have had on his fellow-believers. But, in spite of the visible fortitude with which he endured his imprisonment, he nurtured within him a deep, incurable sadness which he tried to hide from everyone. I lived in the same barrack as he did. Once, at about three o'clock in the morning, I woke up and heard a quiet, restrained sobbing. The old man was sitting on the stove (the same one on which the Bible-reading convict who had tried to kill the Major had sat praying), and was reciting prayers from a handwritten book. He was weeping, and from time to time I could hear him say: 'Lord, forsake me not! Lord, give me strength! My little children, my dear children, we shall never see one another again!' I cannot describe how sad I felt. This was the old man to whom gradually nearly all the convicts began to give their money for safekeeping. Nearly all the convicts were thieves, but for some reason they all became convinced that the old man could not possibly do any stealing. They knew that he hid the money entrusted to him somewhere, but this was such a secret spot that no one would ever be able to find it. He subsequently explained his secret to some of the Poles and myself. In one of the posts of the fence there was a knot that looked as though it had grown firmly together with the wood. But it could be removed, exposing a deep hollow. It was here that 'grandad' used to hide the money and then put the knot back in again on top of it so that no one could ever find anything.

But I have digressed from my story. I was considering the question of why money never remained long in the convicts' pockets. The fact was that quite apart from the trouble of keeping it securely, there was too much in the life of the prison that was dismal; the convicts, on the other hand, were by their very nature creatures so hungry for freedom and, because of their social position, so light-minded and feckless, that it was a matter of course for them to be drawn by the sudden urge to 'spread themselves', to blow all the money they had on wild binges with a great deal of noise and music, trying to forget their misery if only for a minute or two. It was almost uncanny to see how some of them would work themselves half to death without respite for months on end, for the sole purpose of squandering in one day all they had earned, every last penny of it, and how then once again they would toil away until they had enough for another binge. Many of them were fond of buying new clothes, which had to be of the civilian, casual type: informal, black trousers, long-waisted coats, Siberian caftans. Cotton shirts and belts with brass studs on them were also very popular. They dressed up on holidays, without fail, and would go round all the barracks showing themselves off to everyone. Their pleasure in being well-dressed was so great as to be positively childlike; and in many respects the convicts were indeed perfect children. It is true that all these fine garments would suddenly disappear from their owners' possession, they would sometimes be pawned for next to nothing on the very evening of the day for which they had been bought. However, the binge would develop only gradually. It was usually timed to fit in with holidays or namedays. The convict whose nameday it was would get up in the morning, place a candle before the icon and say his prayers; then he would get dressed up and order dinner for himself. He would buy beef and fish. Siberian pelmeni – meat dumplings – would be made; the convict would eat like an ox until he was full, almost always alone, seldom inviting his fellow-convicts to share in the feast. Then the vodka would appear: the man would get as drunk as a lord and would unfailingly sway and stagger his way round all the barracks, endeavouring to show everyone that he was drunk, that he was 'having a good time', and thereby merit general respect. Everywhere among the Russian people a certain sympathy is felt for a man who is drunk; in the prison a drunk man was even treated with deference. Prison drinking had its own brand of aristocraticism. Once he had started his bout of revelling, the convict would hire a musician. In the prison there was a little Pole, a deserter, a thoroughly unpleasant character who none the less played the violin and had his own instrument – his sole earthly possession. He knew no trade whatsoever and his only source of income was hiring himself out to play lively dances for convicts who were on a binge. His task was to keep following his drunken master from room to room, and to saw away on his fiddle for all he was worth. His face would frequently display boredom and depression. But the cry: 'Play, you've had your money!' would force him to start sawing away once more. When he started drinking, the convict could be firmly assured that if he got very drunk, the other convicts would look after him, would put him to bed in time and hide him if the authorities made an appearance, and that they would do all this quite disinterestedly. For their part, the duty sergeant and the veterans who lived in the prison to keep order could also put their minds entirely at rest: there was no possibility of the drunk man's causing any disorder. The whole barrackful of prisoners looked after him, and if he started to get noisy or rowdy he would be restrained at once, even bound hand and foot if need be. For this reason the lower echelons of the prison administration tended to disregard drunkenness, and indeed did not want to know about it. They knew very well that if they did not permit the men to drink vodka it would only be for the worse. But where did the vodka come from?

Vodka was bought in the prison itself from the so-called 'barmen'. There were several of these, and they carried on a steady and successful trade, even though the number of drinkers and 'revellers' was generally small, as drinking required money, which was hard for the convicts to get hold of. Transactions were embarked upon, consolidated and clinched in a rather unusual fashion. A convict might, for example, know no skill and not want to work (there were some like this), yet still want to get his hands on some money, being impatient to strike rich in a hurry. He might have a little money to start out with, and decide to deal in vodka: a bold undertaking, involving a large element of risk. He might have to pay for it with the skin of his back and be simultaneously deprived of both goods and capital. But the 'barman' would be prepared for this. He would not have much money to start out with, and so on the first occasion he would smuggle the vodka into the prison himself and of course sell it at a profit. He would repeat the experiment a second time, and a third, and if he did not fall into the hands of the authorities, he would quickly sell out. Only then would he be able to lay the basis of a real trade on solid foundations: he would become an entrepreneur, a capitalist, employing agents and assistants, with a much lesser degree of risk to himself and a fortune that steadily increased. His assistants would run his risks for him.

In any prison there are always a great many people who have squandered, gambled and drunk away every last penny they own, people who know no trade, pathetic, ragged men who are none the less endowed to a certain extent with boldness and determination.

All that such men have left by way of capital is the skin of their backs; this can still be put to some use, and it is precisely this ultimate capital that the reveller who has squandered all his money decides to put into circulation. He goes to the 'barman' and hires himself out to him as a smuggler of vodka into the prison; a rich 'barman' has several such assistants. Somewhere outside the prison there is someone – a soldier, a tradesman, sometimes even a woman – who uses the 'barman's' money to buy vodka in a tavern for a relatively large commission; this person hides the vodka in some secluded spot where the convicts come to work. The supplier nearly always tests the quality of the vodka first and hard-heartedly replaces what he has drunk with water. It is take it or leave it: a convict cannot afford to be too fussy, and he must be content that at least he has not lost all his money and that he has got his vodka, watered down, maybe, but vodka nevertheless. The smugglers who have been pointed out to him in advance by the prison 'barman' then report to this supplier, bringing with them the intestines of an ox. These intestines are first washed and are then filled with water – in this way they retain their original moistness and elasticity, so that they can eventually be used to contain vodka. Having filled the intestines with water, the convict wraps them around his body, if possible in its most secret parts. It goes without saying that as he does this he displays all the skill and thievish cunning of the smuggler. His honour is in part at stake: he must deceive both guards and sentries. And deceive them he does: a good thief will always get past the guard, who is often merely some new recruit. The guard is of course carefully studied in advance; the time of day and place of work are also taken into account. The convict who is a stovesetter will climb up onto the stove: who can see what he is doing there? It is not the guard's job to climb up after him. When he arrives at the prison he will have a coin in his hand – fifteen or twenty silver copecks, just in case, as he waits for the corporal at the gate. Every prisoner returning from work is examined and frisked by the corporal before being allowed inside the prison. The vodka smuggler usually hopes that the corporal will be too embarrassed to frisk certain parts of his body. But sometimes the corporal reaches these parts, too, and feels the vodka. Then one last resort is left to the convict: without saying a word, out of sight of the guard, he presses the coin he has been hiding in his own hand into that of the corporal. As a result of this manoeuvre he occasionally gets safely into the prison with the smuggled vodka. But sometimes the manoeuvre does not succeed, and then he must pay with his last capital asset, his back. He is reported to the Major, his capital asset is flogged and flogged hard, the vodka is confiscated and the smuggler claims sole responsibility, keeping the 'barman' free of involvement in the matter. It should be noted, however, that he does this not out of any aversion for informing but simply because it is not in his interests to be an informer: he would still be flogged, even if he were to inform; his only consolation would be that both he and the 'barman' would receive punishment. But he will need the 'barman' again, although as a matter of custom and as the result of the prior agreement the smuggler will receive not one penny from the 'barman' for his flogged back. As regards the general matter of informing, it is normally a flourishing business. In prison an informer is not subjected to the slightest humiliation; the thought never occurs to anyone to react indignantly towards him. He is not shunned, the other convicts make friends with him, and if you were to begin to demonstrate to them the utter vileness of informing they would completely fail to understand what you were talking about. The gentleman prisoner, the base and corrupt creature with whom I had severed all relations, was friendly with the Major's personal attendant Fedka, and worked as a spy for him. Fedka would report all that he heard about the convicts to the Major. Everyone in our prison knew this, yet no one would ever have dreamt of punishing the villain or even of reproaching him.

But I have digressed. Of course there are also occasions when vodka is successfully smuggled in; then the 'barman' receives the ox intestines that have been brought to him, pays for them, and begins to estimate what they have cost him. His estimates usually show that the goods have cost him a great deal; and so, for the sake of greater profits, he decants it once more, again adding water to it in almost equal amounts. Then, having thus made all his preparations, he waits for a customer. On the first holiday, and sometimes even on a weekday, the customer will appear: this will be a convict

who has been labouring for months like a harnessed ox and who
has saved up some money so as to be able to spend it all on drink
on a day that he has previously earmarked for this purpose. Long
before it arrives, this day will have been the object of the poor
labourer's imaginings, both in his dreams at night and in happy
reveries at work, and its magic will have sustained his spirit through
the crushing round of prison life. At last the dawn of the bright day
appears in the east; his money is saved up, it has not been confiscated, and he takes it to the 'barman'. The 'barman' starts by
giving him the purest vodka possible, that is to say vodka which
has only been twice diluted; but all that he drinks from the bottle
is immediately replaced with water. For a cup of vodka, the convict
will pay five or six times what it would cost him in a tavern. It may
be imagined how many cups of such vodka must be imbibed and
how much money must be spent in order for a man to get drunk.
But because he has got out of the habit of drinking and because he
has abstained for so long beforehand, the convict gets drunk rather
quickly and usually continues to drink until he has spent all his
money. Then he produces all his new clothes: the 'barman' is also
a pawnbroker. First to fall into his hands are the convict's newly
bought civilian clothes, then he takes his old clothes, and finally he
ends up with the convict's prison clothes as well. When he has
drunk away everything, right to the last rag, the drunkard goes to
bed, and the following day, waking up with the inevitable excrucia-
ting headache, he begs the 'barman' in vain to give him just a sip
of vodka for his hangover. Sadly he endures his misfortune and he
begins work again that very same day; once again he works for
several months without respite or relief, dreaming of his happy day
of drunkenness that has sunk irrevocably into oblivion, and
beginning little by little to take heart again and anticipate another
such day, one which is still far off, but which will eventually in its
turn arrive.

As for the 'barman', he, after making an enormous sum of money
– several dozen rubles – lays in a final stock of vodka. This he does
not dilute with water, since he intends to drink it himself. Enough
of business: now it is his turn to do a little celebrating. There begins
an orgiastic bout of drinking, eating, music. The 'barman's' means

are considerable; he even wins over some of the more directly responsible, lower-ranking prison staff. Needless to say, the vodka that has been laid in is soon drunk; then the reveller goes to other 'barmen' in the prison, who are already expecting him, and drinks away every last penny he has made. No matter how hard the convicts try to hide him, higher-ranking officials – the Major, or the duty sergeant – sometimes catch sight of him. He is taken to the guardroom, his money, if he has any on him, is confiscated, and in conclusion he is flogged. Shaking off the flogging, he comes back to the prison and within a few days is setting up in business as a 'barman' again. Some of these revellers, the rich ones, needless to say, also dream of the fair sex. If they pay a large bribe to a guard, they can sometimes sneak their way out of the fortress with him to a destination somewhere in the outskirts, instead of going to work. There, in some secluded little house somewhere on the very edge of town, an enormous feast is held, and truly gigantic sums of money are squandered. Not even a convict is despised if he has money; the guard who is to accompany him is selected in advance, and will know how to go about his task. Such guards are themselves usually future candidates for prison. However, with money it is possible to do almost anything, and such journeys nearly always remain a secret. It should be added that they take place extremely rarely; a great deal of money is required, and lovers of the fair sex resort to other means, means that are quite without danger.

While I was still in the early days of my prison existence, my curiosity was particularly aroused by a certain young convict, a very good-looking youth. His name was Sirotkin. In some respects he was a rather mysterious creature. I was struck above all by his beautiful face; he was not more than twenty-three years old. He was in the special category, that is to say he was in for life, and this meant that he was considered one of the most serious of the military criminals. Quiet and unassuming, he spoke little and seldom laughed. His eyes were blue, his features regular, his face soft and clear-complexioned, his hair a very light brown. Even his semi-shaven head did not greatly spoil his appearance, so striking were his good looks. He had no trade, but he received small amounts of money quite frequently. He was conspicuously lazy and dressed in a slipshod manner. Someone might occasionally give him some decent clothes to wear, perhaps even a red shirt, and Sirotkin would make no secret of the pleasure he took in his new clothes: he would make the rounds of the barracks and show himself off. He did not drink or play cards, and he practically never quarrelled with anyone. He used to go for strolls behind the barracks, his hands in his pockets, quietly and thoughtfully. It was not easy to imagine what he might be thinking about. Sometimes you might call to him out of curiosity, ask him about something or other, and he would reply at once in a tone of voice that was almost respectful, quite un-convict-like, but always terse and to the point; and he would look at you like a child of ten years old. When he got some money, he spent it not on necessities, such as giving his jacket in to be mended or buying new boots, but on kalatches and treacle cakes which he ate as if he were a child of seven. 'You're a right one, Sirotkin!' the convicts used to say to him, 'you orphan from Kazan!' Out of working hours he would usually wander around the other barracks; almost everyone else would be engaged in their own private tasks, he alone would have nothing to do. If the men said anything to him, it was nearly always something derisive (he and his companions were often made fun of), and he would turn round without saying a word and go to another barrack; sometimes, if the ridicule had been particularly fierce, he would blush. I often used to wonder how this quiet, artless creature had ended up in prison. At one time I was laid up in hospital, in the convict ward. Sirotkin was ill, too, and had the bed next to mine. At some point towards evening we started to talk; he grew unexpectedly animated, and told me in passing how he had been called up into the army, how his mother had wept as she had seen him off, and what a hard time he had had as a recruit. He added that he had found the life of a recruit quite intolerable, because everyone there had been so angry and strict, and the officers had found fault with him almost perpetually ...

'So how did it all end?' I asked him. 'What did you do to finish up here? And in the special category, too ... Ah, Sirotkin, Sirotkin!'

'Well, you see, Aleksandr Petrovich, I was only in the battalion for a year; I was sent here because I killed Grigory Petrovich, my company commander.'

'So I hear, Sirotkin, but I don't believe it. How could a man like you possibly kill anyone?'

'That's what happened, Aleksandr Petrovich. I was dreadfully miserable.'

'But how do other recruits survive? Of course they're miserable at first, but later on they get used to it, and lo and behold they turn out fine soldiers. Your mother must have spoiled you; I bet she fed you on milk and cake till you were eighteen.'

'It's true that my mother was very fond of me. When I went off to join the recruits she took to her bed and I heard that she never got up again ... The recruit life really got to me in the end. My company commander took a dislike to me, he was always having me flogged – and for what? I knuckled under to everyone, minded my *p*s and *q*s; I never touched a drop of vodka, I never got into debt; it's a sorry state of affairs, you know, Aleksandr Petrovich, when a man gets into debt. Everybody in the place was so heartless, there was nowhere to have a decent cry. I used to go away and cry in a corner somewhere. And then there was one time when I was on sentry duty. It was night; I'd been put in the guardhouse next to the armoury. There was a wind blowing: it was autumn, and that dark you couldn't see your hand in front of your face. I felt so wretched, so wretched! I stood my rifle on its end, removed the bayonet and put it down beside me; I took off my right boot, put the muzzle of the rifle against my chest, leaned on it, and pulled the trigger with my big toe. It misfired. I examined the rifle, cleaned the touch-hole, poured in fresh powder, struck the flint and put the barrel to my chest once again. What do you suppose? The powder ignited, but the gun didn't go off. What's this, I thought. I put my boot back on, fixed the bayonet back again and walked about for a bit without saying anything. It was then that I decided to do what I did: I thought, I don't care where they send me, as long as it's out of here. Half an hour later the company commander arrived; he was inspecting the guards. He came right up to me: "Is this any way to stand when you're on duty?" I took hold of my gun and sank the bayonet into him right up to the muzzle. I got four thousand lashes, and was sent here, to the special category ...'

He was not lying. For what other reason would he have been assigned to the special category? Ordinary offences were punished far more lightly. Among his companions, Sirotkin was the only good-looking one. As for the others like him, of whom there were perhaps as many as fifteen in our prison, it was a strange experience to watch them: only two or three of them had faces that were tolerable to look at. The others were an ugly, slovenly, lop-eared bunch. Some of them already had grey hair. If circumstances permit, I shall describe this group in more detail further on. Sirotkin was often on friendly terms with Gazin, the convict I referred to at the beginning of this chapter, when I described how he burst into the kitchen and how he upset my early notions of prison life.

This Gazin was a fearsome individual. He had a terrible and distressing effect on everyone. It always seemed to me that there could be nothing more violent and monstrous than this man. In Tobolsk I once saw the bandit Kamenev, who was notorious for his crimes; later I saw the deserter and terrible murderer Sokolov when he was being tried. But neither the one nor the other repelled me to the extent Gazin did. I sometimes thought I was seeing a huge, outsize spider, the size of a man. He was a Tartar, horribly strong, stronger than anyone else in the prison; he was taller than average, of Herculean build, with an ugly, disproportionately large head; he walked with a stoop, and his face wore a distrustful expression. Strange rumours about him circulated in the prison: it was known that he had been a soldier; but the convicts would have it, I do not know with what justification, that he was an escaped convict from Nerchinsk; that he had already been exiled to Siberia and escaped several times, that he had changed his name and finally ended up in our prison, in the special category. There was also a story that he had been fond of murdering little children, purely for pleasure: he would take the child away to some convenient spot; first he would frighten and torture it, then, delighting in the terror and quaking of his poor little victim, he would quietly and voluptuously slit its throat. This was all quite possibly a fantasy, a consequence of the general aura of unpleasantness with which, for most of the convicts, Gazin was surrounded; but all these fictions somehow suited him, and were in keeping with his appearance. All the same, except for the times when he was drunk, his prison behaviour was very cautious. He was always quiet, never quarrelled with anyone, and avoided the quarrels of others. But this, it seemed, was out of contempt for the other convicts, as if he thought himself superior to all the rest; he spoke very little and was almost purposely unsociable. All his movements were slow, tranquil and confident. From his eyes it was obvious that he was far from stupid, and extremely cunning; but there was always something haughtily derisive and cruel in his expression and his smile. He traded in vodka and was one of the most prosperous 'barmen' in the prison. But perhaps twice a year he experienced a compulsion to get drunk, and it was then that all the brutality of his nature displayed itself. He would get drunk gradually, and he would start by picking on men with taunts of the most vicious kind, calculated and seemingly prepared long in advance; finally, when he was completely intoxicated, he would pass into a fearful rage, grab a knife and go for men with it. The convicts, who knew how appallingly strong he was, would scatter before him and hide: he would go for any man who crossed nis path. But soon a way was found of dealing with him. A dozen or so men from the barrack he belonged to would rush him together and begin beating him. It is impossible to conceive of anything more cruel than this beating: they beat him in the chest, in the heart, in the solar plexus, in the stomach, they beat him long and hard, and only stopped when he was completely unconscious and looked as if he were dead. They could not have brought themselves to beat anyone else like this: to beat a man in this fashion meant to kill him – Gazin, however, they could not kill. After they had beaten him up they would wrap him, quite unconscious, in a sheepskin coat and carry him to the plank bed. 'They say he gets over it once he's had a rest.' And so it was: the next morning he would get up almost well again, and would go out to work morosely and in silence. And every time Gazin got drunk, all the men in the prison knew that the day would end in a beating for him. He knew it too, but he went on getting drunk just the same. At length the men noticed that Gazin was starting to give in. He began to complain of various pains, to look noticeably ill; his visits to the hospital became more and more frequent ... 'He's given in,' the convicts would say to one another

He came into the kitchen in the company of the unpleasant little Pole with the violin, who was usually hired by convicts on drinking bouts for the completion of their entertainment, and stopped in the centre of the kitchen, passing his gaze silently and attentively over all those who were present. No one spoke. Finally, catching sight of me and my companion, he looked at us in malice and derision, smiled a self-satisfied smile, seemed to make some swift, private deduction and, staggering violently, came up to our table.

'Permit me to ask,' he began (he spoke Russian), 'out of what proceeds your honours are pleased to drink tea in here?'

I exchanged glances silently with my companion, realizing that it was best to say nothing and not to answer. The slightest contradiction would have sent this man into a frenzy of rage.

'Got money, have you?' he continued, in his interrogation of us. 'Got a pile of money, have you, eh? Is that what you've come to prison for, to drink tea? Come to drink tea, have you? Say something, God damn you! ...'

But seeing that we had determined to keep quiet and not pay any attention to him, he turned crimson and started to shake with rabid fury. Beside him, in a corner, stood a large tray which was used to contain all the bread that had been cut in slices for the convicts' dinner or supper. The tray was so large that it could hold enough bread to feed half the prison; for the moment, however, it was empty. He seized it in both hands and brandished it above us. A few moments longer and he would have smashed our heads in. In spite of the fact that a murder or an attempted murder threatened the whole prison with extremely unpleasant consequences (searches and friskings would begin, there would be a tightening of restrictions, and so the convicts tried their utmost not to get themselves into such extreme situations): in spite of this, all the men now grew quiet, waiting for what would happen next. No one said one word in our defence; there was not one shout against Gazin, so powerful was their hatred of us. They were quite clearly pleased by the position of danger in which we had been put ... But the incident ended harmlessly: at the very moment he was about to bring the tray down on us, someone shouted from the passage:

'Gazin! Somebody's stolen your vodka!'

He let the tray fall to the floor with a crash, and rushed out of the kitchen as if he had gone insane.

'It's God who's saved them,' the convicts said to one another. And they said this for a long time after. I was never able to find out afterwards whether this message about the stolen vodka had been genuine, or whether it had been invented in order to save us.

In the evening, after it had already grown dark, but before the barracks were locked up for the night, I took a walk round the perimeter fence, and a heavy sadness fell on my heart. Never subsequently, not during all the rest of my life in the prison, did I experience such sadness. The first day of imprisonment is hard to bear, whether it be in gaol, in a fortress or in penal servitude ... But I remember that there was one thought which preoccupied me more than anything else, and which was subsequently to haunt me throughout the whole of my time in the prison. This was a thought involving a problem that was to some extent incapable of solution: the problem of the inequality of punishment for the same crime. It is true that it is impossible to compare one criminal with another, even approximately. For example, there may be two criminals who have both killed a man: all the circumstances of each case are taken into account; and in each case the punishment determined is practically the same. But note what a difference there is between these two crimes. One criminal, for example, may have slit a man's throat just like that, for no reason at all, for the sake of an onion: he has gone out on the road and murdered a peasant who happened to be passing along with nothing on him but an onion. 'What's this, boss? You sent me out to get some loot and all I could find was an onion.' 'You idiot! One onion – that's one copeck! Go and do in a hundred peasants, then you'll have a hundred onions, and that'll make a ruble' (a prison legend). The other criminal has killed to defend the honour of his fiancée, his sister, his daughter against a debauched tyrant. One man has killed because he is a vagrant, beset by a whole regiment of police spies, defending his life and his freedom, often dying of hunger; another slits the throats of little children just for the hell of it, just in order to feel their warm blood on his hands, to savour their terror, their last dove-like quivering under his knife. And what happens? Both men are given penal servitude. There is, it is true, some variation in the length of the sentences they receive. But there are relatively few such variations; while of one and the same crime there is a countless multiplicity of variations. There are as many variations as there are human characters. But let us assume that it is impossible to reconcile, to iron out these differences, that this is an insoluble problem, like squaring the circle, let us assume that this is the case. Consider another difference, one that would exist even if this inequality did not, the difference in the conse-quences of a punishment ... Here is a man who is wasting away in prison, melting down like a candle; and here is another who before he came here had no idea that there was in the world to be found such a merry existence, such an agreeable club of lion-hearted companions. Yes, men like these come to the prison, too. Here, for example, is an educated man with a sensitive conscience, with awareness, heart. The pain in his heart alone will be enough to do away with him, long before any punishment is inflicted upon him. Far more mercilessly, far more pitilessly than the sternest law, he condemns himself for his crime. But here, alongside him, is another man who never once, during the entire duration of his imprison-ment, reflects upon the crime he has committed. He even considers himself to be in the right. And there are still others who commit crimes solely in order that they may be sent to prison and there escape from the infinitely more prison-like existence they led as free men. In freedom a man may have lived in the last stages of degrada-tion, never having enough to eat and working for his employer from morning till night; while in prison the work is lighter than it is at home, there is plenty of bread, and of a high quality the like of which he has never encountered before; on holidays there is beef, there are alms, there is the chance to earn a copeck or two. And the company? A crafty, clever lot who know everything; and so he looks on his companions with respectful wonder; he has never seen men like these before; he considers them the very highest society there is to be found in all the world. Can it really be said that the same punishment is felt by these two men in equal degrees? But what is the use of dwelling on problems that are insoluble? The drum is beating, it is time to go back to our barracks.

* 4 *

FIRST IMPRESSIONS (3)

The final roll-call had begun. After this roll-call the barracks were locked up, each with its own special lock, and the convicts remained confined in them until daybreak.

The roll-call was carried out by the duty sergeant and two soldiers. The convicts were sometimes lined up for it in the court-yard, and the officer of the watch would put in an appearance. But more often the whole ceremony took place in a homely fashion: the roll was called in the barracks. The callers often made mistakes, miscounted, went away and came back again. At last the poor sentries would arrive at the desired figure and lock the barrack door. The barrack held as many as thirty convicts, jammed closely together on the plank bed. It was still too early to go to sleep. Everyone, it seemed, would have to find something to do.

The only representative of the authorities who stayed in the barrack overnight was the veteran I mentioned earlier. Each barrack also had a head convict who was nominated by the Major, for good behaviour, needless to say. These head convicts very frequently ended up by committing serious misdemeanours; then they would be flogged, stripped at once of all rank and replaced by others. The head convict in our barrack was Akim Akimych, who to my surprise would quite often shout at the other convicts. The convicts usually shouted back at him with jeers. The veteran was more sensible, and never interfered: if he did sometimes break his silence, it was only out of a sense of decorum, in order to put his conscience at rest. He usually sat on his camp bed in silence, stitching boots. The convicts paid hardly any attention to him.

On this first day of my prison life I made one observation which the passage of time convinced me was correct. This was that all

those who were not convicts, whoever they were, from those, like
guards and sentries, who were in direct contact with the convicts,
to all those who were in any way connected with prison life, had
a somewhat exaggerated view of the convicts. It was as if they spent
each minute in the uneasy expectation of a convict going for them
with a knife. But what was most remarkable was that the convicts
were aware that they inspired fear, and this obviously gave them
a certain audacity. Whereas the best commander for convicts is one
who is not afraid of them. And indeed, in spite of their audacity,
convicts do generally prefer to be trusted. It is even possible to win
their favour in this way. During my time in prison it happened,
although extremely rarely, that some senior official visited the
prison without a personal guard. It was instructive to see how this
impressed the convicts, and impressed them favourably. A fearless
visitor of this type always aroused their respect, and even if there
was a possibility that something unpleasant might happen, it would
not happen in his presence. The fear that convicts inspire is to be
found wherever there are convicts, and I really do not know what
it springs from. It does of course have some foundation, starting
with the convict's outward appearance, the look of the acknowledged bandit; in addition to this, anyone entering a prison can feel
that this entire body of men has been assembled here against its will
and that, whatever measures are taken, it is impossible to convert
a living man into a corpse: he retains his feelings, his thirst for
vengeance and life, his passions and his desire to satisfy them. Yet,
in spite of this, I am positively convinced that there is no reason
to be afraid of convicts. A man does not so readily or so swiftly go
for another with a knife. In short, even if there is some possible
danger at times, one may conclude from the rarity of such unfortunate incidents that it is not a very great one. I speak here, needless
to say, only of convicted prisoners, many of whom are glad that
they have at last reached the prison (so attractive does a new life
sometimes appear!) and are consequently disposed to behave
quietly and peaceably; and, quite apart from this, their own kind
will not allow the truly restless ones among them to behave with
too much audacity. Every convict, no matter how bold and cheeky,
is afraid of everything in the prison. The prisoner who is awaiting

trial is another matter altogether. He is truly capable of physically assaulting a complete stranger for no reason at all, or only because, for example, he must endure a flogging the next day; and if a fresh charge is brought against him, his punishment will be postponed. In this case, the attack has a cause and a purpose: the purpose is 'to better his lot', at all costs and as rapidly as possible I can even give the details of one strange psychological case of this type. In the military wing of our prison there was one convict who had been a soldier and who had not been deprived of his statutory rights. The court had given him a couple of years' hard labour, and he was the most arrant boaster and coward. As a rule, boasting and cowardice are very rarely met with in the Russian soldier. Our soldiers always seem to be so busy that they would not have time for boasting, even if they wanted to. But if indeed they are boasters, then they are nearly always loafers and cowards, too. Dutov (such was the name of this convict) finally polished off his short sentence and went back to his line battalion. But since all like him who are sent to prison for correction go to the bad for once and for all, it usually happens that after they have been on the loose again for two or three weeks, they end up facing trial once more and turn up in the prison again, this time not for two or three years, merely, but in the 'habitual' category, for fifteen or twenty years. Some three weeks after leaving the prison, Dutov stole something from under lock and key; in addition, he was found guilty of obscene behaviour and brawling. He was brought before the court and sentenced to a severe flogging with hard labour. Reduced to the last stages of terror by the punishment that awaited him, like the most wretched coward, the day before he was to run the gauntlet he took a knife and went for the duty officer who had entered his barrack. Needless to say, he understood very well that by an action like this he would immeasurably increase both the severity of the beating he would receive and the length of the term of penal servitude he would have to do. But his calculations were centred only on postponing, even for a few days, a few hours, the terrible moment when the soldiers would begin to flog him. He was such a coward that when he went for the officer with the knife he did not wound him, but merely went through the motions of an attack for the sake of form, merely in order to establish a new crime for which he would have to be brought before a court once again.

The moment before the flogging that begins his punishment is of course dreadful for the convicted prisoner, and over several years I was to see rather a large number of men on the eve of that day which was so fateful for them. I used to encounter the prisoners awaiting punishment when I was ill in the convict ward of the hospital, which was quite often. It is a fact well-known to all the convicts all over Russia that the people who are most sympathetic towards them are doctors. The doctors never make any distinction between convicts, as almost all non-convicts do, with the exception of the common people. The latter will never censure the convict for his crime, no matter how terrible, and will forgive him everything because of the punishment he has endured and because of his general misfortune. It is not for nothing that the common people throughout Russia call crime a misfortune, and criminals 'unfortunates'. This definition is of profound significance. It is even more important because it is formulated unconsciously, instinctively. And the doctors are a real sanctuary for the convicts in many instances, especially for men who are awaiting punishment and are detained under conditions far more rigorous than those experienced by men who have already been punished ... And so the prisoner who is waiting to be punished, having worked out for himself the probable date of the terrible day, often goes into hospital in an attempt to postpone the dreadful moment if only by a little. When he is discharged from the hospital in the almost certain knowledge that the day that follows will be the fatal one, he is nearly always in a state of violent agitation. Some try to conceal their feelings out of pride, but their clumsy, assumed bravura does not deceive their companions. Everyone knows what is up and keeps quiet out of common kindness. I knew one prisoner, a young man who had been a soldier: he had committed murder and had been sentenced to the maximum number of blows with the sticks. He was so stricken with terror that on the evening before he was due to be beaten[13] he made himself drink a whole jugful of vodka mixed with snuff. Vodka always turns up at a prisoner's side before he is flogged, by the way. It is smuggled in long before the day of the punishment and is obtained in exchange for large sums of money; the convict who is to be punished will gladly deny himself the most rudimentary necessities of life for six months in order to save up the sum needed to buy half a pint of vodka, to be drunk a quarter of an hour before the flogging. There is a general consensus of opinion among the convicts that a man who is drunk does not feel the lash or the sticks so keenly. But I have digressed from my story. The poor young man, having drunk his jugful of vodka, was immediately taken violently ill: he began to vomit blood, and was removed to hospital almost unconscious. This vomiting so ruptured his chest that a few days later he was discovered to have genuine symptoms of tuberculosis, from which some six months later he died. The doctors who treated his tuberculosis could not say what its origin had been.

However, in speaking of the cowardice often encountered in criminals before their punishment, I should add that on the other hand some of them astonish the observer by the extraordinary degree of fearlessness they display. I can remember several instances of bravery that amounted to a kind of insensibility, and these instances were by no means rare. I particularly recall my encounter with one fearsome criminal. One summer day a rumour started to circulate in the convict ward of the hospital that the notorious bandit and deserter Orlov was to be flogged that evening, and that after the flogging he was to be brought to our ward. While they waited for Orlov to arrive, the patients in the ward insisted that the flogging would be a savage one. They were all somewhat agitated, and I must confess that I also awaited the appearance of the notorious bandit with extreme curiosity. I had heard amazing stories about him. He was a villain of a kind that is rare, a man who carved up old men and children in cold blood. He was a man with a terrible strength of will and a proud awareness of his strength. He had confessed to many murders and had been sentenced to run the gauntlet. In the evening they brought him to the wing. It was already dark and the candles had been lit. Orlov was almost unconscious, terribly pale, with thick, tangled, jet-black hair. His back had swollen up and was a bloody blue colour. All night the convicts looked after him, brought him fresh water, turned him over from one side to the other, gave him medicine, as if they were looking after a blood relation or a benefactor. The next day he had regained consciousness and walked twice round the ward! I found this quite amazing: he had arrived in the hospital in such a weak and exhausted state. In one go he had taken the entire half of all the strokes to which he had been sentenced. The doctor had only halted the execution of the punishment when he observed that any further flogging would inevitably bring about the criminal's death. Besides, Orlov was small of build and had a weak constitution; in addition, he was exhausted by the long time he had been held in confinement pending his trial. Anyone who has ever had occasion to meet convicts awaiting execution of their sentence will probably remember their thin, pale, emaciated faces and their feverish stares for a long time afterwards. In spite of that, Orlov quickly recovered. What apparently happened was that his inner psychic energy provided a powerful boost to nature. This man was not really quite an ordinary mortal. I sought closer acquaintance with him out of curiosity and studied him for a whole week. I can say unequivocally that never in my life have I met a man of stronger, more adamantine character. In Tobolsk I once saw a famous criminal of the same type, a former bandit leader. He was just like a wild animal, and as you stood beside him, not yet knowing who he was, you had an instinctive feeling that you were in the presence of a terrible being. The most shocking thing about him for me was his spiritual indifference. The flesh had gained such an ascendancy over all his mental qualities that one glance at his face was enough to tell you that all that was left in him was a savage desire for physical pleasure, for sexual passion and carnal satisfaction. I am certain that Korenyev – that was the bandit's name – would have lost his nerve and would have shaken with terror if faced with an imminent flogging, in spite of the fact that he was capable of carving a man up without batting an eyelid. Orlov was his complete antithesis. This was truly a case of total victory over the flesh. It was evident that this man had boundless self-mastery, that he had nothing but contempt for any kind of torture and punishment, and that he was not afraid of anything under the sun. All that could be seen in him was an infinite energy, a thirst for activity, for revenge, and for the attainment of the goal he had set himself. I was also struck by his strange arrogance. He looked at everything in an incredibly haughty manner, not in such a way as to suggest that he was giving himself airs, but somehow naturally. I do not think that there was any being in the world that could have influenced him by its authority alone. He looked at everything with a kind of unexpected calm, as if there was nothing in the world that could surprise him. And although he was fully aware that the other prisoners looked upon him with respect, he never showed off in their presence. This was particularly interesting, since vanity and arrogance are common to almost all convicts without exception. He had a great deal of common sense and was in some ways strangely outspoken, though not at all garrulous. To my questions he answered bluntly that he was waiting to recover so that he could receive the rest of his punishment as soon as possible, and that before the flogging he had at first been afraid that he would not be able to come through it. 'But now,' he added, winking at me, 'now it's all over. I'll take the rest of the flogging and then they'll send me straight off to Nerchinsk with a working party, but I'll escape on the way there. You bet I'll escape! Just wait till my back recovers!' And all during those five days he waited avidly for the moment when he could apply for his discharge. During this time he was sometimes very given to laughter and geniality. I tried to talk to him about his exploits. He would frown slightly during these questionings, but his replies were always frank. But when he realized that I was trying to get at his conscience, to secure at least some kind of repentance from him, he looked at me contemptuously and haughtily; as though in his eyes I had suddenly become a silly little boy to whom it was impossible to talk as one would to an adult. His features even expressed something approaching pity for me. After a minute or so, he burst out laughing at me in the most artless fashion, without any irony whatsoever, and I am certain that when he was alone once more and remembered what I had said to him, he had several good laughs to himself. In the end he was discharged with a back that had not quite healed; I was also being discharged at this time, and we returned from the hospital together: I to the prison and he to the guardhouse alongside, where he had been held previously. As we said goodbye to one another, he shook my hand, this being a sign of great trust on his part. I think he did this because he was so pleased with himself and the present moment. What it boiled down to was that he could not help despising me and seeing me as a weak, pathetic, submissive creature, in every way his inferior. The next day he was taken out for the second half of his punishment ...

When our barrack was locked it suddenly took on a peculiar aspect – that of a real dwelling-place, a home. Only now could I see my companions, the prisoners, just as they might be at home. During the daytime, NCOs, officers of the watch and senior prison officials generally are liable to come into the prison, and for this reason the convicts behave slightly differently, as though not quite at their ease, as though expecting something to happen at any moment, and in a state of some anxiety. But no sooner was the barrack locked than all the men would sit down calmly, each in his own place, and practically all would begin to work at some handicraft or other. The room would be suddenly flooded with light. Each man had his own candle and candlestick, the latter usually made of wood. One would sit stitching boots, another sewing some garment or other. The foul air of the barrack would grow fouler from hour to hour. A little group of idlers would squat in a corner around a square of carpet spread on the floor, playing cards. Almost every barrack had a convict who owned a small square of threadbare carpet and a pack of incredibly soiled, greasy cards. Such an outfit was known as a *maydan*.[14] Its owner would rent it out to convicts who wanted to gamble at cards, for a charge of fifteen copecks per night; this was how he made his money. The gamblers usually played games like 'three leaves', 'cabinet', and so on. They were all games of chance. Each player placed a heap of copper coins in front of him – all that he had in his pockets – and got up only when he had lost everything or had taken all his companions' money. The game finished late at night, and sometimes lasted until dawn, until the very moment the barrack was unlocked. In our barrack, as in all the others in the prison, there were always some men who were beggars, destitute former nomads who had gambled or drunk all their money away, or who were quite simply beggars by nature. I say 'by nature', and wish to place particular emphasis on this expression. It is a fact that everywhere among our people, whatever the surroundings, under whatever conditions, there are always a few strange characters who are peaceable and by no means lazy, but who seem to have been fated to remain beggars to the end of their days. They are always solitary men without family, they always wear an air of neglect, they always look downtrodden and depressed about something, and they are forever being ordered about by someone, running errands for someone, usually an idler or a nouveau riche. Every original idea, every initiative is a vexation and a burden to them. It is as if they had been born on condition that they initiate nothing themselves, but merely serve and live according to the will of others, dance to another man's tune; their purpose in life is to carry out forever the wishes of someone else. To cap it all, no change of circumstances, no spin of the wheel of fortune can ever make them rich. They remain beggars forever. I have noticed that such characters are encountered not only among the common people, but among all societies, classes, parties, journals and associations. It was the same in every barrack, in every prison: no sooner had a *maydan* been assembled than someone like this immediately appeared in order to service it. And indeed, no *maydan* could function without such an attendant. He was usually hired by all the gamblers together for the whole night, at a rate of around five silver copecks, and his principal duty was to stand on watch all night. He usually froze and shivered in the darkness of the passage for some six or seven hours in a temperature of minus thirty degrees, listening for every tap, every clang, every step that came from outside. The Major or the sentries sometimes appeared in the prison rather late at night. They would enter quietly and discover the card-players, the men at their work, and the extra candles, the light from which could be seen outside. At any rate, when the lock on the door from the passage to the yard began to make sudden clanking sounds, it was too late to hide, to snuff out the candles and lie down on the plank bed. But since the attendant on watch got a very rough reception from the users of the *maydan* afterwards, the number of such unfortunate cases was extremely small. Five copecks is, of course, a ridiculously

small payment, even in prison; but I was always struck by the
hardness and lack of mercy shown by the men who did the hiring,
both in this and in all other cases I witnessed. 'You've had your
money, now get on with the job!' This was an argument that
admitted of no rebuttal. For every half copeck he paid out, the hirer
would take all that he could, he would even take more if possible,
and would still consider he was doing the man a favour. The idler,
the drunkard who threw his money to right and to left without heed
always shortchanged his attendant, and I observed this to be the
case in more than one prison, in more than one *maydan*.

I have already said that almost everyone in the barrack settled
down to some form of occupation: leaving aside the gamblers, there
were not more than five men who were completely idle; they went
to bed immediately the barrack was locked. My place on the plank
bed was right next to the door. On the other side of the planking,
his head next to mine, Akim Akimych had his place. He worked
until about ten or eleven, glueing together a multicoloured Chinese
lantern for some customer in the town who had ordered it and
would pay rather handsomely for it. Akim Akimych was most
adept at making these lanterns, and he worked methodically, without pause; when he had finished working, he cleared everything
neatly away, spread out his mattress, said his prayers and lay down
obediently on the bed. He took this obedience and this sense of
order, it appeared, to the most trivially pedantic extremes; it was
obvious that, like all narrow-minded and limited people, he considered himself to be very clever. I took a dislike to him from my
very first day in the prison, though I recall that on that first day
I thought about him a great deal and found that my main reaction
was one of surprise that such a man, instead of making a success
of his life, had ended up in prison. I shall have occasion to speak
of Akim Akimych several times in what follows.

But let me briefly describe the inhabitants of our barrack. I was
to live many years in it, and all these men were to be my future
barrack-mates and companions. The reader will understand that I
looked at them all with avid curiosity. To the left of my place on
the plank bed a group of Caucasian mountain tribesmen had their
berths. Most of them had been sent here for armed robbery and

their terms were of varying duration. There were two Lezghins, a Chechen and three Daghestan Tartars. The Chechen was a sullen and morose creature; he hardly ever spoke to anyone and constantly looked around him with hatred and mistrust, his smile envenomed and maliciously sneering. One of the Lezghins was an old man, with a long, thin, angular nose, who looked every inch a bandit. But the other one, Nurra, made the most pleasing and likeable impression on me from the first day. He was still young, not very tall, and Herculean in build. His hair was completely blond, and he had light blue eyes; he was snub-nosed, had a face like that of a Finnish woman, and was bow-legged from having spent his earlier life constantly on horseback. His entire body had been hacked and scarred all over by bayonets and bullets. In the Caucasus he had belonged to a peaceful tribe, but had made constant visits on the sly to the hostile mountain tribesmen and had taken part with them in attacks on the Russians. Everyone in the prison was very fond of him. He was always cheerful, had a friendly word for everyone, worked without complaining and was placid and serene, though he often surveyed the vileness and filth of the convicts' lives with indignation and was filled with rage by any kind of thieving, foul play, drunken behaviour or indeed by anything that was dishonourable; but he did not start quarrels, simply turned away in angry disapproval. During the whole of his stay in prison he never once stole anything, never committed one unworthy act. He was extremely religious, and said his prayers devoutly. During the fasts that preceded the Islamic feast days he would go without food and drink like a fanatic, and stand whole nights on end in prayer. He was liked by everyone and everyone believed in his honesty. 'Nurra's a lion,' the convicts used to say; and the nickname 'lion' stayed with him. He was resolutely convinced that when he had served out his prison sentence he would be returned to his home in the Caucasus, and he lived in the hopeful expectation of that day. I think that if he had been deprived of this hope he would have died. From my first day in the prison he struck my attention forcibly. It was impossible not to notice his kindly, sympathetic face among the malicious, sullen and sneering countenances of the other convicts. I had hardly been half an hour in the prison when, walking past me, he patted me on the shoulder, laughing in my face as he did so. At first I did not understand what this meant. Besides, his Russian was very bad. Soon after this he gave me a friendly clap on the shoulder. He did this again and again, and so it went on for three days. As I guessed at the time and as I discovered subsequently to be the case, this meant that he felt sorry for me, that he sensed how difficult it was for me to get my bearings in the prison, that he wanted to show me his friendship, raise my spirits and make me feel assured of his protection. Good, simple-hearted Nurra!

There were three Daghestan Tartars, and they were all brothers. Two of them were getting on in years, but the third, Aley, was no more than twenty-two and looked even younger. His place on the plank bed was next to mine. His handsome, open, intelligent, and at the same time good-naturedly straightforward face drew my heart to him at once, and I was so glad that it was him fate had sent me as a neighbour, and not some other prisoner. All of his soul was expressed in his handsome, one might even say beautiful face. His smile was so full of trust, so childishly guileless; his large black eyes were so soft, so tender that the sight of him brought me a peculiar contentment, even an alleviation of my depression and sadness. I am not exaggerating. Back in Daghestan one of his elder brothers (he had five brothers, who were older than him; two of them had ended up in some factory or other) had once told him to take his sabre and mount his horse, so that they could set off on some kind of expedition together. Respect for older family members is so great among the mountain tribesmen that not only did the boy not dare, he did not even think to ask where they were going. The others did not consider it necessary to tell him. They were all going off on a bandit raid, to ambush and rob a rich Armenian merchant on the road. So it was: they killed the escort, cut the Armenian's throat and pillaged his wares. But the crime was discovered: all six of them were seized, brought before a court, convicted, flogged and sent to Siberia to do penal labour. The only mercy shown by the court to Aley was the reduction in his sentence; he was deported for four years. His brothers had a great affection for him, and this was more of a fatherly than of a brotherly kind. He was a comfort to them in their exile, and they, who were generally morose and sullen, always smiled when they looked at him. When they talked to him (and they spoke to him very little, as if they considered him a boy with whom it was impossible to discuss serious matters), their stern faces relaxed and I would guess that they were talking about something humorous, almost childish; at any rate, they would always look at one another and laugh good-naturedly when they listened to his reply. He himself hardly ever dared to speak to them first, such was the esteem in which he held them. It is difficult to imagine how this boy could have preserved such tenderness of heart throughout all the time of his imprisonment, how he could have nurtured within himself such sincerity, such a likeable disposition, such a resistance to coarseness and profligate behaviour. He was, however, a person of strength and perseverance, in spite of all his obvious gentleness. I got to know him well later on. He was as chaste as a pure maiden, and a base, cynical, filthy, unjust or violent action committed by anyone in the prison lit a fire of indignation in his beautiful eyes, which thereby grew all the more beautiful. But he avoided quarrels and cursing, though he was not generally one to let himself be insulted without getting his own back, and he knew how to stand up for himself. He quarrelled with no one, however: everyone liked him and everyone treated him with affection. To me he was at first merely polite. Little by little I began to hold conversations with him; within a few months he had learned to speak excellent Russian, something his brothers did not achieve in all the time they spent in the prison. He seemed to me an extremely intelligent youth, extremely modest and fastidious; he seemed also to have thought already a great deal about life. It is perhaps as well if I say now in advance that I consider Aley no ordinary human being, and I remember my meeting with him as one of the best I experienced in all my life. There are certain natures so inherently beautiful, so richly endowed by God that the very notion that they could ever alter for the worse seems an impossible one. Your mind will always be at rest where they are concerned. My mind is at rest concerning Aley now. Where is he now? . . .

Once, quite a long time after my arrival in the prison, I was lying on the plank bed thinking miserably about something or other. Aley, normally always active and industrious, had his hands free

for once, even though it was too early to go to bed yet. But this was
the time of their Islamic holiday, and they were not working. He
lay with his hands behind his head, thinking about something.
Suddenly he asked me:

'Are you feeling very miserable just now?'

I looked at him with curiosity; this swift, direct question from
Aley seemed strange to me, Aley who was always so fastidious, so
scrupulous, so clever of heart: but, looking more attentively, I saw
in his face so much anguish, so many painful memories that I
immediately realized he himself was intensely miserable, particularly at that very moment. I told him what I had surmised. He gave
a sigh and smiled sadly. I liked his smile, it was always tender and
full of warmth. Moreover, when he smiled, he exposed two rows
of pearly teeth which might have been envied by the most beautiful
woman in the world.

'Why Aley, I expect you've been thinking about the way they're
celebrating this holiday in Daghestan, haven't you? It's nice there,
I bet?'

'Yes,' he answered with enthusiasm, and his eyes shone. 'How
did you know I was thinking about that?'

'How could I help knowing? Well, is it better there than it is here?'

'Oh, why do you say that? . . .'

'What flowers there must be now in that country of yours, what
paradise! . . .'

'O–oh, don't go on.' He was extremely agitated.

'Listen, Aley, do you have a sister, back there?'

'Yes, but what's it to you?'

'She must be a beautiful woman if she looks anything like you.'

'Like me? She's so beautiful that there's no woman to compare
with her in the whole of Daghestan. My sister! You've never seen
anything like her. My mother's beautiful, too.'

'And did your mother love you?'

'Oh, what are you saying? She's probably died of a broken heart
thinking about me by now. I was her favourite son. She loved me
more than my sister, more than anyone else . . . Last night I dreamed
that she came here and cried over me.'

He stopped talking, and did not say another word that evening.

But from that time onwards he looked for every opportunity of talking to me, although a feeling of respect which for some reason he had for me restrained him from ever being the one to start up our conversations. But he was very pleased if I spoke to him. I questioned him about the Caucasus, about his previous life. His brothers did not prevent him from talking to me, they even seemed to like it. Seeing me grow fonder and fonder of Aley, they became much more friendly towards me.

Aley helped me with my work and did what he could to be of service to me in the barracks. It was evident that he very much enjoyed making things even a little easier for me, that he enjoyed obliging me, and in his endeavour to oblige there was not the slightest element of self-degradation or desire for any kind of advantage, but rather a warm, friendly feeling for me, one which by now he did not trouble to conceal. What was more, he had a great many mechanical skills: he had learned how to do a pretty good job of sewing up a shirt or a set of underwear, he could make a pair of boots, and later on he learned as much carpentry as he could. His brothers praised him and were proud of him.

'Listen, Aley,' I said to him once. 'Why don't you learn to read and write Russian? Don't you know how useful that would be for you here in Siberia later on?'

'I'd like to, very much. But who would give me lessons?'

'There are plenty of educated men here! Well, would you like me to teach you?'

'Oh yes, please do!' And he almost stood up on the plank bed, putting his hands together beseechingly and looking at me.

We started our lessons the following evening. I had a Russian translation of the New Testament – a book that was not forbidden in the prison. Using this book alone, without any alphabet, Aley gained a first-rate reading ability within the space of a few weeks. After three weeks he already had a thorough knowledge of literary Russian. He learned with fervour, with enthusiasm.

We once read the whole of the Sermon on the Mount together. I noticed that he articulated some passages with special feeling.

I asked him if he liked what he had been reading.

He looked up quickly and the colour came flooding to his cheeks.

'Oh yes,' he replied. 'Yes, Jesus is a holy prophet, Jesus spoke the words of Allah. How good it is.'

'Which part do you like best?'

'Where he says: "Forgive, love, don't hurt others and love your enemies, too." Oh, what he says is so good.'

He turned to his brothers, who were listening to our conversation, and began saying something heatedly to them. They had a long, serious talk together, nodding their heads affirmatively all the time. Then with grandly benevolent, that is to say purely Muslim smiles (which I like so much precisely for their grandeur), they turned to me and confirmed that Jesus was indeed a prophet of Allah and that he had performed great miracles; that he had made a bird out of clay, blown on it, and it had flown away ... and that this was written in their books. As they said this, they were quite confident that their praise of Jesus would give me great pleasure, and Aley was obviously overjoyed that his brothers had decided they wanted to please me in this way.

Our writing lessons were also extremely successful. Aley managed to get hold of some paper (and would not allow me to pay for it), pens, ink, and in the space of something like two months had learned to write perfectly. Even his brothers were taken with this. Their pride and satisfaction knew no bounds. They could not thank me enough. If it happened that we were working together, they would vie with one another to help me and considered doing so a great stroke of fortune. That is to say nothing of Aley. He loved me, perhaps, as much as he loved his brothers. I will never forget the day he left prison. He took me behind the barrack and there threw his arms around my neck and burst into tears. He had never kissed me or cried in my presence before. 'You've done so much for me, so much,' he said, 'that my own father and mother could not have done as much: you've made me into a man, God will reward you and I will never forget you ...'

Where are you, where are you now, my dear, dear good Aley? ...

Besides the Circassians there was in our barracks a whole group of Poles, who constituted an entirely separate family, and who had practically no communication with the other convicts. I have already said that for their exclusivity and their hatred of the Russian convicts, they were in their turn hated by the others. These were sick, exhausted men: there were six of them. Some of them were educated; of these I will speak in detail later on. During the final years of my life in the prison I sometimes got books from them. The first book I read had a strong and peculiar effect on me. I will describe these impressions in detail elsewhere. I find them rather curious, and I am sure that they will be quite incomprehensible to most people. It is impossible to judge certain phenomena without having experienced them. I will say one thing: that moral deprivations are harder to bear than any physical torments. When the common man goes to prison he arrives among his own kind of society, perhaps even among a society that is more developed than the one he has left. He has, of course, lost a great deal: his country, his family, everything – but his environment remains the same. An educated man, subject by law to the same punishment as the commoner, often loses incomparably more. He must suppress in himself all his normal wants and habits; he must make the transition to an environment that is inadequate for him, he must learn to breathe an air that is not suited to him ... He is a fish that has been dragged out of the water and onto the sand ... And often the punishment that the law considers equal and apportions equally becomes ten times more painful for him. This is true even if we only take into account the material habits which he must sacrifice.

But the Poles had formed their own private, exclusive group. There were six of them, and they stuck together. Of all the other convicts in our barrack they liked only the Jew, for the sole reason, perhaps, that they found him amusing. However, the other convicts also liked our Jew, though they all without exception laughed at him. He was the only Jew in our barrack, and even now I cannot recall him without laughing. Every time I looked at him I would think of the Jew Yankel in Gogol's *Taras Bulba*[15] who, when he undressed in order to climb, together with his Jewess, into some sort of cupboard, looked uncommonly like a chicken. Isay Fomich, our Jew, was the spitting image of a plucked chicken. He was no longer young, a man of about fifty, of small stature and weak constitution, cunning and at the same time decidedly stupid. He was insolent and

arrogant, and at the same time a terrible coward. He was covered
in a kind of wrinkles, and on his forehead and cheeks there were
brand-marks which had been burned there on the scaffold. I could
not for the life of me understand how he had been able to bear sixty
lashes. He had been sent here on a charge of murder. He carried
hidden on him a prescription which his fellow-Jews had acquired
from a doctor for him immediately after his flogging and branding
on the scaffold. With this prescription he could obtain an ointment
that would remove his brand-marks in a couple of weeks. He did
not dare to use this ointment in the prison and was waiting for his
twelfth year in the prison to be up; after that he would be sent to
be a settler, and he firmly intended then to make use of the prescription. 'If not, so how vood I get married?' he said to me once. 'And
I vant so much to get married.' He and I were great friends. He was
always in the most excellent of spirits. He found life in the prison
easy; he was a jeweller by trade, and he was swamped by orders
from the town, where there was no jeweller, and by this means
escaped work that was physically demanding. Needless to say, he
was a moneylender as well, and he kept the whole prison supplied
with money at interest and on security. He had come here before
me, and one of the Poles described his arrival to me in detail. It is
a very funny story, which I will tell later on; I shall have occasion
to speak of Isay Fomich in several other contexts.

The other inhabitants of our barrack were four Old Believers, old
men who were assiduous and dogmatically literal readers of the
Bible (the old man from the Starodubye settlement was one of
them); two or three Ukrainians, dreary men; a young convict with
a thin face and a thin nose, aged about twenty-three, who had
already murdered eight people; a group of forgers, one of whom
was the life and soul of the whole barrack; and finally a few gloomy,
morose individuals who were unshaven and disfigured, close-jawed
and envious, looked distrustfully and with hatred around them,
and did so intentionally; who would remain frowning, close-jawed
and full of hatred for long years yet to come – for the entire duration
of their imprisonment. All this merely glimmered before my eyes
on this first, joyless evening of my new life -- glimmered amidst the
smoke and soot, the oaths and utter cynicism, in the foul air, to the

clanking of fetters, amidst curses and shameless laughter. I lay on the bare plank bed with my clothes under my head (I did not yet have a pillow then), and covered myself with my sheepskin coat; but I could not get to sleep for a long time, although I was completely exhausted and broken from all the monstrous and unexpected impressions of that first day. But my new life was only just beginning. A great deal still lay ahead of me, things of which I had never had any idea, things I had never foreseen . . .

* 5 *

THE FIRST MONTH (1)

Three days after my arrival in the prison I was told to go out to work. That first day of work has stayed very firmly in my memory, although nothing happened during it that was very unusual, leaving aside, of course, the whole unusual nature of my situation. But it was also one of my first impressions, at a time when I was still trying eagerly to get accustomed to everything. I spent all those first three days in a state of the most painful emotion. 'This is the end of my travelling: I am in prison!' I repeated to myself practically every minute. 'This is to be my refuge for many a long year, this is the corner into which I must creep with such feelings of pain and mistrust . . . But who knows? Perhaps I shall be sorry when in many years' time I have to leave it.' I added, not without a touch of that malicious joy which sometimes becomes a desire to rub salt in one's own wounds, as though one wished to admire one's own pain, as though from the consciousness of the enormity of one's misfortune there were some real pleasure to be derived. The thought that I might in time be sorry to leave this corner filled me with horror: even then I had some inkling of the monstrous extent to which human beings are capable of getting used to anything. But this was all still ahead of me, and meanwhile everything around me was hostile and – terrifying . . . although not everything was in fact so, it seemed to me that way. The savage curiosity with which my new companions, my fellow-convicts, looked me all over, their extra

severity with a novice from the nobility who had suddenly appeared
in their brotherhood, a severity which sometimes almost became
hatred – all this afflicted me to such a degree that I found myself
desperate to be sent to work as soon as possible, so as to discover
and experience the whole extent of my wretchedness at once, to
begin to live as the other convicts did, to get into the same rut as
everybody else. Of course I did not notice or suspect much of what
lay under my very nose: in the midst of that which was hostile I had
not guessed that there might also be happy experiences to be found
here. However, the few kind and friendly faces I encountered even
in these three days cheered me up considerably. The person who
showed the most kindness and friendliness towards me was Akim
Akimych. Among the sullen and hatred-filled faces of the other
convicts I could not also help noticing one or two that were good-
natured and cheerful. 'There are bad people everywhere, but among
the bad there are some good ones,' I hastened to console myself.
'Who knows? Perhaps these people are in no way worse than those
outsiders, those people *outside* the prison.' I thought this and shook
my head at the notion; but – God in Heaven – if only I had known
then to what extent it was true!

There was one man here, for example, whom I only got to know
properly after many, many years, even though he was with me and
constantly near me for almost the entire duration of my imprisonment. This was the convict Sushilov. The mention just now of
convicts who were *no worse* than others immediately brought him
to mind. He used to wait on me. I also had another attendant. Right
at the very beginning of my term, during the earliest days, Akim
Akimych recommended one of the convicts, a man called Osip, to
me, saying that for thirty copecks a month he would make my own
meals for me every day if I really disliked the prison food so much
and had money to buy my own. Osip was one of four cooks chosen
and appointed by the prisoners in our two kitchens, though it was
completely up to the cooks to accept or refuse such appointment.
The cooks did not go out to work, and their duties consisted solely
of baking bread and making cabbage soup. In our barrack they
were not called cooks (*povara*) but 'cookmaids' (*stryapki*, the
feminine noun); but this was not out of contempt for them, all the

more so since the men who were chosen for kitchen duty were an intelligent and relatively honest lot, but as an affectionate joke, one at which our cooks in no way took offence. Osip was nearly always chosen by the men, and he had been a cookmaid for several years, more or less, crying off sometimes only when he was seized by a fit of misery and a desire to smuggle in some vodka. He was a man of rare honesty and gentleness, even though he had been sentenced for smuggling. He was the same tall, sturdy smuggler I made mention of earlier; a coward in every respect, especially where the birch was concerned, meek and mild, kind to everyone, *never* quarrelling with anyone, but in spite of all his cowardice unable to overcome his passion for smuggling. Together with the other cooks, he also traded in vodka, though not, of course, on the same scale as Gazin did, for example, since he was not courageous enough to risk a great deal. I always got along very well with Osip. As for the amount of money needed in order to buy one's own food, the sums involved were minimal. I do not believe I am mistaken if I say that I spent no more than one silver ruble a month on food, apart of course from bread, which was provided by the prison, and sometimes, if I was very hungry, cabbage soup, in spite of my aversion to it, an aversion which, however, vanished almost completely later on. I usually bought a piece of beef, one pound every day. In winter beef cost half a copeck a pound. Our beef was bought at the market by one of the veterans, of whom there was one in each barrack, to supervise the keeping of order and tidiness. The veterans took it upon themselves voluntarily to go to the market every day and do the convicts' shopping; for this they took hardly any payment, just trivial sums. They did this for their own peace of mind, for otherwise they would never have been tolerated by the convicts. So they brought in tobacco, tea-bricks, beef, kalatches and so on and so forth, the only absent item being vodka, though they sometimes made a present of this. Osip cooked the same cut of roast beef for me for years on end. How it was roasted was another matter, but one of less importance. What was remarkable was that over several years Osip and I hardly said a word to one another. I often tried to start a conversation with him, but he seemed somehow incapable of keeping it going: he would smile, or answer *yes* or *no*, and that was that. It was strange to watch this Hercules who was like a seven-year-old child.

Apart from Osip, one of the people who helped me was Sushilov. I did not summon him, and I did not seek him out. He somehow found me himself and attached himself to me; I do not even remember when this happened. He began doing my laundry for me. Behind the barracks a large sluice-pit had been dug for this purpose. The convicts' clothes were washed above this pit in the regulation prison wash-troughs. In addition, Sushilov invented a thousand different duties in order to please me: he put the kettle on to boil for my tea, ran various errands, looked for things for me, took my jacket to the menders, greased my boots about four times a month; he did all this with a great deal of fuss and fervour, as though he had been assigned heaven knows what responsibilities. In short, he had completely identified his lot with mine and had taken on my affairs as his own. For example, he would never say: 'You have so many shirts, your jacket is ripped' and so on, but always: 'We have so many shirts now, our jacket is ripped.' In this way he kept a constant eye on me, and seemed to accept this as his main purpose in life. He knew no trade or, as the convicts say, 'handi-trade', and I seemed to be his only means of earning a copeck or two. I paid him what I could, that is pennies, and he was always meekly satisfied with what he got. It seemed that he had to serve someone, and had singled me out because I was better-disposed than the other prisoners and was more honest about paying up. He was one of those men who could never make enough money or get on in life, the kind who would take the job of acting as look-outs for the *maydans*, standing whole nights in the icy cold of the passage, listening for every sound in the yard in case the Major should arrive. For practically a whole night of such work they would take five silver copecks, and if they were found out they lost everything and paid with their backs. I have already spoken about them. The central characteristic of such men is to efface their personalities at every time and in every place, in front of almost everyone, and in any kind of common concern to play not even a secondary, but a tertiary role. This is all in their nature. Sushilov was a really abject creature, utterly cowed and servile, even downtrodden, although no one in the prison ever laid a finger on him – he was just downtrodden by nature. For some reason I always felt sorry for him. I could not even look at him without feeling this way; but why I was sorry for him I had no idea. I could not engage him in conversation either; he did not know how to converse, and the effort to do so obviously cost him greatly. He would only liven up when, in order to terminate our conversation, I would give him something to do, ask him to go and fetch something for me or run some other errand. In the end I even became convinced that by doing this I was giving him great satisfaction. He was neither tall nor short, handsome nor ugly, stupid nor clever, young nor old; he was slightly pockmarked and had hair that was partly blond. It was impossible to say anything very definite about him. Perhaps only one thing: as far as I could make out, he seemed to belong to the same set as that frequented by Sirotkin, his main qualification being his cowed and downtrodden nature. The convicts would sometimes laugh at him, principally because he had 'swapped himself' on the march to Siberia in the convict gang he had been part of. He had 'swapped himself' for a red shirt and one silver ruble. It was the miserable price for which he had sold himself that the convicts found so amusing. To 'swap oneself' means to exchange one's name, and consequently one's destiny, with that of someone else. However strange this fact may seem it is a fact none the less, and in my time this exchanging of names was very common among convicts *en route* for Siberia, was hallowed by tradition and bound by certain formalities. At first I could not really believe what was going on, although in the end I had to submit to the evidence of my own two eyes.

It is done in the following manner. A gang of convicts under escort is on the march to Siberia, for example. There are all kinds of criminals: some are going to prison, some to penal factories, others are going to the settlements; they are all marching together. At some point along the road, in Perm province, let us say, one of the convicts decides he wants to exchange his name with that of another. For example some Mikhailov or other, a man who has committed murder or some other capital offence, considers that it will hardly be to his advantage to go to prison for many years. Let

us suppose that he is a crafty fellow, an old hand who knows the
ropes; he is looking for a man in the same gang who is preferably
rather simple, downtrodden and cowed, one who has been
sentenced to a relatively light punishment: either a few years in a
factory, or life in a settlement, or even prison, but only for a short
term. At last he comes across Sushilov. Sushilov is a manor serf and
is merely being sent away to a settlement. He has already marched
some fifteen hundred versts without a copeck in his pocket, needless
to say, for Sushilov is incapable of possessing a copeck – marched
in weariness and exhaustion, fed on nothing but the government
rations, without the merest passing morsel of anything tastier,
dressed in prison clothes, waiting on everyone in return for a few
wretched brass bits. Mikhailov starts talking to Sushilov, gets on
close, even friendly terms with him, and finally plies him with vodka
at one of the stops along the way. Now he asks Sushilov if he
wouldn't like to swap names with him. 'My name's Mikhailov,' he
says, 'and I'm going to prison, except it's not really prison, it's some
kind of "special category". Well yes, it is prison, but it's sort of
special, you see, so it's a better class of prison.' There were even
some quite highly placed officials in St Petersburg, for instance,
who had never heard of the special category during all the time of
its existence. It was such a separate and exclusive little niche in one
of the corners of Siberia and its membership was so tiny (in my day
there were no more than seventy men in it) that it was hard to track
it down. I later met people who had done government service in
Siberia and who knew it well, but who first heard about the
existence of the 'special category' from my lips. The Penal Code
devotes a mere six lines to it: 'In such and such a prison a special
category is being instituted, to hold the most serious criminals
pending the opening in Siberia of projects involving the heaviest
penal labour.' Even the prisoners in this 'category' did not know
whether it was for life or merely for a term. No term was specified,
the statute said 'pending the opening ... of projects involving the
heaviest penal labour', and that was all, so it probably was 'for life'.
It was no wonder that neither Sushilov nor any of the rest of the
gang had any idea about this, not even the convict Mikhailov
himself, whose only knowledge of the special category stemmed

from an awareness of the extremely serious nature of his crime, for which he had already received three or four thousand lashes. He had concluded that it was not to any agreeable place that he was being sent. Sushilov, on the other hand, was going to a settlement, what could be more pleasant? 'Wouldn't you like to swap names?' Sushilov, somewhat intoxicated, a simple soul, full of gratitude towards his new friend Mikhailov, does not dare to refuse. What is more, he has already heard from other members of the gang that such an exchange is possible, that others have done it, so that consequently there is nothing unusual or outrageous about it. They arrive at an agreement. The unscrupulous Mikhailov, taking advantage of Sushilov's extraordinary simple-mindedness, buys his name in exchange for a red shirt and a silver ruble, which he gives Sushilov there and then in front of witnesses. The next day Sushilov is no longer drunk, but he is given more vodka to drink, and he feels he cannot go back on his word: the silver ruble has already been spent on vodka, and so, a little later, has the woven red shirt. If you don't want to do it, give the money back. But where is Sushilov to get a whole silver ruble from? And if he doesn't give it back, the artel will force him to: the artel keeps a stern eye on cases of this kind. Then, again, if you've given your word, you must keep it – the artel insists on this, too. Otherwise it will get its teeth into him. The men will beat him up, or perhaps simply kill him; at the very least they will use intimidation on him.

Indeed, if the artel were even once to be lenient in such a case, the custom of exchanging names would go out of existence. If it were possible to break one's promise and rat on a deal that had already been made, after money had changed hands, who would ever keep his word afterwards? In short, this is a concern common to the interests of the whole artel, and it is for this reason that the gang is so strict in such cases. Finally Sushilov sees that he cannot cry off, and decides to comply with the agreement in full. He makes a declaration to the whole gang; anyone else who needs to be bribed or plied with vodka is also present. To them, of course, it is all the same whether it is Mikhailov or Sushilov who goes to the devil, but they have drunk their vodka; they have been treated, so they will keep quiet. At the first stopping-place there will be a roll-call;

Mikhailov's turn will come. 'Mikhailov!' Sushilov will shout: 'Here!' 'Sushilov!' Mikhailov will shout: 'Here!' – and on they will march. In Tobolsk the convicts will be sorted out. 'Mikhailov' will be taken to the settlement, and 'Sushilov' will be escorted under an intensified guard to the special category. No further protest is possible; and how could anything be proved? How many years would such a case drag on? Might it not involve another prison sentence? And finally, where are the witnesses? If there were any, they would deny everything. So the end result of it all is that Sushilov arrives in the 'special category' in exchange for a silver ruble and a red shirt.

The convicts used to laugh at Sushilov – not because he had 'swapped himself' (although men who have exchanged a short sentence for hard labour are generally looked upon with contempt, like any blundering idiot), but because he had only accepted a red shirt and a silver ruble: a payment that was too trivial. Exchanges normally involve large sums of money, relatively speaking, that is. Tens of rubles sometimes change hands. But Sushilov was so submissive, so lacking in individuality, so insignificant in everyone's eyes that somehow it did not even seem worth laughing at him.

Sushilov and I lived in the same barrack for a long time, several years in fact. He gradually became very attached to me; I could not help noticing this, since I too had grown very used to having him around. But once – I will never be able to forgive myself for this – he did not do something I had asked him to do, even though I had just paid him to do it, and I was cruel enough to say: 'Look here, Sushilov, you've taken my money but you haven't done what I asked.' Sushilov said nothing, went off and carried out my errand, but seemed suddenly sad. Two days went by. I thought: it can't be my talking to him that's made him like that. I knew that a certain convict, Anton Vasilyev, had been insistently demanding from him the payment of some trifling debt. On the third day I said to him: 'Sushilov, was it the money to pay Anton Vasilyev you wanted? Here you are.' At that moment I was sitting on the plank bed; Sushilov was standing in front of me. He seemed very taken aback that I had offered him money, had remembered his difficult situation, all the more so since of late he had by his reckoning already taken too much money from me. I went after him and found him behind the barracks. He was standing beside the prison fence pressing his face to it and leaning on it with his elbow. 'Sushilov, what's the matter?' I asked him. He did not look at me, and I, to my great surprise, observed that he was on the point of tears: 'Aleksandr Petrovich, you ... think,' he began in a broken voice, trying to look to one side, 'that I wanted to ... ask you ... for money, but I ... I ... Ach!' Here he turned his head to the fence once more, banging his forehead against it – and how he started to sob! ... It was the first time I had ever seen a man cry in the prison. With difficulty I calmed him down, and even though from that moment on he began to wait on me and 'look after me' even more assiduously than before, if such a thing is possible, some subtle tell-tale signs informed me that in his heart he would never be able to forgive me my reproach. And all the while the other prisoners laughed at him, got at him on every convenient occasion, sometimes showering him with violent abuse. Yet he lived on peaceable and friendly terms with them, and never took offence. Yes, it is very difficult to make a man out, sometimes even when one has known him for many long years!

This is why prison life could not at first glimpse present itself to me as it really was, and as it was to present itself to me later. This is why I have said that even though I looked at everything with keen and avid attention, I could not discern much of what lay right under my very nose. It was of course the major phenomena, the outstanding ones that were the first to impress me, but I tended to interpret these incorrectly and all they did was to leave an impression of pain and hopeless melancholy in my soul. This process was assisted to a considerable degree by my meeting with A—v, a convict who had arrived in the prison a short time before me and who made a very painful impression on me in the first days of my imprisonment. I knew even before my arrival in the prison that I would meet A—v there. He poisoned this difficult early time for me and greatly increased my spiritual torment. I cannot pass him over in silence.

He was the most revolting example of the degree to which a man can lower and debase himself and of the degree to which he is capable of killing every moral feeling in himself, without effort or remorse. A—v was a young man, from the nobility, a fact I mentioned when I described how he reported to the Major everything that happened in the prison, and that he was friendly with the Major's personal attendant Fedka. Here is his story in brief: without managing to finish a course of study anywhere, and after quarrelling with his relatives in Moscow, relatives whom he had terrified by his debauched behaviour, he had arrived in St Petersburg and, in order to get some money, had perpetrated an especially vile bit of informing; he had sold the lives of ten men in order to obtain the immediate satisfaction of his insatiable appetite for the coarsest and most depraved pleasures. Enticed by St Petersburg, by its coffee-houses and Meshchansky Streets,[16] he had fallen such a prey to his own weaknesses that, although he was by no means stupid, he embarked on a crazy and pointless venture. He was soon found out; in his report he had involved innocent people, and had deceived others, and for this he had been sent to Siberia, to our prison, for ten years. He was still very young, his life was only just beginning. One might have thought that this terrible alteration in his fortune would have made an impression on him, called forth some kind of reaction in him, some kind of crisis. But he accepted his new fate without the slightest loss of composure, without the slightest revulsion, even; he felt no moral indignation at it, was not frightened by any aspect of it, except perhaps by the necessity of working and of saying goodbye to the coffee-houses and the three Meshchansky Streets. It even seemed to him that the vocation of a convict had freed his hands for even more repugnant deeds of villainy and baseness. 'A convict is a convict; if you're a convict you can act as dirty as you like and not need to feel ashamed of it.' This, quite literally, was his opinion. I remember this repulsive creature as a phenomenon of nature. Although I lived for several years in the midst of murderers, profligates and inveterate scoundrels I can positively say that never yet in my life have I encountered such complete moral collapse, such resolute depravity and such shameless effrontery as I found in A—v. We had among us a parricide, a man of the nobility; I have already made allusion to him; but

many facts and features helped to convince me that even this man
was possessed of incomparably greater decency and humanity than
A—v. To my eyes, throughout the whole of my life in the prison,
A—v became and remained a kind of lump of meat, with teeth and
a stomach and an insatiable craving for the coarsest, most bestial
physical pleasures, to obtain the least and most whimsical of which
he was capable of knifing, of cold-blooded murder, of anything, in
short, as long as it could be kept hushed up. I in no way exaggerate;
I got to know A—v well. He was an example of what the physical
side of man on its own can produce if unrestrained by any inner
norm or set of laws. And how repulsive I found it to look at his
eternally jeering smile. He was a monster, a moral Quasimodo. Add
to this the fact that he was cunning and clever, of handsome
appearance, even educated to some extent, with talent. No, better
the fire, better plague and famine than to allow such a man into
human society! I have already described how in the prison everything went to the worse from a moral point of view, how spying and
informing flourished, and how the prisoners were in no way angry
about this. With A—v they were all on very friendly terms, and they
used to treat him with much more cordiality than they did us. Our
drunken Major's soft spot for him gave him significance and
importance in their eyes. Among other things, he managed to
persuade the Major that he could paint portraits (he used to assure
the prisoners that he had been a lieutenant in the Guards), and the
Major had demanded that he be sent to work in his house, for the
purpose, needless to say, of painting his, the Major's portrait. It was
here that he got on friendly terms with the attendant Fedka, who
had an extraordinary influence on his master, and consequently on
everyone in the prison. A—v used to spy on us at the request of the
Major, but the Major when he was drunk used to slap him in the
face, shouting abuse at him for being a spy and an informer. It used
to happen that immediately after these outbursts of violence the
Major would sit down on his chair and order A—v to continue
painting his portrait. It seemed that our Major really believed that
A—v was a remarkable painter, almost as good as Bryullov,[17] of
whom he had heard; but he considered he none the less had the right
to slap his face because, he would say, you may be an artist but

you're a convict as well, and even though you're a Bryullov I'm still your commander, and so I'll do what I like with you. Among other things he used to make A—v take off his boots for him and empty his various chamber pots, yet for a long time he could not resist the notion that A—v was a great artist. The painting of the portrait dragged on interminably, for almost a year. Finally the Major realized he was being duped and, fully convinced that the portrait would never be finished, but was instead with every day that passed growing to be less and less like him, he flew into a rage, beat the artist black and blue and had him sent back to the prison to do hard labour. A—v visibly regretted this, and it was very hard for him to renounce his days of idleness, his perks from the Major's table, his friend Fedka and all the delights the two of them had cooked up in the Major's kitchen. But at least when A—v went the Major stopped persecuting M., a prisoner whom A—v had constantly denounced to him, and for this reason: at the time of A—v's arrival in the prison, M. had been alone. He had been very miserable; he had nothing in common with the other prisoners, looked at them with horror and loathing, did not notice or overlooked in them all that might have reconciled him to them, and could not get along with them. They repaid him with their hatred. In general, the situation of men like M. in the prison is a terrible one. M. did not know the reason that had brought A—v to the prison. On the other hand, A—v, guessing the kind of man he had to deal with, hastened to assure him that he had been sentenced for the very opposite of giving false information, almost on the same charge as M., who was overjoyed to have found a companion, a friend. He looked after him, consoled him during his first days in the prison, assuming that he must be suffering dreadfully, gave him the last of his money, gave him food, shared the necessities of life with him. But A—v immediately began to hate M. because M. was well-bred, viewed all baseness with horror, and was totally unlike himself; everything that M. had told him in their earlier conversations about the prison and the Major, A—v now hurried to tell the Major at the earliest opportunity. The Major conceived a fearful hatred of M. because of this and made his life a misery; indeed, if it had not been for the influence of the commander, he would have driven him to suicide.

Not only was A—v quite undismayed when M. later discovered his
base action, but even liked meeting him and looking at him with
a sneer. This evidently gave him pleasure. M. pointed this out to
me several times himself. This base creature subsequently escaped
from the prison with another convict and a guard; I will describe
this escape later on. At first he made every effort to ingratiate
himself with me, thinking I had not heard his story. I repeat that
he poisoned the first days of my life in prison and made them even
more wretched than they were already. I was horrified by this
terrible vileness and baseness into which I had been cast, in the
midst of which I found myself. I thought that everything in this
place was equally vile and base. But I was mistaken: I was judging
all the men by A—v.

During those first three days I trailed miserably about the prison,
lay in my space on the plank bed, had some shirts made for me out
of the regulation prison linen I had received by a trustworthy
convict to whom Akim Akimych had directed me; for these I had
to pay, of course (so many half-copecks per shirt); following Akim
Akimych's insistent advice, I also obtained a folding mattress
(made of thick felt and covered with canvas) which was very thin,
like a pancake, and I got myself a pillow stuffed with wool,
terribly hard if one was not used to it. Akim Akimych made a great
fuss over the business of getting me these things, and got involved
in it himself – with his own hands he sewed for me a blanket made
of scraps of old prison cloth, gathered from worn-out trousers and
jackets which I had bought from the other convicts. Items of prison
property which had lived out their term of service became the
property of the convict; they were immediately sold there and then
in the prison, and no matter how worn-out an article was, the
convict could always hope to sell it at some sort of price. I was very
surprised by all this at first. In general, this period represented my
first contact with the common people. I suddenly found myself
becoming one of the common people, a convict just like they were.
Their habits, notions, opinions and customs also seemed to become
my own, at least as far as outer form and the law were concerned,
though I did not share them inwardly. I was surprised and bewildered, as if I had never before suspected that any of this might

exist and had never heard it talked about, even though I had. But reality makes an impression that is quite different from knowledge and hearsay. Was it possible, for example, that in my previous life I could ever have suspected such clothes as these, such ancient cast-offs, could be considered as being of any use at all? And yet here I was sewing together a blanket for myself out of these very same old cast-offs! It is hard to give an idea of the quality of the cloth that is designated for prison wear. It resembled cloth well enough, it was thick, of the kind favoured by the military; but after it had been worn for just a short space of time it turned into a kind of netting, and developed a shocking number of tears. Cloth garments were only issued for a year, but even so it was difficult to make them last that long. A convict works, carries heavy loads; his clothing soon wears out and develops holes. Sheepskin coats, on the other hand, were issued for three years and usually served during that entire period as clothing, blanket and bedding. But the sheepskin coats were strong, though it was not infrequently that one saw a prisoner towards the end of his third year wearing a sheepskin coat patched with plain canvas. In spite of this, even very worn coats were sold at the end of their official lives for about forty silver copecks. Some which had been kept in better condition were sold for sixty or even seventy silver copecks, and in the prison that was big money.

Money – I have already mentioned this – had a terrible significance and power in the prison. It is safe to say that the convict who had any money at all in the prison suffered ten times less than the one who had none at all, even though the latter was provided with all the regulation prison issue and had, it was thought, according to the administration's reasoning, little use for money. Besides, I repeat that if the convicts had been deprived of the chance of earning their own money they would either have gone insane or would have died like flies (in spite of the fact that they had everything supplied for them) or would have ended by stooping to unheard-of acts of villainy – some out of boredom, others in order to be executed and put out of their misery as soon as possible, or in order by some means 'to change their fortune' (a technical expression). If after earning his copeck by practically sweating blood or by devising extraordinarily complicated ruses, often involving theft and fraud, in order somehow to obtain it, the convict goes on to spend it carelessly like a child, this by no means proves that he does not value it, although it may seem so at first sight. The convict is convulsively, insanely avaricious, and if he does indeed throw his money away like water when he goes on a spree, he is throwing it away on something he considers to be one degree higher in value than money. What is it that has a higher value than money for the convict? It is freedom, or at least the dream of freedom. Convicts are great dreamers. I will say more about this later, but in passing will the reader believe me when I say that I have seen men sentenced to *twenty years* who have quite calmly said to me such things as 'Just you wait till I've done my time and then by God I'll ...'? The whole meaning of the word 'convict' implies a man without a will of his own; when he spends money, however, he is acting from *his own will*. In spite of all the brand-marks, the fetters, and the hateful prison fence, which shuts out God's world and keeps him cooped up like a bird in a cage, he can get hold of vodka, that is to say, of a pleasure forbidden on pain of awesome penalties, he can enjoy women, even sometimes (though not always) bribe his most immediate superiors, the veterans and even the NCOs, who will turn a blind eye to his contravention of law and discipline; he can even strut and swagger in their presence. The convict is inordinately fond of strutting and swaggering, of showing off to his companions and persuading them *if only temporarily* that his freedom and power are infinitely greater than seems to be the case. In short, he can go on the binge, brawl, annihilate someone with crushing insults and prove to him that he *can do* this, that all this is in 'our hands', that is, he can persuade himself of something that is beyond his poor victim's imagining. This, incidentally, may be why among convicts, even when they are sober, there may be observed a general tendency towards swaggering and boasting, and towards a comical and most naïve glorification of their own personalities, even though this may be quite transparently false. But in the end all this excess carries with it its own risk – and this means that it is all imbued with an illusion of life, an illusion, however remote, of freedom. What will a man not give for freedom? What millionaire, if his neck were being strangled by the noose, would not give away all his millions for one gulp of air?

The prison administrators are sometimes surprised that one convict or another can have lived quietly for several years, a model of good behaviour, even being made a head prisoner for good conduct, when suddenly for no apparent reason whatever – as if the devil had got into him – he starts to behave waywardly, to go on binges, get mixed up in brawls, and sometimes even takes the risk of committing a criminal offence: he is openly disrespectful to a senior official, or he commits murder or rape, etc. The administrators view him with astonishment. But all the while the cause of this sudden outburst in the man of whom one least expected it is nothing more than an anguished, convulsive manifestation of the man's personality, his instinctive anguish and anguished longing for himself, his desire to declare himself and his humiliated personality, a desire which appears suddenly and which sometimes ends in anger, in frenzied rage, in insanity, fits, convulsions. So, perhaps, a man who has been buried alive in his coffin and who has woken up in it hammers on its lid and struggles to throw it open, although of course his reason tells him that all his efforts will be in vain. But this it not a matter of reason; rather it is one of convulsions. We must take into account, too, that almost every self-willed manifestation of the convict's personality is considered to be a crime: and for this reason it is naturally all the same to him whether the manifestation is a large or a small one. If he is to go on a binge, then he goes on a binge with a vengeance, if he takes a risk, he risks everything, even murder. It is enough only for him to get started: when the man grows intoxicated, there is no holding him back. And therefore it would be better in every way not to let him get to this point. Everyone would be able to breathe more easily.

Yes; but how can this be done?

* 6 *

THE FIRST MONTH (2)

When I entered the prison I had a small amount of money on me; I carried only a little, apprehensive lest it be stolen from me. For emergencies, however, I kept a few rubles hidden, or rather glued inside the cover of the New Testament which we were allowed to bring into the prison. This book, with the money glued inside it, had been given to me back in Tobolsk by men who had also suffered in deportation, who could count the number of years they had spent in exile in decades, and who had long been accustomed to seeing a brother in every 'unfortunate'. In Siberia there is an almost constant supply of people who seem to have made it the purpose of their lives to look after the 'unfortunates' in a brotherly fashion, piously and disinterestedly, to show the same sympathy and compassion towards them as they would towards their own children. I cannot resist briefly recalling here one particular encounter. In the town where our prison was located there lived a certain lady, a widow called Nastasya Ivanovna. None of us was of course able to become acquainted with her personally during our time as convicts. It seemed that she had chosen it as her purpose in life to help deported convicts, but she showed more concern for us than for the others. Whether it was that some similar misfortune had befallen her own family or that some person who was especially near and dear to her had suffered for some crime, she seemed to consider it a special happiness to do everything for us that she could. There was of course much that she could not do: she was very poor. But languishing there in prison, we felt that there, outside the prison, we had a most devoted friend. Among other things, she often sent us news, which we needed badly. When I left the prison and was setting off for another town, I managed to go and see her and get personally acquainted with her. She lived somewhere in the suburbs, in the house of near relatives. She was neither old nor young, neither particularly good-looking nor particularly ugly; you could not even tell whether she was intelligent or educated. All that could be observed in her at every turn was an infinite kindness, an irresistible urge to oblige, to make things easier for one, to do something pleasant for one. All this could be perceived in her kind, quiet eyes. Together with a friend from the prison, I spent nearly a whole evening in her company. She looked us in the eye, laughed when we laughed, hastened to agree with everything we said; she made a great fuss of us, trying as best she could to play the hostess to us. We were served with tea, hors d'oeuvres and candy, and even if she had had thousands of rubles they would only have brought her any pleasure if she could have used them to make life pleasanter and easier for our companions who were still in prison. When we were saying goodbye she produced a cigarette case for each of us, as a souvenir. She had glued these cigarette cases together for us herself out of cardboard (heaven knows how she had done it!), and had pasted coloured paper round them, exactly the same kind of paper as is used for the covers of children's school arithmetic primers (and perhaps some such primer had indeed been used for the purpose). Both cigarette cases were decorated with a fine border of gilt paper, which she had probably had to go to the shops especially for. 'You smoke cigarettes, so maybe it will be of some use to you,' she said timidly, almost as if making an excuse for her present ... Some people say (I have heard this and read it) that the most elevated love of one's neighbour is at one and the same time the greatest egoism. What egoism there could be in this instance I cannot for the life of me imagine.

Although I did not have very much money on me when I entered prison, I could not really bring myself to be angry with those convicts who, having already once taken me in, during almost the very first hours of my imprisonment came to me in the most naïve fashion a second, a third, and even a fourth and a fifth time to borrow money from me. But I will make one frank confession: I found it very annoying that all these men with their naïve ploys evidently considered me a simpleton and a fool and found me ridiculous just because on their fifth request I would give them money. They quite obviously thought that I was taken in by their deceits and ploys, and if only I had been able to refuse them and tell them to go away I am certain that they would have begun to have much more respect for me. But no matter how angry I got, I could not bring myself to refuse them. The reason for my anger was that all during those first days in the prison I was seriously and carefully deliberating how and on what kind of footing I should try to establish myself in the prison, or rather on what kind of footing I should try to establish myself with the other convicts. I sensed and realized that this whole environment was utterly new to me, that I was completely in the dark, and that I could not go on living in the dark for all those years. I had to prepare myself. I naturally decided that above all I must act directly, as my inner feelings and my conscience dictated. But I also knew that this was after all just words, and that before me there lay a practical test that would demand all my powers of anticipation.

And so, in spite of all the trivial worries connected with my getting settled down in the barrack, worries which I have already mentioned and in which Akim Akimych was principally responsible for getting me involved, in spite of the fact that to some extent they helped to keep my mind off other things, I was increasingly tormented by a terrible, devouring anguish. 'The house of the dead!' I would say to myself sometimes, looking in the twilight from the entrance to our barrack at the convicts who were returning from work, lounging idly about the drill square in the prison's courtyard, drifting from the barracks into the kitchen and back again. I studied them closely, and by their faces and movements tried to determine what sort of men they were and what their characters were like. They loafed about in front of me with faces that were either sullen or excessively gleeful (these two facial expressions are the ones most frequently encountered and may almost be said to be characteristic of life in prison), swore and cursed at one another or simply talked together, or, finally, walked alone with light, quiet steps, as if reflecting about something, some with a look of tiredness and apathy, others (even here!) with one of arrogant superiority, their caps worn at an angle, their sheepskin coats thrown over their shoulders, an insolent, crafty look in their eyes and with faces that wore a jeering, independent expression. 'All this is my new environment, the world in which I must live now, whether I like it or not ...' I would think to myself. I used to try to find out about the convicts by questioning Akim Akimych, with whom I liked very much to drink tea, so as not to be alone. Tea, by the way, was about my only sustenance in this early period of my imprisonment. Akim Akimych was not averse to a glass of tea and himself used to set up our ridiculous little home-made tin samovar, which M. had lent me. Akim Akimych would usually drink one glass (he had glasses, too), drink it silently and sedately, return it to me, thank me, and immediately set to work on my blanket. But he was unable to tell me what I wanted to know and could not even understand why I was so interested in the characters of the convicts around us. He would listen to me with a sort of canny smile which I remember very vividly. 'No, it's obvious that I'll have to find out by experience, not by question and answer,' I thought.

Early in the morning of the fourth day, just as they had been on the day I had gone to have the new fetters put on me, the convicts were formed up into two rows on the drill square in front of the guardhouse by the prison gates. In front of them, facing them, and behind them soldiers stood to attention with loaded rifles and fixed bayonets. A soldier has the right to kill a convict if he attempts to escape; but at the same time he is responsible for this action if he carries it out under circumstances that are not those of the utmost necessity; the same applies in cases of open revolt by the convicts. But who would ever think of trying to escape in broad daylight? An officer of the engineers, a works supervisor and some engineer NCOs and soldiers who were also in charge of the prison work all made their appearance. The roll was called; the convicts who worked in the tailoring shop were the first to set off; the engineer officers were not concerned with them; they worked exclusively for the prison and made all the clothes for it. Then other groups set off for the workshops and yet others for ordinary hard labour. I too set off in a group of about twenty other convicts. Behind the fortress, on the frozen river, there were two government barges which because they were no longer serviceable had to be broken up so that at least the old timber might not go to waste. Yet all this old material was apparently worth very little, and indeed had almost no value at all. Firewood could be bought in the town at a very low price, and all round there were forests in plenty. The convicts were really sent here to work in order to give them something to do, and they understood this very well. They always set about such work listlessly and apathetically; it was quite another matter when the work they were given to do had a sense and a value and, especially, when they could ask to be given a fixed assignment. Then they seemed to grow animated, and although there was no advantage for them in this, they would exert every effort in order to finish the job as quickly and as well as possible; it even seemed that their self-respect was somehow at stake. But with the kind of work we had to do at present, work that was done more for the sake of form than out of any necessity, it was hard to get a fixed assignment, and men had to work right up until the drum that beat the signal for them to return to barracks at eleven o'clock in the morning. It was a warm, misty day; the snow was almost beginning to melt. Our entire group had set off in the direction of the river bank behind the fortress, with a faint clanking of chains, which although they were concealed under our clothes, none the less made a thin, sharp metallic sound with each step we took. Two or three men went to the storehouse for an implement they needed. I walked with the others and even felt my spirits revive a little: I wanted to find out as soon as possible what the work was like. What was this penal labour really like? How would it be to work for the first time in my life?

I remember everything right down to the last detail. At one point along the way some kind of artisan with a beard met us, stopped and stuck his hand in his pocket. A convict immediately came forward from our group, took off his cap, accepted the alms the man offered him – five copecks – and swiftly returned to his mates. The artisan crossed himself and continued on his way. The five copecks were all spent that same morning on kalatches, which were equally divided among our gang.

In this band of convicts there were some who were sullen and untalkative, others who were indifferent and listless, yet others who spent the time lazily chatting to one another. There was one man who for some reason always seemed overjoyed and in the best of spirits; as we moved along he sang and well nigh danced, making a clanking sound with his fetters every time he jumped in the air. This was the same short, stout convict who on my first morning in the prison had had the quarrel with the other at the water-pail during wash-time, because the other had had the effrontery to make the senseless declaration that he was a king cockerel. This cheerful character's name was Skuratov. At length he started to sing a song of which I remember the refrain:

           I was married when I wasn't there –
           I was working in the mill.

Only the balalaika was missing.

Needless to say, his unusually cheerful disposition immediately aroused the indignation of several of our party. It was even construed as something approaching an insult.

'He's started his howling again!' said one prisoner reproachfully, though it was no business of his.

'The wolf knows one song and you've stolen it, you Tula git,' observed another in morose, Ukrainian intonations.

'All right, so I'm from Tula,' came Skuratov's swift retort, 'but at least I'm not like you Poltavans, choking yourselves with dumplings all day.'

'Get out of it! What did you ever get to eat? All you used to do was slurp soup out of your shoes.'

'And now he looks as if the devil's been feeding him on cannonballs,' added a third.

'It's quite true, my dear lads, that I'm just spoiled and pampered,' Skuratov replied with a gentle sigh, as if he felt remorse for being pampered, addressing everyone in general and no one in particular; 'I was martyred on prunes and French crussants from my earliest childhood (he meant nurtured. Skuratov got words mixed up intentionally), my brothers still have their own shop in Moscow to this day, doing a roaring trade down a little alley, wealthy merchants, they are.'

'And what did you sell?'

'Oh we had a number of lines. It was then you know, dear lads, that I got my first two hundred ...'

'Not rubles?' one inquisitive convict chimed in, positively aquiver at the mention of so much money.

'No, dear laddie, not rubles – whacks. Luka, hey, Luka!'

'There's some as calls me Luka, but to you I'm Luka Kuzmich,' a thin little convict with a pointed nose answered unwillingly.

'All right, then, Luka Kuzmich, if that's the way you want it.'

'There's some as calls me Luka Kuzmich, but to you I'm just plain "Uncle".'

'Oh, all right, Uncle, it's not worth trying to talk to you. But you'd have liked what I was going to say. Well, that's how it was, dear lads, that I didn't make much money in Moscow; in the end they gave me fifteen strokes of the lash and sent me out here. So I ...'

'What did they send you here for?' interrupted one man who had been assiduously following Skuratov's story.

'Oh, for going into the isolation blocks, for drinking vodka out of the barrels, for talking a whole lot of rot; so I didn't really manage to make a whole lot of money in Moscow, one way and the other. And I really, really, really wanted to be rich. I can't tell you how badly I wanted it.'

Many of the men burst out laughing. Skuratov was evidently one of nature's entertainers, or rather clowns, who seem to see it as their mission to cheer up the lives of their gloomy companions and, needless to say, receive nothing but abuse for their pains. He belonged to an individual and remarkable type, about which I shall perhaps have more to say elsewhere.

'Well, but now they'll be able to go shooting you instead of the sable,' observed Luka Kuzmich. 'Man, but your clothes alone must be worth a hundred rubles.'

Skuratov was wearing the most threadbare, soiled old sheepskin coat imaginable; it was covered all over with conspicuous patches. He surveyed it with a kind of attentive indifference, up and down.

'But my head's worth a lot, dear chaps, my head!' he replied. 'When I said goodbye to Moscow, the only consolation I had was taking my head with me. Goodbye, Moscow, thank you for the steam bath, thank you for the whipping you gave me afterwards! And there's no use looking at my coat ...'

'Maybe I should look at your head, then?'

'His head doesn't belong to him, either, he got given it for charity,' interjected Luka again. 'He was given it in Tyumen out of Christian charity when his gang was passing through.'

'Tell us, then, Skuratov, did you have a trade?'

'What sort of trade could he ever have? He used to lead blind beggars around and steal their money off them,' observed one of the sullen convicts, 'that's the only trade he ever knew.'

'In factual act, I did try my hand at making boots,' replied Skuratov, completely ignoring this barbed remark. 'But I only ever made one pair.'

'And did anyone buy them?'

'Yes, there was one chap who turned up, obviously had no fear of God in him, no respect for his father and mother; God punished him – he bought them.'

All the men around Skuratov split their sides laughing.

'And I did one more job, in this place,' Skuratov continued with the utmost composure. 'I stuck some uppers on Stepan Fedorych Pomortsev's, the lieutenant's, boots.'

'And was he satisfied?'

'No, dear chaps, he was not satisfied. He cursed me to kingdom come and gave me a knee in the backside as well. He was very angry. Aye, cheated me, my life has, cheated me, this convict life.

After just a little while
Akulina's husband went ...

he suddenly started to sing buoyantly, without any warning, stamping his feet in a hop, skip and jump.

'That bloke's a disgrace,' muttered a Ukrainian who was walking alongside me, squinting at Skuratov with malevolent contempt.

'He's no use at all,' observed another in a serious, conclusive tone of voice.

I had no idea why the men seemed to be angry with Skuratov, and why in general, as I had already noticed during these early days, all the cheerful convicts seemed to be held in a certain degree of contempt. I put the Ukrainian's anger and that of the other convicts down to a conflict of personalities. But it had nothing to do with personalities, it was anger because Skuratov had no self-control, did not display the stern consciousness of personal dignity with which the entire prison population was infected – and, in short, because he was, to employ the expression they used, 'no bloody use at all'. However, they did not extend their anger to all the cheerful convicts and did not treat all of them as they did Skuratov and others like him. It was a matter of what types of behaviour were permissible; a man who was good-natured and unassuming was immediately subjected to humiliation. I was quite taken aback by this. But there were also some cheerful convicts who could and did stand up for themselves and who gave no quarter: the other convicts were compelled to respect them. There was one of these caustic tongues right here in the group I was with, really a most cheerful spirited and amiable man, though I was to get to know this side of him only later on. He was a big, portly fellow with a large wart on his cheek and a very comical expression on his face, which was however rather handsome and intelligent. The men called him the Pioneer, because he had once served in the Pioneers; now he was in the special category. I shall have more to say about him later on.

Not all the 'serious' convicts were as expansive as the Ukrainian who had expressed indignation at Skuratov's cheerfulness, however. In the prison there were men who had aspirations to superiority, to a knowledge of everything that went on, to resourcefulness, character and intelligence. Many of these men really were intelligent, had strong characters and really did attain what they aspired to, namely superiority and a considerable moral influence on their companions. These intelligent convicts were often deadly enemies – and each of them had many ill-wishers. They regarded the other convicts from a position of dignity and even condescension, did not start needless quarrels, were on good terms with the administration, and played a kind of managerial role at work. Not one of them would ever pick on another convict for a thing like singing: they did not stoop to such trivialities. All the men of this type were remarkably polite to me during my entire stay in prison, though I did not find them very talkative; their dignity also seemed to be involved here. I shall also talk about them in more detail.

We arrived at the river bank. Below, frozen into the ice of the river, lay the old barge we were to break up. On the other side of the river one could see the blue of the steppe; it was a cheerless, lonely view. I expected everyone to throw themselves into the work right there and then, but nothing seemed to be further from their minds. Some of the men sat down on the logs that had been washed up onto the bank; nearly all pulled from their boots pouches of the local tobacco which was sold by the leaf at the market for three copecks a pound, and short Turkish pipes made of willow-wood with home-made wooden mouthpieces. The pipes were lit: the guards formed a cordon round us and kept watch over us with an appearance of utter boredom.

'And whose idea was it to break up this barge, anyway?' said one convict, seemingly to himself, not addressing anyone in particular. 'Have they run out of wood chippings, or something?'

'He wasn't scared of us, whoever it was,' observed another.

'Here, where are those peasants off to?' asked the first man after a pause, ignoring the answer to his previous question and pointing into the distance at a group of peasants who were setting off somewhere across the untrodden snow in single file. All the convicts turned lazily in their direction and began to mimic them, for want of anything else to do. One of the peasants, the last one in the line, had a particularly comical way of walking, his arms thrown wide apart and his head, on which he wore a tall, cone-shaped felt hat, like a buckwheat loaf, hung down. His whole figure was clearly delineated against the white snow.

'Ar, brother Petrovich, look how he's got himself up, then,' observed one convict, mimicking the way in which the peasants spoke. It was noticeable that the convicts tended in general to look down on the peasants slightly, even though half of them came of peasant stock.

'The way the one at the back walks, lads, you'd think he was sowing radishes.'

'He's got his thinking cap on, 'cos of all that money of his,' observed a third.

They all laughed, but lazily, as if reluctant to do so. Meanwhile one of the kalatch sellers had arrived, a pert and sprightly woman.

The man who had been given the five copeck piece bought kalatches with it, and these were immediately distributed equally among the men.

The young convict who sold kalatches in the prison took two dozen and got into a heated argument trying to get three kalatches instead of two, the extra kalatch being his usual commission. But the woman would not agree to this.

'Right, so you're not going to give it me, then?'

'Why should I?'

'So the mice don't get it.'

'Go on and get out of it,' shrieked the woman, laughing.

Finally the foreman, an NCO with a stick, came over.

'Here, you men, what are you sitting around here for? Get on with your work!'

'Come on, Ivan Matveich, give us an assignment,' said one of the 'managerial' convicts, slowly getting up.

'You should have asked for that earlier on. Breaking up the barge, that's your assignment.'

Somehow everyone finally got up and trudged off down to the river with reluctant, trailing steps. Some 'managers', in word at least, immediately made their appearance among the crowd of men. It turned out that the barge was to be broken up for a purpose, after all: we were to preserve as much of the timber as we could, especially the *kokory*, which were hoops fixed to the bottom of the boat along its whole length with wooden nails – work that would be prolonged and tedious.

'Right, first of all we'll have to pull out that big beam over there. Get going, lads,' observed one man who was certainly not a 'manager' or an administrator, but simply an ordinary labourer, a quiet, humble type who up till now had not said a word. Bending down, he took hold of a thick beam, waiting for other men to come to his assistance. But no one helped him.

'Going to lift that, are you? You'll never lift it, not even your bear of a grandad could,' someone muttered through his teeth.

'Come on, lads, what are you waiting for? I don't know ...' said the volunteer in a puzzled tone of voice, letting go of the beam and getting up.

'Work all day and you won't be done ... what did you volunteer for?'

'He couldn't feed three hens without getting it wrong, and here he is wanting to be first ... Big mouth!'

'Here, lads, I didn't mean no harm,' the puzzled convict tried to excuse himself. 'I just ...'

'What am I supposed to do with you lot, put dust-covers on you or something? Or do you want pickling for the winter?' shouted the foreman again, looking in bewilderment at the twenty-strong crowd of men who did not know how to start work. 'Get busy! At the double!'

'The more haste, the less speed, Ivan Matveich.'

'But you're not doing a bloody thing! Hey, Savelyev! Talkalot Petrovich! I'm asking you, what are you standing there idle for? Get started!'

'I'm not going to do it on my own, am I?'

'Give us an assignment, Ivan Matveich.'

'I've told you, you're not getting any assignment. Get that barge broken up and then you can go back to barracks. Get busy!'

At last the men set to work, listlessly, reluctantly and clumsily. It was almost irritating to watch this crowd of big, hefty workmen who seemed to have absolutely no idea of how they should go about their task. No sooner had they started to remove the first, smallest hoop when it turned out that it was falling apart, 'falling apart of itself', as the men expressed it to the foreman; it was concluded that the work could not be undertaken in this way, and that some other method would have to be found. There ensued a long discussion among the men about the right method to use. This, needless to say, soon turned into a cursing session that threatened to go even further . . . The foreman started to shout again and waved his stick, but once again the hoop fell apart. It finally became evident that axes were not sufficient for the job, and that some other implement would have to be used. A couple of men were immediately dispatched under escort to the fortress in order to get these other tools, and while they waited the others sat down on the barge in perfect peace and quiet, taking out their pipes and lighting them again.

At last the foreman spat.

'Well, you'll never make the work pay. Ach, what a bunch, what a bunch,' he muttered, making an angry gesture, and went back to the fortress, waving his stick in the air.

An hour later the works supervisor arrived. When he had listened quietly to all that the convicts had to say, he announced that he was going to set them an assignment: they were to remove another four hoops, but to do it so they did not break but remained intact; he also designated a large section of the barge that was to be taken apart. after which the men would be allowed to return to barracks.

It was a hefty assignment, but how those men set to it. There was no sign now of laziness or bewilderment. The axes began to thud as the wooden nails were wrenched out. The rest of the men placed thick poles underneath the hoops and, bearing down on the poles with the weight of twenty hands, smartly and adroitly prised up the hoops, which now to my surprise came away all in one piece and undamaged. The work went like lightning. No one wasted any words, there was no swearing, each man knew what to say, what to do, where to go, what to suggest. Exactly half an hour before the drum was beaten, the assignment was completed and the convicts went back to barracks, weary but entirely satisfied, though they had only saved some thirty minutes of the whole time allotted. But with regard to myself, I noticed one strange thing: wherever I went in order to try to be of help, I was always out of place, in the way, and the men would drive me away with a curse.

The very lowest ragamuffin, himself the most inferior of workmen, not daring to utter a word in the presence of the other convicts, who were more alert and intelligent than he, even such a man thought himself entitled to shout at me and drive me away if I happened to be standing next to him, on the pretext that I was in his way. At last one of the alert convicts said casually to my face: 'Who told you to shove your nose in? Beat it. Quit pushing in where you're not wanted.'

'You're in prison now,' said another man immediately, taking up the refrain.

'You'd do better to get yourself a tin mug,' said a third, 'and go and do a bit of begging for yourself, there's nothing for you to do here.'

I was compelled to stand apart on my own; but to stand apart while everyone else is working makes one feel somehow guilty. When I really did move away to the end of the barge, however, the men started to call out:

'Look at the workmen they've given us; what can you get done with the likes of them? Not a thing!'

This was all of course intentionally staged as a kind of entertainment for everyone. It was essential that a former nobleman be given a rough time, and they were of course glad of the opportunity to do it.

The reader will now readily understand why, as I have already said, the first question that preoccupied me when I entered the prison was the one of how I should behave, on what sort of footing I should try to set myself with these men. I knew in advance that I would often have confrontations with them such as the one I was now having at work. But confrontations or no confrontations, I was determined not to alter the plan of action I had already partly thought out at this time; I knew that it was the right one. I had decided that I must behave as straightforwardly and as independently as I could, under no circumstances make any particular attempt to approach them, but not reject them if they wished to approach me. Under no circumstances should I be afraid of their threats and hatred, and I should pretend as far as possible to ignore these. Under no circumstances should I approach them on certain points, and should not indulge certain of their habits and customs; in short, I should not ask to be fully accepted by them as one of their companions. I guessed at first glance that they would be the first to despise me if I did this. However, according to their scheme of things (I later discovered this to be the case beyond any doubt) I was supposed to assert my noble origins and show them that I respected these; in other words, I was expected to pamper myself, to give myself airs, to show disdain for them, to sniff at everything, to act the fine gentleman. This was their conception of what a nobleman was. They would, of course, have given me a rough time for behaving like this, but they would none the less have respected me for it. Such a role did not suit me; I had never been their sort of nobleman. On the other hand, however, I promised myself never by any action of mine to debase in their eyes either my education or my way of thinking. If, in order to please them, I had started to curry their favour by agreeing with them, behaving familiarly with them and lowering myself to the level of their various 'qualities', they would have immediately supposed that I was doing this out of fear and cowardice, and would have treated me with contempt. A—v was no example to follow: he was on close terms with the Major, and the men were afraid of him. On the other hand, I did not want to shut myself off from them in a chilly, inaccessible politeness as the Poles did. I understood very clearly now that the men despised me because I wanted to do the same work as they did, because I did not pamper myself or put on airs in their presence; and although I knew with certainty that they would later be compelled to alter their opinion of me, the thought that at present they had, in some sense, a right to despise me, thinking that I was trying to ingratiate myself with them at work – this thought hurt me bitterly.

When the afternoon's work was over, and I returned to the prison in the evening, weary and exhausted, a terrible feeling of anguish once again overcame me. 'How many thousands of days like this one still lie ahead of me,' I thought, 'all of them like this one, all of them the same.' When it was already getting dark, I was wandering silently and alone behind the barracks, following the line of the prison fence. Suddenly, I saw our dog Sharik running towards me. Sharik was our prison mascot, just as there are regimental, battery and squadron mascots. This dog had lived in the prison longer than anyone could remember, belonged to no one, considered everyone his owner and was fed on scraps from the kitchen. He was quite a large dog, black with white spots, a mongrel, not very old, with intelligent eyes and a fluffy tail. No one ever fondled him or paid him the slightest attention. From my first day, I stroked him and gave him bread out of my hand. When I stroked him he would stand quietly and look at me affectionately, gently wagging his tail as a sign of pleasure. Now, not having seen me, the first person to fondle him in several years, for a long time, he had been running around looking for me among all the other convicts, and finding me behind the barracks came rushing towards me with a yelp of joy. I don't know what came over me, but I rushed forwards and kissed him, throwing my arms around his head; in one running leap he placed his forepaws on my shoulders and began to lick my face. 'So this is the friend that has been sent to me by fate,' I thought, and every time I returned from work during those early, sombre days, the first thing I did, before going anywhere else, was to hurry behind the barracks with Sharik jumping up in front of me, yelping with delight, embrace his head and kiss it again and again, while a sweet and yet agonizingly bitter sensation gnawed at my heart. And I remember that I would derive great satisfaction from the thought – as though taking pride in my own agony of spirit – that there was in the whole world left to me only one creature that loved me, that was devoted to me, my friend, my only friend – my faithful dog Sharik.

* 7 *

NEW ACQUAINTANCES. PETROV

But time went by, and little by little I began to settle down. With every day that passed, the ordinary scenes and events of my new life had a less and less disturbing effect on me. Incidents, surroundings, people all became familiar. It was impossible to grow reconciled to this life, but it was high time I accepted it as an established fact. If I still had any misapprehensions, I tried to keep them as deeply hidden as possible. I no longer trailed around the prison like a lost soul, nor did I betray anguish. The savagely inquisitive eyes of the convicts were no longer trained on me so often, or with such manifest insolence. I also seemed to have become familiar to them, a circumstance for which I was very glad. Already I walked about the prison as though I were at home, I knew my place on the plank bed and even seemed to have managed to get used to things I never would have believed I could in all my life have grown used to. I went regularly each week to have half of my head shaved. Every Saturday, in our free time, we were summoned one by one from the prison to the guardhouse (a convict who did not go had to make his own arrangements for shaving) and there the battalion barbers washed our heads with soap and cold water and scraped them mercilessly with the bluntest of razors. The memory of this torture still gives me a gooseflesh. However, I soon found a remedy: Akim Akimych directed me to a military convict who for a copeck would shave anyone's head with his own razor, and who had built a business out of this. Many of the convicts went to him in order to avoid the prison barbers, though they were no milksops. Our convict-barber was called *the major*, though I have no idea why, and I could not see how he resembled the real Major in any way. Now, as I write this, I see this 'major' before me, a tall, lean and taciturn fellow, rather on the unintelligent side, forever absorbed in his occupation and never to be seen without a strop in his hand, sharpening his utterly worn-out razor. He seemed wholly taken up with this occupation, and appeared to have accepted it as his mission in life. He was always very happy when his razor was sharp and someone came along wanting to be shaved: his lather was warm, his hand light, giving a shave as smooth as velvet. He obviously took both pleasure and pride in his art and he would accept the copeck he had earned carelessly, as though what really mattered was the art, not the money. A—v once got a real dressing-down from the Major proper when in one of his sneaking reports about the other convicts he once mentioned the name of our prison barber and incautiously styled him *the major*. The real Major flew into a violent rage. 'I'll show you who's the Major round here,' he shouted, foaming at the mouth, as he dealt with A—v in his usual fashion. 'Have you any idea what a major is? Here's some villain of a convict, and you dare to call him a major, right to my face, in my very presence! ...' Only someone like A—v could get along with such a man.

From my very first day in the prison I began to dream about freedom. It became my favourite occupation to calculate, using a thousand different measurements and methods, how long it would be before my years of imprisonment were over. The subject dominated all my thoughts, and I am certain that anyone who has been deprived of freedom for any length of time finds this to be the case. I have no idea, of course, whether the other convicts thought and calculated as I did; but the astonishing lightheadedness of their hopes struck me from the very outset. The hope of a prisoner who has been deprived of freedom differs completely from that of a man who is living a normal life. The free man has hopes, of course (for a change in his fortunes, for example, or for the success of some undertaking), but he lives, he acts; he is carried along entirely in the whirl of real life. Not so the convict. He also has a kind of life, it is true – that of a prisoner, a convict. But whoever a convict is and whatever the term of his sentence, he is emphatically, instinctively unable to accept his fate as something positive and final, as a part of real life. No convict feels *at home* in prison, but rather as if he were on a visit there. He contemplates twenty years as though they were two, and is quite certain that when he leaves prison at the age of fifty-five he will be the same strapping fellow he is now at thirty-five. 'I've got a bit to live yet!' he thinks, obstinately repelling all doubts and troublesome thoughts. Even the lifers who belonged to the special category sometimes counted on the imminent arrival from St Petersburg of a special authorization: 'to be transferred to the Nerchinsk mines, and their sentences fixed'. Then everything would be fine: for one thing, it took nearly six months to march to Nerchinsk, and marching in a convict gang was infinitely preferable to being in prison! Then they would serve their time in Nerchinsk, and then ... There were even grey-headed old men who used to make this kind of calculation.

In Tobolsk I saw men who had been chained to the wall. They were put on seven-foot-long chains and slept on camp beds placed alongside them. The convicts chained in this way were men who had committed particularly atrocious crimes here in Siberia. They were kept chained up like this for five, even ten years. Most of them were bandits. I only saw one man among them who looked as though he might have some sort of rank: he had once worked in government service somewhere. He spoke rather quietly and subserviently, with a lisp; his smile had a saccharine sweetness. He showed us his chain, and the most comfortable way of lying on the bed. When he was at large he must have been quite a character. These men were all generally well-behaved and seemed contented, but each one of them wanted to serve out his sentence as soon as possible. What for, one asked oneself. Just so they could get out of this dank room with its low brick vaults and walk around the prison courtyard and ... that was all. They would never be let out of prison. They themselves knew that men who were released from their chains were kept in the prison for the rest of their days, until they died, wearing fetters. They knew this, and yet they had a terrible desire to serve out their enchainment as quickly as possible. Without this desire, how could they stay chained up for five or six years on end and not die or go out of their minds? Was there any man who could have endured it?

I had a feeling that work could be my salvation, that it could strengthen my body and my physical health. The continual mental unease, the nervous irritation and closed atmosphere of the barrack could destroy me completely. 'If I get out in the open air more often, work every day until I'm tired, get used to carrying heavy weights, then at least I will save myself,' I thought. 'I will strengthen myself, I will leave prison healthy, fit and strong, not old.' I was not mistaken: the work and physical activity did me a power of good. I looked with horror upon one of my companions (a nobleman) who was wasting away in prison like a candle. He had come here at the same time as myself, had been young, handsome and cheerful, but left half-destroyed, grey-haired, suffering from shortness of breath and hardly able to walk. 'No,' I used to think, looking at him, 'I want to live, and I will live.' The convicts gave me a hard time at first because of my love of work, and they poisoned my life for a long time with their mockery and contempt. But I paid no attention to anyone, and would cheerfully go off somewhere, even if only to bake and pound alabaster, for example, one of the first jobs I learned. That was easy work. The works administrators were prepared to do everything in their power in order to make the work of the gentleman convicts easier. This was by no means an indulgence, however, but merely what was right and proper. It would have been a strange thing if a man of half the strength, who had never worked in his life before, had been expected to carry out the same assignment as that given a real labourer. But this 'spoiling' was not always done, and when it was, it was done as it were on the sly; such matters were subject to strict supervision. The convicts were quite often required to do hard physical labour, and then of course the noblemen suffered twice as much as the other convicts. The work on the alabaster usually involved the detailing of three or four old men or weaklings (that included us, of course); in addition, one real workman who knew the job was sent along with them. The same man was usually chosen for several years on end; his name was Almazov, a lean, austere, swarthy character, already getting on in years, surly and taciturn. His contempt for us was

profound. He was so untalkative, however, that he could not even
be bothered to grumble at us. The shed in which the alabaster was
baked and pounded also stood on the steep, deserted river bank.
In winter, especially if the day was gloomy and overcast, the view
across the river of the opposite bank in the far distance was a
melancholy one. There was something dreary and heart-searing
about this wild, empty landscape. But it was perhaps even more
painful when the sun shone on the endless white sheet of the snow;
if only one could have flown away somewhere into those steppes,
which began on the opposite bank and spread out to the south in
a single unbroken expanse for some fifteen hundred versts to the
south. Almazov usually set to work in austere silence; we would
experience a kind of shame at not being able to help him properly,
while he would purposely cope with all the work on his own,
declining to ask us for any kind of assistance, as if in order to make
us feel the whole burden of our guilt before him and regret our own
uselessness. Yet all his task consisted in was firing the oven and
baking the alabaster we hauled in for him. The next day, when the
alabaster was thoroughly baked, the work of unloading it from the
oven began. Each of us took a large wooden mallet, put some
alabaster into a special box, and set about pounding it. This was
very agreeable work. The fragile alabaster quickly turned into a
white, gleaming dust, so well and easily did it crumble. We brandished our heavy mallets and made such a banging and a crackling
that we all delighted in it. At last we grew tired, and our spirits were
improved; our cheeks glowed red, our circulation was faster. At this
point Almazov would begin to look at us condescendingly, as one
might look at young children; condescendingly he would smoke
his pipe for a while, though when in the end he opened his mouth to
speak, he could not resist having a good grumble at us. He was,
however, always like this, and was basically a good man, I think.

Another kind of work I was sent to do was rotating the lathe in
the workshop. The wheel of the lathe was large and heavy. Considerable exertion was required in order to rotate it, especially when
the lathe operator (one of the engineer workmen) was making some
item of regulation furniture for a prison official, a banister, say, or
a leg for a table so big that almost a whole log was required for the

purpose. In such a case one man would not have the strength to rotate the wheel on his own, and so two were usually sent – myself and another of the noblemen, B. For a period of several years this task was always allocated to us whenever there was anything to be turned. B. was a frail, puny man, still young, who suffered from a weak heart. He had arrived in the prison the year before me together with two companions – one of these was an old man who said his prayers day and night (the convicts respected him greatly for this) and who died while I was still there. The other was a man still young, fresh-skinned, ruddy-cheeked, strong and courageous, who had carried the exhausted B. the whole latter half of the march to the prison, a distance of some seven hundred versts. The friend-ship between them was something to watch. B. was a man of great education and nobility of spirit, with a character that was mag-nanimous, but had been vitiated and exasperated by illness. We rotated the wheel together, and found that this absorbed our inter-est. This work was magnificent exercise for me.

I also particularly enjoyed shovelling snow. This was usually done after blizzards, and was a very frequent occurrence in winter. After a twenty-four-hour blizzard, some of the houses would be covered with snow up to the middle of the windows, while others would be snowed up almost entirely. Then, when the blizzard had stopped and the sun had come out, we would be chased outside in large groups, sometimes all of us together, to shovel the drifts of snow away from the government buildings. Each man received a shovel, and a common assignment was given, sometimes an assign-ment such that it might well be wondered how it could ever be completed, and then all the men set to work simultaneously. The powdery, freshly fallen snow, slightly frozen on top, was easily shovelled up in enormous lumps which turned into glittering dust as we scattered them about. Our shovels cut straight into the white mass that sparkled in the sunshine. The convicts were nearly always cheerful when they did this work. The fresh winter air and the physical exercise warmed them up. Everyone grew cheerful; laughter, shouts, jokes rang out. Some of the men would begin to throw snowballs at each other, not, needless to say, without the ensuing shouts of the cautious prisoners, who were indignant at any laughter or jocularity, and the general animation usually ended in an exchange of violent abuse.

Little by little I began to widen the circle of my acquaintance. Acquaintances were not, however, uppermost in my mind: I was still restless, gloomy and mistrustful. My acquaintanceships began of their own accord. One of the first people to start visiting me was the convict Petrov. I say 'visit' and wish to place particular emphasis on this word. Petrov was in the special category and lived in the barrack furthest from mine. It might have appeared that there could be no communication between us whatever; we also had and could have absolutely nothing in common. And yet in these early days, Petrov seemed to consider it his duty to come to my barrack to see me or to catch me during the work break when I was walking behind the barracks, concealed as far as possible from human eyes. At first I did not care for this. But he somehow managed to contrive it so that I began to find his visits entertaining, in spite of the fact that he was by no means a particularly communicative or talkative individual. He was a short, sturdily built man, adroit and unable to keep still; his face was quite pleasant, pale, with broad cheekbones, his eyes bold, his teeth small, white and closely set, with an everlasting pinch of snuff just inside his lower lip. Putting snuff or tobacco inside one's lip was a habit that was common to many of the convicts. He seemed younger than his years. He was about forty, but looked more like thirty. To me he always spoke quite freely, and he treated me as an equal in every respect, that is to say with the utmost decency and tact. If he noticed, for example, that I wanted to be alone, he would talk to me for a couple of minutes and then immediately leave me, each time thanking me for the attention I had paid him, something which, needless to say, he never did for any of the other convicts. It was an interesting fact that our relations continued like this not only during the early days of my sentence, but for several years on end, and almost never became any closer, though he was truly devoted to me. Even now I cannot decide what it really was he wanted from me, and why he came to see me every day. Although he had occasion to steal from me later on, his stealing was somehow done *by accident*; he almost never asked me for money, so it was not for the sake of money or with any ulterior motive that he came to visit me.

I do not know why, but it always seemed to me that he was not living in the prison at all, but far away in some other place in town, only visiting the prison in passing so as to obtain the latest news, to call on me, to see how we were all getting along. He was always hurrying off somewhere, as if he had left someone waiting for him, some business unfinished. Yet he never seemed particularly flustered. The expression of his eyes was rather strange: fixed, with a touch of boldness and mockery, but directed as though into the distance, as though he were looking through and beyond the objects that met his gaze at some other objects that were further off. This gave him an absent-minded look. Sometimes, for fun, I would look to see where Petrov went after he left me. Where was it that people were waiting for him? But when he left me he would hurry off to a barrack or kitchen, and sit down there beside one of the men who were chatting, listening attentively to their conversation; sometimes he would engage in the conversation himself, quite heatedly, it seemed, and then break off and grow silent. But whether he was speaking, sitting or just being silent, it was none the less evident that he was only passing through, and that somewhere he had business to attend to, where people were waiting for him. What was strangest of all was that he never had any kind of business whatsoever; he lived a life of complete idleness (apart from the prison work, of course). He had no trade, and hardly ever had any money. But he did not seem to lose any sleep over money. What was it he talked about with me? His conversation was as strange as the man he was. For example, he would see me walking alone somewhere at the back of the prison and would suddenly make a sharp turn in my direction. He always walked fast, and turned round abruptly. He would stride towards me, yet would appear to be running.

'Hello.'

'Hello.'

'I'm not disturbing you, am I?'

'No.'

'I wanted to ask you about Napoleon.[18] He's related to the

Napoleon who was here in 1812, isn't he?' (Petrov was a Kantonist and was educated.)

'Yes, he is.'

'How is it he's a president, then?'

He always asked his questions rapidly and curtly, as if he needed to know whatever it was as soon as possible. It was as though he were carrying out an investigation into some extremely important matter which would not brook the slightest delay.

I explained how it came to be that he was a president and added that it was possible he would soon be an emperor.

'How come?'

I explained this too, as well as I was able to. Petrov listened attentively, understanding all that I said and quickly thinking it over, even tilting his ear towards me as he did so.

'Hm. I wanted to ask you, Aleksandr Petrovich: is it true, as they say, that there are monkeys with arms that reach down to their feet and which are as big as the tallest man?'

'Yes, there are monkeys like that.'

'What do they look like?'

I explained this too, as best I could.

'And where do they live?'

'In hot countries. There are some on the island of Sumatra.'

'Is that in America? Is that the country where they say people walk around on their heads?'

'Not on their heads. You're thinking of the Antipodes.'

I explained what America was and, to the best of my ability, what the Antipodes were. Once again he listened attentively, as though he had come especially to hear about the Antipodes.

'Aha! I read about Countess Lavallière[19] last year, Arefyev brought the book over from the adjutant's. Is it true, or is it just made up? It's written by Dumas.'

'It's made up, of course.'

'Well, I must be off now. Many thanks.'

And Petrov disappeared. Our conversations never really varied much from this model.

I started to glean some facts about him. When M. found out about our acquaintanceship he went so far as to warn me. He told me that many of the convicts had inspired him with horror, especially at first, in his early days in the prison, but that none of them, not even Gazin, had made such a fearsome impression on him as this Petrov.

'He's the most determined, the most fearless of all the convicts,' said M. 'He's capable of anything; he'll stop at nothing if some whim crosses his fancy. He'd kill you, if the notion took him, just like that, kill you without batting an eyelid or feeling the slightest remorse. I think he may not be in his right mind.'

I found this opinion very interesting. But M. was somehow unable to give me his reasons for thinking this way. And it was a strange thing: I was subsequently to know Petrov for several years on end, and talked to him every day; all during this time he was sincerely devoted to me (though I really do not know why) – and in all those years, although he lived a regular, well-behaved life in the prison and did nothing very dreadful, every time I looked at him and talked with him I became convinced that M. was right and that Petrov was indeed a most determined, fearless man who would submit to no restraint. Why this seemed to me to be so, I cannot say.

I will observe, however, that this Petrov was the same man who, when he had been led out for his flogging, had tried to kill our Major when the latter had been 'saved by a miracle', as the convicts said, leaving the prison just before the very moment the flogging was due to begin. On another occasion, before he had gone to prison, it had happened that the colonel had struck him during drill. He had probably been hit like this many times before; but this time he refused to put up with it and stabbed the colonel openly in broad daylight, in front of the assembled battalion. However, I do not know all the details of his story; he never told it to me. These were, of course, only sudden fits, when his nature would suddenly display itself in its entirety. But these fits of his were very rare. He was really well-behaved and even submissive. Passions lurked within him, and they were strong, virulent ones, but the hot coals were kept constantly strewn with ashes and smouldered away quietly. I never observed a trace of boasting or vanity in him, as I did in others. He seldom quarrelled, but on the other hand was not particularly

friendly with anyone except Sirotkin, and then only when he needed
to obtain the latter's services. Once, however, I saw him get seriously angry. Something was being refused him; he was being done
out of his rightful share. The man he was arguing with was a tall,
athletic convict; his name was Vasily Antonov, a vicious jeering
bully who was no coward, either; he was in the civilian category.
They had been shouting at one another for a long time, and I
thought that the affair would end with at most a few punches, since
Petrov occasionally, though very rarely, fought and swore like the
very worst of convicts. But this time it was different: Petrov suddenly grew pale, his lips quivered and turned blue; he began to
breathe with difficulty. He got up from where he had been sitting
and slowly, very slowly went up to Antonov with bare feet (he was
very fond of going barefoot in summer). Everyone in the noisy,
shout-filled barrack suddenly grew quiet; one could have heard the
sound made by a fly's wings. They were all waiting for what would
happen next. Antonov leapt towards him; he looked terrible ... I
could stand it no longer and left the barrack, fully expecting that
before I had gone down the front steps I would hear the shriek of
a man who had been murdered. But this time, too, the matter came
to nothing: before Petrov could get to him, Antonov quickly and
silently threw him the item of contention. (The whole fuss was
about some pathetic rags, some kind of cloths used for binding up
their legs and feet.) Antonov, of course, snarled some abuse at him
for a couple of minutes, so as to cleanse his conscience, and out of
a sense of propriety, in order to show that he was not a complete
coward. But Petrov paid not the slightest attention to the abuse,
and did not even bother to reply: the matter had nothing to do with
abuse, and it had been settled in his favour; he was very satisfied
and took the rag. A quarter of an hour later he was loafing around
the prison with an air of utter idleness as if he were looking for
someone to tell him about something interesting so he could poke
his nose in and listen. It seemed that everything was of interest to
him, but he seemed to remain somehow indifferent to most of what
went on, and spent his time strolling idly around the prison, carried
aimlessly here and there. He could be compared to a workman, a
good, strong workman who could really get cracking on a job, but

who was temporarily unemployed and was sitting playing with the little children while he waited for something to turn up. I could not really understand why he stayed in the prison, why he did not run away. He would have run away without the slightest hesitation if he had really wanted to. With men like Petrov, reason is in control only for as long as they do not want anything. Then their desire is not to be deflected by any obstacle upon earth. And I am certain that he could have made a most skilful escape, could have given everyone the slip, could have holed up somewhere in the woods or in the reeds of the river bank, going without food for a week. But he had evidently not hit on this idea yet, did not *completely* desire this. I never observed in him any great powers of judgement, any particular common sense. People like this are born with one idea which drives them unconsciously to and fro throughout the whole of their lives; so they move aimlessly through life until they find something that is thoroughly consonant with their desires; then they lose their heads over it. It sometimes surprised me that a man like this, who had killed his colonel for striking him, could lie down so unquestioningly under the birchings he received. He was sometimes whipped, too, when he was caught with vodka. Like all convicts who had no trade, he sometimes got involved in vodka smuggling. But he would submit to the birch as though by his own consent, as if he were perfectly aware that he had done wrong; if this had not been the case, nothing, not even the threat of death itself, could have induced him to submit. It also surprised me when, in spite of his evident devotion to me, he stole from me. This seemed to go in phases with him. He was the man who stole my Bible from me, when I had asked him to take it from one place to another. It was only a matter of a few yards, but he managed to find a buyer on the way, sold the Bible and drank the proceeds forthwith. He probably wanted to drink very badly, and since he wanted it so badly, it *had* to be done. This is the kind of man who will kill someone in order to get twenty-five copecks to buy a bottle of vodka, although at another time he would let the same man walk by with a hundred thousand rubles in his pocket. In the evening he himself told me that he had robbed me; he spoke without a shadow of embarrassment or remorse, with complete indifference, as if he were telling me about the most ordinary occurrence. I started to give him a good talking-to; I was annoyed about not having my Bible any more, after all. He listened without irritation, almost meekly; he agreed that the Bible was a very useful book, was genuinely sorry for having stolen it; he looked at me with such self-confidence that I immediately stopped scolding him. He had put up with my reprimands, probably reckoning that since he was not going to get away with such an action without a dressing-down like this, it was as well that I should let myself go and derive both relief and pleasure from scolding him; but that it was really a lot of nonsense, such nonsense that anyone who was serious would be ashamed to talk the way I was doing. I had the impression that he regarded me as some sort of a child, as an infant, even, who had no understanding of the most elementary realities of life. If, for example, I started to talk to him about anything other than books or learning, he would, it is true, reply to me, but his reply would be made only out of politeness, as it were, limited to the very briefest of answers. I often used to wonder what there could possibly be for him in all the bookish knowledge he was in the habit of asking me about. It would sometimes happen that during these conversations I would cast a sidelong glance at him to see if he were not laughing at me. But no; he would usually be listening seriously and attentively, though not greatly so, and this used sometimes to annoy me. His questions were precise and definite, but he would seem little surprised by all the information he received from me and would accept it with something approaching absent-mindedness ... I had the feeling that it had not taken him long to decide that it would be impossible to talk to me as one might to other people, that apart from books there was nothing I understood, or was capable of understanding, and that he might as well leave me alone.

I am certain that he was fond of me, and this impressed me very much. Whether it was that he considered me an immature, incomplete person, or whether he felt for me that peculiar kind of compassion which every strong being feels for every weak one, having identified me as such, I do not know. And although all this did not prevent him from stealing from me, I am certain that at the same time as he stole from me he felt sorry for me. 'Dear me!' he may have thought as he laid his hands on my earthly possessions. 'What kind of a man is this who can't even stand up for his own belongings?' But this it was, apparently, that made him feel fond of me. He once said to me, almost by accident, as it were, that I was 'far too good-natured', and 'a walkover, such a walkover that a fellow feels sorry for you. Only don't take that as an insult, Aleksandr Petrovich,' he added after a minute or two; 'I was just saying what I really feel.'

In life such people occasionally make a sudden and dramatic appearance at moments of general and violent action or social cataclysm and in so doing find their true vocation overnight. They are not men of words[20] and are incapable of being instigators or the leading lights in any cause; they are, however, the chief executors of causes and are the first to engage in action. They do this simply, without fanfare, but they are the first to leap over the main obstacles, moving forwards at full tilt without fear or reflection – and everyone rushes blindly after them, right to the last barricade, where they usually lay down their lives. I do not think Petrov will come to a good end; he will wind everything up in one minute flat, and if he has not yet died it is only because his time has not yet come. However, who can tell? It may be that he will live to have grey hair, and will wander here and there before he dies very quietly of old age. But I think M. was right when he said that Petrov was the most desperate man in the whole prison.

* 8 *

DESPERATE MEN. LUKA

It is hard to say much about men who are desperate; in prison, as elsewhere, they are rather few in number. A man might look fearsome; you would take into account the stories that were told about him, and steer clear of him. An instinctive feeling made me avoid these men at first. Later on, my view of even the most terrible murderers was to change in many respects. One man who had never killed anyone could be more terrifying than another who had been sentenced for six murders. It was hard to form even the most elementary impression of some crimes, so strange were the circumstances in which they had been committed. I say this because among the common people some crimes have the most astonishing motives. There is, for example, one type of murderer that is quite often encountered. He lives quietly and humbly, enduring the vicissitudes of fortune. He may be a peasant, a house serf, an artisan or a soldier. Suddenly, without warning, something within him snaps; his endurance runs out and he plunges a knife into his enemy and oppressor. Something strange now begins to happen: the man seems to go temporarily berserk. He began by murdering his oppressor, his enemy; this, although criminal, is understandable; here there was a motive. But then he starts murdering people who are not his enemies, but just those who happen to cross his path, and he murders them for amusement, because of an insult or a look, for the sake of a string of beads, or simply, as way of saying 'Out of the way, don't let me catch you, here I come!' It is as if the man were drunk, or in delirium. As if, having overshot some sacred limit within himself, he begins to exult in the feeling that there is no longer anything sacred in him; as though he felt an irresistible longing to overshoot all law and authority in one go, and to delight in the most unbridled and boundless freedom, to delight in the sinking sensation in his heart which is caused by his own apprehension of himself. He knows, too, that a dreadful punishment awaits him. This is all, perhaps, similar to the feeling a man has when he looks down from a high tower into the depths below his feet, until he would be glad to throw himself downwards head first, so as to make an end of it all as soon as possible. And this can happen even in the case of the most submissive and hitherto unobtrusive men. There are even some who show off in this bemused state. The more downtrodden he was before, the more he is now seized by the urge to cut a dashing figure, to inspire terror. He delights in the terror he causes, loves the disgust he arouses in others. He affects a kind of *desperation*, and a 'desperate' man like this often longs for punishment, longs to be *dealt with*, because in the end his affected *desperation* has become too much for him to bear. It is interesting to observe that for the most part this state of mind, this affectation is sustained right up to the scaffold, and is then switched off: as if this were some formal interval designated in advance with certain rules and regulations. Now the man suddenly resigns himself, withdraws into the background, becomes a limp rag. On the scaffold he whines and snivels, begging the onlookers for forgiveness. When he arrives in the prison, you look at him and behold such a slobbering, snivelling, abject creature that you find yourself wondering if this can really be the same man who murdered five or six people.

Of course, there is another kind of man in the prison, one who does not submit so easily. He preserves a certain swagger, a certain boastfulness: 'Look,' he says, 'I'm not who you think I am; I'm in here for six murders.' But in the end he submits nevertheless. Only occasionally does he amuse himself by recounting his past bold exploits, the wild orgies he once had when he was a 'desperate' man, and if only he can get hold of some simple soul there is nothing he likes better than to show off and boast to this man with a suitably important air, holding forth about his heroic achievements, but taking care not to show that he is bursting with impatience to do so. 'Look,' he says, 'that's the kind of man I was!'

And with what finesse this self-regarding caution is observed, how insolently careless such a story sometimes is! What studied affectation is displayed in the narrator's tone of voice, in his every word. And where do these uneducated men learn it all?

Once during these early days, as I lay idly and miserably on the plank bed one long evening, I listened to a story of this kind and because of my inexperience took its narrator for some monstrous, terrible villain, for some character of outrageously iron will, while at the same time I hardly took Petrov seriously at all. The story was about how this man, Luka Kuzmich, for no other reason but his own satisfaction, had *wiped out* a certain major. This Luka Kuzmich was the same young, thin little Ukrainian convict with the pointed nose from our barrack whom I have already mentioned somewhere. He was really a Russian, but had been born in the south, where he had been a house serf, it appeared. There really was something sharp and overweening about him: 'the bird is small, but its claw is sharp.' But the convicts see through a man instinctively. He was held in very low esteem, or as they say in prison 'held in every low esteem'. His vanity was incredible. That evening he was sitting on the plank bed sewing a shirt. Sewing linen was his trade. Beside him sat a tall, sturdy, slow-witted lad of restricted intelligence who was none the less kind and good-natured; this was his neighbour on the plank bed, the convict Kobylin. Since they were neighbours, Luka often quarrelled with him, and in general treated him condescendingly, in a jeering and despotic manner, which Kobylin did not always notice because of his simple-heartedness. He would knit away at a woollen stocking, listening to Luka with indifference. Luka was telling his story in a voice that was loud and clear. He wanted everyone to hear, though he tried to make it sound as though it were Kobylin alone he was talking to.

'Well, my friend, they sent me away from our village,' he began, as he picked away with his needle, 'to Ch—v²¹ for vagrancy, you see.'

'When was that, a long time ago?' asked Kobylin.

'It'll be a year ago come next pea-picking. Well, when we reached K—v²¹ they stuck me in the prison for a bit. I looked round: there were twenty men in there with me, Ukrainians, all of them, tall, healthy, strapping fellows like bulls. And peaceful, like: the food was terrible, their major could twist them round his little finger, at his worship's excretion (Luka got the word wrong on purpose). After I'd been inside for a couple of days, I saw they were a bunch of cowards. "What are you giving a fool like that such an easy time for?" I asked them. "You go and try talking to him yourself!" they smirked back at me. I didn't say any more after that.

'And there was one really funny Ukrainian there, lads,' he added suddenly, turning away from Kobylin and addressing all the men together. 'He used to tell us about his trial and all the things he told the judge, and the tears would stream down his face as he sobbed about how he'd left his wife and kids behind. And he was a really hardened criminal, a massive grey-haired fellow. "I says to him: no! But there he sits, the little devil, writing and writing. Well, I says to myself, I hope you choke, I'd like that. But on he went, writing and writing away, until he'd finished . . . And what he'd written was my undoing." Give us a bit of thread, Vasya; this stuff's no good.'

'It's from the market,' replied Vasya, giving him some thread.

'The stuff we use in the tailoring shop's better. They sent the veteran for some the other day, but I don't know what mean old woman he buys it from,' continued Luka, holding his needle up to the light in order to thread it.

'Must be somebody he knows.'

'That's it, must be somebody he knows.'

'Well, so what about the major, then?' asked the completely forgotten Kobylin.

This was all that Luka required. However, he did not continue his story at once, almost as if Kobylin were not worthy of his attention. He calmly straightened his threads, calmly and lazily crossed his legs beneath him and at last began to speak:

'I finally managed to rouse my Ukrainians, and they asked to see the major. That morning I'd managed to borrow a knife from a neighbour of mine; and I hid it just in case it was needed. The major was furious when he arrived. Right, I said, don't you chicken out now, you Ukrainians. But their tails were right down between their legs, they were fairly shaking with fright. The major came running in, drunk. "Who's this? What's this? I'm the Tsar, and I'm God as well!"

'When he said: "I'm the Tsar, and I'm God as well",' Luka continued, 'I edged forward with the knife hidden in my sleeve.

'"No, your honour," I said, getting closer and closer to him, "how can your honour be our Tsar, and God as well?"

'"Aha, so it's you, is it?" cried the major. "You mutineer!"

'"No," I said (still getting closer and closer), "no, your honour, as you yourself may know, our God the Omnipotent and Omnipresent is One," I said. "And our Tsar is One, too, and he's been placed over us all by God Himself. He's a monarch, your honour," I said. "But you, your honour," I said, "are only a major and our commanding officer, your honour, by the favour of the Tsar and your merits," I said.

'"What-what-what-what?" he clucked like a hen, unable to speak properly, and choking. He was really surprised.

'"This is what," I said; and I suddenly went for him and stuck my knife in his belly right up to the hilt. It worked like magic. He rolled over and twitched his legs a bit and that was that. I threw the knife away.

'"Have a look at him now, Ukrainians, now you can lift him up,"
I said.'

Here I wish to make a digression. Unhappily, expressions like
'I'm the Tsar, and I'm God as well' and many other similar ones
were very frequently used by many commanding officers in the old
days. It must be confessed, however, that there are only a few such
officers left now; indeed, they may have died out altogether. I will
also observe that it was for the most part the officers who had risen
from the lower ranks who used and were particularly fond of using
such expressions. The rank of officer seems to have the effect of
turning everything in them, including their mental faculties, upside
down. After groaning long years under the weight of drudgery,
after progressing through all the degrees of subordination, they
suddenly realize that they are officers and gentlemen, commanders,
and in their first intoxication, from want of habit, they exaggerate
the notion of their power and importance; only, needless to say, in
relation to the ranks subordinate to them. Their attitude to their
superiors is, as before, one of servility, now quite unnecessary
and even offensive to many superior officers. Some of these yes-
men even rush to declare to their commanders, with a peculiar
display of tender feeling, that they have come from the lower ranks
and that even though they are officers they 'will always remember
their place'. But in relation to the lower ranks they become almost
unconditional despots. Of course, nowadays it would be hard to
find an officer who would say 'I'm the Tsar, and I'm God as well.'
But even so, I will none the less observe that nothing irritates
convicts, and indeed all the lower ranks, as much as these expressions employed by their superior officers. This self-aggrandizing
insolence, this exaggerated notion of their own impunity will
engender hatred in the most obedient of men and will drive them
beyond the bounds of patience. All this is now happily a thing of
the past – even in the old days such behaviour was severely
prosecuted by the authorities. I know several examples of this.

And indeed the lower ranks are irritated by any condescending
off-handedness, any disdain that is shown to them. There are some
who think, for example, that as long as one feeds a convict, looks
after him well, does everything according to the law, the matter is

at an end. This is a mistaken view. Everyone, whoever he is and however lowly the circumstances into which he has been pushed, demands, albeit instinctively and unconsciously, that respect be shown for his human dignity. The convict knows he is a convict, an outcast, and he knows his place *vis-à-vis* his superior officer; but no brands, no fetters will ever be able to make him forget that he is a human being. And since he really is a human being, it is necessary to treat him as one. Merciful heavens! *Human* treatment may even render human a man in whom the image of God has long ago grown tarnished. It is these 'unfortunates' that must be treated in the most human fashion. This is their salvation and their joy. I have met such good and noble commanding officers. I have seen the effect they produced on these degraded creatures. A few kind words – and the convicts experienced something approaching a moral resurrection. Like children, they rejoiced, and like children they began to love. I will observe one more thing that is strange: convicts do not like prison officials to behave too familiarly or *too* good-naturedly towards them. They want to respect the officials, and such behaviour somehow prevents them from doing so. The convicts like the officer in charge of them to have a decoration, to be important-looking, to be in the good books of some high-up official; they like him to be strict, dignified and fair-minded, and to respect his own personal worth. The convicts like such men better than any others: they see that he preserves his own dignity and does not insult them, and for them this means that everything is as it should be.

'I bet you got a roasting for that,' observed Kobylin, calmly.

'Hm. A roasting, my friend, too true, a roasting. Aley, give me the scissors. So then, friends, is there no *maydan* today?'

'The money's all gone on drink,' observed Vasya. 'If it hadn't, there'd be a *maydan*.'

'If! They give you a hundred rubles for "if" in Moscow,' observed Luka.

'And how many did they give you, Luka, all in all?' began Kobylin again.

'My dear man, they gave me a hundred and five. And I'll tell you something else, friends, they nearly killed me,' said Luka quickly, once again turning away from Kobylin. 'The way they gave me my hundred and five was to take me out in full parade. Before that I'd never had a taste of the lash. Crowds of people were flocking round as far as the eye could see, the whole town had turned out: "They're going to flog a bandit, that means he must be a murderer." Those crowds were so stupid, I can't tell you. The executioner stripped my clothes off, flung me on the ground and yelled: "Lie still, I'm going to burn your hide off!" I waited for what was coming next. When he landed the first one on me I wanted to howl, I tried to open my mouth but there wasn't any howl left in me. My voice had gone. When he landed the second one, believe it or not, I couldn't even hear them counting "two". When I came to again, I heard them counting "seventeen". They took me down from the crossbar four times after that, gave me half an hour's rest each time: they poured water over me. I looked at them all with my eyes bursting out of my head and thought: "Now I'm going to croak ..."'

'And didn't you?' asked Kobylin, naïvely.

Luka surveyed him with a glance that was filled with the utmost contempt; some of the men burst out laughing.

'The man's a blethering idiot.'

'He's not all there on top,' observed Luka, as if regretting ever having started to talk to such a man.

'He's off his head, you mean,' said Vasya, in support of this.

Although Luka had killed six people, no one in the prison was afraid of him, even though he himself had a secret desire to be thought a fearsome character.

9

ISAY FOMICH.
THE BATH-HOUSE.
BAKLUSHIN'S STORY

The feast of Christmas was approaching. The convicts were looking forward to it with a kind of solemn expectancy, and as I watched them I also began to anticipate something unusual. Four days before the holiday we were taken to the bath-house. In my time, especially in my first years in the prison, the convicts were seldom taken to the bath-house. All the men were filled with jubilation and started to get ready. Arrangements had been made for us to go there after dinner, and during these after-dinner hours no one did any work. The man in our barrack who was most jubilant and excited of all was Isay Fomich Bumshteyn, a Jewish convict, whom I have already mentioned in Chapter 4 of my story. He liked to steam himself until he was in a torpor, until he lost consciousness, and whenever, turning over old memories in my mind, I remember our prison baths (which truly deserve not to be forgotten), the face that appears in the foreground of the picture is that of our most bliss-fully happy and never-to-be-forgotten Isay Fomich, my prison companion and barrack mate. My goodness, what an extremely amusing fellow he was! I have already said a few words about his appearance: he was aged about fifty, puny and wrinkled with the most fearsome brands on his cheeks and forehead; his thin, white body recalled that of a chicken. His facial expression displayed a constant, unshakeable self-satisfaction, a kind of blissfulness, even. He seemed in no way to regret having ended up in prison. Since he was a jeweller, and since there was no jeweller in the town, he received a constant stream of commissions from the noblemen and the government officials there, and occupied himself solely with this work. Even though it was not very much, he did receive some payment for what he did. He was by no means hard up, was even 'well off', but he salted his money away and lent it at interest to any convict who asked. He had his own samovar, a good mattress,

cups, a whole dinner service. The Jews of the town did not refuse
him their acquaintance and protection. On Saturdays he would go
to the town synagogue (this was permitted by the regulations), and
all in all he lived in the lap of luxury; not, however, without the
impatient expectation of the day when his twelve-year sentence
would be up and he could 'get married'. There was in him the most
comical mixture of naïveté, stupidity, cunning, insolence, simple-
heartedness, timidity, boastfulness and effrontery. I found it very
strange that the other convicts did not treat him with derision, but
merely pulled his leg on the odd occasion. Isay Fomich was evidently a diversion for them, someone who could always cheer them
up. 'There's only one Isay Fomich, don't you dare lay a finger on
him,' the convicts used to say, and Isay Fomich, although he knew
what they meant, was none the less clearly proud of the importance
he had. This amused the convicts no end. His arrival in the prison
was quite killingly funny (it was before my time, but the other
prisoners told me about it). Suddenly, early one evening, when
work was over for the day, a rumour spread through the prison that
a Jew had been brought in, that he was being shaved in the guardroom and would be coming in very soon. There was not a single
Jew in the prison at that time. The convicts awaited his arrival with
impatience and immediately flocked round him when he walked
in through the gates. The duty sergeant led him into the civilian
barrack and pointed out a berth on the plank bed to him. Isay
Fomich was holding a bag which contained both his own things and
his prison issue. He put down the bag, clambered up onto the plank
bed and sat down, tucking his legs under him, not daring to raise
his eyes and look at anyone. All round him reverberated laughter
and prison jokes about his Jewish origin. Suddenly a young convict
forced his way through the crowd, carrying his very oldest, dirtiest
and most tattered pair of wide, summer trousers, together with his
prison-issue foot-rags. He sat down beside Isay Fomich and
clapped him on the shoulder.

'Well, my dear friend, I've been waiting for you here these last
six years. Hey, look, what'll you give me for this lot?'

And he laid out in front of him the rags he had brought.

Isay Fomich, who had been so timid upon entering the prison

that he had not even dared to raise his eyes and look at the crowd of jeering, disfigured and terrible faces which surrounded him densely on all sides, and who because of his timidity had not yet managed to get a word out, catching sight of the man's pledge suddenly mustered his forces and began to run his fingers through the rags with great self-confidence. He even held them up to the light. Everyone was waiting for what he would say.

'Come on now, you'll surely give me a silver ruble for them, won't you? They're worth it, after all,' continued the prospective client, winking at Isay Fomich.

'A silver ruble's out of the question, I can let you have seven copecks.'

These were the first words uttered by Isay Fomich in the prison. Everyone fairly rocked with laughter.

'Seven copecks! All right, then, give me seven; you're in luck! Here, look, take the clothes; if you lose them I'll have your hide.'

'The interest will be three copecks, that's ten you'll have to pay if you want them back,' the Jew continued abruptly in a quavering voice, putting his hand in his pocket for the money and casting a fearful glance at the other convicts. He was terrified, yet he wanted to do business.

'That's yearly interest, is it, the three copecks?'

'No, not yearly, monthly.'

'You've got close fists, Jew. What do they call you?'

'Isay Fomich.'

'Well, Isay Fomich, you're going to go places in here! Goodbye.'

Isay Fomich examined the rags again, folded them up and carefully put them into his bag to the continued accompaniment of the convicts' laughter.

Everyone really seemed fond of him and none of the men ever harmed him, although they were nearly all in debt to him. He himself was as meek as a hen and, seeing that he was generally regarded with favour, even felt encouraged to strut about a bit; this he did in such a simple-hearted and comical fashion, however, that everyone immediately forgave him. Luka, who had known a lot of Jews in his time, often used to tease him, not out of any malice, but

simply for the sake of amusement, as one might amuse oneself with
a dog, a parrot or any kind of trained animal. Isay Fomich knew
this very well, took not the slightest offence, and laughed it off most
skilfully.

'Hey, Jew, I'll finish you off!'

'You hit me one and I'll hit you ten,' Isay Fomich would reply
with a swagger.

'Goddam mangy scab.'

'So what if I am?'

'Mangy Jew.'

'So what? I may be mangy, but I'm rich; I have money.'

'You sold Christ.'

'So what if I did?'

'Well done, Isay Fomich, good man! There's only one Isay
Fomich, don't you lay a finger on him,' the convicts shouted,
laughing.

'Hey, Jew, you'll get a flogging, you'll go to Siberia.'

'Already I'm in Siberia.'

'They'll send you even further.'

'And is our Lord God there?'

'I expect so.'

'So what, then; as long as I have the Lord God and my money,
I'll be all right anywhere.'

'Good man, Isay Fomich, it's obvious you're a good man!' men
shouted all around, and Isay Fomich, though he could see they
were laughing at him, did his best to keep his spirits up; the
universal chorus of praise gave him obvious satisfaction, and he
began to sing to the whole barrack in a thin little descant: 'La – la
– la – la – la!' It was some inane, ridiculous little tune, the only song
(it had no words) he ever sang during all the time he was in the
prison. Later, when he had formed a closer acquaintance with me
he would solemnly swear to me that this song was the same one that
the Jews, all six hundred thousand of them, great and small, had
sung as they crossed the Red Sea, and that all Jews are commanded
to sing this tune at the moment of triumph and victory over their
enemies.

On Friday evenings men from the other barracks used to come

over specially to our hut in order to watch Isay Fomich celebrate his Jewish Sabbath. Isay Fomich was so innocently vain and boastful that he even enjoyed the curiosity of the convicts. With pedantic, affected gravity he placed a cloth on his little table in a corner, opened his holy book, lit two candles and, muttering some secret words, began to array himself in his robe (*riza*, or *rizha*, as he pronounced it in his Polish accent). This was a gaily coloured woollen cloak which he preserved carefully in his locker. He tied leather phylacteries on both his hands, and on his head, right on his very forehead, by means of a bandage he fastened a kind of small wooden box, so that it looked as though some sort of ridiculous horn were coming out of his forehead. Then he began his prayers. He recited them in a sing-song voice, shouting, spraying himself with spittle, turning round and round in circles and making wild, ridiculous gestures. Of course, all this was prescribed by the prayer ritual, and there was not really anything strange or funny about it; but what was funny was that Isay Fomich gave the impression that he was showing off to us and making a spectacle out of his prayers. Now he would suddenly bury his face in his hands and begin to recite in a sobbing voice. His sobs would increase in intensity, and nearly wailing, in a state of exhaustion, he would lower his head, crowned with the wooden box, onto the holy book; but then again, suddenly, in the midst of the most violent sobbing, he would begin to roar with laughter and recite something in singsong fashion, his voice moved and solemn, as if weakened by an excess of happiness. 'Aye, the spirit's taken him,' the convicts used to say. I once asked Isay Fomich what the sobs and sudden solemn transitions to happiness and bliss meant. Isay Fomich liked it a great deal when I asked him questions of this kind. He explained to me at once that the weeping and sobbing denoted the idea of the loss of Jerusalem, and that the holy law directed believers to sob as violently as possible at this thought, and to beat their breasts. But that at the moment of the most intense sobbing, he, Isay Fomich, *must suddenly*, as if by chance, remember (this *suddenly* was also prescribed by the law) that there exists a prophecy concerning the return of the Jews to Jerusalem. At this memory he must immediately break out into joy, singing and laughter, and must

utter his prayers in such a way that his voice expressed as much
solemnity and nobility as possible. Isay Fomich was extremely fond
of this *sudden* transition and of its absolute obligatoriness: he saw
it as an especially clever, cunning machination, and told me with
a somewhat boastful air about this complicated ordinance. Once,
when his prayers were in full swing, the Major walked into the
room accompanied by an officer of the watch and some guards. All
the convicts stood to attention beside their places on the plank bed,
except for Isay Fomich, who began to shout and gesticulate even
more wildly than before. He knew that his prayers were allowed by
the prison regulations, holy law demanded that he should not
interrupt them and, of course, there was no risk in his shouting like
this in front of the Major. But he greatly enjoyed putting on airs
in front of the Major and showing off to the rest of us. The Major
walked up to within one pace of him: Isay Fomich turned round
with his back to his little table and began to recite his solemn
prophecy in sing-song tones, right in the Major's face, waving his
arms about as he did so. Since at that moment it was prescribed for
him to express in his features an extreme degree of happiness and
nobility, he lost no time in doing so, screwing up his eyes in a
curious fashion, laughing and nodding at the Major. The Major
was startled; but finally he snorted with laughter, called Isay
Fomich a fool to his face and left, Isay Fomich continuing to shout
louder and louder all the while. An hour later, when Isay Fomich
was having his supper, I asked him: 'What if the Major had been
stupid and got angry with you?'

'What Major?'

'What do you mean, what Major? Didn't you see him?'

'No.'

'But he was standing two feet away from you, right under your
nose.'

But Isay Fomich began most earnestly and in categorical tones
to assure me that he had not seen any Major, that during these
prayers he fell into a kind of trance, and saw and heard nothing of
what was going on around him.

I can see Isay Fomich now (as if it were yesterday), wandering
around the prison on Saturdays the way he used to, idly, with

nothing at all to do, and trying with all his might not to engage in any activity, as was prescribed for the Sabbath by holy law. What impossible stories he would tell me each time he came back from his synagogue; what unheard-of items of St Petersburg news and gossip he used to bring me, assuring me that he had them from his fellow-Jews, and they at first hand.

But I have spent too much time talking about Isay Fomich.

There were only two public bath-houses in the whole of the town. One was run by a Jew and consisted of private rooms that cost fifty copecks a time. It was intended for people high up on the social scale. The other was by and large a plebeian establishment, dilapidated, cramped and dirty, and it was to this bath-house that we convicts were taken. It was a frosty, sunny day; the convicts were happy to be getting out of the fortress and having a look at the town. There were jokes and laughter all the way. A whole platoon of soldiers with loaded rifles escorted us, to the wonderment of the whole town. Once in the bath-house, we were divided into two shifts: the second shift had to wait in the cold antechamber, while the men on the first shift took their bath. This arrangement was necessitated by the cramped nature of the building. But even so, the place was so cramped that it was hard to imagine how even half of our men could ever fit into it. Petrov, however, did not leave my side; without my having to ask him, he leapt to my assistance and even offered to wash me. Baklushin, a convict from the special category, also offered his services to me at the same time as Petrov. Baklushin was nicknamed 'the pioneer', and I have already mentioned him earlier as being one of the most cheerful and sympathetic of the convicts, which indeed he was. We already knew one another slightly. Petrov even helped me to undress, as not being used to it I undressed slowly, and it was cold in the antechamber, almost as cold as it was outside. I may as well note here that a convict finds it very hard to undress if he has not completely mastered the art of doing it. The first thing he must be able to do is to undo his fetter straps. These fetter straps are made of leather, are about seven inches long, and are fixed round the legs of one's long johns, just below the iron ring that surrounds one's leg. A pair of fetter straps costs no less than sixty silver copecks, but every convict buys a pair at his own expense, of course, because without them it is impossible to walk. The fetter-ring does not fit the ankle tightly, and one can insert a finger into the space between. The iron ring knocks and rubs against one's ankle, and in one day a convict without fetter straps can rub his legs raw. But taking the straps off is not difficult. What is more difficult is to learn how to extricate one's long johns from the fetters. This is a real conjuring trick. In order to get the garment off one's left leg, say, one must first pass it through the space between one's leg and the fetter ring; then, when one has freed the leg, the garment has to be pushed back through the ring; then all that one has taken off one's left leg must be passed through the ring on one's right ankle; then all this must be pulled back towards oneself. The same procedure has to be followed when one is putting on fresh underwear. A novice finds it hard even to guess how it is done; we were first taught the correct procedure in Tobolsk by a convict named Korenyev, a former bandit leader who had spent five years chained to the wall. But the convicts grew used to it and could soon manage it without the slightest difficulty. I gave Petrov a few copecks to buy some soap and a bast sponge; it is true that soap was also issued to the convicts by the prison free of charge, each man receiving a piece the size of a two copeck bit, about as thick as the slices of cheese served up at the evening parties of people of 'modest means'. Soap was also sold here in the antechamber, along with spiced fruit tea, kalatches and hot water. By arrangement with the proprietor of the bath-house, each convict received just one small tubful of hot water; if a man wanted to be any cleaner, he could pay half a copeck and receive another tubful, which was handed into the bath itself from the antechamber through a hatch especially designed for this purpose. When he had undressed me, Petrov led me by the arm, having noticed that I was finding it very difficult to walk in my fetters. 'You have to pull them higher up, onto your calves,' he kept saying, supporting and steadying me as though he were my tutor, 'and take care, there's a step here.' I even felt slightly ashamed; I wanted to assure Petrov that I could manage alone, but he would not have believed this. He treated me just as if I were a child, a clumsy minor whom everyone must help. Petrov was in no way a servant, above all not a servant; if I had once offended him, he would have known how to deal with me. I never promised him any money for his services, and he never asked for payment. What was it that induced him to look after me in this way?

When we opened the door into the bath itself, I thought we were walking into hell. Imagine a room about twelve paces long and roughly the same in width, into which were packed as many as a hundred, or probably at the very least eighty men at once, since the convicts were divided into two shifts, and up to two hundred of us had arrived at the bath-house. Steam that swathed one's eyes, soot, dirt, the place so crowded that there was nowhere to stand. I took fright and was about to turn back, but Petrov instantly gave me reassurance. With the greatest of difficulty, we somehow managed to squeeze our way through to the wall benches by stepping over the heads of the men who were sitting on the floor, and asking them to bend down so we could get past. But all the places on the benches were taken. Petrov told me we would have to buy places, and he at once began to haggle with a convict who was sitting near the hatch window. For a copeck this man gave up his place, taking the money there and then from Petrov, who had brought it with him clutched in his fist for just such an eventuality. The man immediately dodged under the bench, straight below my place, where it was dark and dirty and where a sticky condensation floated everywhere to a depth of nearly half a finger. But even the places under the benches were all occupied; there, too, a mass of humanity seethed. On the whole floor area there was not a space the size of a man's palm on which convicts were not sitting huddled, splashing themselves from their tubs. Others stood erect in their midst and, holding their tubs in their hands, washed themselves standing up; the dirty water streamed off them straight onto the shaven heads of the men sitting below. On the shelf and on all the ledges that led up to it men sat washing themselves, huddling and stooping. They did not wash very much, however. The common people do not wash much with soap and hot water; they only steam themselves an inordinate amount and then pour cold water over themselves – that is their kind of bath. On the shelf about fifty birch switches rose and fell in unison; each man was lashing himself into a state of intoxication.

More steam was manufactured every minute. This was not heat any longer; it was an inferno. All was yammering and cackling, accompanied by the sound of a hundred chains being dragged along the floor ... Some men, wanting to get through, became entangled in the chains of others, and got their own chains caught on the heads of those who were sitting lower down; they would fall cursing and dragging behind them those with whom they had become entangled. Filthy water poured everywhere. Everyone was in a kind of intoxicated, aroused state of mind; shrieks and cries reverberated. Beside the hatch window that gave through to the antechamber from where the water was handed in, there was a continual swearing and jostling, a general fracas. When the hot water was distributed it was splashed on the heads of those who were sitting on the floor before its bearer managed to carry it to his place. Every few moments the bewhiskered face of a soldier who had his rifle at the ready would look in through the door that had been set ajar, to see there were no breaches of the regulations. The convicts' shaven heads and their bodies scalded red by the steam seemed more monstrous than ever. On a back that is exposed to steam the weals once made by whips and staves generally stand out vividly; and so now all these backs looked as though they had been freshly lacerated. Fearsome weals! My skin used to crawl at the sight of them. More steam was made, enshrouding the entire bath chamber in a thick, hot cloud; all was screaming and yammering. Through the cloud of steam one caught a glimpse of mercilessly beaten backs, shaven heads, doubled up arms and legs; and, to cap it all, Isay Fomich yammering loudly at the top of his voice, on the very highest shelf. He was steaming himself into oblivion, but it seemed that no amount of steam could ever satisfy him; for a copeck he had hired the services of a bath attendant, but this man's patience broke at last, he threw down the switch and ran off to pour cold water over himself. Isay Fomich did not lose heart and hired a second attendant, a third: on an occasion such as this he had decided that money was no obstacle and changed attendants as many as four times. 'He's a wizard at steaming himself, good man, Isay Fomich!' shouted the convicts from below. Isay Fomich himself felt at this moment that he was indeed higher up than anyone else, and had beaten them all to it; he exulted and screeched out his aria in a mad little voice: 'La – la – la – la – la,' drowning out all the other voices. It occurred to me that if at some later date we should all find ourselves together in hell, it would be very similar to this place. I could not resist telling Petrov this idea of mine; he merely looked around him and said nothing.

I was going to buy him a place beside me; but he sat down at my feet and declared he was fine as he was. Baklushin meanwhile bought water for us and brought it to us in case we needed it. Petrov declared he was going to wash me from head to foot, so that 'you'll be all nice and clean', and he tried very hard to make me steam myself. This I did not intend to risk. Petrov rubbed me all over with soap. 'And now I'm going to wash your footsies,' he added in conclusion. I was on the point of retorting that I was perfectly capable of washing myself, but I did not want to contradict him and gave myself completely into his care. There was not a trace of servility in his use of the diminutive form 'footsies'; quite simply, it was probable that Petrov could not bring himself to call my feet 'feet', as he might in the case of other people, real people who had feet, whereas I as yet had only 'footsies'.

When he had finished washing me, he delivered me back to the antechamber with the same ceremony, supporting me and warning me at every step as if I were made of porcelain; he helped me to put on my underwear, and only when he had quite finished with me did he rush back into the bath to steam himself.

When we got back to barracks I offered him a glass of tea. This he did not refuse; he drank it down and thanked me. It occurred to me that I might be generous and treat him to a noggin. There was a noggin in our barrack, too. Petrov was highly delighted, drank the vodka, grunted and, observing that I had thoroughly revived him, set off in a hurry for the kitchen, as though there were some business there that could not be settled without him. Another of my companions, Baklushin ('the pioneer'), whom I had also invited to have tea with me, took his place.

I do not know a man more sympathetic than Baklushin. It is true that he gave no quarter to anyone, quarrelled frequently, did not like others to meddle in his affairs – in short, he knew how to stand up for himself. But his quarrels did not last long, and I think we were all fond of him. Wherever he went, people were pleased to see him. Even in the town he was known as the most entertaining man around, one who never lost his cheerful disposition. He was a tall young fellow of about thirty, with a boyish, simple-hearted face that was quite good-looking, though it had a wart on it. He would sometimes twist this face of his into the most killingly funny impersonations of all and sundry, so that everyone around him could not help roaring with laughter. He was also a great master of telling jokes; but he had no time for our fastidious enemies of laughter, and consequently no one ever swore at him for being 'idle and useless'. He was full of fire and life. He made my acquaintance during the first days of my imprisonment and told me that he had been a Kantonist, that he had subsequently served in the Pioneers and had even attracted the notice and the affection of several highly placed persons, something he remembered with great pride. He began at once to ask me about St Petersburg. He even read books. When he came to have tea with me, he made all the men in the barrack laugh with a story of how that morning Lieutenant Sh. had given our Major a dressing-down. Then he sat down beside me and told me with a look of satisfaction that it seemed the stage show would be going ahead as planned. Some of the prisoners had started to get together a stage show for the holidays. Men had come forward to be actors, and a bit of scenery had been put together on the quiet. Some of the townspeople had promised to lend clothes for the actors' costumes, even the female ones; through the good offices of a certain personal attendant it was even hoped to obtain an officer's uniform with shoulder knots. If only the Major did not take it into his head to forbid the show, as he had done the year before. But that Christmas the Major had been in a bad mood. He had lost money at cards somewhere, and besides there had been some fooling around in the prison, so he had forbidden the show out of spite; this year, however, he might not stand in its way. In short, Baklushin was in a state of some excitement. He was apparently one of those most closely involved in getting the show together, and I promised myself there and then that I would do my best to be present at this performance. I found Baklushin's simple-hearted joy in the show's success very appealing. One thing led to another, and we fell into conversation. Among other things he told me that he had not always served in St Petersburg; that he had been found guilty of some misdemeanour there and had been sent, now as a non-commissioned officer, however, to a garrison battalion in Riga.

'And it was from there that they sent me here,' observed Baklushin.

'But what for?' I asked him.

'What for? What do you think it was for, Aleksandr Petrovich? It was for falling in love!'

'Come on now, they haven't started sending people here for that yet,' I retorted, laughing.

'I have to admit,' Baklushin added, 'I have to admit that in the middle of that affair I did shoot one of the Germans over there with a pistol. But is shooting a German reason enough to deport a man, answer me that?'

'But how did it happen? Tell me, I'm interested.'

'It's a ridiculous story, Aleksandr Petrovich.'

'So much the better. Tell me.'

'You want me to tell you? Well, since you're listening ...'

I heard the story of a murder which, although it was not entirely ridiculous, was none the less distinctly odd.

'It happened liked this,' Baklushin began. 'When I was sent to Riga, I saw it was a fine, big town, only there were a lot of Germans. Well, of course, I was still a young man, I was well in with the officers, walked around with my cap at an angle, I knew how to pass my time, in other words. I used to wink at the German girls. There was one of them who took my fancy, called Louise. She and her aunt both worked as laundresses, only handling the very finest linen. Her aunt was old, a posh sort of woman, and they were quite well-do-do. At first I just used to walk past their windows, but later on I got really friendly with them. Louise spoke good Russian, except it sounded as though she had a frog in her throat – a real sweetie, she was, I've never met another like her. At first I wanted to try a bit of this and that, but she said to me: "No, don't do that, Sasha, because I want to keep myself for you, so I can be a good wife for you," and she would only caress me and laugh such a tinkling laughter ... she was such a pure little creature, I've never seen another like her. She herself suggested we get married. Well, how could I resist marrying her, just imagine! I got ready to go to the lieutenant-colonel with a request for permission ... Quite suddenly, Louise didn't turn up for one of our rendezvous; she missed a second, and a third ... I sent her a letter; there was no reply. What's this? I thought to myself. If she had been playing me false she would have acted clever, replied to my letter and kept our rendezvous. But she wasn't capable of telling a lie; so she just broke the whole thing off. It's the aunt, I thought. I didn't dare to go and see her aunt; although she knew all about it, we still did everything in secret, softly softly. I ran about like a madman, wrote her a final letter in which I said that if she didn't come to meet me I'd go and see her aunt. She took fright and came to meet me. She was crying; she said that a German, a distant relative of hers, a rich and elderly watchmaker by the name of Schultz, had stated that he wished to marry her – "he said he wanted to make me happy, and not be left without a wife in his old age; he said he loved me and had been meaning to propose to me for a long time, but had kept quiet until he made his mind up. You see, Sasha," she said, "he's rich, and that's a bit of luck for me; you don't want to deprive me of my good luck, do you?" I saw she was crying, putting her arms round me ... Well, I thought, she's talking sense, really. What good is there in marrying a soldier, even if he is an NCO! All right then, Louise, I said, goodbye, and God be with you; I don't want to deprive you of your happiness. What's he like, handsome, is he? "No," she said, "he's sort of old, with a long nose ..." She even started laughing herself. I left her; oh well, I thought, it's not to be. The next morning I went round by his shop – she had told me which street it was in. I looked in the window: the German was sitting there making his watches. He was about forty-five or so, and he had a hook nose, staring eyes and was wearing a dress coat and a tall, stand-up collar, an important-looking number. I fairly spat; I was just about to smash his window for him when I thought, better leave him alone, it's no good crying over spilt milk. I went back to barracks when it was getting dark, I lay down on my camp bed and, would you believe it, Aleksandr Petrovich, I started to cry ...

'Well, a day went by, and another, and then another. There was no sign of Louise. But meanwhile I heard from a gossip (she was an old woman, another laundress whom Louise sometimes went to see) that the German knew about our love and for this reason had determined to ask her to marry him as soon as possible. Otherwise he would have waited for another couple of years. He had apparently made Louise take some vow that she wouldn't see me again; he seemed to be treating both her and her aunt very badly, and there was a possibility that he might change his mind – he hadn't yet come to a firm decision. The gossip also told me that he'd invited them both to have coffee with him in two days' time, on Sunday morning, and that another relative of his would also be present, an old man who had been a merchant but was now extremely poor and worked as a caretaker in some cellar or other. When I found out that on Sunday the whole affair might be settled, I was seized with such anger that I lost control of myself. All that day and all the next I could think of nothing else. I could eat that German alive, I thought.

'On Sunday morning I still didn't know what I was going to do, but when the service was over I leapt to my feet, pulled on my overcoat and set off for the German's. I thought I would catch them all there. As for why I was going to the German's, and what it was I wanted to say to him, I myself had no idea. But I stuck a pistol in my pocket, just in case. I had this miserable little pistol, with an old-style cocking-piece; I had used it when I'd been a boy. It was no earthly use whatsoever. None the less, I loaded it with a bullet; I thought: if they start kicking me out and swearing at me I'll produce the pistol and scare them all. I got there. There was nobody in the workshop, they were all sitting in a room at the back. It was just them, no one else, no servants. He only had one servant, a German woman who was his cook as well. I walked through the shop; I could see that the door in there was shut, and that it was an old door, on a hook. My heart was beating fast, I stopped and listened: they were talking in German. I kicked the door as hard as I could and it opened at once. I saw that the table was laid. There was a large coffee pot on the table, and the coffee was boiling on a spirit burner. There were rusks; on another tray there was a decanter of vodka, with herring and sausage, and also a bottle of some kind of wine. Louise and her aunt, both dressed in their finest, were sitting on the sofa. Opposite them, in a chair, sat the German, the bridegroom, with his hair neatly combed, wearing a dress coat and the kind of collar that sticks out in front. And to the side, on another chair, sat another German, a fat, grey-haired old man who never said a word. When I went in, Louise turned pale. Her aunt started to get up, but she sat down again, and the German knitted his brows. He was really angry; he got up and came towards me:

'"What," he said, "do you want?"

'Normally I would have been covered in confusion, but my rage had taken a powerful hold of me.

'"Oh," I said, "anything you like. Since I've come as your guest you can pour me some vodka. I've come to visit you."

'The German thought about this, and then said:

'"Sit down."

'I sat down.

'"Well," I said, "what about some vodka?"

'"Here is vodka," he said; "drink, please."

'"What about some of your good vodka?" I said. My rage had really taken me over by now.

'"This is good vodka."

'I was beginning to find it offensive, his way of treating me as though I was his inferior. All the more so because Louise was watching. I drained my glass, and said:

'"Why so uncivil, German? You want to be friends with me, I've come on a friendly visit."

'"I cannot be your friend," he said: "you are a simple soldier."

'Well, that sent me into a frenzy.

'"You stuffed shirt," I said, "you sausage merchant. Do you realize that at this moment I can do with you exactly as I please? How would you like me to shoot you with a pistol?"

'I took out my pistol, stood in front of him and pointed the muzzle straight at his head, point-blank. The others just sat there, more dead than alive, afraid to utter a word. The old man was shaking like a leaf; he said nothing, his features were utterly pale.

'The German was surprised, but he soon regained his composure.

'"I am not afraid of you," he said, "and I implore you, as a man of integrity, to have done with your joke this instant; but I am not at all afraid of you."

'"Not so," said I, "you're afraid!" And what did I see but that he didn't dare to move his head away from the pistol; he just went on sitting there.

'"No," he said, "you will never dare to do it."

'"And why," I said, "wouldn't I dare to do it?"

'"Because," he said, "it is strictly forbidden and you will surely be punished for it."

'God knows what was the matter with that German. If he hadn't got my wick he'd still be alive; it was the argument that did it.

'"So," I said, "you think I don't dare to?"

'"Yes."

'"I don't dare to?"

'"You absolutely do not dare to do this to me."

'"Well, try this then, bratwurst!" And I shot a bullet into him, and he rolled off his chair. The women shrieked.

'I put the pistol back in my pocket, and off I went. As I was going into the fortress, I chucked the pistol into the nettles right beside the gate.

'I went back to my barrack, lay down on my camp bed and thought: they'll come and arrest me right away. An hour passed, and another – nobody arrested me. And just before twilight a terrible anguish descended on me; I went out; I simply had to see Louise. I walked past the watchmaker's shop. I saw there was a crowd there, and police. I went to see the gossip: send for Louise! I waited for a bit, then I saw Louise running towards me. She threw her arms round my neck, she was in tears. "It's all my fault," she said, "it's all because I listened to my aunt." She also told me that after what had happened, her aunt had gone home and had been so scared that she had been taken ill and was unable to say a word. She had not told anyone about it and forbade me to tell anyone; she was afraid; let them do what they liked. "Nobody saw us," said Louise. "He'd sent his servant away because he was scared of her. She'd have scratched his eyes out if she'd known he was intending to get married. None of the workmen were in the building that day, either; he'd told them all to go home. He made the coffee and the snacks and sandwiches himself. And as for the old man, he's never spoken a word in all his life, he didn't say anything, and when that happened that morning he was the first to take his hat and leave. And he'll probably go on saying nothing," said Louise. So it was. Two weeks went by without anyone arresting me, and I was not under the slightest suspicion. Those two weeks, believe it or not, Aleksandr Petrovich, were the happiest two weeks of my life. I met Louise every day. And how very, very attracted to me she was now! She would say to me in tears: "I'll follow you wherever you're sent, I'll give up everything for you!" I nearly decided to have done with my life there and then, such pity did I feel for her. Well, when two weeks were up I was arrested. The old man and the aunt had come to some sort of agreement and had given evidence against me ...'

'But wait a minute,' I interrupted Baklushin. 'They could only have give you ten or at most twelve years in the civilian category for that; but you're in the special category. How come?'

'Oh, that was something quite different,' said Baklushin. 'When I was brought before the court the captain started flinging obscene abuse at me in front of the judge. I wasn't going to stand for it, and I said to him: "You watch your language! You villain, that's the Tsar's emblem[22] you're sitting looking at, in case you hadn't noticed." Well, from then on things took a different turn, they started the trial over again and sentenced me for everything together: I got four thousand, and sent here to the special category. And when they took me out to be flogged, they took the captain out, too: I got the green street, and he was stripped to the ranks and sent to serve as a private in the Caucasus. Goodbye, Aleksandr Petrovich. Come and see our show.'

10

THE FEAST OF
CHRISTMAS

At last the holidays arrived. On Christmas Eve very few convicts
went out to work. A few went to the sewing sheds and the workshops; the rest of the men merely attended the work detail, and
although they were assigned to various locations, almost all of
them, either singly or in groups, went straight back to the prison,
and after dinner no one left it at all. Even during the morning the
majority of the convicts went about exclusively on their own business, and not on official tasks: some busied themselyes with the
illicit provision of vodka and the ordering of new supplies; others
to see friends of both sexes, or to collect before the holiday the small
amounts of money owing to them for work done earlier in the year.
Baklushin and the men who were taking part in the stage show went
to see certain acquaintances, mostly in the officers' detachment,
and to obtain the necessary costumes. Some men walked around
looking preoccupied and fussed simply because others did, and
although some, for example, had no prospects of getting any money
from anywhere, they none the less acted as though they were indeed
about to get some; in short, everyone seemed to be expecting some
sort of a change to take place on the following day, something out
of the ordinary. Towards evening the veterans who had gone to the
market to do the convicts' errands came back laden with many
different kinds of things to eat: beef, sucking-pigs, even geese.
Many of the convicts, even the most plain-living and thrifty ones,
who saved up their copecks all year round, considered it their duty
to spare no expense on this occasion and to celebrate the end of the
fast in a proper manner. The day that would come tomorrow was
a real holiday, which the convicts could not be deprived of –
it was formally recognized by law. A convict could not be sent out
to work on this day; there were only three such days in the year.[23]

And really, who can tell how many memories must have stirred
in the souls of these outcasts as they rose to meet such a day! The

days of the great feasts are sharply imprinted on the memory of the common people, beginning in childhood. These are the days when they rest from their strenuous labours, days when families gather together. In prison they must have been remembered with torment and anguish. Respect for the solemn feast even acquired a certain ritual majesty among the convicts; there was little merrymaking, everyone was serious and seemingly preoccupied with something, although many had practically nothing at all to do. But even the idlers and the merrymakers tried to preserve a certain air of importance ... It was as if laughter had been forbidden. The prevailing mood was one of a certain exaggerated punctiliousness and irritable impatience, and any man who did anything to disturb this general atmosphere, even accidentally, would be set upon with shouts and curses by the others, as if he had aroused their anger by not having sufficient respect for the holy feast. This mood of the convicts was remarkable, and could even be quite moving. In addition to his inborn sense of reverence for the great day, each convict had an unconscious feeling that by observing this feast he was in some way coming into contact with the whole world, that consequently he was not altogether an outcast, a lost man, a severed limb, and that as it was in the world of men, so it was in prison. They felt this; it was obvious and understandable.

Akim Akimych too was very busy preparing for the holiday. He had no family memories, for he had grown up as an orphan in a house belonging to strangers and had begun an arduous military service from the age of fifteen: there had been no particular happiness in his life, because he had always lived it with such regularity and monotony, afraid to stray even by a hair's breadth from the path of duty that had been marked out for him. He was not particularly religious, either, since probity had apparently swallowed up all his other human endowments and attributes, his passions and desires, good and bad. Consequently he was preparing to greet the solemn day without fuss or agitation, without being troubled by any anguished and entirely futile memories, but with a quiet, methodical probity which was exactly as great as was necessary for the execution of his duties and the performance of a ritual that had been established for once and for all. In general, he was not one to give matters much reflection. It seemed that he never bothered his head about the meaning of any fact; but once rules were explained to him, he would carry them out with religious exactitude. If tomorrow he had been required to do the exact opposite, he would have done it with precisely the same obedience and thoroughness. Once, once only in his life had he attempted to live according to his own perceptions – and had ended up in prison. The lesson had not been lost on him. And although fate had decreed that he should not have even the slightest understanding of what it was he had been found guilty of, he had none the less deduced from his adventure one saving maxim: never under any circumstances to use his reason, since this was 'no business of his mind', as the convicts expressed it among themselves. In his blind devotion to ritual, he even regarded his Christmas sucking-pig, which he had stuffed with buckwheat porridge and roasted (with his own hands, for he knew how it was done), with a kind of anticipatory respect, as if this were no ordinary sucking-pig, which one could buy and roast any time one liked, but a special, Christmas one. It is possible that he had been used from childhood onwards to seeing a sucking-pig on the table when Christmas Day came round, and I am convinced that if even once he had missed his taste of sucking-pig on that day he would have been left for the rest of his life with a nagging sense of guilt at not having done his duty. Until the holiday arrived he went around in an old jacket and a pair of old trousers, which although they were quite respectably darned were none the less threadbare. It now transpired that he had carefully preserved in his locked box the new suit of jacket and trousers which had been issued to him about four months previously, and had not touched it, smiling at the thought of how he would put it on for the first time when it was Christmas. And that was what he did. On Christmas Eve he took out the new suit, unfolded it, examined it, gave it a brush, blew the dust off it and, when he had attended to all this, tried it on. The suit fitted him perfectly, it turned out; everything was as it should be, the jacket buttoned all the way to the top, the collar, as if it were made of cardboard, propped his chin up high; the jacket was even drawn in at the waist, reminding one of a military uniform, and Akim Akimych fairly beamed with pleasure, turning from side to side, not without a certain dash and swagger, in front of his tiny looking-glass, the rim of which he had once, long ago, in a moment of idleness, decorated with a border of gold paper. There was only one little hook on the jacket collar which did not seem to be in quite the right position. Taking note of this, Akim Akimych decided to move the hook; this he did, tried the jacket on again, and this time everything seemed fine. Then he folded the garments once more and hid them in his locked box with his mind at ease until the next day. His head was shaven in the approved manner; but as he viewed himself attentively in the looking-glass, he noticed that his head did not appear to be entirely smooth on top; a few little tufts of hair were just visible, and he went straight off to 'the major' to have himself shaved properly and according to the regulations. Although no one was going to inspect him the following day, he had himself shaved, purely in order to satisfy his conscience, so as to have carried out all his Christmas duties. A reverence for buttons, epaulettes and stripes had been indelibly impressed upon his mind from childhood onwards as a kind of unquestionable obligation, and upon his heart as an image of the highest degree of beauty a decent man could attain to. When he had set everything to rights, as the head convict in the barrack he gave orders for hay to be brought in, and carefully supervised the spreading of it over the floor. The same was done in the other barracks. For some unknown reason hay was always spread on the barrack floors at Christmas.[24] Then, when he had completed his labours, Akim Akimych said his prayers, lay down on his camp bed and immediately fell into a peaceful slumber like that of a young infant; so as to wake up as early as possible in the morning. All the convicts acted in exactly the same manner, however. In all the barracks the men went to bed far earlier than they usually did. Their usual evening occupations were neglected; no one even mentioned *maydans*. Everyone was waiting for the morning that followed.

At last it arrived. Early, before it was light, as soon as reveille had been sounded on the drum, the barracks were unlocked and the duty sergeant wished them all a merry Christmas. The men did likewise, replying in a friendly, affectionate tone. After hurriedly saying their prayers, Akim Akimych and a lot of other men whose geese and sucking-pigs were cooking in the kitchen rushed off to see what was being done to them, how they were being roasted, where they were being put, and so on. Through the small, snow-and-ice-encrusted windows of our hut we could see out across the darkness to where in all six ovens of both kitchens bright fires were burning, having been kindled well before dawn. Convicts were already poking about the courtyard in the dark, wearing their sheepskin coats either arm-in-sleeve or thrown carelessly over their shoulders; they were all swiftly heading for the kitchen. There were some, however, only a very few, it must be admitted, who had already managed to pay a visit to the 'barmen'. These were the most impatient ones. In general, all the men behaved in a decent manner, peaceably and with a decorum that was somehow unusual for them. None of their usual quarrels and bad language were to be heard. They all knew that it was a day of great importance, a religious holiday of the first magnitude. There were some who went round the other barracks to give their greetings to men from their part of the country. Something akin to friendliness made its appearance. I will observe in passing that friendliness was something one hardly ever saw among the convicts: I allude not to any general spirit of friendliness – that was even less in evidence – but simply to the private friendship of one convict with another. This was something almost completely absent in the prison, and it was a remarkable feature of our life: things are different in freedom. All the men in the prison, with very rare exceptions, were callous and sour in their dealings with each other, and this was a form of behaviour that had been accepted and established once and for all. I also left the barrack; it was just beginning to get light; the stars were growing faint; a thin, frosty mist was rising into the air. The kitchen chimneys were emitting columns of smoke. Some of the convicts I met as I walked wished me a merry Christmas spontaneously and with real affection. I thanked them and responded in kind. Some of them were men who until now had not said a word to me all during the past month.

Right outside the kitchen I was accosted by a convict from the military barrack, his sheepskin coat thrown over his shoulders. He saw me from halfway across the yard, and shouted to me:

'Aleksandr Petrovich! Aleksandr Petrovich!' He was on his way to
the kitchen and in a hurry. I stopped and waited for him. He was
a round-faced lad with a quiet expression in his eyes; he was very
untalkative with everyone, and had not said a single word to me
or paid me the slightest attention since I had entered the prison; I
did not even know his name. He ran up to me breathlessly and
stood right in front of me, staring at me with a meaningless, yet
somehow blissful smile on his face.

'What do you want?' I asked him, not without astonishment, in
view of the fact that he was standing and staring, smiling at me with
all his might, yet not having started up any sort of conversation
with me.

'Well, I mean, it's Christmas ...' He muttered and, having
surmised that there was nothing more to talk about, he left me and
rapidly set off for the kitchen.

I will observe, incidentally, that we never had any close dealings
with one another after this, and hardly said a word to one another
for all the rest of my time in the prison.

Around the blazing ovens in the kitchen there was a great deal
of bustle and jostling, quite a crowd. Each man was looking after
what was his; the cooks were getting on with the preparation of the
prison food, for dinner would be eaten earlier than usual today. No
one had begun to eat yet, however; although some would have liked
to, they desisted out of a sense of decorum in the presence of the
others. A priest was expected, and only after his visit would the
breaking of the fast begin. In the meanwhile it was still not quite
light, when outside the prison gate the corporal's summoning cry
began to ring out: 'Cooks!' These cries rang out practically every
minute and continued for almost two hours. The cooks were needed
to receive the gifts of food which had been brought to the prison
from every quarter of the town. The food arrived in enormous
quantities in the form of kalatches, bread, curd tarts, pastries, buns,
blintzes and other fancy confections. I don't believe there was one
merchant or artisan housewife in all the town who had not sent
some of her baking as a Christmas present for the 'unfortunates',
the convicts. Some of this charity was extremely generous – there
were fancy loaves made of the finest flour, sent in large quantities.

Some of it was very meagre – a half-copeck kalatch and two rye buns with a thin smearing of sour cream on them: this was the gift of pauper to pauper, from the last there was to spare. Everything was accepted with equal gratitude, without respect of gifts and donors. As they accepted the gifts, the convicts took off their hats, bowed, wished the donor a merry Christmas and took the offering back to the kitchen. When heaps of bakeries had accumulated, the head convicts from each barrack were sent for, and they distributed all the items equally among the barracks. There was no quarrelling, no bad language; the distribution was done fairly and equitably. Our barrack's share was divided up in the barrack itself by Akim Akimych and another convict, who made the division and distributed the bakeries to each convict personally. There was not the slightest objection, not the slightest envy; everyone was pleased with what he got; there was not even any suspicion that the offerings might have been hidden or unevenly distributed. When he had seen to his business in the kitchen, Akim Akimych proceeded to his investiture; he dressed with the greatest of decorum and solemnity, not leaving one hook unfastened, and when he had finished he at once began to pray in earnest. He spent quite a long time in prayer. Many convicts, the elderly ones for the most part, were already standing at prayer. The younger convicts did not pray much: some of them might cross themselves when they got up in the morning, but that was all, even on a feast day. When he had finished praying, Akim Akimych came up to me and rather solemnly wished me a merry Christmas. I at once invited him to have tea with me, and he offered to share his sucking-pig with me. After a bit Petrov, too, came running up to me to wish me the season's greetings. It seemed he had had a few drinks already, and though he was out of breath when he came running up to me, he did not say much, but merely stood in front of me for a short while and soon went off in the direction of the kitchen. In the military barrack the men were making preparations to receive the priest. This barrack was designed differently from the rest: in it the plank bed extended around the walls, and not into the middle of the room, as in all the other barracks, so that it was the only room in the prison that was not cluttered up in the middle. It had probably been designed in this

way so that all the convicts could be mustered here if necessary. A
small table, covered with a clean towel, had been placed in the
centre of the room; an icon had been placed on the table, and a lamp
lit. At last the priest arrived with the cross and the holy water. After
he had prayed and sung the liturgy in front of the icon, he stood
before the convicts, and they all came forward to kiss the cross with
genuine reverence. Then the priest went round all the barracks,
sprinkling them with holy water. In the kitchen he praised our
prison bread, which was renowned for its fine taste in the town, and
the convicts immediately expressed a desire to have two freshly
baked loaves sent to him; a veteran was immediately charged with
this task. The convicts escorted the cross out of the prison as
reverently as they had received it among them. Almost immediately
afterwards, the Major and the prison governor arrived. The
governor was liked and even respected by the men. He made the
rounds of all the barracks accompanied by the Major, wished each
man a merry Christmas, went into the kitchen and tried the prison
soup. The soup was delicious; almost a pound of beef per convict
had been added to it. In addition, millet porridge had been prepared
and the men could have as much butter as they wanted. When he
had seen the governor off, the Major gave orders for the meal to
begin. The convicts tried not to catch his eye. They did not like the
spiteful looks he gave them from behind his spectacles, through
which even now he was looking to right and to left, to see if there
were not any breaches of the regulations, or anyone he could catch
red-handed.

We began to eat. Akim Akimych's sucking-pig was done to a
turn. I don't know how it was, but immediately after the Major's
departure, about five minutes after he had gone, there suddenly
seemed to be an unusually large number of drunken convicts. Yet
only five minutes earlier, nearly all the men had been completely
sober. There were a lot of glowing, beaming faces. Balalaikas were
produced. The little Pole with the violin was already following
around some reveller who had hired him for the whole day to saw
out lively dance-tunes for him. The conversation was growing
noisier and more drunken. But the meal passed off without any
serious disturbances. Everyone was full. Many of the older and

more sedate convicts went away to sleep, as did Akim Akimych, in
the apparent assumption that this was what one always did after
dinner on a major holiday. The old man from the religious settlement at Starodubye took a short nap and then climbed up on the
stove, opened his Bible and continued to pray far into the night,
almost without interruption. He found it painful to watch the
'disgrace', as he called the convicts' general free-for-all. All the
Circassians had sat themselves down on the front steps and were
observing the drunken crowd with curiosity and not a little distaste.
I came across Nurra: '*Yaman, yaman!* (bad, bad!),' he said to me in
Tartar, shaking his head in pious indignation. '*Ukh, yaman!* Allah
will be angry!' With stubborn aloofness Isay Fomich had lit a
candle in his corner and had ostentatiously set to work, showing
that he did not give a fig for the holiday. In corners here and there
maydans had been set up. The card-players were not afraid of the
veterans, but men were put on watch in case the duty sergeant
turned up, although he was trying not to notice anything. The
officer of the watch looked in about three times during the entire
day. But when he appeared the drunken convicts were hidden and
the *maydans* removed, and it seemed that he too had decided not
to pay any attention to minor infringements of the regulations.
Little by little the crowd grew livelier. Quarrels started to break out.
Sober convicts were still by far the more numerous, however, and
they looked after the drunken ones. On the other hand, the men
who had started drinking put away enormous quantities of liquor.
Gazin was in his element. He was strolling about looking pleased
with himself near his place on the plank bed, beneath which he had
placed the vodka he had been keeping for this occasion somewhere
in a hidden place in the snow behind the barracks; he chuckled slyly
as he watched his customers arrive. He himself was sober and had
not touched a drop. He intended to have his binge at the end of the
holiday, after he had relieved the convicts of all the money in their
pockets. Songs rang out through the barracks. But the men's
drunkenness was already turning into a reeking stupor, and from
their songs it was not far to tears. Many of the convicts were
strutting around, their sheepskin coats thrown over their shoulders,
plucking the strings of their balalaikas with a sprightly swagger. In

the special category the convicts even formed an eight-part choir. They sang magnificently to an accompaniment of balalaikas and guitars. Few of the songs were authentic Russian folk-songs. I remember only one, which they sang valiantly:

> A young wife, at eve
> I sat with the feast.

And now I heard a new version of this song, one I had not heard before. Several lines had been added on at the end:

> A young wife, I
> Have tidied up my house:
> I've washed my spoons clean,
> Poured soup in the tureen;
> I've scrubbed the doorposts down,
> Made pies for everyone.

Most of the songs were the so-called 'prison' songs, but they sang only the well-known ones. One of them was a humorous song that describes how a man, when he was free, lived the carefree life of a gentleman, but is now locked up in prison. The song describes how in his former existence he used 'to touch up blancmange with champagne', but now

> They give me cabbage leaves and water –
> I wolf them down for all I'm worth.

Another song they sang was the somewhat overworked

> I used to have a gay time,
> Some capital I had.
> I spent it in my May-time,
> Now I'm in gaol instead,

and so on. The convicts did not say 'capital' but 'copital', pronouncing the word as though it derived from the Russian verb *kopit*, 'to save up'. Mournful songs were sung as well. One of them was a real convict song; it is also well-known, I think:

The sky with light begins to glisten,
Reveille on the drum does sound,
The headman tries the door-bolt. Listen:
The tally clerk is coming round.

No one sees us in our prison,
How we live, together tossed;
God our Heavenly Creator's with us,
Even here we are not lost,

and so on.

Another was even more melancholy than this one, but it had an attractive tune, and had probably been composed by some deported convict; its words were artificially sweet and a bit on the ungrammatical side. I can only remember a few lines of it now:

My eyes will never see that land again,
The land where I was bore;
For without guilt to suffer pain
I'm doomed for evermore.

Upon the roof the owl does hoot,
Cries out on woodland air.
My heart grows mournful at its note,
For I cannot be there.

This song was often sung in our prison, not as a chorus, but by convicts singly. Someone might, in an idle moment, go out onto the steps leading up to the barrack, sit down, fall into reflection, face in hand, and begin to intone it in a high falsetto. The sound of it would somehow stir you to the depths of your being. Some of the men were rather good singers.

Meanwhile it had begun to get dark. Sadness, depression and stupor began to show painfully through the drunkenness and merrymaking. A man who had been laughing an hour ago was now sobbing to himself somewhere, having drunk more than he could manage. Others had already contrived to get into a couple of fights. Yet others, pale and hardly able to stand, staggered about the barracks, picking quarrels with anybody they met. The very same

men whose initial intoxication had been of the least provocative
kind now looked in vain for friends in order to lay bare their souls
to them and sob out their drunken misery. All this pathetic crowd
had wanted to have a good time, to spend the great holiday in high
spirits and good humour. Yet God, how dreary and dismal the day
was for nearly everyone. Everyone spent it looking as though they
had been disappointed in some hope. Petrov dropped in to see me
a few more times. He had drunk very little all day and was almost
completely sober. But right up to the very last minute of the day
he still seemed to be expecting something unusual, something
festive and hilarious. Though he kept quiet about this, it could be
seen in his eyes. He scurried indefatigably from barrack to barrack.
But nothing in particular happened or was encountered except for
drunkenness, senseless drunken bad language and heads that were
stupefied with intoxication. Sirotkin, too, was wandering around
the barracks, looking washed and wearing a new woven red shirt;
he too had a quiet, naïve look, as though he were expecting something. Gradually the atmosphere in the barracks had become sick-
ening and unbearable. Of course, there was also much that was
comical, but I had come to feel a kind of sadness and pity towards
all these men, felt oppressed and suffocated in their midst. Here
were two convicts arguing with one another about who should
stand the other a treat. It was obvious that they had been arguing
for a long time already, and that they had quarrelled about this
before. One of the men in particular had some long-held grievance
against the other. He was complaining, and endeavouring to prove,
in slurred tones, that the other had treated him unjustly: last year
at Shrovetide some sheepskin coat or other had been sold, and the
money hidden away somewhere. There was something else, besides
... The accuser was a tall and muscular fellow, mild-tempered and
by no means stupid, but who when drunk felt an irresistible urge
to make friends with everyone and pour out his sorrows. He was
abusing his adversary and showing that he had a grudge against
him so that the eventual reconciliation he would have with him
would be all the more conclusive. The other man was a short,
thickset, stocky fellow; his round face expressed cunning and an
ability to intrude on the business of others. He had if anything

drunk more than his companion, but was only slightly drunk. He possessed character, and was reputed to have money, but for some reason it seemed to be in his interests now not to irritate his expansive friend, and he was taking him to the 'barman'; the friend was insisting that he did this 'if he had a spark of decency left in him'.

With a certain respect for his client and a shade of contempt for the expansive friend, because the latter was not buying his drink with his own money but was being treated, the 'barman' produced a cup and filled it with vodka.

'No, Styopka, you have to do it,' the expansive friend was saying, observing that he was in luck, 'because it's your duty.'

'I'm not going to waste any more of my breath talking to you!' replied Styopka.

'No, Styopka, you're wrong,' said the other firmly, taking the cup from the 'barman'. 'You owe me money; you've no shame in you; even your eyes don't belong to you, you borrowed them off somebody. You're a villain, Styopka, that's what you are; in one word, a villain!'

'Stop snivelling, you've spilt your vodka! The man's doing you the favour of buying you a drink, so drink!' the 'barman' shouted at the expansive friend. 'I'm not going to wait here all night for you!'

'All right, I'm going to drink it, what are you shouting at? Merry Christmas, Stepan Dorofeich!' he said politely, with a little bow, cup in hand, to Styopka, whom he had only just finished calling a villain. 'May you live in health for a hundred years, not counting the ones you've lived already!' He drank up, grunted and wiped his mouth. 'In the old days I could hold a lot of liquor, boys,' he observed with a look of earnest dignity, addressing everyone and no one. 'But now it seems the years are catching up with me. I thank you, Stepan Dorofeich!'

'That's quite all right.'

'So what I want to tell you, Styopka, apart from the fact that you're the biggest villain I know, what I want to tell you is ...'

'And I know what I want to tell you, you drunken son of a bitch,' Styopka chipped in, having lost all patience. 'You listen here and mark every word: we're going to divide the world up between us, you and me: you can take one half, and I'll have the other. Now go away and don't let me set eyes on you again. I've had enough of you!'

'So you're not going to give me my money back?'

'What money, you drunken buffoon?'

'Eh-heh, you'll come crawling to me on your hands and knees in the next world asking me to take it, but I won't! We earn our money by hard work and the sweat of our brows and the blisters on our hands and feet. You'll rot with my five copecks in the next world.'

'Aw go to hell.'

'Don't aw at me; I'm not a packhorse.'

'Go on, get out of it.'

'Villain!'

'Con!'

And the exchange of swearing and abuse started again, even worse than before.

Two friends were sitting apart from one another on the plank bed. One of them was a massive, tall, beefy fellow, a real butcher of a man; his face was red. He was almost in tears, because he was very moved. The other was a thin, feeble-looking man with a long nose that had a drip on the end of it, and little piggy eyes that were trained on the ground. He was a crafty, educated man; he had once been a clerk and rather looked down on his friend, which the latter in secret fiercely resented. They had spent the whole day drinking together.

'He dared me,' the beefy man was shouting, violently shaking the clerk's head with his left arm, which he had placed around it. 'Dared' meant 'hit'. The beefy man, who had been an NCO, secretly envied his emaciated friend, and so they were both competing with one another to find the most exquisite terms of abuse.

'And I'm telling you you're wrong . . .' the clerk began dogmatically, stubbornly refusing to raise his eyes and surveying the ground in a self-important manner.

'He dared me, do you hear!' his friend interrupted, pulling at his boon companion even harder. 'You're the only friend I have left in the world, do you hear? That's why I'm telling you and you alone: he dared me . . .'

'And I say again: such a sour excuse, my dear friend, is but withered laurels on your head,' the clerk retorted in a polite, delicate little voice. 'You would do better to admit, dear friend, that all this drunkenness comes of your own irresponsibility . . .

The beefy man staggered back a few places, dully fastened his drunken eyes on the complacent little clerk and suddenly, quite unexpectedly, rammed his enormous fist as hard as he could into the clerk's little face. That was the end of a friendship that had lasted all day. The dear friend went flying unconscious under the bed . . .

Into our barrack came a friend of mine from the special category, a young fellow of infinite good nature and high spirits, quite intelligent, and unusually straightforward, as convicts go. He was the same man who, on my first day in the prison, had asked during dinner where he could find the rich peasant, had said he had 'his pride' and had drunk tea with me. He was about forty years old, with an unusually large lower lip and a large, meaty nose that was covered in blackheads. In his hands he held a balalaika, the strings of which he strummed carelessly. He was followed, as by some sycophant, by a tiny convict with a large head, whom I had seen very little of up till now. But no one paid him any attention. He was a strange character, mistrustful, always silent and serious; he worked in the sewing shed and evidently tried to keep aloof and have nothing to do with the other convicts. Now he was drunk, however, and had attached himself to Varlamov like a shadow. He was following him around in a state of terrible agitation, waving his arms about, beating with his fists on the wall and the plank bed, and was almost in tears. Varlamov appeared to be paying no attention to him, as if he were not at his side at all. Remarkably, these two men had earlier had practically nothing to do with one another; they had nothing in common as regarded either their occupations or their characters. Even the categories they belonged to were different, and they lived in different barracks. The little convict's name was Bulkin.

When Varlamov saw me, he grinned. I was sitting on my place

on the plank bed beside the stove. He was standing some way from me, figuring something out; swaying on his feet, he approached me with uneven steps. He struck a defiant pose with the whole of his body. Then, lightly plucking the strings of his balalaika, he chanted in a recitative, as he gently tapped his foot:

> Her face is round, her face is pearly,
> She sings like the tomtit early,
>   My sweet love is she;
> In her satin dress she dances,
> Whirls its pretty, fancy flounces,
>   She's as fair can be.

This song seemed to drive Bulkin out of his wits; he waved his arms about and, addressing everyone, shouted:

'He's lying, boys, he's lying! There's not a word of truth in it, he's lying.'

'To old man Aleksandr Petrovich!' said Varlamov, looking me in the eye with a mischievous laugh, and made as if to clamber up and kiss me. He was pretty drunk. The expression 'to old man such-and-such ...', meaning 'my respects to such-and-such ...', is used by the common people all over Siberia, even when addressing a young man of twenty. The expression 'old man' has a respectful, deferential, even flattering shade of meaning.

'Now then, Varlamov, how are you?'

'Oh, living one day at a time. If you like Christmas, you start getting drunk early; you'll have to excuse me!' said Varlamov in a rather sing-song voice.

'He's lying, he's lying again!' shouted Bulkin, pummelling the plank bed in a kind of despair. But Varlamov seemed to have vowed to himself not to pay him the slightest attention, and this created an extremely comic situation, since Bulkin had latched onto Varlamov ever since early that morning for no other reason than that Varlamov was 'lying', as it seemed to him. He flitted after him like a shadow, worrying over his every word and wringing his hands, which he had beaten on the walls and the bed until they were almost bleeding; he was in agony, visible agony over his conviction that Varlamov was 'lying'. If he had had any hair on his head he would probably have torn it out in chagrin. It was exactly as if he had taken upon himself the obligation of answering for Varlamov's every action, as if all Varlamov's defects lay on his conscience. But what made this so absurd was the fact that Varlamov never even glanced in his direction.

'He's lying, he's lying, he's lying! Not one word of it fits with the facts!' howled Bulkin.

'What's it got to do with you?' asked the convicts, laughing.

'I'll tell you one thing, Aleksandr Petrovich: when I was young I was very good-looking and the girls used to fancy me a lot ...' began Varlamov suddenly, for no apparent reason.

'He's lying! He's lying again!' Bulkin interrupted, with a kind of squeal.

The convicts roared with laughter.

'And I used to cut a fine figure in front of them: I used to wear my red shirt and my wide velveteen trousers; I'd lie there like Champagne Charlie, as drunk as a lord – in short, I had it made!'

'He's lying!' Bulkin asserted, affirmatively.

'And in those days I had a two-storeyed stone house that my father had left me. Well, in two years I managed to spend both those storeys, and all I had left was the gate and no posts. That's money for you – easy come, easy go.'

'He's lying!' asserted Bulkin, even more affirmatively.

'So when I'd come to my senses I sent my people a real tear-jerker of a letter; I thought maybe they might send me a bit of money. It was because of that they said I'd turned against my parents. Disrespectful, they said I was. It's seven years now since I sent that letter.'

'So there was no reply?' I asked, laughing.

'No, there wasn't,' he answered, suddenly starting to laugh, too, and bringing his nose closer and closer to my face. 'But you know, Aleksandr Petrovich, I've got a mistress here ...'

'You? A mistress?'

'Only the other day Onufriyev said to me: "Mine may be pock-marked and ugly, but she's got a lot of clothes; yours is pretty but she's broke, she has to go begging."'

'And is it true?'

'It's true she's broke,' he replied as he shook with inaudible laughter; the men in the barrack also burst out laughing. They all knew he really had taken up with some destitute woman, a beggar, and had given her only ten copecks in six months.

'Well, and so?' I asked, in a desire to be free of him.

He said nothing for a moment, looked at me full of sweetness and light, and said fondly:

'So since that's how it is, I wonder if you might see your way to standing me a noggin? After all, Aleksandr Petrovich, I've had nothing to drink except tea all day,' he added with tender emotion, accepting the money I gave him, 'and I've been knocking that tea back till I couldn't get my breath, and it's been sloshing about in my belly like it's in a bottle . . .'

As he took my money, Bulkin's mental derangement reached an acme of intensity. He gesticulated like a man in despair, practically in tears.

'Good people!' he shouted, addressing the whole roomful of men in a frenzy. 'Look at him! He's lying! Whatever he says, he's lying, lying, lying!'

'But what's it got to do with you?' the convicts shouted to him, astonished at his fury. 'You silly man!'

'I won't let him lie!' Bulkin shouted, his eyes glittering as he thumped his fist on the bed with all his might. 'I don't want him to lie!'

All the men roared with laughter. Varlamov pocketed the money, took his leave of me and, making a great show, hurried out of the barrack – he was going to the 'barman', of course. Only now did he seem to become aware of Bulkin's presence.

'All right, come on then!' he said to him, pausing in the entrance, as if he really did need Bulkin for some purpose or other. 'Wooden-top!' he added, with contempt, allowing the aggrieved Bulkin to go first, and starting to strum his balalaika once more . . .

But what is the point of describing this drunken scene? At last the claustrophobic day was at an end. The convicts fell asleep heavily on the plank bed. They talked and raved in their sleep even more than on other nights. Here and there men still sat at *maydans*.

The long-awaited holiday was over. Tomorrow would be an ordinary day, with work again ...

* 11 *

THE STAGE SHOW

On the evening of the third day of Christmas, the first performance of our stage show took place. The actors had probably gone to a great deal of trouble to get the performance together, but they had taken it all upon themselves, so that none of the rest of us had any idea of how things were going. We did not even really know what the performance was to consist of. During these three days the actors had done all they could to get hold of costumes when they went out to work. Whenever I met Baklushin, all he could do was to snap his fingers in delight. Even the Major seemed in a good mood, though we were completely in the dark as to whether he knew about the show or not. If he did know, had he given his formal permission or had he simply decided to keep quiet, giving the whole thing up as a bad job and figuring that at least no regulations were being broken? My own opinion is that he did know about the show, indeed could not help knowing about it; but that he did not want to interfere, perceiving that that might make matters worse: the convicts would only begin to fool around and get drunk, and it was far better for them to have something to keep them busy. The only reason I suppose this to have been the Major's line of reasoning is that it is the most natural, proper and sensible one. One might even put the matter this way: if the convicts had not had their Christmas show or some such similar occupation, the prison authorities would have had to devise one for them. But since our Major was distinguished by a mode of thought that ran quite counter to that of the rest of mankind, it may very well be that I commit a grave error in supposing that he knew about the show and had given his permission for it. A man such as the Major must forever be bearing down on someone, taking something away, depriving someone of a right – establishing discipline, in short. The whole town knew about this aspect of the man. What did he care that it was just these very restrictions of his that caused all the fooling around in the prison? There were penalties for fooling around (reasoned men like our Major), and all that was required in dealing with these convict villains was severity and the constant, literal application of the law. These inept executors of the law decidedly fail to understand and are incapable of understanding that its literal application, without any understanding of its sense or its spirit, leads straight to its being broken, and indeed has never led to anything else. 'It's the law, what more do you want?' they say, and are genuinely bewildered when they are asked for common sense and a sober head as well. They seem to consider the latter in particular to be a superfluous and outrageous luxury, an intolerable constraint.

But whatever the case, the senior duty sergeant did not go against the convicts, and that was all that mattered to them. I can say quite positively that the show and the men's gratitude for its being permitted were the reasons for there not being one serious disturbance in the prison during the holiday period: not one malignant quarrel, not one case of theft. I saw for myself how the men required nothing but the threat that the show might be forbidden for them to quiet down those who were drunk or quarrelsome. The duty sergeant made the convicts promise him that there would be no trouble and that they would behave themselves. They gladly agreed, and kept their promise faithfully; they were also very flattered that anyone should trust them like this. It should be said, however, that it cost the authorities nothing to permit the show, no sacrifices whatsoever. No space was marked out specially for the purpose in advance: the show could be assembled and dismantled in some fifteen minutes. It lasted an hour and a half, and if any order had suddenly come down from on high for the performance to be stopped, it could have been carried out instantly. The convicts kept their costumes in their locked boxes. But before I describe how the show was put together and what the costumes were actually like, let me describe the playbill, what it was proposed to perform, in other words.

There was no written playbill as such. On the second and third performances a sort of programme did, however, materialize,

written by Baklushin for the officers and the other distinguished
visitors who had favoured our show with their presence at its first
performance. The officer of the watch usually came, and once the
watch commander himself put in an appearance. On one occasion
the officer of the engineers also came along. It was for visitors like
these that the programme was compiled. It was supposed that the
renown of the prison show would echo far through the fortress and
even the town, all the more so since the latter had no theatre. There
was a rumour that some amateurs had once joined forces for a
single performance, but that was all. The convicts were like
children, delighting in the smallest success, and even vain about it.
'Who knows,' the men thought to themselves, and said to one
another things like: 'maybe even the real high-up ones'll get to hear
about it; they'll come and have a look; then they'll see what us
convicts are all about. This isn't just a soldiers' pantomime with
stuffed dummies and boats that float and dancing bears and goats.
There's actors here, real actors doing classy plays; there's nothing
like this in town. They say there was a theatrical evening at General
Abrosimov's house and there's apparently to be another; well,
maybe their costumes'll be better than ours, but as far as the
dialogue's concerned who can beat our boys? Maybe the governor
will get to hear about it, and – you never know – maybe he'll want
to come and see it, too. There's no theatre in the town . . .' In short,
the convicts' imaginations were inflamed to such a pitch of high
fever during the holidays, especially after their first success, that
they almost fancied they might receive a reward or a reduction in
their sentence, though as they did so they at once began to laugh
very good-naturedly at their own foolishness. In short, they were
children, utter children, even though some of them were over forty.
But in spite of the fact that there was no programme, I already knew
the main outlines of the proposed entertainment. The first piece was
a vaudeville, entitled *Filatka and Miroshka*, or *The Rivals*.[25] A week
before the performance, Baklushin had bragged to me that the role
of Filatka, which he had taken, would be played better than it had
ever been played in the theatres of *Saint* Petersburg. He strode up
and down the barracks, boasting mercilessly and shamelessly, yet
at the same time with the best of good humour; from time to time

he would suddenly let fly with something 'theatrical', a bit of his
part, in other words – and everyone would roar with laughter,
regardless of whether what he had spouted was funny or not. It
must be admitted, however, that even in doing this, the convicts
knew how to restrain themselves and preserve their dignity:
enthusiasm for Baklushin's capers and prattle about the forthcoming show was displayed only by either the very youngest and
inexperienced convicts, who lacked self-discipline, or by the most
senior ones, whose authority was firmly established, so that they
had nothing to fear in expressing their feelings, whatever they might
be, even ones that were most forthright (in prison terms, the most
improper) and simple. The others listened to the rumours and
gossip in silence. It is true that they did not condemn Baklushin or
contradict him, but they tried for all they were worth to show
indifference to the rumours about the show, and even in some
degree to treat them with condescension. It was only at the very
end, almost on the eve of the performance, that everyone started
to show interest: what would they see? What were our boys like?
What was the attitude of the Major? Would the show be as good
as it was last year? ... and so forth. Baklushin assured me that all
the actors had been perfectly cast for their parts. There would even
be a curtain. Sirotkin was going to play Filatka's fiancée, 'and just
wait till you see what he looks like dressed up as a woman!' he said,
screwing up his eyes and clicking his tongue. The Lady Bountiful
was to have a dress with a flounced skirt, a cape and a parasol, while
the Lord Bountiful was to appear in an officer's uniform with
epaulettes, carrying a cane. Then a second piece would follow, a
dramatic one, called *Kedril the Glutton*.[26] The title interested me
greatly; but no matter how hard I tried, I could not obtain any
information about the play in advance. All I could find out was that
it was not taken from any book but was to be acted 'from the copy';
that they had got the play from some retired NCO who lived in an
outlying part of the town and who had probably once taken part
in a performance of it himself as an item in some soldiers' theatri-
cals. It really is the case that in our remote towns and provinces
there are plays which, it would appear, no one has ever heard of
and which have probably never appeared in print, but have popped

up out of nowhere and are an indispensable part of every people's theatre in a certain area of Russia. Incidentally, speaking of 'people's theatre', it would be a very, very good thing if one or other of our researchers would make a fresh study, more thorough than has hitherto been the case, of this form of theatre, which is healthy and flourishing and is even, perhaps, not quite without significance. I cannot believe that all I subsequently saw in our prison show was thought up by the convicts themselves. There must be some continuity of tradition, certain established techniques and concepts which are handed on from generation to generation by force of habit. They are to be found among soldiers, factory workers, in factory towns, and even among the artisans and shopkeepers in a few obscure and impoverished little places. They have survived, too, among the servants of the large landowners' houses in villages and small provincial towns. I am even inclined to believe that many of these old plays have been kept alive in Russia from one generation to the next by means of written copies made by the servants of landowners' houses. In the old days, the landowners and Moscow nobility had their own theatres, staffed by actors who were serfs. It was in these theatres that our popular dramatic art, the signs of which are unmistakable, had its beginnings. As for *Kedril the Glutton*, despite all my curiosity, I could find out nothing about it in advance except that evil spirits appeared on the stage and carried Kedril off to hell. But what was the significance of the name Kedril, and why was it 'Kedril' and not 'Kirill'? Was this name Russian, or was it of foreign origin? I could obtain no answers to these questions. It was announced that to conclude the show there would be a 'pantomime with music'. All this was, of course, quite fascinating. There were some fifteen actors, a gallant, energetic lot. They made themselves busy in secret, got on with their rehearsals, behind the barracks sometimes, anywhere that was out of the public eye. They really wanted to surprise us all with something out of the way and unexpected.

On ordinary working days the prison was locked up early, as soon as it started to get dark. For the days of Christmas an exception was made: the barracks were not locked until the evening drum was beaten. This privilege was granted especially in order to facilitate the holding of the show. During the holiday someone was usually sent early each evening to the officer of the watch with the humble request 'to permit the show and not lock the barracks for a while longer yet', adding that the show had also taken place the previous evening, that the locking-up had been postponed then, too, and that there had been no trouble. The officer of the watch reasoned as follows: 'It's true there wasn't any trouble yesterday; and if they're promising that there won't be any today either that means they'll see to it themselves, and that's the best bet of all. And anyway, if they're not allowed to have their show (who knows what that bunch of convicts might get up to?) they might start fooling around out of spite and make trouble for the guards.' And then, finally, it was a boring task, standing on watch, and here there was a show, not just a soldier's entertainment but a convict show, and convicts were interesting people: it would be fun to go and have a look. The officer of the watch always has the right to have a look.

The duty officer would show up: 'Where's the officer of the watch?' 'He's gone to the prison to count the convicts and lock up the barracks' – a straightforward answer and a straightforward excuse. By not locking the barracks until the evening drum, the officers of the watch allowed the show to take place every night for the entire duration of Christmas. The convicts knew in advance that the guards would not interfere and so their minds were at rest.

At around seven o'clock Petrov came for me, and we set off together to see the performance. Nearly everyone in our barrack went, with the exception of the Chernigov Old Believer and the Poles. The Poles only went to the very last performance on the fourth of January, and then only after they had been assured over and over again that the show was good and entertaining and that they would not get into trouble if they went to it. The Poles' finickiness in no way upset the convicts, and when they arrived on the fourth of January they were welcomed very politely. They were even given the best places in the house. As for the Circassians and Isay Fomich, our show was a real delight to them. Isay Fomich contributed three copecks on each of his visits; on the last night he put ten copecks in the plate, and his face wore an expression of rapture. The actors' plan was to collect from each member of the audience what he could afford; the money was to cover the costs of putting on the show and for the actors' 'refreshment'. Petrov assured me that I would be given one of the best positions, no matter how packed the house, since being better-off than the other men I could be expected to contribute more, and also since I knew more than they did about what they were doing. This turned out indeed to be the case. But first I must describe the theatre and the way in which the show was staged.

The military barrack in which the show was performed was about fifteen paces long. From the courtyard one climbed a flight of steps up to the passageway, and from the passageway one entered the barrack. This long barrack was, as I have already mentioned, of a design different from that of the others: in it the plank bed extended along the walls, so that the middle of the room remained empty. One half of the room, that nearest to the exit via the steps, was designated for the audience; the other half, which adjoined another barrack, was used as the proscenium. The curtain was what struck me most of all. It stretched for a distance of some ten paces the entire width of the barrack. A curtain like this was such a luxury that it really was something to be marvelled at. What was more, it had been painted on with oils: here were trees, arbours, ponds and stars. It was made of bits of cloth, old and new; everyone had contributed or sacrificed something, old footcloths and shirts had been sown together somehow into one enormous width. The part of the curtain for which there had not been enough cloth was made of paper that had been begged by the sheet from the various offices and departments. Our painters, among whom the prison 'Bryullov' A—v was prominent, had made it their task to paint it and colour it. The effect was overwhelming. A luxury such as this was enough to gladden the hearts of even the most sullen and starchy convicts who, when it came to the show, proved without exception to be just as much children as the most hot-headed and impatient men. All the men were very pleased with themselves, almost boastfully so. The lighting consisted of a few tallow candles cut into pieces. In front of the curtain stood two of the kitchen benches, and in front of the benches there were three or four chairs which had been provided in case of visits by senior officers. The benches were for the NCOs and the engineer clerks, the supervisors and similar persons who, although they represented the authorities, were not of officer rank, just in case they looked in at the prison. In the event, there was a constant stream of visitors from outside throughout the entire holiday period; on some evenings there would be more than on others, and on the last night there was not one empty place on the benches. Finally, behind the benches there stood the convicts; they stood out of respect for the visitors, without their caps on, wearing their jackets or sheepskin coats in spite of the stifling, vapour-laden atmosphere of the room. Needless to say, not enough space had been provided for all the convicts. It was not merely that some were literally sitting on top of others, especially in the back rows – the plank bed and the stage wings were also jammed with men, and there were even some theatre-lovers who watched the show every night from the adjoining barrack behind the stage. The crowding in the front half of the room was unbelievable and might have stood comparison with the crowding and jostling I had only recently witnessed in the bath-house. The door into the passage was open; even in the passage, where the temperature was twenty degrees below zero, crowds of people were standing. Petrov and I were immediately let through almost as far as the benches, where the view of the stage was much better than in the rows further back. I was regarded in part as an adjudicator and connoisseur who had been in theatres rather different from this one; the men saw that Baklushin constantly came to ask me for advice and that he treated me with respect; and so I now received a place of honour. It might be thought that the convicts were all extremely vain and frivolous; but all this was a pose. The convicts might laugh at me, observing that I was a poor helpmate to them at work. Almazov might look at us gentry with contempt as he showed off to us his skill at baking alabaster. But mingled in with their victimization of us and jeering at us was another element: we had once been noblemen; we belonged to the same class as their former masters, of whom they could have no good memories. Yet now, at the show, they stepped aside for me. They recognized that in this matter I was better equipped to judge than they, that here my experience and knowledge were greater than theirs. Even the least well-disposed towards me (I know this for a fact) now wanted me to praise their show, and ushered me to the best place without the slightest self-abasement. I realize this now, remembering the impression I had at the time. I remember how it seemed to me then: their desire for a just assessment of their performance was in no way self-deprecatory, but was rather an expression of their own personal dignity. The best and most outstanding characteristic of our common people is their sense of justice and their desire for it. The cockerel-like habit of always wanting to be first in every situation, and *at all costs*, and whether one is worthy of it or not – this is unknown among the common people. One has only to remove the outer, superficial husk and look at the kernel within attentively, closely and without prejudice, and one will see in the common people things one had no inkling of. There is not much that our men of learning can teach the common people. I would even say the reverse: it is they who should take a few lessons from the common people.

As we were on our way to the show, Petrov told me with simple candour that I would be let through to the front of the house because I would contribute more money. There was no fixed entry price: each man gave what he was able to give or what he wished to give. Almost everyone put in something when the plate was brought round, even if it was only half a copeck. But this willingness of the men to let me through to the front, even though it stemmed partly from a desire for money, from a belief that I would contribute more than others, what a sense of personal dignity it contained! 'You're better off than I am, so you go in front; even if we are all equal here you'll make a bigger contribution: so the actors will prefer a visitor like you – but also, you'll get a place at the front because we're all here not because of money but because we've got respect for what we're doing, and so we must sort ourselves out in our own way.' How much genuine, noble pride there was in this! This was respect not for money, but for oneself. In the prison money and riches were not generally held in great regard, especially if one considers the convicts *en masse*, as members of the artel. I can hardly remember one instance of anyone seriously demeaning himself for the sake of money, not even isolated instances. There were cadgers, and they used to ask me for money. But their cadging was more mischief and foolery than any real desire for gain; it was rather a kind of simple-hearted playfulness. I do not know if I am making myself clear ... But I am forgetting the show. To the matter in hand.

Before the curtains were raised the entire room presented a strange and animated spectacle. For a start, there was the crowd of spectators, packed, squeezed and jammed on every side, awaiting the beginning of the performance with a look of patience and happy anticipation on their faces. In the back rows were the men who had climbed on top of one another. Many of them had brought logs of wood from the kitchen with them; when he had somehow managed to place the thick log against the wall, the man would clamber up onto it in a standing position, supporting himself with both hands on the shoulders of the man in front, and would continue to stand like this, without changing position, for the next two hours perfectly satisfied with himself and the place he had. Others managed to get a foothold on the lower step of the stove and remained standing there all the time, supporting themselves on the backs and shoulders of the men in front of them. This was in the rows at the very back of the room, by the wall. There was also a tightly packed crowd of men who had clambered up onto the plank bed, at one side of the room, above the musicians. These were good positions. Five or so men had clambered up onto the stove itself and were lying on top of it, looking down. Now they were happy! The windowsills on the other side of the room were also packed with crowds of latecomers or men who had been unable to find a good place. Everyone behaved quietly and with decorum. Everyone wanted to present the best possible appearance to the officers and visitors. Every face wore an expression of the most artless expectation. The men's faces were red and wet with sweat from the heat and stuffiness. What a strange reflection of childlike joy, of pure, good-natured contentment shone on these furrowed, branded cheeks and foreheads, on these gazes which had hitherto expressed only gloom and sullenness, on these eyes which sometimes sparkled with a terrible light! None of the men wore caps, and as far as I could see, every head was shaven on the right-hand side. But now there were sounds of activity from the stage. In a moment the curtain would be raised. The orchestra struck up . . . This orchestra is worthy of note. At one side of the room, seated along the plank bed were some eight musicians: there were two violins (one belonged to the prison, while the other had been borrowed from someone in the fortress, though the man who played it was also a convict), three balalaikas, all home-made, two guitars and a tambourine in lieu of a double bass. The violins did nothing but screech and saw, the guitars were pathetic, but the balalaikas were out of this world. The agility with which the musicians shifted their fingers on the strings stood comparison with the deftest conjuring trick. They played one dance tune after the other. In the liveliest passages the balalaika players knocked against the sounding-boards of their instruments; the tone, taste, execution, the style of playing and the interpretation of the melodies were all unique, original and specific to the convict milieu. One of the guitarists also had an excellent mastery of his instrument. This was the man of noble origin who had murdered his father. As for the convict who played the tambourine, he performed wonders: he whirled it around on his finger, and drew his thumb across its parchment. Strong, clear beats that were swift, resonant and even would suddenly be broken up into countless tiny, jangling, whispering sounds. At length two accordionists also appeared. To tell the truth, I had previously had no idea of the possibilities of these simple folk instruments; the harmony and ensemble, and most important of all, the spirit and character of the melodic interpretation were simply remarkable. Now for the first time I perceived what was truly extravagant and dashing in the reckless bravura of the Russian melodies. At last the curtain was raised. Everyone stirred, shifting their weight from one leg to the other, the men at the back standing on tiptoe; someone fell off his log; every single member of the audience opened his mouth and fixed his eyes on the stage, and the most complete silence reigned . . . The performance ; began.

Aley was standing beside me, surrounded by a group that included his brothers and all the other Circassians. They had all become great devotees of the show and went to it every evening.

I noticed on more than one occasion that all the Muslims, Tartars and so on were extremely fond of any kind of spectacle. Isay Fomich had also squeezed in beside them; from the moment the curtain rose he seemed transformed into pure seeing and hearing, and into the most ingenuous, avid expectation of marvels and delights. It would have been tragic indeed if he had been disappointed. Aley's good-natured countenance shone with such beautiful, childlike joy that I confess the sight of him filled me with happiness, and I remember that each time one of the actors did something particularly amusing or clever I found myself involuntarily turning in Aley's direction and glancing at his face. He did not see me; he had other things to think about. Standing quite near me on my left was an elderly convict whose face always wore a frown, a man forever peevish and discontented. He had also noticed Aley, and I saw him turn round several times to look at him, smiling slightly as he did so: such a sweet boy! The man called him 'Aley Semyonych', I don't know why. The performance of *Filatka and Miroshka* got underway. Baklushin was truly magnificent in the role of Filatka. He played the part with astonishing lucidity. One could see that he had given careful consideration to every phrase, every movement. He knew how to lend significance to his every least word and gesture, a significance that was fully in keeping with the character of his part. Add to this painstaking effort and study an astonishing, authentic gaiety, straightforwardness and a lack of artifice and you would certainly have agreed, had you seen Baklushin, that he was a genuine, natural actor of great talent. I have seen *Filatka* performed several times on the stages of the Moscow and Petersburg theatres, and I can positively say that in each city the actor who played Filatka was not as good as Baklushin. Compared with him they came across as *paysans* and not as authentic peasants. They were trying too hard to be peasants. Baklushin had the additional advantage of being spurred on by rivalry; everyone knew that in the second piece the part of Kedril was to be played by the convict Potseykin, an actor whom all the men considered to be better and more gifted than Baklushin, and Baklushin was as distressed by this as a child might be. Time after time during those last days before the performance he came to me and poured out his feelings. Two hours before the show was due to start he was shaking with a kind of fever. When the spectators laughed and shouted from their places 'Bravo, Baklushin! Good lad!' his whole face shone with happiness and his eyes gleamed with genuine inspiration. The scene in which Filatka and Miroshka kiss, when Filatka shouts to Miroshka beforehand 'Wipe your nose!' and wipes his own came out just right, and was killingly funny. Everyone fairly rocked with laughter. But it was the audience that interested me most; here the men lost all their inhibitions. They gave themselves up wholeheartedly to their enjoyment. Their cries of approval resounded more and more frequently. One man kept nudging his neighbour, hurriedly giving him his opinion of the acting, not caring and in all probability not even seeing who it was standing next to him during the comic scenes; another would suddenly turn to the crowd in a rapture of enthusiasm, as though urging everyone to laugh, wave his arm in the air and once again turn towards the stage in eager absorption. A third could do nothing but click his tongue and snap his fingers and was unable to keep still; and as there was no room for him to move about, he just kept shifting from one foot to another. The general mood of exhilaration reached its highest pitch towards the end of the play. I do not exaggerate in the slightest. Imagine the prison, with its fetters and servitude, its long, dismal years stretching ahead, its life as monotonous as the dripping of rainwater on an autumn day – and then suddenly all these oppressed and tyrannized, confined men being allowed for a brief space of time to unwind, to enjoy themselves, to forget their bad dream, to put on a show and to do it as if to say proudly to the astonished townsfolk: 'Look, this is the stuff we're made of!' The townspeople naturally found the whole thing quite fascinating, the costumes, for example. They were terribly curious to see convicts like Vanka Otpety, Netsvetayev or Baklushin dressed in clothes that were completely different from the ones they had been used to seeing them wearing for so many years. 'He's only a convict, after all, you can hear his fetters clanking, but here he is now coming on stage wearing a frock-coat and a round hat and a cloak, just like a regular citizen! He's got a moustache, and hair on his head. Look, he's taken a fine handkerchief out of his pocket, he's fanning himself with it, he's playing the part of a gentleman, he damn well *is* a gentleman!' And they would all be beside themselves with excitement. The Lord Bountiful came on wearing an adjutant's uniform, a very old one, it was true, with epaulettes and a cap with a cockade. The effect was remarkable. There had been two contenders for this part, and – was it to be believed? – they had fought one another like little children over who should get it: they both wanted to appear in an officer's uniform with shoulder knots! The other actors had kept them apart, and by a majority of votes had decided that Netsvetayev should have the part, not because he was more personable and better-looking than the other convict, and so resembled a gentleman more, but because Netsvetayev had told everyone that he would appear on stage with a cane and would wave it in the air and twirl it over the ground like a real gentleman and dandy of the first order, which Vanka Otpety would be unable to do, since he had never seen real gentry. And true enough, when Netsvetayev appeared before the public with his lady, he did nothing but twirl the thin reed cane he had procured from somewhere swiftly and agilely over the ground, probably in the belief that this was the very height of upper-class refinement, elegance and fashion. At some time in his house serf's childhood, as a bare-footed little boy, he had probably seen some handsomely dressed gentleman with a cane and had been captivated by the gentleman's ability to twirl it; this image had been indelibly stamped upon his memory, so that at thirty years of age he could remember everything just as it had been, and could thoroughly fascinate and enthrall the whole prison with it. Netsvetayev was so engrossed in this occupation that he no longer had eyes for anyone or anything; he would even speak his lines without raising his eyes, and simply continued to follow the movements of the tip of his cane. The Lady Bountiful was also very remarkable in her own way: the man who played her appeared in an old, threadbare muslin dress that looked as though it might once have been a floorcloth, bare-armed and bare-legged, his face smeared excessively with powder and rouge; he wore a calico nightcap tied under his chin, held a parasol in one hand and in the other a painted paper fan with which he fanned himself constantly. The lady was greeted by a great howl of laughter; the lady herself could not hold back her mirth and burst out laughing at several points. The lady was played by the convict Ivanov. Sirotkin looked very sweet dressed up as a girl. The satirical songs also went off very well. In short, the piece was played through to everyone's complete and general satisfaction. There was no adverse criticism, nor could there be any.

The orchestra played the overture 'Hall and Home' again, and once more the curtain was raised. This was *Kedril the Glutton*. *Kedril* is a play in the 'Don Juan' genre; at any rate, devils carry both master and servant off to hell towards the end of it. The convicts presented a whole act, but this was apparently only a fragment; the play's beginning and ending had been lost. What we saw made not the slightest sense whatever. The action took place in Russia, at an inn somewhere. The innkeeper was showing a gentleman in an overcoat and a battered round hat to his room. Behind him followed his servant Kedril, carrying a trunk and a chicken wrapped in brown paper. He was wearing a sheepskin coat and a footman's cap. Kedril was the glutton of the title, and was played by the convict Potseykin, Baklushin's rival. The gentleman was played by Ivanov, the same man who had played the Lady Bountiful in the first piece. The innkeeper, played by Netsvetayev, warned the two men that the room was haunted by devils, and disappeared. The gentleman, looking gloomy and preoccupied, muttered to himself that this was nothing new to him and told Kedril to unpack their stuff and get the supper ready. Kedril was a coward and a glutton. When he heard about the devils he grew pale and trembled like a leaf. He would run away if he could, but he had a cowardly fear of his master. Also, he was hungry. He was pleasure-loving, stupid, cunning in his own way, and a coward; he duped his master at every step and at the same time went in fear of him. This servant character was a remarkable one, in which the features of Leporello might be glimpsed distantly and vaguely, and it was played in truly remarkable fashion. Potseykin had real talent, and was in my view a better actor than Baklushin. Of course, when I met Baklushin the following day I did not say as much outright: I should have hurt his feelings too much. The convict who played the gentleman also acted quite well. His lines were the most dreadful rubbish, unlike anything on earth; but his diction was correct and aggressive, his gestures correspondingly so. While Kedril was busy with the trunk, his master strolled meditatively around the stage, and announced to all and sundry that this evening marked the end of his travels. Kedril listened with curiosity, made faces, delivered asides and had the audience laughing at every word he uttered. He did not care about his master; but he had heard about the devils; he wanted to know what they were like, and he started to talk and ask questions. The master finally told him that once, when he had been in some kind of trouble, he had invoked the powers of hell, and the devils had come to his aid and rescued him; but that today the term of his contract expired, and the devils would perhaps come that very day to carry off his soul, as agreed. Kedril began to get very frightened. But the master did not lose heart and told him to make the supper. At the mention of supper, Kedril brightened up, took out the chicken, produced the vodka, and nipped off a piece of the chicken in his fingers and sampled it. The audience roared with laughter. Then the door gave a creak, and the wind banged the shutters; Kedril shivered and hastily, almost unconsciously, stuffed into his mouth an enormous gobbet of chicken which he was unable to swallow. Again there was laughter. 'It is ready?' cried the master, pacing about the room. 'I'll have it ready for you ... in a tick, sir,' said Kedril, sitting down at the table and quite serenely proceeding to tuck in to his master's meal. It was evident that the audience relished the seryant's agility and cunning and the fact that the master had been made a fool of. Potseykin, it must be admitted, really did deserve the praise he got. His delivery of the line: 'I'll have it ready for you ... in a tick, sir' was magnificent. When he sat down at the table he began to eat voraciously, starting up at his master's every footstep, afraid that the latter would find him out; as soon as the master turned round, he hid under the table, taking the chicken with him. At last his initial hunger was satisfied; it was time to think of the master. 'Kedril, how long are you going to be?' cried the master. 'It's ready, sir!' replied Kedril jauntily, suddenly remembering that there was practically nothing left for his master. In fact, all that was left on the plate was a single leg of chicken. The master, gloomy and preoccupied, sat down at the table without noticing anything, while Kedril stood behind his chair with a napkin. Kedril's every word, gesture and grimace as, turning to the audience, he nodded at his dunce of a master, were met with unrestrained roars of laughter from the audience. Then, as soon as the master had begun to eat, the devils appeared. This part of the play was quite incomprehensible, and the entry of the devils was really far too outlandish: a side door opened in the wings, and there appeared something shrouded in white, with a candle lantern instead of a head; a second phantom also had a lantern for a head and carried a scythe. What were the lanterns, what was the scythe, why were the devils dressed in white? No one had any explanation to offer; but then no one gave the matter the slightest thought. This was probably as it should have been. The master turned to the devils with a fair amount of courage and shouted to them that he was ready, that they could carry him off now. But Kedril was as frightened as a rabbit; he crawled under the table, but in spite of all his terror he did not forget to take the bottle of vodka with him. The devils disappeared for a moment; Kedril crawled out from under the table; but as soon as the master sat down to his chicken again, the three devils burst into the room once more, seized the master from behind and carried him off into the nether world. 'Kedril! Save me!' cried the master. But Kedril was occupied with other matters. This time he had taken the bottle, the plate and even the bread under the table with him. Now he was alone, the devils were gone, the master too. Kedril crawled out, looked about him, and a smile lit up his face. He screwed up his eyes mischievously, sat down at his master's place, and giving a nod to the audience, said in a semi-whisper:

'Well, now I'm on my own ... without the master!'

Everyone laughed at Kedril's being without a master; but then he added, once more in a semi-whisper, confidentially addressing the audience and winking at them more and more high-spiritedly:

'The devils have carried off the master!'

The audience's enthusiasm was unbounded! Quite apart from the fact that the devils had carried off the master, Kedril spoke the line with such mischievousness, such a mockingly triumphant grimace,

that it was really impossible not to applaud. But Kedril's good
fortune did not last for long. No sooner had he taken possession
of the bottle, filled his glass and brought it to his lips than the devils
suddenly returned, crept up behind him on tiptoe and grabbed his
arms. Kedril bawled at the top of his voice; he was too scared to
turn round. And he could do nothing to ward the devils off: he was
holding the bottle and the glass, neither of which he was strong-
willed enough to part with. His mouth wide open with horror, he
sat still for a moment, his eyes goggling out of his head at the
audience, with such a killingly funny expression of abject conster-
nation on his face that he would have made a fitting subject for a
painting. At last he was borne aloft and taken away, bottle and all,
kicking his legs and bawling for all he was worth. His bawling could
still be heard after he had been carried off the stage. But the curtain
fell and everyone laughed, everyone was wild with enthusiasm ...
The orchestra struck up the Kamarinskaya.[27]

The music began quietly, almost inaudibly, but the melody grew
louder and louder, the tempo faster, the knuckles of the balalaika-
players struck the sounding boards with bravura ... This was the
Kamarinskaya in full swing, and it would really have been a fine
thing if Glinka could have heard it as it was played in our prison.
The 'pantomime with music'[28] was beginning, the Kamarinskaya
being heard throughout its entire duration. The set depicted the
interior of a hut. A miller and his wife were on the stage. In one
corner the miller was mending a harness, while in another his wife
was spinning flax. Sirotkin played the wife, Netsvetayev the miller.

I should observe that our scenery was very meagre. In this, as in
the preceding piece and others, we fleshed out the scene in our
imagination rather than seeing it with our eyes. Instead of a back-
drop there was something resembling a carpet or horsecloth; at the
side there were some wretched screens. The left side was not
blocked off at all, so that the plank bed was visible. However, the
spectators were an undemanding lot and were willing to flesh out
the reality in their imaginations; indeed, this was something the
convicts were very good at: 'If it's supposed to be a garden, right,
then it's a garden; same if it's supposed to be a room or a hut – no
problem.' Sirotkin looked very sweet dressed up as a young girl.

Some of the spectators paid him muttered compliments under their breath. The miller finished the work he was doing, took his cap and his whip, went over to his wife and made signs to her indicating that he must leave, but that if she were to let anyone in while he was gone, then ... and he pointed to the whip. His wife listened to him and nodded her head. This whip was most likely very familiar to her: she was in the habit of amusing herself when her husband was away. The husband went out. As soon as he was out of the door, his wife shook her fist after him. But now there was a knocking; the door opened, and this time a neighbour appeared, also a miller, a bearded peasant wearing a kaftan. He was carrying a gift, a silk handkerchief. The woman laughed; but no sooner had the man made as if to embrace her than there was another knock at the door. Where could he hide? The woman quickly hid him under the table, and sat down again at her spinning wheel. Another admirer appeared: he was a clerk, wearing a military uniform. Up till now the pantomime had gone irreproachably, every gesture had been just right. Once could not help thinking in astonishment, as one watched these makeshift actors, of how here in Russia so much vigour and talent goes almost entirely to waste in captivity and bitter misfortune. But the convict who played the clerk had probably once been in a provincial or amateur theatre, and in his view not one of our actors had any understanding of the art, nor did they comport themselves properly on stage. And so when he came on, he made his entrance in the style in which classical heroes are supposed to have been acted in the old days: he took a long stride, and without yet moving his other leg suddenly stood still, throwing back the whole of his body and his head, looked around him with supercilious dignity and – took another stride. If such a gait looked ridiculous when adopted by the actors who played the classical heroes, it looked even more so when it was employed by an actor playing a military clerk in a comic scene. But our audience thought this was no doubt the way it was supposed to be, and accepted the lanky clerk's long strides more or less uncritically as a *fait accompli*. Hardly had the clerk got as far as the middle of the stage when yet another knock was heard: once again the woman took fright. Where was she to hide the clerk? It turned out that the chest had fortunately been left unlocked, and the clerk was able to climb into it and hide. The woman shut the lid. This time the guest who appeared was somewhat different – he was also an admirer, but of a rather peculiar kind. He was a Brahmin, and was even dressed as one. The audience exploded with laughter. The Brahmin was played by the convict Koshkin, and played brilliantly. He really did look like a Brahmin. In his gestures he expressed all the extremity of his love. He raised his arms to the sky, then placed them on his breast, his heart; but no sooner had he exposed his tender feelings than there came a loud bang at the door. The loudness of the bang indicated that it was the husband. The woman was beside herself with terror, the Brahmin hurtled around like a madman, imploring her to hide him. She quickly pushed him behind the cupboard, rushed back to her spindle without even remembering to open the door, and continued to spin, deaf to her husband's knocking. In her fright she twisted in her fingers thread that was not there and turned an imaginary spindle, while the real one lay on the floor, forgotten. Sirotkin portrayed her terror very well and effectively. But the husband broke the door in with his foot and bore down on his wife with his whip in his hand. He had seen everything, secretly spying, and he showed her with his fingers that he knew there were three men hidden in the room. Then he set about looking for them. First he found the neighbour, and saw him off the premises with cuffs about the ears. The panic-stricken clerk was about to try to escape, raised the lid of the chest with his hand and by so doing gave himself away. The husband lashed him with his whip, and on this occasion the lovelorn clerk scuttled off in a decidedly unclassical manner. There remained the Brahmin; the husband spent a long time looking for him, and at last found him in the corner behind the cupboard, bowed to him politely and yanked him out by his beard into the middle of the stage. The Brahmin tried to defend himself, shouting: 'Accursed, accursed!' (the only words uttered during the whole pantomime), but the husband did not pay any attention and dealt with him in his own way. The wife, seeing that her turn was coming next, threw away her thread and spindle and ran from the room; the spinning board crashed to the ground and the convicts rocked with laughter. Aley pulled at my arm without looking at me and shouted to me: 'Look! The Brahmin! The Brahmin!' and simply could not stop laughing. The curtain fell. The second scene began ...

But there is no point in describing all the scenes. There were two or three more. They were all funny and full of unfeigned high spirits. Even if the convicts had not actually devised them themselves, at least they had put something of themselves into each one. Practically every actor improvised something of his own, so that an actor played the same role slightly differently every evening. The last pantomime, fantastic in character, concluded with a ballet. A corpse was being buried. Together with a multifarious retinue, the Brahmin was intoning various chants above the coffin, but to no avail. Finally 'The Sun is Going Down' rang out,[29] the dead man came back to life and everyone began to dance for joy. The Brahmin danced with the man he had raised from the dead, a very peculiar sort of Brahmin's dance. With this the show was over until the following evening. The convicts went their separate ways cheerfully and with satisfaction, praising the actors and expressing their thanks to the duty sergeant. No quarrelling was heard. Everyone seemed somehow unusually satisfied, even happy, and fell asleep not in their usual way but almost at peace with themselves – and for what reason, one might wonder? This was no fiction of my imagination. It really was so. All that was needed was for these poor men to be allowed to live in their own way for a bit, to enjoy themselves like human beings, to escape from their convict existence just for an hour or so – and each individual underwent a moral transformation, even if it only lasted for a few moments ... But now it was darkest night. I started and woke up for some reason. The old man was still sitting on the stove saying his prayers; he would remain there praying until daybreak. Aley was sleeping quietly beside me. I recalled that even as he had fallen asleep he had been laughing still, discussing the show with his brothers, and I found myself looking involuntarily at his peaceful, childlike face. Piece by piece, I remembered everything: the day that had just been, the holidays, that whole month ... In terror, I raised my head and looked around me at my companions who were sleeping in the dim light of a six-to-a-pound prison candle. I looked at their wretched faces, their wretched beds, at all this utter misery and poverty. I scrutinized it, and it was as if I were trying to convince myself that all this was real, and not the continuation of some monstrous dream. But it was real: I could hear someone groaning; someone let his arm fall heavily, jangling his chains. Another man started and began to talk in his sleep, while the old man on the stove prayed for all 'Orthodox Christians', and one could hear him quietly and evenly intoning: 'Lord Jesus Christ, have mercy upon us . . .'

'I'm not going to be here forever, after all – just for a few years!' I thought, and laid my head on my pillow once again.

PART TWO

✻

1

THE HOSPITAL (1)

Shortly after Christmas I was taken ill and was admitted to the military hospital. The hospital stood on its own, about half a verst from the fortress. It was a long, single-storeyed building, painted yellow. In summer, when repair work was done, a very large quantity of ochre was used to freshen up its appearance. Offices, living quarters for the senior medical personnel, and other accommodation stretched around the enormous courtyard. The main building housed only medical wards. There were a great many wards, but only two had been set aside for the convicts, and these were always very crowded, especially in summer, so that the beds often had to be moved closer together. The convict wards were filled with all kinds of 'unfortunates'. Our people came here, as did various soldiers awaiting court martial, who were detained in various guardhouses and were divided into three categories: sentenced, unsentenced and transit; there were also men from the corrective battalion – a strange institution, to which soldiers who had committed an offence or were thought to be unreliable were sent in order to receive corrective discipline, and from which they usually emerged some one, two or more years later as the most recondite of villains. Convicts who were taken ill generally reported the fact to the duty sergeant in the morning. Their names were immediately taken down in a book and they were sent with this book, under escort, to the battalion infirmary. There the doctor made a preliminary examination of all the sick men from the fortress's various military commands, and admitted to hospital all those he found to be suffering from some genuine illness. My name was taken down in the book, and at some time between one and two o'clock, when all our men had left the prison for the afternoon's work, I was admitted to hospital. A sick convict usually took with him as much money and bread as he could – he could not expect to be given any rations at the hospital that day – a tiny pipe, a pouch of tobacco, and a flint and steel. These last items he would keep

carefully hidden in his boots. I entered the hospital precincts not
without a certain curiosity about this new and as yet unfamiliar
variation on our daily convict life.

It was a warm day, dismal and overcast, one of those days when
an institution like a hospital takes on a particularly sour, depressing, workaday appearance. With my escort I went into the reception area, where there were two copper baths. Another two
patients, prisoners as yet unsentenced, were already hanging
around with their escorts in expectation of being seen to. A doctor's
assistant came in, looked us over in a lazy, authoritative manner
and then set off in even more leisurely fashion to make his report
to the doctor on duty. The doctor soon appeared; he examined us,
was very kind to us and issued us each with 'complaint sheets'
(medical charts) which were marked with our names. The task of
writing a description of the illness, of the medicines prescribed, the
diet to be followed, and so forth, was given to the intern who was
in charge of the convict wards. I had already heard that the convicts
could not praise their doctors highly enough. 'They're like a father
to a man,' they had said in answer to my questions, when I had been
on my way to the hospital. Meanwhile, we changed. The outer
clothing and underwear in which we had arrived was taken from
us, and we were issued with hospital undergarments to wear, and
also long stockings, slippers, nightcaps, and thick, brown cloth
dressing gowns lined with something that was probably canvas but
that might also have been a kind of sticking plaster. Not to put too
fine a point on it, the dressing gown was utterly filthy; but it was
not until later that I appreciated this fully. Then we were taken to
the convict wards, which were located at the end of a very long,
clean, high-ceilinged corridor. The standard of outward cleanliness
was generally very high; everything one saw fairly glistened. However, this may just have been the way it seemed to me after prison.
The two unsentenced prisoners went into the ward on the left, I into
the one on the right. By the door, which was bolted with an iron
bar, stood a sentry with a rifle, and beside him a sub-sentry. The
junior NCO (one of the hospital guard) gave orders for me to be
let through, and I found myself in a long, narrow room, along both
sides of which beds had been placed, some twenty-two in number;

three or four of these were not yet occupied. The beds were made of wood and were painted green; they were of a type that is all too familiar to us in Russia – the kind of beds that are guaranteed, by a kind of predestination, never to be free of bedbugs. I found a place for myself in the corner, on the other side of the room, where there were windows.

As I said earlier, there were convicts from our prison here, as well. Some of them already knew me or had at least seen me before. But far more of the men were unsentenced prisoners and convicts from the corrective battalion. Seriously ill patients, ones unable to get out of bed, were not very numerous. The others, the only slightly ill or the convalescent, either sat on their beds or walked up and down the room, where a space wide enough for walking had been left between the two rows of beds. An extremely oppressive hospital smell permeated the ward. The air was contaminated with various unpleasant vapours and the stench of medicines, even though the stove in the corner was kept alight practically all day. My bed was covered with a striped quilt, which I removed. Beneath the quilt there was a cloth blanket, lined with canvas, and thick bedlinen of very doubtful cleanliness. Beside the bed stood a small table, on which stood a jug and a tin cup. For the sake of propriety, all this was covered by a little towel which was part of the hospital issue. Under the table there was a shelf: there the patients kept jugs of kvas, or teapots, if they drank tea, which only a few did. On the other hand, the patients' pipes and tobacco pouches, which they almost all had, the consumptive cases included, were hidden under their beds. The doctor and the other medical personnel hardly ever examined the beds, and if they did discover anyone with a pipe, they pretended not to notice. None the less, the patients themselves were very cautious in this regard, and if they wanted to smoke their pipes they would do so over by the stove. Only at night did they smoke in bed – but at night no one made the rounds of the ward, except, occasionally, the commander of the hospital guard.

I had never before this time been in hospital as a patient; and so everything around me was completely new to me. I noticed that I attracted a certain amount of curiosity. The other men had already heard about me, and they looked me over without ceremony, even

with a shade of superiority, in the way schoolboys look over a new
pupil, or government officials a petitioner. Beside me on my right
lay an unsentenced prisoner, a clerk, the illegitimate son of a retired
captain. He was being tried for forgery and had already spent a year
in the hospital without apparently being ill in any way, although
he kept assuring the doctors that he had an aneurism. He had got
what he wanted: he escaped both penal labour and corporal punishment, and a year later was sent to T—k[30] to be remanded at the
hospital there. He was a thickset, stocky fellow, aged about twenty-
eight; he was an out-and-out villain with a detailed knowledge of
the law, was very shrewd, an extremely self-confident and over-
familiar individual. He was possessed of a morbid vanity, and had
very seriously convinced himself that he was the most honourable
and upright person in the whole world, and that he was indeed quite
innocent – the certainty of this had remained with him permanently. He was the first to talk to me; he began to question me with
curiosity and gave me a rather detailed account of the day-to-day
running of the hospital. Needless to say, he began by telling me he
was the son of a captain. He very much wanted to be seen as a
nobleman, or at least as 'well born'. His place was taken by a patient
from the corrective battalion who came up to me and began to
assure me that he knew many of the exiled noblemen, referring to
them by their first names and patronymics. He was a soldier whose
hair was already grey; one could read by his face that he was making
it all up. His name was Chekunov. It was obvious that he was trying
to ingratiate himself with me, probably suspecting that I had
money. Noticing my package of tea and sugar, he at once offered
me his services: he would obtain a teapot and brew some tea for
me. M—cki had promised to send me a teapot from the prison the
following day via one of the convicts who went to the hospital to
work. But Chekunov was as good as his word. He managed to get
hold of a cast-iron teapot and even a cup, he boiled the water and
generally put himself out for me with extraordinary alacrity, a
circumstance which immediately drew some malevolent jeers at his
expense from one of the patients. This was a consumptive by the
name of Ustyantsev, who had the bed opposite mine, an unsentenced soldier, the same one who in his fear of a flogging had

drunk a jugful of vodka mixed with a large quantity of snuff, and had thereby contracted tuberculosis; I have already made allusion to him. Until now he had lain in silence, having difficulty with his breathing, gazing at me steadily and earnestly and following Chekunov's movements with indignation. The extraordinarily bilious quality of his earnestness somehow lent his indignation a particularly comic tinge. At last he could restrain himself no longer:

'Ach, the groveller! He's found a master!' he said in a voice that halted and gasped with weakness. He was living out the very last days of his life.

Chekunov turned to him indignantly:

'Who's a groveller?' he blurted out, looking at Ustyantsev contemptuously.

'You are!' replied the other in such a confident tone of voice that it appeared he considered he had a perfect right to give Chekunov a good dressing-down and had even been appointed for that purpose.

'I'm a groveller, am I?'

'That's right. Do you hear him, good people, he doesn't believe it! He's surprised!'

'So what? Ach, he's as helpless as a man with no arms. He's not used to being without a servant, he doesn't know what to do. Why shouldn't I look after him, you shaggy snout of a joker?'

'Who's a shaggy snout?'

'You are.'

'I'm a shaggy snout, am I?'

'That's right!'

'And I suppose you're the handsome one? If I'm a shaggy snout, you've got a face like a crow's egg.'

'Shaggy snout is what you are! The man that God strikes down should at least have the decency to lie down and die. But no, you keep on getting up again. What do you keep on getting up again for?'

'What for? I'll kiss a boot, but not a shoe. My father never lowered himself, and he told me not to, either. I . . . I . . .'

He was about to continue, but was suddenly racked by a terrible fit of coughing which lasted for several minutes; he spat blood.

Soon a cold sweat of exhaustion stood out on his narrow forehead.
If it had not been for the coughing, he would still have been talking;
from his eyes it was evident how much he would have liked to have
gone on with the exchange of abuse; but in his weakness he merely
waved his arm . . . So that in the end Chekunov forgot all about him.

I had a feeling that the consumptive man's fury was directed
more at me than it was at Chekunov. Chekunov's desire to put
himself at my service and thereby earn himself a copeck or two
would not have been viewed by any of the men with anger or
especial scorn. Everyone understood that he was simply doing it for
money. The common people are not over-fussy on this account,
and have a fine nose for such matters. What Ustyantsev objected
to was me: he objected to my tea and the fact that even wearing
fetters I still appeared to be his social superior, unable to manage
without a servant, even though I had never asked for one and did
not want one. I really did always want to do everything for myself,
and I had a particular desire not to give the impression of being lily-
fingered or spoiled, or of playing the gentleman. In this my own
self-respect was partially at stake, if the truth be told. But it was
always happening – and I really have no idea why this should have
been so – that I found myself unable to refuse all sorts of assistants
and right-hand men who would batten onto me of their own accord
and end by taking me over completely, so that they were really my
masters, and I their servant; but on the surface I must admit that
it really did look as though I was the nobleman, that I was unable
to manage without a servant, and that I gave myself airs. Naturally,
I found this very annoying. But Ustyantsev was a consumptive, a
man of irritable temper. The other patients kept up an air of
indifference, with even a shade of superciliousness. I remember that
they were all preoccupied with one matter in particular: from their
conversation I discovered that a convict, who at that very moment
was being beaten with rods, was to be brought to our prison that
same evening. The convicts were waiting for the new arrival with
a certain amount of curiosity. They said, however, that the beating
the man was receiving was not a severe one – only five hundred
strokes altogether.

Gradually I began to look around me. As far as I could see, most of the really ill patients here were suffering from scurvy and eye infections – the local diseases in this part of the world. There were several such men in the ward. The other really ill ones were suffering either from fevers, sores of various kinds, or from tuberculosis. Unlike in other wards, here there was a grouping together of patients suffering from all kinds of diseases, even venereal ones. I say *really* ill ones, because there were some men who had come here without being ill at all, simply in order 'to have a rest'. The doctors willingly admitted them out of compassion, especially when there were a lot of empty beds. Conditions in the guardhouse and the prison seemed so bad compared with those in the hospital that many convicts came here only too gladly, in spite of the stuffiness and the locked ward. There were even some men who were special connoisseurs of lying in bed and of hospital life in general; most of these came from the corrective battalion, however. I examined my new companions with interest, but I remember that there was one man in particular, a convict from our prison, who aroused my curiosity. He was dying, was also consumptive, and was also living out the terminal stage of his illness; he occupied the bed next to Ustyantsev, and so was almost opposite me. His name was Mikhailov; two weeks earlier I had seen him in the prison. He had been ill for a long time and should have been receiving medical attention long before now; but he had quite unnecessarily kept a stiff upper lip, and had only gone into hospital at Christmas, to die three weeks later of the most terrible consumption. It was as if he had burned to a cinder. I was struck now by his terribly altered face – a face which was one of the first I had noticed upon entering the prison; then it had somehow galvanized my attention. In the bed next to him lay one of the soldiers from the corrective battalion, a disgustingly filthy and unkempt old man … But it is not possible for me to describe all the patients individually … I am reminded of this old man now for the sole reason that he made a certain impression on me then and in the space of a single moment managed to give me a full conception of certain features of the convict ward. I remember that at the time this old man had a terrible cold. He sneezed constantly, and continued to sneeze for a whole week, even in his sleep. His sneezes seemed to come in volleys, five or six

at a time, and after each one he would say: 'Lord, what a visitation!'
At that moment he was sitting on his bed, avidly stuffing his nose
with snuff from a paper package, so as to be able to sneeze with
even greater vehemence and efficiency. He sneezed into a cotton
handkerchief, one of his own, which had a checked pattern; it had
been washed countless times and was terribly faded. As he sneezed
he furrowed his small nose strangely into countless little wrinkles,
and the stumps of old, blackened teeth appeared with his red,
dribbling gums. Whenever he had finished a sneeze, he would open
the handkerchief out and closely examine the abundant gobbets of
snot in it, whereupon he would immediately smear it all over his
brown prison dressing gown, so that all the snot stayed on the
dressing gown and the handkerchief was left only slightly damp. He
continued to do this all week. The painstaking, miserly saving of
his own handkerchief at the expense of the prison dressing gown
drew not the slightest protest from the other patients, even though
one of them would have to wear the dressing gown after him. But
our common people are astonishingly lacking in squeamishness. As
for myself, at that moment I recoiled, and at once found myself
beginning to examine with revulsion and curiosity the dressing
gown I had only just put on. I then reflected that for a while now
it had been drawing my attention by its strong smell; by now it had
grown warm from the heat of my body, and it was smelling increasingly strongly of medicines, sticking plaster and, it seemed to me,
some kind of pus, which would not have been surprising, since it
had been worn on the backs of patients from time immemorial.
Perhaps the back part of its canvas lining had been washed
occasionally; but I could not be certain of this. Just now, at any
rate, this lining was saturated in all kinds of unpleasant secretions,
lotions, suppurations from broken blisters, and the like. What was
more, these wards frequently admitted convicts who had just been
beaten with rods until their backs were flayed raw; their wounds
were treated with medicated lotions, and so the dressing gown,
which was donned straight on top of the man's wet shirt, could not
possibly help getting wet too, and the whole mess stayed on it. And
during the whole of my time in the prison, all those several years,
every time I was in the hospital (and I was there often) I would put

on those dressing gowns with apprehension and mistrust. I particularly detested the large, remarkably fat lice that were sometimes found in them. The convicts used to take great satisfaction from killing them, so much that when one of these dead lice crunched under a convict's thick, clumsy fingernail, one could see by the expression on the executioner's face the degree of pleasure he obtained. The men also particularly loathed bedbugs, and sometimes, on long, tedious winter evenings the whole ward would be turned upside down in an effort to get rid of them. And although, apart from the unpleasant smell, everything in the ward was as clean as it could be on the surface, underneath, as one might put it, was a different story. The patients were used to this state of affairs, even believing it to be a necessary one. The hospital's arrangements and regulations were not particularly conducive to cleanliness either. But I will speak of these later ...

No sooner had Chekunov made some tea for me (with, I will observe in passing, the ward water which was carried in once every twenty-four hours and which was all too swiftly contaminated by the stinking air) than the door opened with a certain amount of noise, and the soldier who had just been beaten with rods was brought in escorted by a reinforced guard. This was the first time I had seen a man who had received a judicial beating. Later on such men were frequently led in, some were even carried (the ones who had not been able to withstand the beating), and these occasions were always a great source of diversion for the patients. The men usually greeted these victims of the law with an exaggeratedly stern expression on their faces, even a certain stiff earnestness. However, the kind of reception accorded was dependent to some extent on the gravity of the crime, and consequently also on the number of strokes that had been administered. A man who had been very severely beaten and also had the reputation of being a serious criminal received a proportionately greater degree of respect and attention than some recruit who had deserted, such as the man who had just been brought in. But whatever the case, no special condolences or especially irritable remarks were ever made. In silence the convicts would come to the unhappy man's assistance and look after him, especially if he could not manage without such aid. The

doctors' assistants were perfectly aware that they were delivering
the man who had been beaten into experienced and skilful hands.
The aid that was given usually involved the necessary process of
frequently changing a sheet or shirt soaked in cold water and
applying it to the man's lacerated back, especially if he himself was
unable to look after himself. Another form of aid was the deft
extraction of wooden splinters from the blisters. These splinters
were often left behind in a man's back by rods that had broken.
Such an operation was usually very painful for the patient. But in
general I was always surprised by the extraordinary capacity for
enduring pain that was shown by those who had been beaten. I saw
so many of them, sometimes beaten beyond endurance, and yet
hardly one of them ever uttered a groan. Only their faces seemed
to alter and grow pale; their eyes would burn; their gaze would be
distraught, restless, their lips would tremble so that the wretched
fellows would bite them compulsively until they almost drew blood.
The soldier who had come in was a young lad of about twenty-
three, of strong, muscular build, handsome-featured, tall, slender
and dark of skin. His back, however, had been fairly beaten about.
His body had been stripped bare to the waist; a wet sheet had been
thrown over his shoulders, and this was making him shiver in every
limb as if he had a fever. For something like an hour and a half he
walked up and down the ward. I looked into his face: he did not
seem to be thinking about anything at all at that moment; his eyes
were strange and wild, giving fleeting glances and apparently
unable to rest on anything with focused attention. I had the impression that he was staring at my tea. The tea was hot; steam was rising
from the cup, and the poor, wretched man was cold and shivering,
so that his teeth chattered. He turned towards me suddenly, without saying a word, took the cup, drank the tea standing up and
without sugar, and performed the whole action in a terrible hurry,
trying not to look at me in the process. When he had drunk the
tea he put down the cup without saying anything, and without even
giving a nod in my direction, began to scurry up and down the ward
again. But what use had he for words or nods? As for the convicts,
they all of them at first avoided any kind of conversation with the
flogged recruit; although they had aided him initially, for some

reason they all seemed to be trying not to pay any more attention to him, perhaps out of a desire to give him as much peace as possible and not to burden him with any further questions or 'commiserations', and with this state of affairs he seemed perfectly content.

Meanwhile it was getting dark, and the night-light was lit. Several of the convicts, but not many of them, had their own candle-holders. Finally, when the doctor had finished his evening rounds, the duty sergeant arrived to count all the patients, and the ward was then locked, the night pail having first been carried in ... I discovered to my surprise that this pail stayed in the ward all night, even though there was a proper toilet only a couple of paces down the corridor. But such was the way things had been arranged. During the day the convict patients were permitted to use the toilet in the corridor; at night they were not under any circumstances given permission to do so. The convict wards were not like the ordinary wards – the convict patients had to go on being punished even when they were ill. Who was responsible for this regulation I do not know; all I know is that it was no sort of regulation at all, and that the whole futile sterility of bureaucratic red tape was nowhere more strongly in evidence than in this case. Needless to say, the regulation was not the doctors' doing. I repeat: the convicts could not praise their doctors highly enough; they revered them as if they had been their own fathers. Each man got a kind look and a friendly word from them. This was especially appreciated by a convict, a man who had been rejected by all and who could for this reason see that such kindness and sincerity were genuine. It might not have been this way – no one would have questioned the doctors if they had treated the convicts differently, in a rougher, less humane fashion: consequently, their kindness stemmed from a genuine philanthropy. And of course they understood that a patient, whoever he was, convict or no convict, had the same need of fresh air, say, as any other patient, even one of the very highest rank. The patients in the other wards, the convalescents, for example, were allowed to wander freely about the corridors, take proper exercise, breathe an air that was less contaminated than that of the stuffy ward, which was always inevitably full of suffocating odours and exhalations. It is both terrible and stomach-turning for

me to comprehend how putrid our already stinking air must have
been at night, when this pail was brought in, given the overheated
atmosphere of the ward and the fact that many of the patients were
suffering from diarrhoea. In saying (as I have just done) that a
convict had to go on being punished even when he was ill, I did not
and do not suppose that a regulation such as that affecting the toilet
was enforced merely as an extra punishment. That would of course
be a senseless libel on the authorities. It is futile to punish a man
who is ill. And since that is the case, it naturally follows that some
stern, severe necessity had probably compelled the authorities to
take measures so damaging in their consequences. What could that
necessity be? What is so troubling is that there was nothing that
could in any way account for the necessity of these measures and
indeed many others which were so incomprehensible that one could
not even begin to find any explanation for them. How was this
senseless cruelty to be accounted for? On the pretext that a convict
might have entered the hospital, pretending to be ill, deceived the
doctors, gone out to the toilet at night and run away under the cover
of darkness? It is almost impossible to demonstrate the full
absurdity of such a notion. Where would the man run to? How
could he even run? What clothes would he have? During the day
the patients were allowed out one at a time; it would have been
perfectly possible for the same procedure to have been followed at
night. A sentry with a loaded rifle stood by the door. The toilet was
literally two paces away from the sentry, but in spite of this each
patient was escorted to the toilet by a sub-sentry who kept his eyes
on him continuously. The toilet had only a single double window
with an iron grille. Under the window, in the courtyard, beside the
windows of the convict wards, a sentry marched up and down all
night. In order to get out of the window, the man would have had
to break through both the double window and the iron grille. It
should be noted that the warders slept right next to the sentry, and
ten yards away, outside the other convict ward, stood another
sentry armed with a rifle, with beside him another sub-sentry and
more warders. And where would the man have run to in winter,
wearing nothing but his stockings and slippers, his hospital dressing
gown and his nightcap? And if this was so, if there was so little risk

of any breach of security (none at all, in actual fact), what was the purpose of making things so very difficult for these patients in what were possibly the last hours and days of their lives, these men for whom fresh air was even more necessary than it is for those who are well? What was it? I could never make head nor tail of this ...

In this connection I cannot help mentioning something else that I found bewildering, something that struck me during all those years as an utter enigma, to which I could not for the life of me find any answer. I feel I must at least say something about this before I continue with my account. I have in mind the fetters, from which no illness can free the sentenced convict. Even the consumptive patients died before my very eyes wearing their fetters. And yet all the men were used to their fetters, they all regarded them as an accomplished fact with which it was useless to argue. It is unlikely that anyone ever gave the matter an instant's thought, since during all those years it never even once occurred to the doctors to petition the authorities for the removal of the fetters from a convict who was seriously ill, especially in cases of tuberculosis. Admittedly the fetters in themselves are, God knows, not such a very great encumbrance. They generally weigh from eight to twelve pounds. A weight of ten pounds is not a great burden for a man in good health to carry around with him. I was told, however, that after a few years of wearing fetters a man's legs begin to wither. I am uncertain whether this is true or not, though there is probably something in it. Any burden, even one of only ten pounds, if it is permanently affixed to a man's leg, will inevitably increase the limb's weight abnormally and may over a protracted length of time produce a certain harmful effect. But even supposing this to be of little account to a man in good health, can we say the same of one who is ill? It may even be of small account to a man who is only moderately ill. But, I repeat, can the same be said of the seriously ill, of the consumptive patients whose arms and legs are already withering before the fetters get to work and for whom the slightest straw is an intolerable burden? And, in fact, even if the medical authorities were only to obtain clemency for the consumptive patients, this would in itself be a real and great blessing. It may be objected by someone that a convict is a villain and so unworthy of blessings; but can it be right to aggravate the punishment of those whom the wrath of God has smitten in this way? It is impossible to believe that this was done for the sake of punishment alone. Even the law exempts consumptives from corporal punishment. In that case, some mysterious and important precaution must be involved here, one taken in the interests of preventive security. However, I was never able to work out what it was. There could hardly have been any fear that the consumptive patients would have escaped. Which of them would have thought of such a thing, especially after a certain stage in the development of this sickness? To pretend that one has tuberculosis, to deceive the doctors in order to make one's escape – that is impossible. The disease is not like that; it is obvious at first glance. One point in passing: were these fetters put round the legs of these men for the sole purpose of preventing them from escaping or from trying to escape? Absolutely not. The fetters were simply a public dishonour, a disgrace, and a shameful physical and moral burden. This was at least the intention. They could never have prevented any man from running away. The most inept and clumsy convict knew how to saw through them or knock their rivets out with a stone. The leg fetters were really no prevention of anything; and if this was the case, if they were fitted to the sentenced convicts solely as a punishment, then once again I ask: was it right to punish men who were dying?

As I write this, I have a vivid recollection of one of these dying patients, a consumptive, the same Mikhailov who occupied the bed nearly opposite mine, not far from Ustyantsev's, and who died, I remember, on the fourth day I spent in the ward. It may be the thoughts and impressions that occurred to me at the time of his death which prompted me to speak of the consumptive patients just now. I did not know Mikhailov very well, however. He was still quite young, only twenty-five, no more, tall, thin and extremely good-looking. He was in the special category and was taciturn to the point of abnormality, with a perpetual quiet and peaceful sadness. It was as if he was 'withering away' in prison. This at least was how the convicts, among whom he was remembered with affection, expressed it. All I can remember is that he had wonderful eyes, and I do not really know why I recall him so vividly. He died at about three o'clock in the afternoon one clear, frosty day. I remember the strong, slanting rays of the sun as they shone through the green, slightly iced windowpanes of our ward. The unhappy man was bathed in a flood of these rays. He was unconscious when he died, and his departure from this life was long and agonizing, lasting some several hours. Since morning he had begun not to recognize those who approached him. The men wanted to bring him some relief, as they could see what agony he was in; he was breathing with difficulty, deeply and with a hoarse wheezing; his chest arched high in the air each time he inhaled, as though he could not get enough air into his lungs. He had thrown off his blanket and all his hospital clothes, and finally he began to tear off his shirt as well: even that seemed too great a weight for him to bear. The men came to his aid and helped him to take off his shirt. It was terrible to see that long, thin body with its arms and legs that had withered away to the bone, with its sagging belly, its arched chest, its ribs showing as clearly as the ribs of a skeleton. All that remained on his body was a wooden crucifix with an amulet, and his fetters, from which it appeared he could now have removed his withered legs at will. Half an hour before his death all the convict patients seemed to grow quiet, and began to conduct their conversations in a near whisper. Anyone who moved about did so almost inaudibly. The men talked little among themselves; if they did talk it was mostly about other matters, and only from time to time would they cast a glance at the dying man whose wheezing was getting louder and louder. At last he felt for the amulet on his chest with a wandering, shaky hand and began to pull it off, as if it too was a burden that was pressing on him and making him anxious. Someone removed the amulet as well. Ten minutes later he was dead. The men knocked on the door of the ward to let the sentry know. The warder came in, looked stupidly at the corpse and went off to get the doctor's assistant. The assistant soon appeared, a good-natured young fellow a little too concerned about his own appearance, which was actually quite attractive. He went up to the dead man with rapid steps that resounded loudly in the hushed ward, and with a particularly off-hand manner which he seemed to have studied especially for just such an eventuality as this, took the dead wrist, felt for the pulse, and with a wave of his arm marched out again. Messengers were sent at once to inform the guard: the dead man was a serious criminal from the special category and could be certified as dead only after certain specially ordained ceremonies had been gone through. As they waited for the sentries to arrive, one of the convicts suggested in a quiet voice that it might be a good idea to close the dead man's eyes. When he saw the crucifix lying on the pillow he picked it up, examined it and put it back around Mikhailov's neck, also without saying a word; when he had done this he made the sign of the cross over himself. Meanwhile the dead man's face was showing signs of rigor; a ray of sunlight was playing on it; the mouth was half open, and two rows of white, young teeth gleamed through the delicate lips which had congealed fast to the gums. At last the duty sergeant came in; he was wearing his helmet and carrying a sabre, and he was followed by two warders. He approached the corpse, walking more and more slowly, and looking bewilderedly at the hushed convicts who were staring grimly at him from all sides. When he was about a yard away he stopped dead as though suddenly abashed. The sight of the completely naked, withered corpse, wearing nothing but its fetters, made a deep impression on him, and he suddenly unfastened his sword-belt, took off his helmet – something no regulation required him to do – and made the sign of the cross broadly over himself. This man was a hardbitten, grey-headed soldier who had put in many years of service. I remember that at that same moment Chekunov, another grey-haired man, was also standing close by. He was looking steadfastly, without saying a word, into the duty sergeant's face, observing his every movement with a strange attentiveness. But their eyes met, and for some reason Chekunov's lower lip suddenly started to tremble. He contorted it strangely, baring his teeth and, as if inadvertently drawing the duty sergeant's attention to the corpse, said quickly:

'He had a mother too!' and walked away.

I remember that these words seemed to pierce me through ... And why had he said them, what had put them into his head? But now they were beginning to lift the corpse on the bed; the straw rustled, the fetters fell jangling on the floor amidst the general silence, still attached to the dead man. Someone picked them up. The body was carried away. Suddenly everyone started to talk in loud voices. The duty sergeant, who by now was out in the corridor, could be heard sending someone off to get the smith. The corpse would have to have its fetters removed ...

But I digress.

* 2 *

THE HOSPITAL (2)

Every morning the doctors made a round of the ward; at about eleven o'clock they would all appear in our midst together, accompanying the senior hospital doctor. They were preceded about an hour and half earlier by the convicts' intern, who also visited our ward every day. At this time our intern was a young doctor who knew his job, a kind, friendly man of whom the convicts were very fond. They could only find one thing wrong with him: 'He's too soft.' And indeed he was rather at a loss for words, and seemed somehow uncomfortable in our presence, almost on the point of blushing; he would alter a patient's diet practically on the first request, and even appeared to be willing to prescribe whatever medicines the men asked for. However, he was a fine young fellow. It must be admitted that many doctors in Russia have the love and respect of the common people; as far as I have been able to observe, this is true without exception. I realize that my words will seem paradoxical, particularly considering the common people's universal distrust of medicine and of drugs imported from abroad. A man of the people, even if he is suffering from the most serious illness, will continue for years on end to visit the local quack or treat himself with his own domestic remedies (which are by no means to be despised), rather than go to the doctor or enter hospital. But one other very important consideration is involved here, too, one that has nothing at all to do with medicine, namely the common people's universal distrust of anything that bears the stamp of government authority and officialdom. Then again, the people suffer from fears

and prejudices about hospitals, fed by various scares and rumours
that are often absurd, but sometimes have a basis in reality. What
frighten them most, however are the German-type systematization
of the hospital, the strangers who surround them all the time they
are ill, the strictness of the diet, the stories about the ruthless
severity of the medical assistants and the doctors, about the dissec-
tion and disembowelling of corpses, and so forth. What is more, the
way the common people see it is that they are to be given treatment
by their masters, for the doctors belong to a higher social class than
they. However, when they get to know the doctors better (though
there are exceptions, this is mostly true) all these terrors disappear,
a fact which to my mind redounds to the honour of our medical
men, most of whom are quite young. The majority of them know
how to win the respect and even the love of the common people.
At any rate, I am writing about what I have seen and experienced
for myself on many occasions and in many places, and I have no
reason to believe that the situation is very much different elsewhere.
Admittedly, there are a few doctors in some out-of-the-way places
who take bribes, exploit their hospitals to their most immediate
personal advantage, neglect their patients almost entirely and even
forget all the medicine they have ever learnt. This still goes on; but
I am talking about the majority, or rather about the spirit, the new
trend that is to be observed in the medical world of our time. Those
others, those renegades to the cause, those wolves among the sheep,
whatever they may bring in their own defence, such as, for example,
the *milieu* in which they work and which has devoured them too,
will forever be in the wrong, particularly if they have lost their sense
of philanthropy. A philanthropic approach, kindness, a fraternal
compassion are sometimes more necessary to a patient than any
medicaments. It is time we stopped complaining apathetically
about our *milieu*, claiming that it has devoured us. It is admittedly
true that it does indeed devour a great many things in us, but not
everything; a cunning and practised villain will often find that by
appealing to the influence of his *milieu* he can cover up and justify
not only his weakness, but also in many cases his own villainy,
especially if he is an eloquent talker or writer. However, I have once
more wandered off my subject; all I wish to say is that the mistrust

and hostility of the common people are directed at the medical administration, and not at their doctors. When they find out what their doctors are really like, they quickly lose many of their prejudices. The rest of our hospital arrangements are to this day out of touch with the Russian character in many respects; the systematization is still alien to the habits of our ordinary folk, and cannot win their full confidence and respect. So at least it seems to me on the basis of some of my own impressions.

Our intern usually stopped in front of each patient, examined him and questioned him with seriousness and the utmost attention, and prescribed the appropriate medicines and diet. Sometimes he would notice that there was nothing at all the matter with a patient; but since the convict had come here in order to get a rest from the prison work or to lie for a bit on a mattress instead of on bare boards, or quite simply just in order to be in a warm room instead of the damp guardhouse crowded with tightly jammed masses of pale, emaciated prisoners awaiting trial (all over Russia, unsentenced prisoners are nearly always pale and emaciated, a sign that both the conditions of their detention and their mental state are in all probability worse than those of convicts who have been sentenced), our intern would quietly put him down as a case of *febris catarrhalis*, say, and would sometimes allow him to stay in hospital for as long as a week. We all used to laugh about this *febris catarrhalis*. We knew very well that by a mutual, unspoken agreement between doctor and patient this was the accepted formula used to designate a fictitious illness – 'reserve collywobbles', as the convicts translated *febris catarrhalis*. Sometimes a patient would take advantage of the doctor's kindness and prolong his stay in hospital until he had to be thrown out by force. Then it was worth seeing how our intern would noticeably appear to grow shy, as if afraid to tell the patient to his face that he had practically recovered and should ask to be discharged as soon as possible, even though he had every right to have the man discharged right there and then, without any further coaxing or argument, writing down on his 'complaint sheet' the words *sanat est*. He would start by dropping the odd hint, and would then almost beg the man: 'Don't you think it's time, hm? After all, you are almost well now, and the ward's so crowded,' and so on and so forth, until the patient started to feel guilty and finally asked to be discharged of his own accord. The senior hospital doctor, although he was a decent, philan- thropic individual (the patients were very fond of him, too), was infinitely more snappish and decisive than the intern, and even displayed on occasion a kind of grim severity for which the men particularly respected him. He always appeared in the company of the other hospital doctors after the intern had gone; he too exam- ined the men individually, giving special attention to those who were seriously ill. He always had a kind, encouraging, even heartfelt word for them and in general made a good impression on all the patients. Never would he refuse to admit, never did he send back men who came to the hospital with 'reserve collywobbles'; but if a patient obstinately malingered, he would discharge him there and then: 'All right, my lad, you've been here long enough, you've had your rest, now off you go and don't take advantage of our hospi- tality.' The really stubborn malingerers were usually either men who were too lazy to work, especially in summer when the work was long and hard, or else they were prisoners awaiting trial and an eventual beating or flogging. I recall especial severity, cruelty even, being used on one of these men in order to make him dis- charge himself. He had arrived at the hospital with an eye infection: his eyes were red, and he was complaining of a violent, stabbing pain in them. Treatments were begun, including blisters, leeches, the spraying of the eyes with a corrosive fluid, and so on, but the infection persisted and the man's eyes did not clear. The doctors gradually surmised that the infection was not genuine: the inflam- mation was continuously slight, grew no worse nor better, ap- peared to be static – a dubious state of affairs. All the convicts had known for ages that the man was shamming, although he himself would not admit it. He was a young lad, and quite handsome, but he made an unpleasant impression on us all: he was reserved, suspicious, wore a constant frown; he never spoke to anyone, his face had a sullen look, and he hid from everyone as though he suspected us all of something. I remember that some of us even thought he might do something drastic. He had been a soldier, had become mixed up in large-scale robbery, had been brought to court and sentenced to a thousand strokes of the sticks, and the convict battalions. As I have already mentioned, the convicts sometimes devise extraordinary methods of putting off the moment of pun'sh-ment: on the eve of his flogging a man might thrust a knife into one of the prison officials or even into one of his own mates, be sent for retrial, have his punishment deferred for a couple of months, and thus realize his aim. It did not seem to matter to such men that in another two months' time they would receive a punishment of twofold, even threefold severity; all they cared about was to delay the dreaded moment, even if only by a few days, no matter what it cost them – so low did their spirits sometimes sink. Some of the convicts had already begun to whisper among themselves that this man ought to be watched: he might slit someone's throat in the night. However, this was merely what people said, and not even the men whose beds were next to his bothered to take any special precautions. But it was noticed that he rubbed his eyes with lime from the plaster on the wall and also with some other substance, so as to make them appear red in the morning. Finally the senior hospital doctor threatened to apply a seton. In cases of persistent eye infections lasting over a long period of time, when all other medical expedients have been tried, in order to save a man's sight the doctors resort to a drastic and extremely painful operation: they apply a seton, following the manner in which this is done to horses. But even then the poor man would not agree to get better. Whether it was that he was too stubborn, or just too scared, I do not know; but the fact is that the application of a seton, though not as bad as a beating, is still an extremely painful process. As much of the skin as can be gathered in one hand is bunched up at the back of the patient's neck and is skewered with a knife, producing a long, broad wound in the nape. A broad cloth tape of almost a finger's width is passed through this wound; then every day at a given time this tape would be given a tug, thereby opening the wound again, so that it festered continually and did not get a chance to heal. The poor man endured this ordeal for several days, suffering dreadfully, and finally agreed to discharge himself. In a single day his eyes were restored to health, and as soon as his neck had healed up he went off to the guardhouse in order the following day to receive his one thousand blows with the sticks.

Of course, the moment before a beating or flogging is a cruel one, so cruel that I am perhaps wrong to call this fear faintheartedness and cowardice. It must be cruel if men are prepared to take twice or three times the amount of their punishment if only it is not administered immediately. I have also made mention, though, of those men who themselves asked to be discharged as soon as possible, even though their backs had not yet healed from the first part of their punishment, in order to receive the rest of their strokes and thus be released from pre-sentence detention. This detention in the guardhouse pending sentence was for all the prisoners much worse than prison itself, of course. But, quite apart from any difference in temperaments, some men find that they are capable of much fearless determination because beatings . nd punishments have become an ingrained habit with them. A man who has been beaten many times seems to grow hardened both in spirit and in back, and comes in the end to view such beatings sceptically, almost as a minor inconvenience, losing his fear of them. As a general rule, this is true. A convict of ours in the special category, a Kalmyk who had been christened with the name Aleksandr, or Aleksandra, as the men called him, a strange fellow, villainous, fearless and at the same time very good-natured, told me how he had got through his first four thousand strokes; as he did so, he laughed and told jokes, but he swore very earnestly that if he had not been used to being whipped from childhood, his very earliest, most tender childhood, so that his back had not once been free of scars during all the time he had spent with his horde, he would never have been able to endure those four thousand strokes. From the way he told me his story it appeared that he considered this education under the lash a great blessing. 'I was beaten for everything, Aleksandr Petrovich,' he told me as he sat on my bed one evening before the candles were lit, 'for everything you can imagine, everything under the sun, I was beaten for fifteen years on end from as far back as I can remember, several times each day; I was beaten by anyone who felt like beating me; so that in the end I got quite used to it.' How he had got into the army I do not know. I don't remember: he may have told me, however; he was an inveterate runaway and vagrant. I can only remember his story about the fear and horror he had felt when he had been sentenced to four thousand strokes for murdering an officer. 'I knew that my punishment would be severe and that I might not survive my beating, and even though I was used to the lash, four thousand strokes seemed like some kind of a joke. What was worse, the whole of the officer corps was out to get me. I knew, I knew for a fact that I was not going to make it, that they wouldn't let me out from under their sticks alive. The first thing I thought of was trying to get myself christened. I thought, maybe they'll pardon me, and although my own people told me at the time that nothing would come of it, that I wouldn't receive a pardon, I still thought that I'd try none the less, that they'd feel sorrier for a fellow who'd been christened. Well, I was christened and during the ceremony I was given the name Aleksandr. But that didn't do anything to alter the number of strokes I got. They might at least have reduced it by one, I thought; I even got quite offended. I thought to myself: just you wait, I'll make real jackasses of you all; and what do you suppose, Aleksandr Petrovich? I did! I was really good at playing dead, not completely dead, you know, but sort of like my last hour had come. They took me out and gave me a thousand: that feels hot, I shouted; they gave me another thousand: well, I thought, it's all up with me, they'd beaten me out of my senses, my legs were cracking up, I went crashing to the ground: my eyes looked like a corpse's, my face was blue, I'd stopped breathing, I was foaming at the mouth. Up came the doctor: "He's going to die any minute," he said. They hauled me off to the hospital, and I perked up straight away. They took me out two more times after that, and they were that mad at me, really mad, and two more times I fooled them; I only felt one of the third thousand before I passed out, and when it came to the fourth, each stroke cut me like it was a knife going through my heart, each stroke felt like three, they were laying into me that hard. They'd really gone over the top with me. That mean old last thousand (God rot it) was equal to all the other three put together, and if I hadn't played dead just before the end (there was only two hundred strokes left to go) they'd have beaten me to death right there and then. Well,

I wasn't going to stand for that: I fooled them again, and passed out; again they were taken in, and how could they not have been? The doctor himself was. So the last two hundred they gave me, they laid into me really viciously, they made it feel worse than the first two thousand put together, but no, they didn't kill me, and why didn't they kill me? Only because I'd grown up with the lash since I'd been a child. That's why I'm alive today. Oh, they beat me all right, they gave me some beatings in my time!' he added, as he concluded his story in a sort of sad, meditative tone of voice, as if he were trying to remember and count the number of times he had been beaten. 'But no,' he added, after a moment's silence, 'I can't even count the number of times I was beaten; and what would be the point? No counting's ever going to be enough to do justice to the likes of that.' He looked at me quickly and laughed, but so good-naturedly that I could not help smiling back at him. 'You know, Aleksandr Petrovich, whenever I dream at night, I dream they're laying into me: I never dream about anything else.' And indeed he often used to cry out in his sleep at night, yelling at the top of his voice so that the others would waken him with prods and shoves: 'Here, mate, what are you yelling about?' He was a short, sturdy fellow of about forty-five, restless and good-humoured, and he got along very well with everyone; he was very addicted to thieving and often got beaten by the men because of it, but then which of us did not do a bit of thieving, and which of us was not beaten because of it?

I will add one more thing: I was always surprised at the extra-ordinary good humour, the lack of vindictiveness with which all these men used to describe how they had been beaten, and by whom. There was very rarely even the slightest hint of spite or hatred to be detected in such accounts, which always used to seize my heart at once, making it beat louder and faster. They, on the other hand, laughed and talked like children. There was M—cki, for example, who told me about his punishment; he was not a nobleman, and had been given five hundred strokes. I learned about this from the other men, and asked him if it were true. He answered somewhat tersely, as though suffering some inner pain, trying not to look at me, and his face reddened; after a short while he did look at me, his eyes glittering with hatred and his lips quivering with indignation. I felt that he would never be able to forget that episode of his past. But the convicts, almost all of them (I will not swear that there were no exceptions), looked upon this matter from quite a different point of view. I would sometimes reflect that they could not possibly feel guilty and deserving of punishment, especially when it was not against their own kind that they had transgressed, but against authority. The majority of them did not feel that they had done any wrong whatsoever. I have already said that I did not observe any pangs of conscience in them, even in those cases where the crime was against one of their own kind. Crimes against representatives of authority were simply beneath their notice. It sometimes used to seem to me that in these latter cases the men had their own special, as it were practical or factual view of the matter. Account was taken of fate, of the irrefutability of accomplished fact, and this was done not in any calculated fashion, but unconsciously, as out of a kind of faith. Although a convict is always inclined to consider himself in the right with regard to crimes against figures of authority, so that no question ever arises in his mind, he is none the less perfectly aware that the authorities look upon his crime from quite a different standpoint, and that therefore he must be punished, so that they may be quits. Here there is a two-sided struggle. Besides, the criminal knows for a certainty that he will be acquitted by the judgement of his own people, who will never finally condemn him and who will for the most part fully acquit him, as long as his crime is not against one of his own kind, his brothers, his common kith and kin. His conscience is untroubled; and this freedom from moral embarrassment gives him strength, and that is the main thing. He feels that he has something to lean on, and so he feels no hatred, but accepts what has happened to him as an unavoidable circumstance, one which was not initiated with him and will not terminate with him but which will continue to exist for a long, long time yet as a part of a long-established, passive but insistent conflict. What soldier feels any personal hatred for the Turk he is fighting against? Yet the Turk slashes, stabs and shoots at him. However, not all the men's stories were entirely cold-blooded and indifferent. Of Lieutenant Zherebyatnikov, for example, they would talk with a certain shade of indignation, though not a very pronounced one. I became acquainted with this Lieutenant Zherebyatnikov in the first days of my stay in hospital, not directly, but through the convicts' stories about him. Later on I did occasionally see him in the flesh when he was on guard duty at the prison. He was a tall, fat, oily man of about thirty, with red, pudgy cheeks, white teeth and a booming laugh like that of Gogol's Nozdryov.[31] From his face it was obvious that he was an extremely unreflective individual. He was very fond of administering floggings and beatings whenever it was his turn to do so. I hasten to add that even then I looked on Lieutenant Zherebyatnikov as a monster among my own kind, and that was how the convicts themselves regarded him. There were other officials besides him, in former days of course, those days of which 'the legend's fresh, but scarce to be believed',[32] who were also fond of performing their duty with zeal and eagerness. But most of the officials did this work in a straightforward fashion, and without any special liking for it. The lieutenant, on the other hand, was a sort of ultra-refined gourmet in this sphere. He loved, he passionately loved the art of administering corporal punishment, and he loved it for its own sake. He took real pleasure in it, and like some patrician from the time of the Roman Empire, worn out in delights and amusements, he devised various refinements, various unnatural practices, in order to arouse and agreeably titillate his greasy sensibilities. A convict might be taken out for punishment with Zherebyatnikov as the officer in command. One glance at the long lines of men drawn up with thick sticks would be enough to fill the lieutenant with inspiration. He would stride complacently around the ranks, earnestly impressing on each man that he must carry out his duty zealously and conscientiously, or else ... But the soldiers knew what that 'or else' meant. Then the offender would be brought out, and if he was not already familiar with Zherebyatnikov, if he had not heard of all his ins and outs, the lieutenant would play on him the trick described in what follows. (Needless to say, this was only one trick out of a hundred; the fertility of the lieutenant's imagination was inexhaustible.) Every convict, at the moment when he is stripped and his hands are tied to the rifle-butts by which the NCOs drag him the whole length of the 'green street' – every convict, following a universal custom, always begins at this point to beseech the commanding officer in a tearful, plaintive voice to soften the punishment and not let the beating be of excessive severity: 'Your honour,' cries the unfortunate man, 'have mercy, be a good father, make me pray for you all the rest of my days, don't do me in, spare me!' This would be precisely the cue that Zherebyatnikov had been waiting for. He would stop the proceedings at once and begin to engage the man in a rather sentimental kind of conversation:

'My friend,' he would say, 'but what am I do do with you? It isn't I who's punishing you, it's the law.'

'Your honour, it's all in your hands, spare me!'

'And do you think I don't feel sorry for you? Do you think I'm going to enjoy watching them beat you? I'm a man too, you know! Or maybe you think I'm not human?'

'We know, your honour, we know: you're our father and we're your children. Be a good father to us!' the convict would cry, already beginning to hope.

'But my friend, judge for yourself; you're a bright fellow after all, you can judge: I know that all the rules of humanity command me to look upon even a sinner like yourself with lenience and mercy.'

'Your honour, that's God's truth you're speaking.'

'Yes, to look upon you with mercy, no matter how sinful you may be. But it isn't up to me, it's up to the law. Think about it! After all, I'm at the service of God and my country; I take a grievous burden of sin upon myself if I weaken the law, just think about that!'

'Your honour!'

'Well, what of it! All right, just this once, seeing it's you. I know I'm acting wrongly, but that's the way it must be ... I'll let you off lightly this time. But what if that's just another way of doing you harm? What if I let you off lightly this time and you go away thinking that it'll be like that next time as well, and commit some crime, what then? It'll be my fault ...'

'Your honour! I swear before my friends and my enemies! Before the throne of the Heavenly Creator ...'

'Well, all right, all right! But will you swear to me that you'll behave yourself in future?'

'May the Lord strike me dead, so in the next world I ...'

'Don't swear, man, it's a sin. I'll accept your word for it, will you give me your word?'

'Your honour!!!'

'Now listen, I'm only letting you off because you're crying like an orphan. Are you an orphan?'

'Oh yes, your honour, I'm all alone, no mother, no father ...'

'Right, then, it's because you're crying like an orphan; but remember, this is the last time ... Take him!' he would add in such a lenient tone of voice that the convict would be able to find no prayers worthy of such forgiveness. But at that point the terrible procession would start to move, and the man would be taken out; the drum would start to thunder, and the sticks would start to flail ... 'Mangle him!' Zherebyatnikov would bellow at the top of his voice – 'Burn him! Thrash him, flog him! Set him alight! More, more! Hit the orphan harder, hit the villain harder! Hammer him, hammer him!' And the soldiers would lay into the man as hard as they could, the poor wretch would see sparks, he would begin to yell, and Zherebyatnikov would run along the line after him, laughing and laughing, bursting, holding his sides with laughter, unable to straighten up, so that at last one even felt sorry for him, the kind-hearted fellow! He would be overjoyed, delighted, and only occasionally might one hear his hearty, booming laughter, and the words: 'Thrash him, flog him! Set him alight, the villain, set the orphan alight! ...'

Or he might think up another variation. The man would be taken out to be beaten. The convict would again start his beseeching. This time Zherebyatnikov would not put on airs or tease the man, but start out in all frankness:

'Look here, my good fellow,' he would say, 'I'm going to have you properly punished, you've deserved it. But I'll tell you what: I'm not going to tie you to the rifle-butts. You're going to take your punishment alone, in this new way I've thought up. You must run as fast as you can down the whole line! That way, even if every stroke lands on you, it'll still be over with sooner. What do you think? Want to try it?'

The convict would listen in bewilderment and distrust, thinking it over. 'Who knows,' he would reflect, 'maybe it really would be better that way; if I run as fast as I can, the pain'll be five times less, and maybe not every stroke will land on me.'

'All right, your honour, I agree.'

'Well, I agree too, so off you go! Look sharp now, no nodding off!' he would shout to the soldiers, knowing in advance, however, that not one stick would fail to land on the man's back; any soldier who missed knew very well what he could expect. The convict would start to run along the 'green street' for all he was worth, but needless to say he would not get any further than the fifteenth man in the line; the sticks would suddenly pelt down on his back like a tattoo of drums, like a flash of lightning, and the poor wretch would fall to the ground with a shriek, like one felled by a bullet. 'No, your honour, it's better the old way,' he would say, slowly raising himself, pale and frightened, and Zherebyatnikov, who had known in advance the effect his trick would have, would roar with laughter until his sides split. But it is not possible for me to describe all the amusements he devised for himself, or to relate all the tales the convicts told about him.

The men used to tell tales of a slightly different kind, different in mood, about a certain Lieutenant Smekalov who had been acting prison governor before our Major was appointed to that post. They used to talk about Zherebyatnikov more or less indifferently, without any special animosity, but none the less his exploits were not admired by them, they had no praise for him, and he was clearly the object of much loathing. Their contempt for him even had a slightly condescending edge to it. Lieutenant Smekalov, on the other hand, they remembered with delight and satisfaction. The fact was that he was not a great devotee of flogging; he had none of Zherebyatnikov's pure love of the art. On the other hand, he was not against corporal punishment; but his floggings were remembered almost lovingly – so well was he able to please the convicts. What was his secret? What did he do to deserve such popularity? It is true that convicts, like all the Russian people, perhaps, are prepared to forget the most prolonged tortures for the sake of a single word of kindness; I say this as a fact, without attempting to

weigh its significance from one side or the other. It was not difficult
to please these men and gain popularity for oneself. But Lieutenant
Smekalov had gained an *especial* popularity – such that even the
beatings he administered were remembered almost with tender
emotion. 'We didn't need a father,' the convicts would say, and they
would utter sighs as they compared their memories of their previous
governor with the Major they now had in charge of them. 'That
man had a heart of gold!' Smekalov was a simple man, and was
indeed possibly kind-hearted in his own way. It is occasionally the
case that an official is not only kind-hearted but even magnani-
mous; yet what happens then? None of the men likes him, and
indeed he may even become the object of their derision. The fact
of the matter was that Smekalov somehow had the knack of making
all the convicts accept him as *one of their own kind*. This is a great
skill, or rather it is an inborn talent, the possessors of which never
give it a second's thought. It is a strange thing: some of these men
are completely lacking in good nature, yet they sometimes attain
great popularity. They are not overly discriminating, not easily
repelled by the convicts beneath their command; and this, it seems
to me, is the principal reason for their success. There is no aura of
the lily-fingered lordling about them, no trace of an overweening
manner; instead, they exude a certain special atmosphere of the
common man, something they are born with – and, goodness, how
sensitive the common people are to this atmosphere! What will they
not give for it? They are prepared to exchange the most lenient
commander for one who is much stricter, just as long as this new
man partakes of their own homespun ambience. And if this con-
genial fellow is also genuinely good-natured into the bargain, albeit
in a rather eccentric fashion? He is beyond price! As I have already
said, Lieutenant Smekalov, too, sometimes administered a cruel
flogging – but he somehow possessed the knack of doing it so that
not only did the convicts not resent the 'tricks' he played during the
punishment, they remembered them long afterwards with amusement and satisfaction. Smekalov only had a few such 'tricks',
however – he was lacking in creative imagination. In actual fact he
really knew only one single trick, which he had made last almost
a whole year; but its charm was possibly derived from its being his

only one. It was really very straightforward. The guilty convict
would be led out. Smekalov would come out to the punishment area
smiling an ironical smile and making a few jokes. He would start
to question the guilty man right there and then about certain
extraneous matters, about his personal life as a convict in the
prison, not at all with any ulterior motive in view, or out of any
desire to tease, but simply because he *genuinely wanted to know
about these matters*. The birches would be brought, and a chair for
Smekalov; he would sit down on the chair, and might even light his
pipe. He had one of those long pipes. The convict would start to
entreat him . . . 'No, my friend, lie down, that's no good . . .' Smekalov would say. The convict would give a sigh and lie down. 'Right
then, my good fellow, do you know a certain prayer?' 'Of course,
your honour, I was christened, you know, I've known it ever since
I was a child.' 'Right, then get on and recite it.' The convict would
know what to recite, and he would also know what would happen
when he recited it, as this trick had been played thirty times previously on other convicts. Even Smekalov was aware that the convict
knew this; he was aware that even the soldiers standing with their
birches raised over their prostrate victim had witnessed this trick
far too often, yet he went on repeating it. Maybe it was such a
perennial source of enjoyment to him because he had made it up
himself, out of literary vanity. The convict would begin to recite,
the soldiers would wait with their birches, and Smekalov would
bend practically double on his chair, raise his hand and stop
smoking his pipe as he waited for a certain word. After the first line
of the well-known prayer the convict would come to the words 'in
heaven'. That was the signal. 'Stop!' the lieutenant would shout,
suddenly inflamed, and he would turn to the first soldier, whose
birch was raised and ready, and bawl, with the gesture of one
inspired: 'Sock him for seven!'

And he would roar with laughter, fit to burst. The soldiers
standing around him would also grin: the man who was doing the
flogging would grin, even the victim himself would almost grin,
even though at the word 'seven' the birch would already be
whistling through the air, one split second later to cut like a razor
into his guilty body. And Smekalov would be pleased, because he it

was who had devised this so cleverly, had himself had the idea of coupling 'in heaven' with 'sock him for seven' and had even invented a rhyme, what was more. And Smekalov would leave perfectly pleased with himself, and the man who had been flogged would also leave almost pleased with himself and with Smekalov, and half an hour later you would see him telling the men in the prison how the trick that had been played thirty times previously had now been played for the thirty-first time. 'The man has a soul! What a sense of humour!'

At times there was even a touch of Manilov-like sentimentality[33] about some of the men's recollections of the kind lieutenant.

'You'd be walking along, lads,' a convict might say, his face beaming with the memory, 'you'd be walking along and he'd be sitting there at his window in his dressing gown, drinking his tea, smoking his pipe. You'd take off your hat. "Where are you off to, Aksenov?" he'd ask. "To work, Mikhail Vasilich, I've got to go to the workshop right away, first thing." He'd laugh to himself about that ... The man had a soul! A real soul!'

'And we'll never see another like him!' one of the men who were listening would say.

* 3 *

THE HOSPITAL (3)*

The reason I have spoken here about punishments and about the various people who had the task of performing these interesting duties is that it was only when I went into hospital that I received my first real glimpse of all these matters. Until then I had known about all this only from hearsay. Our two wards held all the convicts who had been punished by line beating with rods; the men came from all the battalions, the convict divisions and the other military commands that were stationed in our town and its

* Everything I write here concerning punishments and tortures relates to the time I spent in prison. I have since heard that all this has changed and is continuing to change. (*Note by F. M. Dostoyevsky.*)

environs. In that early period, when I was still fascinated by everything that took place around me, all these customs that were so
strange to me, all these victims of floggings and men who were
getting ready to be flogged naturally made a very deep and vivid
impression on me. I was agitated, confused and frightened. I
remember that at the same time I began with sudden impatience to
try to make sense of every detail of these new phenomena, listening
to the men's conversations and stories concerning this subject,
asking them questions and trying to obtain answers. Among other
things, I wanted to find out all there was to know about all the
degrees of sentencing and punishment, all the gradations of punishment, and how the convicts themselves viewed them; I attempted
to re-create in my imagination the psychological condition of men
who were going out to be flogged. I have already said that there are
few men who can face their punishment with equanimity, and this
even includes those who have already received many beatings and
floggings in the past. At this point a keen, but purely physical terror
usually descends on the condemned man. It is a terror that is
involuntary and inexorable, and it overwhelms a man's entire
moral being. Even later on, indeed during all those few years of my
life in the prison, I would find myself casting an involuntary glance
at those men who, having come to hospital after the first part of
their punishment and having stayed there long enough for their
backs to heal, had discharged themselves only in order to go out
and receive the other half of the strokes to which they had been
sentenced. This division of the punishment into two parts always
occurred on the ordering of the doctor who is present when the man
is flogged. If the crime entailed a large number of strokes, so many
that the victim could not take them all at once, the flogging was
divided into two or even three parts, depending on the doctor's
opinion, once the flogging had got under way, as to whether the
man would be able to go on walking up and down the line, or
whether this would put his life at risk. Sentences of five hundred,
a thousand or even fifteen hundred strokes were normally taken in
one go; but if the sentence called for two or three thousand, its
execution would be divided into two or even three parts. Those men
who, once their backs had healed after the first part of their

sentence, left hospital in order to receive its second part, were
usually morose, sullen and unsociable on the day of their discharge.
They would display a kind of stupefaction, a weird absent-
mindedness. Such men would not enter into conversation and
normally never uttered a word; what was most interesting of all was
that not even the convicts themselves would ever speak or try to
speak to such a man about what was in store for him. Not a word
was wasted; there was no attempt to console; as a general rule, the
convicts even tried to pay as little attention as possible to such a
man. This was of course better for him. There were exceptions, like
Orlov, for example, of whom I have already spoken. After he had
taken the first part of his punishment, the only thing that troubled
him was that his back was taking such a long time to heal and
that he would not obtain a speedy discharge so as to be able to
go out and receive the rest of his strokes, be dispatched with a
convict gang to the place of exile that had been allotted to him, and
make his escape en route. But this ambition was a source of diversion for him, and God knows what else was on his mind. He was
a fiery, volatile individual. He was very self-satisfied and was
constantly in an excited state of mind, but he repressed his feelings.
The fact was that before the first part of his punishment he had
thought he was not going to survive the beating and that it was
intended he should die. Various rumours about how the authorities
proposed to treat him had reached him while he had been detained
awaiting sentence; it was at that time that he had begun to prepare
himself for death. But when he survived the first part of the beating,
his spirits revived. He had been brought to the hospital half beaten
to death; I have still to this day never seen wounds such as those
he had then; but he arrived among us with joy in his heart, in the
hope that he would survive, that the rumours had been untrue; here
he was, after all, after his long period of confinement as he had
awaited trial and sentence, he was already beginning to dream of
the road, of escape, of freedom, the fields and woods ... Two days
after his discharge from hospital he died in the same hospital, in the
same bed, having failed to survive the second half of his sentence.
But I have made allusion to this already.

The very same men who had passed such troubled days and

nights before their punishment bore its execution with fortitude, and this was true even of the least brave. I seldom heard any groans, not even during the first night after their arrival, not even from the most severely beaten; as a general rule the common people have a great ability to endure pain. I asked the men a lot of questions about the pain. Sometimes I had a desire to find out just how great this pain was, and to learn with what it might be compared. I really don't know why this was. All I remember is that it was not out of any idle curiosity. I repeat that I was agitated and shaken. But no matter whom I asked, I could not obtain any reply that satisfied me. 'It's a burning sensation, like having a fire burning on top of you' – that was all I could get out of them, and that was how they all described it. 'It's a burning sensation' – and that was that. In these early days I started to get friendly with M—cki, and I tried asking him about it, too. 'It hurts like nothing on earth,' he replied, 'and it feels like a fire burning you; as if your back was being roasted in the very hottest of fires.' In short, they all gave the same description. I remember, however, that at this time I noticed something strange, though I will not swear as to the accuracy of the observation; it was, however, lent strong support by the common consensus of the men. This was that the birch, if a large number of strokes were administered with it, was the most severe punishment of all those in use in our prisons. This may at first glance appear absurd and impossible. However, it is possible to flog a man to death with only four hundred strokes of the birch; and with anything over five hundred, death is almost certain. Not even a man of the very strongest constitution can take a thousand strokes of the birch at once. On the other hand, five hundred strokes of the sticks can be taken without the slightest danger to a man's life. Even a man of less than iron constitution can take a thousand strokes of the sticks without his life being put at risk. Even two thousand strokes of the sticks are not enough to kill a man of average strength and healthy constitution. 'The birch stings more,' they would say, 'the pain's worse.' And of course the birch is indeed more painful than the cane. Its effect is more strongly irritant, it has a more drastic effect on a man's nervous system, stimulating it to excess, and straining it more than it can bear. I don't know how it is nowadays, but in the not so distant past there were certain gentlemen who obtained from the freedom to flog their victims something that was reminiscent of the Marquis de Sade and the Marquise de Brinvilliers. There was, I believe, something about this sensation that made the hearts of these gentlemen stop beating, something at once sweet and painful. There are people like tigers, who thirst for blood to lick. Whoever has once experienced this power, this unlimited mastery over the body, blood and spirit of another human being, his brother according to the law of Christ; whoever has experienced this control and this complete freedom to degrade, in the most humiliating fashion, another creature made in God's image, will quite unconsciously lose control of his own feelings. Tyranny is a habit; it is able to, and does develop finally into a disease. I submit that habit may coarsen and stupefy the very best of men to the level of brutes. Blood and power make a man drunk: callous coarseness and depravity develop in him; the most abnormal phenomena become accessible, and in the end pleasurable to the mind and the senses. The human being and the citizen perish forever in the tyrant, and a return to human dignity, to repentance, to regeneration becomes practically impossible for him. What is more, the example, the possibility of such intransigence have a contagious effect upon the whole of society: such power is a temptation. A society which can look upon such a phenomenon with indifference is already contaminated to its foundations. Put briefly, the right given to one man to administer corporal punishment to another is one of society's running sores, one of the most effective means of destroying in it every attempt at, every embryo of civic consciousness, and a basic factor in its certain and inexorable dissolution.

Ordinary executioners are shunned by polite society, but gentleman executioners are far from being so. It is only recently that a contrary opinion has been expressed, and that only as an abstract theory, in books. Even those who express it have not all been able to suppress in themselves their need for despotic powers. Every manufacturer, every employer cannot help sometimes feeling a certain irritable satisfaction at the thought that his employees and all their families are exclusively dependent on him. This is certainly the case; not so swiftly does a generation tear itself away from that which heredity has implanted in it; not so swiftly does a man renounce that which has entered his bloodstream, that which he has, in a sense, received in his mother's milk. Such lightning changes of heart do not take place. To confess one's guilt and one's original sin is little, very little; one must wean oneself away from them completely. And that takes more than a little time.

I was speaking about the executioner. The qualities of the executioner are found in embryonic form in almost every modern person. But these bestial qualities do not develop to an equal degree in every individual. If in developing they overwhelm all a person's other qualities, that person naturally becomes a fearsome monster. There are two kinds of executioner: voluntary ones and involuntary, conscripted ones. A voluntary executioner is of course in every respect more debased than an involuntary one; the latter, however, is shunned and abominated by the convicts with horror and loathing, with an uncontrollable, almost mystical terror. What is the reason for this almost superstitious fear of the one kind of executioner and for such indifference, bordering on approval, accorded to the other? There are some extremely strange examples: I have known honest men, respected in society, who were for example unable to rest easy unless the man who was being flogged screamed under the birch, unless he begged and prayed for mercy. This was the accepted form; it was considered both proper and necessary, and when on one occasion the victim refused to scream, the executioner, whom I knew, and who in other contexts might have been considered a decent fellow, took it as a personal affront. At first he had inended to go easy on the man, but when he failed to hear the customary 'your honour, beloved father, have mercy, make me pray for you till the end of my days', and so on, he flew into a mad fury and gave the man fifty extra strokes of the birch in an effort to extract both scream and prayers – and got them. 'He couldn't be allowed to get away with it, sir, it's rank insubordination,' he said to me, very earnestly. As for the real executioners, the involuntary, conscripted ones, it is a well-known fact that these were convicts who had been condemned and sentenced to deportation, but had been kept on as executioners. At first these men were sent to study the art of flogging under another executioner, and when they had learned it from him they were kept on permanently at the prison, where they were confined separately, had their own special rooms and even their own housekeeping arrangements, although they were more or less constantly under guard. Of course, a human being is not a machine; although the executioner carried out the flogging because he had to, he too sometimes got carried away; but although it was not without personal satisfaction that he administered the flogging, he practically never felt any personal animosity towards his victims. His skill in applying the strokes, his knowledge of his craft, his desire to show off to his companions and to the public excited his self-esteem. He really put himself out for the sake of his art. Moreover, he knew very well that he was a universal outcast, that everywhere he went he was met and followed with a superstitious fear, and it was impossible to be certain that this might not have its effect on him, intensifying his fury and his bestial proclivities. Even the children knew that he had 'disowned his father and his mother'. It was strange, however, that all the many executioners I chanced to encounter were without exception educated men, men of sense and intelligence, possessed of an unusual self-esteem, not to say pride. Whether it was that this pride developed in them as a counter to the universal contempt in which they were held, or whether it was strengthened in them by their consciousness of the terror they inspired in their victims, and by their sense of mastery over them, I do not know. It may be that even the very spectacle and theatrical pomp of the surroundings in which they appear before the public on the scaffold contribute to the development in them of a certain superciliousness. I remember that at one time I frequently had occasion to meet with and closely watch a certain executioner. He was a fellow of medium height, muscular, lean, aged about forty, with a fairly pleasant and intelligent face and a mop of curly hair. He also wore an unusually dignified and tranquil air; he kept up a gentlemanlike appearance, and always answered my questions briefly, thoughtfully and even kindly, but with a kindness that had a touch of superciliousness about it, as if he were boasting about something to me. The officers of the watch often used to talk with him when I was there, and they did so with what seemed to be genuine respect. He was aware of this, and in the presence of any officer he would redouble his politeness, his dourness and his sense of his own worth. The more kindly the officer talked to him, the more unyielding he would appear, and although he did not relax his most refined politeness one iota, I am none the less certain that at that moment he considered himself immeasurably superior to the officer who was talking to him. This was written all over his face. It sometimes happened that on very hot summer days he would be sent off under guard with a long, thin pole to kill the town's stray dogs. In our town there were an extraordinary number of dogs which belonged to no one and which multiplied with unusual rapidity. During the hottest part of the summer they became dangerous, and the executioner was sent in on the instructions of the authorities in order to exterminate them. But it appeared that he did not even find this depressing duty in any way humiliating. It was a sight worth seeing, the dignity with which he strode about the streets of the town accompanied by a weary guardsman, terrifying the old women and children merely by his appearance, the tranquil, even supercilious manner in which he gazed at everyone he met. But by and large the executioners led an untrammelled existence. They had money, they ate very well, they had vodka to drink. They got their money from bribes. A civilian prisoner who was being taken out to be flogged always scraped enough money together, even if it was his very last penny, to give the executioner a present before the punishment commenced. In the case of rich prisoners, however, the executioner would demand a sum that was fixed according to the victim's supposed means; this might be as much as thirty rubles, and sometimes even more. With very rich prisoners the haggling would be quite intense. Of course, the executioner could never really let a man off lightly; he would answer for that with his own back. On the other hand, he would promise his victims not to lay into them too hard. The prisoners nearly always agreed to his terms; if they did not, the executioner would flog them in truly barbaric fashion; it was quite within his power to do so. In some instances he might even impose a considerable financial demand on a poor prisoner; the man's relatives would come to haggle and sue, and woe betide them if they did not satisfy the executioner's request. In such cases the executioner would be

very much assisted by the superstitious terror he inspired. What
wild stories were told about executioners! The convicts used to
assure me that an executioner could kill a man with a single blow.
But really, when was this ever put to the test? However, it may have
been so. The men's assurances were too positive. The executioner
himself promised me that he could do this. The men also said that
he could land a swinging blow on his victim's back without raising
even the slightest weal on it and without the victim ever feeling the
slightest pain. But the stories about all these tricks and subtleties
were legion. Even though the executioner had taken the bribe that
was supposed to make him go easy on a man, he would nevertheless
administer the first stroke as hard as he was able, with all his might.
This had even become a custom with the executioners. He would
moderate the subsequent strokes, especially if a payment had been
made to him in advance. But whether he had been paid or not, the
first stroke was up to him. I really do not know why they went about
it like this. It might have been in order to habituate the victim to
the strokes that were to follow, on the principle that one very severe
stroke would make the lighter ones seem less painful; or they may
have simply wished to show off to their victims, to scare them a bit
and pull them up sharply, so that they should know with whom they
had to deal – to announce themselves, in short. Whatever the case,
before he began the the flogging the executioner was in an excited
state of mind, he felt his power, had a consciousness of his mastery.
At that moment he was an actor; the public would watch him with
wonder and terror, and of course it was not without satisfaction
that he shouted to his victim before he administered the first stroke:
'Lie still, I'm going to burn your hide off!' – the usual and fatal
words on such occasions. It is hard to imagine the degree to which
human nature may become distorted.

In those early days I spent in the hospital, I listened to those
stories told by the men with appreciation. We all found it very
boring lying there. All the days were alike. In the morning we had
the diversion of the doctors' visit and then, soon after they had
gone, we had dinner. In conditions of such monotony, eating was
of course a major diversion. The food provided followed the
various diets that were prescribed for the patients' illnesses. Some

men only got soup thickened with a kind of groats; others got nothing but porridge; yet others were given semolina pudding, which was very popular among the men. The convicts grew soft while they were in hospital, and developed a sweet tooth. Convalescent patients, and those who had almost recovered, got a piece of boiled beef, or 'bull' as the men called it. Best of all was the diet prescribed for the men who had scurvy – they got beef and onions, with horseradish and so on, and sometimes a measure of vodka. Bread was black or brown, again depending on what form of illness a man had, and it was tolerably well baked. The official nature and the subtlety of the diets prescribed used to make the men laugh. Of course patients who were suffering from certain illnesses could not eat anything at all. On the other hand, those who did have an appetite could eat whatever they liked. Some men exchanged their dishes, so that the diet that had been prescribed for one case went to a completely different one. Others who were on a restricted diet would buy beef, or the scurvy diet, and drank kvas or the hospital beer, again buying it from those who had had it prescribed for them. These dietary items were sold or resold for money. The beef diet was especially prized – it cost five copeck bills. If no one in the ward had anything worth buying, the warders would be sent over to the other convict ward, and if there was nothing there, either, they would go to the military wards – the 'free' wards, as the convicts called them. There were always patients who wanted to sell their meals. They had to subsist on nothing but bread, but they pulled in a fair bit of money. Poverty was, of course, the rule, but those who had any money were able to send out to the bazaar for kalatches, and even for sweets and candies. Our warders carried out all these commissions quite disinterestedly. The most tedious part of the day began after dinner; because they had nothing to do, the men slept, talked idly, quarrelled, told stories. If no new patients were brought in, this time of the day would be even more tedious. The arrival of a new patient nearly always created something of a stir, especially if it was a man nobody knew. The men would look him over and try to find out who he was, what he was like, where he had come from and what he had done. They were particularly interested in transit prisoners: they always had something to tell,

though they did not talk about matters that affected them personally; unless a man started talking about those of his own accord,
no one ever questioned him about them. All they were asked about
was where they had come from, with whom, what the journey had
been like, where they were being taken, and so forth. As they
listened to some such new tale, one or two of the men might be put
in mind of their own story, with its various transits, gangs, executioners and officers. Men who had run the gauntlet also
appeared at about this time of day, towards evening. They always
created something of a stir, as I have already mentioned; but they
were not brought in every day, and a day on which they did not
make their appearance was somehow robbed of its interest for us;
it was as if we had all grown very tired of each other's company,
and quarrels would start to break out. We were even glad to see the
insane prisoners who were brought in for clinical tests. The trick
of pretending to be insane in order to escape punishment was one
resorted to from time to time by prisoners awaiting sentence. Some
were quickly found out, or rather they themselves would alter the
strategy of their behaviour; a prisoner who had been carrying on
absurdly for two or three days would suddenly return to his senses,
calm down and gloomily begin to ask to be discharged. Neither the
convicts nor the doctors ever reproached such a man, nor did they
try to shame him by reminding him of his recent antics; he would
be discharged without anyone saying a word, and in two or three
days he would appear back at the hospital again, having received
his punishment. Such cases were, on the whole, rare, however. But
the really insane prisoners who were brought in for tests were a
plague and an affliction to the whole ward. Some of these madmen,
the violent ones, who shouted, danced and sang, were at first
greeted by the convicts with something approaching delight.
'Here's a bit of fun!' they would say, looking at some grotesque
creature who had been brought in. But I found the spectacle of
these unfortunate men both painful and distressing. I could never
look at an insane prisoner with indifference.

However, the incessant antics and agitated buffoonery of these
madmen who were at first received by the men with howls of
laughter ended by boring everyone to death, and after a day or two

our patience would be finally exhausted. One of these madmen was kept in with us for nearly three weeks, and he made life in the ward really insufferable. As luck would have it, another madman was brought in at the same time. This one made a particular impression on me. It was the third year of my penal servitude. During the first year, or rather the first months of my life in the prison, in the course of the spring, I used to set off with a gang to work at a brick factory two versts away, where I carried bricks of the stove-makers who were repairing the kilns, getting them ready for the summer brick-making. At the factory that morning M—cki and B. introduced me to the works superintendent who lived there, an NCO by the name of Ostrozhsky. He was a Pole, an old man of about sixty, tall and lean, extremely good-looking and even somewhat majestic in appearance. He had been stationed in Siberia for very many years, and although he was of common peasant stock and had come here as a soldier after the Polish Uprising of 1830, M—cki and B. loved and respected him. He was constantly reading the Catholic Bible. I used to talk with him, and he spoke so kindly, so sensibly, told such interesting stories, looked at one in such a good-natured, sincere way. I did not see him again for about two years. All I heard was that he had got involved in some trouble and was under investigation. And then suddenly he was brought to our ward making the most indecent and vulgar gestures. The patients were wild with delight, but I was filled with such sadness ... After three days we no longer knew what to do with him. He quarrelled, fought, shrieked, sang, even at night, and got up to such disgusting antics that we all simply began to feel sick. He was afraid of no one. They put him in a straitjacket, but this made things even worse for us, even though without the straitjacket he had been picking quarrels and trying to fight with practically everybody. During these three weeks the whole ward sometimes rose up as one man, begging the senior doctor to move our 'treasure' to the other convict ward. A couple of days later the men there would be likewise asking to have him moved back in with us. And since there were two insane convicts in the hospital, both of them restless and violent, each ward exchanged its madman with the other. Neither, however, was any better than the other. All the patients gave a sigh

of relief when at last the two madmen were taken away somewhere ...

I recall another strange madman. One day in summer, a prisoner
awaiting the execution of his sentence was brought in. He was a
robust, very awkward-looking man of about forty-five, with a face
that had been disfigured by smallpox. The lids of his small, red eyes
were swollen, and he appeared very gloomy and morose. He was
put in the bed next to mine. He turned out to be a very quiet fellow,
never spoke to a soul and sat as though he were thinking something
over. Darkness began to fall, and he suddenly turned to me. Out
of the blue, without any preliminaries, but giving the impression
that he was telling me his most intimate secret, he began to inform
me that in a few days' time he was supposed to be given two
thousand strokes, but that the flogging would not take place,
because the daughter of Colonel G. was interceding for him. I
looked at him in bewilderment and replied that in a matter of this
kind a colonel's daughter would not be able to have much influence.
As yet the true state of affairs had not filtered through to me; the
man had not been brought in as an insane prisoner, after all, but
as an ordinary patient. I asked him what illness he was suffering
from. He replied that he did not know. He had been sent here for
some reason, but was perfectly healthy, and the colonel's daughter
was in love with him. On one occasion two weeks ago she had
driven past the guardhouse as he had been looking through the iron
grille of the small window. She had fallen in love with him as soon
as she had set eyes on him. And since then she had visited the
guardhouse three times on various pretexts. The first time she had
called with her father to visit her brother, an officer who was on
watch duty there. The second time she had come with her mother
to distribute alms; as she had passed him she had whispered to him
that she loved him and was going to save him. It was strange, the
way he filled this absurd tale with such minute details, a tale which
needless to say was entirely the product of his own poor, disordered
brain. He had a devout belief that he would escape his punishment.
He talked calmly and positively about this lady's passionate love
for him and, quite apart from the general absurdity of the story,
it was bizarre to hear such a romantic tale about a love-lorn maiden

from the lips of a man who was nearly fifty and whose features were so despondent, so bitter and so disfigured. It was strange what the fear of a flogging had managed to do to this timid soul. Maybe he really had seen someone through the window, and the madness which fear had inculcated in him and which was increasing with every hour had suddenly found its outlet and its appropriate form. This unhappy soldier, who had possibly never once thought about young ladies in all his life before, suddenly dreamed up an entire romance, instinctively clutching at this straw. I listened without saying anything, and later told the other patients what I had heard. But when the other men started to grow curious, he remained chastely silent. The next day the doctor spent a long time questioning him, and since the man told him there was nothing the matter with him and since the examination proved this to be indeed the case, he was discharged. However, we learned that he had had *sanat* entered on his 'complaint sheet' only after the doctors had left the ward, and it was thus too late for us to tell them what was wrong with him. Indeed, we ourselves had not fully realized what the matter was. The whole fault lay in the mistake made by the authorities in sending the man to the hospital without explaining why he had been sent. Some administrative slip had been made. Perhaps even the officials who had sent the man here had not been certain that he was insane, but had acted on hearsay and had sent him in for tests. Whatever the truth of the matter, two days later the unhappy man was taken out and flogged. The suddenness with which this happened was apparently a great shock to him; right up to the last moment he had continued to believe that he would not be punished, and when he was taken out between the lines of soldiers he began to shout for help. Because there were no spare beds in our ward he was put in the other one. I made inquiries about him and learned that he had not said a word to anyone for a whole week, had been in a state of distress and extreme melancholy ... Later, when his back had healed, he was sent away somewhere. At any rate, I heard nothing more of him after that.

As regards the general question of treatment and drugs, so far as I was aware the patients with minor ailments hardly ever followed the instructions of the doctors or took the medicines pre-

scribed for them; on the other hand, the more serious cases and in
general those patients who really had something wrong with them
derived great satisfaction from their treatment, and took their
mixtures and powders conscientiously. But it was the external
remedies that had the greatest popularity among the men. Cupping
glasses, leeches, poultices and bloodletting, the remedies so loved
and trusted by our common folk, were all accepted by the men with
willingness and even pleasure. There was one strange thing that
interested me. The same men who had so patiently borne the most
agonizing pain when they had been flogged with the birch or the
sticks frequently complained, made faces and even groaned when
the cupping glasses were being applied. I do not know how to
explain this: it may have been that they had grown very soft, or they
may have just been giving themselves airs. It is true that the cupping
glasses in use in our ward were of a peculiar kind. The little machine
that was used for piercing the skin had long ago been lost or broken
by the medical assistant, or had possibly worn out, so that the
assistant had to make the necessary incisions with a lancet. About
twelve incisions were made for each cupping. If the machine was
used, the operation was painless. The twelve small blades pene-
trated the skin at the same time, instantly, and no pain was felt. But
with incisions using the lancet it was a different matter. The lancet
pierced the skin relatively slowly. And since if ten cuppings were
made it was necessary to perform one hundred and twenty such
incisions, the effect of them all together was rather painful. I have
had this treatment, but although it was both painful and a nuisance,
it was not so bad as to make one groan out loud. It was quite absurd
to see some great, lanky fellow writhing about and starting to
whine. All this could be compared to the way a man who is calm
and resolute in any matter of serious importance will occasionally
fall into a mood of bilious caprice at home when he has nothing
to do: he will not eat the food that is brought to him, he scolds and
curses, nothing is to his liking, everyone gets on his nerves, everyone
is insulting him, everyone is harassing him – in short, 'he's too
damned comfortable', as is sometimes said of such gentlemen who,
however, are also to be found among the common people. In our
prison, where we all lived on top of one another, they were all too

common. Such mollycoddled individuals were usually teased by the other patients, some of whom used indeed to curse and abuse them outright. The man under attack would fall silent, as though he had been waiting for the other men's abuse in order to be able to do so. Ustyantsev was one of those who particularly could not abide these men, and he never let go an opportunity of taking them to task: he never let go an opportunity of taking anyone to task, for that matter. This was his entertainment, and it was a real need with him. It goes without saying that it stemmed from his illness, but it was also due in part to his stupidity. At first he would glare earnestly and fixedly at the man; then he would start to upbraid him in a voice of serene conviction. He poked his nose into everything that went on; it was as though he had been given the job of seeing that order and morality prevailed among us.

'He gets everywhere,' the convicts used to say, laughingly. But they spared his feelings and avoided quarrels with him, and only occasionally did they laugh at him like this.

'The amount he talks! You'd need a train of wagons to carry it off.'

'He talks a load of rubbish. I've no respect for an idiot like that. What does he howl for, when he gets the lancet? If you can't stand the heat, stay out of the kitchen, that's what I say.'

'What's it to you?'

'No, lads,' one of the convicts interjected, 'the cups are nothing, I've had them. But there's nowt so painful as somebody pulling you by the ear for a long time.'

All the men laughed.

'Somebody been pulling your ear, then?'

'Do you think I'm not serious? Of course they have.'

'That must be why your ears stick out, then.'

Shapkin, the convict in question, really did have very long sticking-out ears. He had been a vagrant, and was still young, a quiet, sensible man who always spoke with a kind of grave, repressed humour, which gave some of the stories he told a sharply comic edge.

'What would I think you'd got your ear pulled for, anyway? How would I get an idea like that, you stupid man?' Ustyantsev inter-

posed again, addressing Shapkin indignantly, even though the
latter had not been speaking to him, but to all the men collectively
– but Shapkin did not even cast a glance in his direction.

'Who pulled it then?' asked someone.

'Who? The district police officer, of course. You see, lads, it was
because I was a vagrant. The two of us had just got to K., me and
another vagrant, Yefim his name was, he had no other. On the way
we'd not done too badly out of a peasant in Tolmino, that's a
village, you know. Well, we went into K. and had a look round:
maybe we could do ourselves a bit of good here and all, and then
scarper. We weren't exactly town mice, if you'll take my meaning.
Well, the first thing we did was, we went into a public house. We
had a look round. This old geezer comes up to us, a regular dosser
he was, with raggedy elbows, wearing an old suit he was. We got
talking about this and that.'

'"And how, may I ask, are you travelling?" he says. "With
documents?"*

'"No," we says. "Without documents."

'"I see, sir. Like myself, sir. I have a couple of sterling companions here with me," he says. "They're in the pay of General
Cuckoo, too.† So I take the liberty, seeing as how we've been out
on the town for a while and haven't as yet managed to pull in a
farthing, of asking you to buy us a pint of vodka."

'"With the greatest of pleasure," we says. Well, so all had a
drink, see. And then they showed us a job right up our street, called
for a bit of breaking and entering, it did. There was this house on
the outskirts of town, with a wealthy tradesman living in it, a whole
lot of goodies there was in there, so we decided to suss it out one
night. The only trouble was, when we did the joint we all got caught,
all five of us. They took us off down the nick, and we were hauled
in before the district police officer himself. "I'll question these men
myself," he said. He came in with his pipe, had them bring him a
cup of tea. He was a big chap with sideburns. He sat down. They
brought in three other blokes as well, they was vagrants, too. A

* With passports. (*Note by F. M. Dostoyevsky.*)
† i.e. in the woods, where the cuckoo sings. He means that they are vagrants, too. (*Note by F. M. Dostoyevsky.*)

vagrant is a rum bird, lads: he can't remember anything, he's so pigheaded, he forgets everything, doesn't know his arse from his elbow. The district police officer says to me: "Who the hell are you, then?" He's bellowing at me, like he's shouting out of a barrel. Well, of course, I say: "Your honour, I don't remember, your honour I've forgotten."

'"Hang on a minute," he says. "I want to have a word with you, I know your face." He's staring at me with his eyes popping out of his head, but I've never seen him before. Then he says to the next fellow: "And who might you be?"

'"Scarper, your honour."

'"That's your name, is it, Scarper?"

'"That's my name, your honour."

'"Right, then, you're Scarper, and who are you?" he says to the third man.

'"Scarper'n all, your honour."

'"And is that your name?"

'"That's my name. Scarper'n all, your honour."

'"And who gave you a name like that, you villain?"

'"Kind folk did, your honour. There's kind folk in the world, you know, your honour."

'"And who were these kind folk?"

'"I don't remember, your honour, begging your honour's pardon."

'"You can't remember any of them?"

'"No, your honour."

'"But you had a father and a mother, didn't you? Don't you remember them?"

'"I suppose I must have done, your honour, but I've forgotten them, too; maybe I did, your honour."

'"And where have you been living until now?"

'"In the woods, your honour."

'"Only in the woods?"

'"Yes."

'"But what about the winter?"

'"I can't remember the winter, your honour."

'"Well, and what about you, what's your name?"

'"Axehead, your honour."

'"And yours?"

'"Grindsharp, your honour."

'"And yours?"

'"Sharpgrind, your honour."

'"And none of you remembers anything?"

'"Not a thing, your honour."

'He stands there and laughs, and they look back at him, smirking. Another time he might just as easily have kicked our teeth in, you could never tell. But these men were all big healthy brutes, solid like.

'"Take them to the prison," he said, "I'll deal with them later; but you there, you stay behind." That was me he was talking to. "Come over here and sit down!" I looked: there was a table with pen and paper on it. I thought to myself: "I wonder what he's got up his sleeve?" "Sit down on that chair," he said. "Take the pen and write." And he grabbed hold of my ear and pulled me along by it. I looked at him like he was mad or something. "I can't write, your honour," I said. "Write!" he said.

'"Have a heart, your honour." "Write as best you're able to write!" And he kept pulling me by the ear, pull, pull, pull, and then he gave it a twist. I tell you, lads, I'd sooner he'd given me three hundred of the birch. I saw stars! "Get on and write, and stop your fussing."

'Gone off his rocker, had he?'

'No, he'd not gone off his rocker. The thing was, there was this clerk in T—sk who'd pulled off a stunt not so long ago: he'd embezzled some state funds and made off with them, and he had sticking-out ears, too. Well, they were looking for him everywhere. Apparently I looked like this bloke, so the DPO was trying to find out if I could write and if so, what my handwriting was like.'

'What a caper! And did it hurt?'

'You're telling me it did.'

Laughter broke out all around.

'Well, and so did you write something?'

'How would I write? I started trailing the pen across the paper, and then he gave up. Well, he slapped me in the face a dozen times or so and then let me go, back to the prison, that is.'

'And can you write?'

'I used to be able to, but when pens came into fashion I sort of got out of the habit ...'

This, then, was the type of story, the chatter, rather, with which we sometimes used to while away our dreary hours. Lord, how tedious it was! Long, stuffy days, one after the other, all identical. If only there had been a book to read! All the same, I used to visit the hospital frequently, especially in the early days of my imprisonment; sometimes I was ill, at other times I simply went there in order to get a rest, to get away from the prison. Life was oppressive there, even more so than in hospital: it was morally more oppressive. Spite, animosity, quarrelling, envy, the eternal faultfinding of the other convicts with us, the noblemen; the spite-filled, threatening faces! Here in the hospital everyone was more or less on equal terms with everyone else, there was a more companionable spirit. The most melancholy part of the whole day came in the evening, when the candles were lit, and night began. A dim night-light glowed far away over by the door, a bright point of light; but our end of the ward lay in semi-darkness. The air would grow stuffy and foul. Someone might not be able to get to sleep, and would get up and sit on his bed for an hour or so, inclining his head in its nightcap as though thinking about something. You would watch him for a whole hour and try to guess what it was he was thinking about, just to kill time. Or else you might start to dream as you remembered the past, your imagination filling with vivid, expansive images; you would remember details you would not remember at another time, ones you would not ever feel as acutely as you did now. Or else you would try to guess about the future: would you ever get out of prison? If you did, where would you go? When would it be? Would you ever get back to your own part of the world again? You would think and think, and hope would begin to stir in your soul ... Another time you might simply start counting: one, two, three and so on, to make yourself fall asleep. I used sometimes to count up to three thousand without falling asleep. Someone would start to toss and turn. Ustyantsev would cough his wet, consumptive cough

and groan weakly, each time with the words: 'Lord, I have sinned!'
And it would be strange to hear this sick, broken, whimpering voice
in the silence of the ward. Somewhere in a corner there would be
others who were awake, talking as they lay in their beds. One man
might start to tell something of his past, of far-off, long-ago events,
of his vagrancy, his children, his wife, the way he had once lived.
From his remote whisper alone you would sense that none of the
things he was talking about would ever come back to him and that
he himself was a severed chunk torn from that life. Another man
would listen to him. All you would hear would be that quiet, even
whisper, like the purling of water somewhere far away ... I remember hearing one of these stories in the course of one long winter's
evening. At first it seemed to me like some nightmare, as if I were
lying in delirium and had dreamed it all in the heat of my fever ...

* 4 *

AKULKA'S HUSBAND: A STORY

It was late at night, after twelve. I had dozed off, but I suddenly
woke up. The dim, meagre glow of the distant night-light was
barely enough to show up the outlines of the ward ... Practically
all the men were already asleep. Even Ustyantsev was sleeping, and
in the stillness one could hear how hard it was for him to catch his
breath, the mucus rattling in his throat every time he breathed in
and out. Suddenly, from far away, out in the passage, there came
the sound of the heavy footsteps that heralded the approach of the
relief sentry. There was the slam of a rifle-butt hitting the floor. The
door of the ward was opened; the lance-corporal, stepping gingerly,
counted the patients. A minute later the ward was locked again, and
silence reigned as before. It was only now that I noticed, a little way
from me on my left, two men who were still awake and who seemed
to be whispering to one another. This was quite a common occurrence in the wards: sometimes two men would lie next to one
another for days and months without ever saying a word to each
other, and then suddenly start talking to one another, their tongues

loosened in the darkness, and one would begin to relate his entire past to the other.

It appeared that they had already been talking for some considerable time. I had not caught the beginning, and could not now catch all they were saying. Little by little, however, I attuned my ear and began to pick up everything. I could not get to sleep: what else was there to do but listen? ... One of the men was telling the other something heatedly, propping himself up in a semi-reclining position with his head lifted and his neck craned in the direction of his neighbour. It was obvious that he was worked up, excited about something; he wanted to talk about something that had happened to him. His listener was sitting on his bed, with his legs stretched out along the mattress, in complete and sullen indifference; from time to time he would mumble something by way of reply, or to show that he was sympathetic, but this seemed to be more for the sake of propriety than for any genuine reason. Every few minutes or so he would stuff his nose with snuff from a snuffbox. This was the correctional soldier Cherevin, a sullen pedant of about fifty, a soulless rationalist and a conceited idiot. The man with the story to tell, Shishkov, was a man still young, about thirty years old, one of the civilian convicts who worked in the sewing shed. Until now I had not given him much attention, and I somehow did not feel greatly inclined to have much to do with him later on in my prison life either. He was a shallow, unstable man. Sometimes he would give up talking altogether, and behave sullenly and coarsely, not saying a word for weeks on end. But sometimes he would suddenly poke his nose into some business or other, would start to spread scandalous rumours, get worked up over trifles, scurrying from one barrack to the other, passing on news, talking nineteen to the dozen and generally quite beside himself with excitement. The men would beat him up, and he would stop talking once more. He was a cowardly, insipid creature. Everyone treated him with a kind of contempt. He was short and thin; his eyes were restless, but sometimes expressed a kind of gormless reverie. Occasionally he would tell some story or other; he would start in a great fever of excitement, waving his arms about – and then he would suddenly break off or change the subject, get carried away by some new details and forget what it was he had begun with. He was always getting into quarrels, and he would never fail to reproach the other man for some wrong he imagined the latter had done him. He would talk with emotion, almost in tears ... He played the balalaika quite well and enjoyed playing; on holidays he would even dance, and he danced well when he was made to by the men ... It was very easy to make him do anything ... It was not that he was particularly dutiful, but he enjoyed making friends and would do whatever he had to in order to win them.

It was a long time before I could make head or tail of what he was talking about. He seemed, at the beginning at any rate, to keep wandering off the subject, getting bogged down in things that were irrelevant. It may have been, too, that he had noticed Cherevin showed practically no interest in his story, but that he wanted to persuade himself that his listener was all ears, and it might have upset him too much if he had been persuaded that the contrary was true.

'... He used to go to the bazaar,' he continued. 'Everyone would bow to him, treat him like royalty – he was a rich man, after all.'

'He had a business of some kind, you said?'

'Yes, that's right, he did. We were all poor, us folk who worked there. Beggars, really. The women used to carry water up a steep bank from the river to water the vegetable patch; they'd work their fingers to the bone, but by autumn they'd not even have enough cabbage to make a soup. We were destitute. Well, he had a big holding, hired men to work his land, three of them, there were; he had his own beehives, and sold honey, and he dealt in cattle, too, around our parts – so naturally he was looked up to a bit. He was really old, about seventy, he had trouble shifting his old bones; grey-haired, he was, a big fellow. He'd go down to the bazaar wearing a fox-fur coat and everyone would pay their respects to him. They could tell who he was, you see. "Good day to you, Ankudim Trofimych, sir!" "Good day to you," he'd say, for he never left anybody out. "May you live forever, Ankudim Trofimych!" "And how are things with you?" he'd ask. "Oh, about as right as soot is white," we'd say. "And how are you, sir?" "Oh, I get by, for all my sins, standing in the way of the sun like the rest of you." "May you live forever, Ankudim Trofimych!" He'd never leave anyone out of the conversation, but when he opened his mouth it was as if every word was worth a ruble. He was a fanatical Bible reader, educated, he was, always reading some religious stuff or other. He'd sit his old woman down in front of him: "Now listen to this, wife, and take it to heart!" he'd say, and start expounding it all to her. And the old woman wasn't that old, either, she was his second wife, to get children, you see, his first wife hadn't given him any. Well, this second wife, Marya Stepanovna she was called, had given him two sons – they were still only little, he was sixty when the younger one, Vasya, was born, and his daughter, Akulka, was the eldest child, she was nearly eighteen.'

'Was she your wife, then?'

'Hang on a minute, will you? First there was all the trouble with this chap called Filka Morozov. "I want my share," Filka said to Ankudim. "Give me my four hundred rubles: I'm not your employee, you know. I don't want to be your partner and I don't want to marry Akulka either. I'm going to enjoy myself now," he said. "My parents are both dead, so I'm going to spend the money on drink. Then I'm going to join the army and in ten years' time I'll be back here having been made a field marshal." So Ankudim gave him the money, squaring the debt completely, as Morozov's father and the old man had started their business on joint capital. "You're a hopeless case," said Ankudim. And Filka said: "Hopeless I may or may not be, greybeard, but you'd try to teach a man to eat his porridge with an awl. Pinching pennies is all you know about; look at all that useless junk you've collected just because you think it might come in handy one day. I'd like to spit on it all. You scrape and save and you end up with damn all. I've got more self-respect than that. And I don't want your Akulka," he said. "Anyway, I've already slept with her ..."

"What do I hear?" said Ankudim. "Do you dare to shame an honest father, an honest daughter? When did you sleep with her, you snake, you reptile?" And he started to shake all over. Filka told him.

'"And not only will she not marry me," he said, "but I'll see to it that your Akulka won't marry any man – nobody'll take her, not even Mikita Grigorich'll take her, 'cos she's gone and disgraced herself. I've been having it off with her ever since the autumn. And I wouldn't take her now even if you offered me a hundred lobsters. Here, go on, try offering me a hundred lobsters – I won't take her ..."

'And did he enjoy himself, that man! He had such a good time, he made the earth shake and the rafters ring. He got a bunch of cronies together, and a great pile of money, and the binge lasted three months – he blew the lot. He would say: "When I've spent all the money I'll sell the house, I'll sell everything and blow that, too, and then I'll either join the army or take to the open road." He'd be drunk from morning to night, and he used to drive a pair of horses with bells on. And the girls fell for him in droves. He used to play the *torban*[34] not half badly.'

'So he'd been having it off with Akulka before, had he?'

'Hang on, will you? My dad had died only recently, and my mum used to bake cakes, working for Ankudim, see, that was how we made a living. It wasn't much of a living, though. Well, we had a bit of land behind the wood, a holding, we used to sow it with grain, but everything went after my dad died, 'cos I went enjoying myself too, lad. I used to beat my mum up, just to get the money off her ...'

'That's terrible, that is, beating your mum up. It's not right.'

'I used to be drunk, my lad, from morning to night. The house we had was all right, even if it was falling down it was our own, but there wasn't a thing in it. We used to go hungry, with hardly a bite to eat for weeks on end. My mum used to go on and on at me, but what did I care? ... I never used to leave Filka Morozov's side in those days. I was with him from morning to night. "Play the guitar and dance for me," he used to say, "and I'll lie here and throw money to you, because I'm a very wealthy man." And what didn't he get up to? But the one thing he wouldn't do was receive stolen goods. "I'm not a thief, I'm an honest man," he used to say. "But let's go and throw tar on Akulka's gate, because I don't want Akulka marrying Mikita Grigorich, that's all I care about now," he said. The old man had been meaning to marry the girl off to Mikita Grigorich for a long time. Mikita was an old man, too, a widower, he wore glasses, had some business or other. When he heard there were rumours about Akulka going around he went back on his word: "It would be a terrible disgrace for me, Ankudim Trofimych," he said, "and anyway I'm too old to get married." So we threw tar on Akulka's gate. And did they give that girl a hiding ... Marya Stepanova shouted: "I'll thrash her to death!" And the old man said: "In the olden days, in the time of the virtuous patriarchs, I'd have dismembered her at the stake; but nowadays all is darkness and corruption in the world." All the neighbours in the street could hear Akulka's howling: she was thrashed from morning to night. And Filka shouted so the whole bazaar could hear it: "Akulka's a great girl to share a bottle of vodka with. She's dressed just right, she's dressed in white, who's the lucky man tonight?" He said: "I rubbed their noses in it, so they won't forget in a hurry." It was about that time that I once met Akulka carrying her pails, and I shouted to her: "How do you do, Akulina Kudimovna! Greetings to your charming self, you're dressed just right. Where do you get the money from? Aren't you going to marry that man you're living with" – that was all I said; but she just stared at me with those big eyes of hers, she was as thin as a rake. The way she was staring at me her mother thought she was sharing a joke with me and laughing, and she shouted through the gateway: "What are you showing your teeth for, you shameless hussy?" And that day her mother started thrashing her again. She used to thrash her for an hour solid. "I'm thrashing her because she's not my daughter any more," she would say.'

'So Akulka was a loose woman, was she?'

'Just you listen, my friend. Me and Filka used to be drinking every day together, and one time my mum came to see me. I was lying down: "What are you lying there for, you villain?" she said. "You're nothing but a bandit." She started yelling at me, see. "Marry Akulka," she said. "They'll be glad to get rid of her to you, they'll give you three hundred rubles to do it." "But she's been publicly disgraced," I replied. "And you're a fool," she said; "the altar covers everything; it'll be all the better for you, she'll be beholden to you all her days. And we could use their money; I've already discussed it with Marya Stepanovna. She's most amenable to the idea." "Give me some money," I said. "Twenty rubles on the nail, and I'll marry her." And believe it or not, I was drunk without a break right up to the time of the wedding. Filka Morozov kept threatening me meanwhile: "So you're going to be Akulka's husband, are you? I'll break every bone in your body and sleep with your wife every night of the week if I want," he said. And I said to him: "Shut your gob, you hunk of dogmeat." Well, I mean, he'd insulted me right in front of the whole street. I ran off home: "I'm not getting married," I said, "unless I get fifty rubles right now."'

'And did they let her marry you?'

'Let me? Why not? We weren't in disgrace. My father had only been ruined by a fire right at the end of his life, before that we'd been better off than they were. Ankudim said: "You're nothing but beggars." I replied: "That's a nice bit of tar you've got on your gate." He said: "Are you trying to intimidate us or something? You've got no proof whatsoever that she's been whoring, but you can't stop idle mouths from talking. There's the door, you don't have to take her. Just give me back the money I gave you." Well, then I'd had it with Filka. I sent Mitri Bykov to tell him that I was going to drag his name in the mud before the whole world; and I was drunk, my friend, right up to the wedding itself. I only sobered up on the altar. When we'd left the altar and sat down again, Mitrofan Stepanych, that's my uncle, said: "It may not be pure as snow, but it's a marriage, and it's all settled now." Old man Ankudim was drunk, too, and crying, he sat there with the tears trickling into his beard. Well, my friend, what I did next was this: I'd taken a whip along in my pocket, I'd been keeping it specially for the wedding; I'd had the idea of giving Akulka a bit of fun, to teach her a lesson for her cheating about the marriage and to show people she hadn't married an idiot.'

'That's the way! So she'd get the right idea straight off ...'

'No, my friend, you just keep quiet ... In our part of the world the custom is for the married couple to be led straight from the altar to a private room, while the others carry on drinking. So there they'd left us in the private room, Akulina and me. Akulka was sitting there as white as a sheet, not a trace of colour was there in her cheeks. She was scared, see. Her hair was white as snow, too.

She had these great big eyes. And she was dead quiet, too, all the time, it was like she was dumb. A queer kind of girl, she was. And so, friend, can you imagine it: I got my whip out and put it right beside the bed – but it turned out that she hadn't done anything she didn't ought to have done.'

'What?'

'Not a thing had she done wrong. She was a decent girl from a decent home. And so why had she had to put up with all that, my friend? Why had Filka Morozov dragged her name in the mud before the whole world?'

'That's right.'

'So then I got down on my knees to her, right beside the bed, and I clasped my hands together. "Forgive me, Akulka Kudimovna, fool that I am, for thinking badly of you. Forgive me, villain that I am." And she sat there on the bed looking at me, put both her hands on my shoulders, and she laughed, but meanwhile the tears were flowing down her cheeks; she was laughing and crying at the same time ... Then I went out to them all: "Right," I said. "If Filka Morozov ever crosses my path again I'll wipe him clean off the face of the earth." And the old couple, they just couldn't find prayers enough; the mother just about fell at her feet, wailing away. And the old man said: "If we'd known this, beloved daughter of ours, we'd never have married you to a man like him." The first Sunday we went to church, I was wearing my astrakhan hat, my best caftan, and my velveteen breeches; she was wearing a new hare-fur coat and a silk kerchief – just like we were made for each other, that's the way we looked! People looked at us admiringly; I was as ever is, and Akulka, though she hadn't got anything to brag about, didn't look so bad either, the best of the dozen, she was ...'

'Well, that was all right then.'

'Just you wait and hear. The day after the wedding, when I was still drunk, I gave the wedding-guests the slip; I just ran away. "Let me at him, that good-for-nothing Filka Morozov – let me at him, the villain!" I went round the bazaar shouting like that! But I was drunk; they caught me over at the Vlasovs' place, and it took three men to drag me back home again. People in the town had started to talk. The lasses at the bazaar were saying to one another: "You

know what, girls? Akulka's turned out an honest woman after all."
And a bit later on, Filka said to me in front of everybody: "Why
don't you sell your wife? Then you can get drunk! Our soldier
Yashka got married just for that reason alone: he never slept with
his wife, but he was drunk for three years," he said. I said to him:
"You villain!" And he said: "You're nothing but a fool. Anyway,
you were pissed when they married you. How could you know what
was what?" When I got home, I yelled at the old couple: "You
married me to her when I was drunk!" The mother started arguing
back. "Your ears are stopped up with gold, mother," I said. "Let
me at Akulka!" Well, and then I started beating Akulka up. I hit
her and hit her and hit her. My friend, I went on hitting her for two
days, till I couldn't stand up myself no more, either. She had to stay
in bed for three weeks.'

'That's just a matter of course,' observed Cherevin, phlegmatic-
ally. 'If you don't beat them, they ... But did you catch her with
her lover, then?'

'No, I didn't,' said Shishkov with an effort, after a moment's
silence. 'I'd got really offended, people were jeering at me, and
Filka was the ringleader in all this. "That's a model of a wife you've
got, everyone can have a look at her." He invited us over to his
place, and his opening shot was: "He's got a wife that's nice, kind,
well brought up and charming – that's what he thinks. But have you
forgotten, lad, that you threw tar on her gate?" I was sitting there,
drunk, and right there and then he grabbed me by the hair and
pulled me down by it: "Dance," he said, "husband of Akulka, I'm
going to hold you by the hair like this and you're going to dance
and give me a bit of fun!" "You villain!" I shouted. And he said
to me: "I'll bring some of my pals over and I'll thrash your Akulka
with a birch rod, as much as I want to." So you'll be able to imagine
that after that I was too scared to go out of the house: I thought,
he'll come and make a laughing-stock of me. So I started beating
her, just for that ...'

'What did you beat her for? You can tie a man's hands, but you
can't tie his tongue. Too much beating's no good. Give her a hiding,
teach her what's what, and then be nice to her. That's what a wife's
for.'

Shishkov said nothing for a while.

'I felt offended,' he began again, 'and I just got into the habit of it; some days I used to beat her from morning to night: she could do nothing right, the way I saw it. If I didn't beat her, I would get bored. She used to sit not saying a word, looking out of the window, crying . . . She was always crying, I'd start feeling sorry for her, but still I'd beat her. My mother kept on shouting at me about her: "You villain," she'd say, "you no-good convict!" "I'll kill her," I'd yell back, "and don't anyone dare say a word: for you married me to her under false pretences." At first old Ankudim took her side, came to me himself: "I don't know what kind of man you are," he said, "but you're not up to much; I'll see justice is done to you!" But later on he just gave up. And Marya Stepanovna knuckled under completely. She came to me once and said, in a voice full of tears: "I have a favour to beg of you, Ivan Semyonych, it isn't much, but it would be a great blessing. Let me live to see the light again, master," and she bowed down. "Relent, forgive her! Wicked people have been saying bad things about our daughter: you yourself know that she's an honest woman . . ." She bowed deeply, and cried. But I was still throwing my weight around: "I don't want to hear another word out of you! I'll do whatever I like to you all now, for I've lost control of myself; but Filka Morozov's my buddy and my closest friend . . ."'

'So you went on the binge together again, did you?'

'Not a bit of it! There was no talking to the man. He was drinking himself berserk. He'd spent all his money and had hired himself out to a tradesman. He'd joined the army in place of the tradesman's son. In our part of the world, if you do that, right up to the day they come to take you away everyone and everything in the house is at your disposal, and you're number one. When you enlist you get the money in full, and until then you live in the master's house for up to half a year, sometimes. The things they do to those masters, it's a crying disgrace! I'm joining up instead of your son, they say, so that means I'm your benefactor, and you've all got to show me respect, or else I won't do it. So Filka had really let fly at the tradesman's place, he was sleeping with the daughter, he used to pull the master's beard after dinner every day – he did anything

he liked for his own amusement. He took a bath every day, and they
had to make the steam for it using vodka instead of water; the
womenfolk had to carry him into the bath-house in their arms.
When he came back to the house after he'd been out drinking, he'd
stand out in the street: "I don't want to go in by the gate, take the
fence down." And they'd have to make a hole in the fence for him
to walk through. It all came to an end eventually, they came to take
him away, sobered him up. There were crowds of people all down
the street: "They're taking Filka Morozov away to enlist!" And
Filka bowed to everyone. At about this time Akulka happened to
be passing on her way from the kitchen garden; when Filka saw her
right outside our gate, he shouted "Stop!" jumped down from the
cart and bowed down to the ground before her. "My darling," he
said, "my sweet, I have loved you for two years and now they're
taking me away to be a soldier. Forgive me," he said, "honest
daughter of an honest father, because I am a villain before you –
it's all my fault!" And again he bowed down to the ground before
her. At first Akulka looked frightened, but then she bowed to the
waist and said: "Forgive me, too, kind man; I feel no malice
towards you." I went after her into the house. "What did you say
to him, you evil whore?" And believe it or not, she looked at me,
and said: "I love him now more than anyone else in the whole
world!"'

'Well I never ...'

'And all that day I didn't say one word to her ... Only when
evening came, I said: "Akulka! I'm going to kill you now." That
night I couldn't get to sleep, I went out to the passage to get myself
some kvas to drink, and it was already starting to be daylight. I
went into the house. "Akulka," I said, "get yourself ready and
come out to the holding." I'd been getting ready to go there before,
and my mother knew we were going. "That's it," she said. "It's the
busy season now and I hear that the labourer's been in bed for three
days with a bad stomach." I harnessed up the cart, didn't say
anything. When you get out of our town there's pine forest for
fifteen versts and our holding lies on the other side of the forest.
We'd gone about three versts through the forest when I stopped the
horse: "Stand up, Akulina," I said: "your final hour has come."

She looked at me in fear, stood up in front of me, and didn't say a word. "I've had enough of you," I said; "say your prayers!" Then I grabbed her by the hair: she had these long, thick plaits, I wound them round and round my hands, and I stuck my knees in her back, took out my knife, bent her head back and slit her throat like she was a calf ... She started screaming, the blood spurted out, I threw the knife away, and took hold of her in front with both my arms. I laid her down on the ground, embraced her and then started screaming over her body, yelling my head off; she was screaming and I was screaming; she was shaking all over, trying to break free of my arms, and the blood was gushing, really gushing all over my face and my arms. Then I left her, I got scared, I left the horse, too, and ran home by the back lanes as fast I was able, and went into the bath-house: we had one of those old bath-houses, it wasn't used; I hid myself under the ledge and stayed there until nightfall.'

'And what about Akulka?'

'She must have got up after I'd left and set off home. They found her a hundred yards from the place later on.'

'You didn't kill her, then?'

'No ...' Shishkov paused for a minute.

'There's this vein,' observed Cherevin. 'If you don't cut it at first go, the person will struggle and struggle, and no matter how much they bleed, they won't die.'

'Oh, she died all right. They found her body in the evening. They reported it, and a search was started for me – they found me when it was dark, in the bath-house ... This is the fourth year I've spent in here,' he added after a moment.

'Hm ... Well, of course, you do have to beat them, no good will come of it if you don't,' Cherevin observed coolly and exactly, taking out his snuffbox again.

'Besides, lad,' he continued. 'From your story you seem to have acted very stupidly. I once caught my wife with a lover, too. So I told her to go into the barn and I folded my reins double. "Who did you swear to honour and obey? Who did you swear to?" I said. Then I thrashed her, with the reins, thrashed her and thrashed her, thrashed her for an hour and a half, till she screamed: "I'll wash your feet and drink the water." Advotya, my wife's name was.'

5

THE SUMMER

But now it was the beginning of April, and Holy Week was approaching. Little by little, the summer tasks got underway. The sun grew warmer and brighter with every day that passed; the air smelt of spring and had a disturbing effect on the organism. The onset of the fine weather was unsettling even to a man in fetters, it aroused in him indefinite desires and aspirations, a vague melancholy. A man seems to pine for freedom even more in the sun's bright rays than he does on a wet day in winter or autumn, and this was true of all the convicts. They seemed pleased with the fine days, but at the same time a kind of impatience and fidgetiness quickened in them. In fact, I observed that quarrels among the men were more common in the prison during the spring. There was a greater frequency of noise, shouting, hubbub, various kinds of escapades; but out at work you would also sometimes suddenly notice someone looking thoughtfully and fixedly into the blue distance, across at the opposite bank of the Irtysh, where the untrammelled Kirghiz steppes begin, stretching like an immense tablecloth for more than a thousand versts; you would hear someone give a deep sigh, as deep as he could make it, as if he longed to breathe that free and distant air and so bring relief to his oppressed and fettered soul. '*Ekh-ma!*' the convict would exclaim at last, suddenly, as though shaking off dreams and musings. With sullen impatience he would take up his shovel, or the bricks which he had to shift from one place to another. A moment later he would have forgotten his sudden rush of feeling and would have begun to laugh or curse, according to his temperament; or he would suddenly begin his assignment, if he had one, with extraordinary ardour, far more than was required, and start to work – work as hard as he was able, as if he were trying to suppress something that was choking and oppressing him from within. All these men were strong, most of them were in the flower of their maturity and strength ... Fetters were hard to bear at such a time! I am not making up any poetic fancies, and am certain of the truth of my observation. As well as this being the time when in the warmth of the bright sun you feel with all your soul, with all your being the boundless strength of nature as once more it rises from the dead all round you, the time when the closed-in prison, the guards and the will of others become even more difficult to bear; this is also the time when, with the first skylark, vagrancy begins all over Russia and Siberia: God's people escape from prison and take to the forests. After airless dungeons, after courtrooms, fetters and floggings they wander at will, wherever they choose, wherever looks most attractive and most favourable; they eat and drink whatever they can find, whatever God sends them, and at night they fall asleep somewhere in the forest or the fields, free of their great trouble, free of the anguish of prison, like the birds of the forest, with no one but the stars to say good-night to, under the eye of God. Who will deny that it is a hard life, 'serving under General Cuckoo'? Sometimes a man will not see bread for whole days on end; he will have to hide, and remain hidden; he will have to steal and rob, and sometimes even kill. 'The settler's like a little child – by what he sees his eye's beguiled' is a Siberian proverb about the convict settlers. It is a saying that applies, and even more than applies, to the vagrants. The vagrants are quite often bandits, and nearly always thieves – more by necessity than vocation, of course. There are some men who are really addicted to vagrancy. Some even run away from the settlements to which they are sent when they have finished their sentences. You might think that a man would be content to live in a settlement and have all his needs provided for, but this is not the case: something pulls him, calls him away. The life he leads in the forests is a poor one, with many terrors, but it is free and filled with adventure, there is something alluring about it, it has a mysterious charm for those who have experienced it. You may even see a man now sober and correct of bearing, who has promised to become a sedate, well-behaved citizen and a busy farmer, run away to the forests like this. A man may even get married, have children, live for five years in the same spot and then suddenly vanish into the unknown one fine morning, leaving his wife, his children and the whole of the district he belongs to wondering what has happened to him. One of these men was pointed out to me in the prison. He had not committed any particular crime, at least no one ever talked about him as though he had, but had run away, and indeed had spent the whole of his life running away. He had been out beyond the Danube on the southern Russian border, he had been in the Kirghiz steppes, in Eastern Siberia, in the Caucasus – everywhere, in fact. Who knows but that in other circumstances he might not have become a second Robinson Crusoe, filled as he was with a passion for travelling? I was told all this by the other prisoners, however; he himself rarely indulged in conversation, and when he did utter a word or two it was only in cases of great necessity. He was a peasant of very small build, about fifty years old, extremely mild-tempered, with an extremely placid and even stupid face, placid to the point of idiocy. In summer he liked to sit in the sunshine and hum a song to himself, but so quietly you could not hear him five paces away. His features looked as if they were made of wood; he ate little, mostly bread; he never bought a single kalatch or a measure of vodka; it was unlikely that he ever had any money or that he could count. He was completely indifferent towards everything. He would sometimes feed the prison dogs with his own hands, something no one else ever did. Indeed, Russians are in general not great believers in feeding dogs. The men said he had been married twice; they said he had some children somewhere ... I really do not know how he had ever managed to end up in prison. Everyone in the prison expected him to slip away from there, too; but either the time for him to do that had not yet arrived or it was already past, for he continued to live there, adopting a contemplative attitude towards this alien environment. However, with him nothing was certain; though, really, why should he have run away, and what advantage would there have been in it for him? None the less, the life of a vagrant in the forest was paradise compared to the life the men led in prison. That was easy to understand; there could be no comparison. Though the life was hard, it was one's own. That is why every convict in Russia, wherever his prison may be, grows restless with the coming of spring and the first friendly rays of the spring sunshine. It is not every convict who plans to run away. Because of the difficulties that are involved, and the consequences if one is caught, it is safe to say that only one convict in a hundred ever decides to do it; yet the other ninety-nine do at least dream of escaping and of where they might escape to; they cheer their hearts with the mere desire, with the mere idea of such an escape being possible. Some may recall how they escaped on some other occasion . . . I speak now of those men who are already serving their sentences. But of course it is the unsentenced prisoners who far more often make their escape. Those men who have been sentenced for a given term are likely to try to escape only at the beginning of their time in prison. By the time he has put in two or three years of penal servitude, a convict has already begun to attach some value to those years, and he gradually concedes to himself that it will be better for him to finish his sentence properly and leave for a settlement at the end of it, rather than expose himself to such a risk and such dire penalties if his escape attempt fails. And failure is so likely. Perhaps only one man in ten succeeds in *changing his fortune*. Then again, sentenced convicts who have been condemned to very long terms of imprisonment are more likely than others to try to escape. Fifteen or twenty years seem like an infinity, and a man who has been given such a sentence is forever ready to dream about a change in his fortunes, even though he has already been in prison for ten years. The brand-marks on the convicts' faces naturally have an effect in deterring them from running away. *Changing one's fortune* is a technical term. It happens during interrogations, when men are caught trying to escape, that they will say they were trying to change their fortune. This slightly bookish expression is a perfectly literal description of what is actually the case. No man who runs away really plans to escape into total freedom – he knows that this is well-nigh impossible – but either to end up in another institution, to get into a settlement, or to be retried for a fresh crime which he will commit during his vagrancy. In short, he plans to go anywhere except back to the old, over-familiar place, the prison he was in before. If during the course of the summer these escaping convicts are unable to find some out-of-the-way spot where they can spend the winter, if, say, they do not come across someone who is willing, for a fee, to screen them from the authorities, if they are unable, by killing somebody, to acquire some passport or other which will entitle them to live anywhere, then when autumn comes most of them, if they have not already been caught, will come crowding into the fortresses and prisons and give themselves up. The charge will be vagrancy, and they will go into the gaols to spend the winter, not, of course, without the hope of escaping again the following summer.

The spring used to have its effect on me, too. I can remember how I would sometimes look avidly through the cracks in the stockade, and stand for a long time with my head pressed against our palings, feasting my eyes on the green of the grass on our fortress ramparts, on the ever-deepening blue of the distant sky. My restlessness and anguish would grow with every day that passed, and the prison would come to seem more and more hateful to me. The hostility of the other convicts, to which as a nobleman I was constantly exposed in the first years of my sentence, would become intolerable to me, poisoning my whole existence. During those early years I often used to go into hospital, even though there was nothing the matter with me, just in order to get out of the prison for a while, to escape from that insistent, universal hatred, which nothing could appease. 'You're iron noses – you nosed us to death,' the convicts used to say to us. How I envied the convicts of common peasant stock! They immediately made friends with everybody. And so the spring, the spirit of freedom, the universal rejoicing in nature also had a depressing and irritating effect on me. At the end of Lent, I think it was during its sixth week, I was to take Holy Communion. From the very first week of the fast, the whole prison was divided by the senior duty sergeant into seven shifts, one for each week, so that all the men could take the sacrament. There were thirty men in each shift. I enjoyed the weeks of fasting very much. We used to go to the church, which was situated not far from the prison, two or three times every day. I had not been in a church for a very long time. The Lenten ritual, so familiar to me from my parents' home back in the distant days of my childhood, the solemn prayers, the prostrations – all this stirred up the far, remote past in me, reminding me of the years when I had been a child, and I remember how pleasant I found it when each morning we were taken out by guards with loaded rifles to walk to the church over ground that had frozen hard overnight. The guards did not come into the church, however. In the church we stood in a huddle right by the doors, in the very last row, where all we could catch of the service was the full-throated voice of the deacon and from time to time a glimpse of a black vestment, or the bald head of a priest through the crowd. I would remember how, standing in church as a child, I would sometimes look at the peasants who crowded at the entrance, moving aside deferentially to make way for someone wearing thick epaulettes, or a fat landowner, or a frilled and flounced, but extremely devout lady – people for whom nothing less than the very front row would do, and who were instantly ready to fight each other for a place at the front. It used to seem to me that back there by the entrance people prayed differently from us – they prayed humbly and fervently, and they prostrated themselves as though fully admitting their own lowly station.

Now it was my turn to stand back there, and even further back: we were in fetters, and exposed to public disgrace; everyone avoided us, feared us, even, and on each occasion we were given alms. I remember that I found even this pleasant – it was an experience that contained a peculiar, subtle flavour of enjoyment. 'If this is how it is to be, so be it,' I would think. The convicts took their prayers very seriously, and each time they came to church each one of them would bring his widow's mite with which to buy a candle or contribute to the collection. 'I'm somebody, too,' was what they thought or felt as they gave it up – 'Everyone's equal before God ...' We took communion at early mass. When, with the chalice in his hands, the priest came to the words '... receive me, O Lord, even as the robber',[35] nearly all the convicts fell kneeling to the ground with a jangling of fetters, apparently interpreting these words as a literal expression of their own thoughts.

But now it was Holy Week. The authorities presented each man with an egg and a hunk of white milk bread. Once again the priest came visiting with his cross, again there were visits from officials, the thick, substantial soup, the drunkenness and loafing around – all just as it had been at Christmas, with the only difference being that now one could walk around in the prison yard and bask in the sun. Things felt lighter and more spacious than they had done in winter, but at the same time they somehow seemed more melancholy. The long, endless summer days somehow grew peculiarly intolerable on holidays. At least work made the ordinary days seem shorter.

The tasks we had to do in summer proved to be much more arduous than the winter ones. Most of the summer work was centred around various engineering and construction projects. The convicts did bricklaying and dug foundations; there were others who worked as carpenters, locksmiths or as painters, carrying out repair and maintenance work on the government buildings. Yet others went to the brickworks to make bricks. The men considered this the most arduous work of all. The brickworks were situated some three or four versts from the fortress. Throughout the summer, at about six o'clock each morning, a gang of fifty convicts was sent off to make bricks. The men who were chosen for this job were manual workers, men who had no skill or trade. They took bread with them, as the site was too far away to make it worth their coming back in the middle of the day to eat, and thereby have to walk eight versts extra. They ate their main meal of the day in the evening, when they returned to the prison. The assignment was given for the whole day, and it was such that a convict could scarcely complete it in the time allotted. First one had to dig up clay and carry it to the site; then one had to fetch water and trample the clay in a clay pit; and finally one had to make from the clay a very large number of bricks, about two hundred, I think it was, or maybe even two hundred and fifty. I only went to the brickworks on two occasions in all. The brick-makers used to come back in the evenings tired and exhausted, and all summer long they would reproach the other convicts with the fact that they were doing the heaviest work. In this they seemed to find some consolation. None the less, there were some men who even showed a certain willingness to go to the brickworks; for one thing, the work took one away from the town; the worksite was open and unconfined, on the banks of the Irtysh. At any rate, it was a lot more cheerful to be able to look around one for a change instead of at those dreary prison surroundings. One could smoke if one wished, and even lie down for half an hour – a great treat. As for myself, I either carried on going to the workshop as before, or hauled bricks on one of the construction sites. Doing this latter work, I once had to haul bricks from the bank of the Irtysh to a barracks that was being built some two hundred yards away on the other side of the fortress rampart, and this work continued for some six months without a break. I found that I almost liked the work, even though the rope in which I had to haul the bricks constantly rubbed my shoulders raw. What I liked was that this work was quite visibly developing my physical strength. At first I could only haul eight bricks at a time; each brick weighed twelve pounds. But later on, I could haul up to twelve and fifteen bricks at a time, and this pleased me greatly. Physical, no less than moral strength is required in penal servitude if one is to survive all the material deprivations of that accursed existence.

And I wanted to go on living after I had left prison . . .

I liked hauling bricks, however, not only because the work strengthened my body, but also because it was done on the banks of the Irtysh. I speak of this river bank so often because it was only from there that one could see God's world, the pure, clear distance, the free, uninhabited steppes, the desolation of which had a strange effect on me. It was only on the river bank that one could turn one's back to the fortress and shut it from sight. All the other places where we worked were either inside the fortress or alongside it. From my very earliest days in it, I conceived a deep aversion for this fortress and especially for certain buildings in it. The house of our Major seemed a particularly foul and accursed place, and I looked at it with loathing whenever I passed it. But on the river bank one could forget oneself: one would look at that immense, vacant landscape in the way a prisoner looks out at freedom from the window of his cell. Everything here was beloved and enchanting to me: the brilliant, hot sun in the bottomless blue sky, and the distant singing of a Kirghiz peasant floating across from the Kirghiz side of the river. One would scrutinize the distance for a long time and at last make out the poor, smoke-stained yurt of some nomad; one would see a wisp of smoke above the yurt, a Kirghiz woman fussing over her two rams. The whole scene would be one of poverty and a primitive wildness. One would catch a glimpse of a bird in the blue, transparent air and follow its flight for a long time, attentively: now it would skim the water, now disappear into the blue, then appear again, a barely decipherable moving point ... Even a poor, unhealthy-looking flower which I found during the early spring in a cleft of the rocky river bank exercised a morbid fascination on me. The anguish, the depression I experienced during that first year were unbearable, and they made me bitter and irritable. Because of them I failed to notice much of what was going on around me in the first year. I closed my eyes to it all and did not want to look. I did not notice, among the malicious, hostile convicts who were my companions, the good men, the men who were capable of thinking and feeling in spite of this repellent outer crust. In the midst of all the caustic remarks I would sometimes fail to notice words that were kind and friendly, and which were all the more welcome because spoken without any ulterior motive, often straight from the heart, by men who had perhaps suffered and endured more than I had. But why waste space on this? I was extremely glad if I managed to be thoroughly tired out when I got back to barracks: I might get to sleep! For sleeping was atrociously difficult in summer, almost more so than in winter. It is true that the evenings were sometimes very pleasant. The sun, which had hung above the prison yard all day, would begin to move down the horizon at last. The air would grow cooler, and then the almost cold (relatively speaking) night of the steppe would fall. The convicts used to wander in droves about the yard as they waited to be locked up for the night. Most of them would herd together in the kitchen, though. In there, crucial questions of prison were constantly being discussed, there were debates on all kinds of questions; sometimes there would be an investigation of some rumour, often something which was absurd, but which excited to an extraordinary degree the interest of these men who had been suspended from contact with the rest of the world. There was, for example, a rumour that the Major was to be given the sack. The convicts were as gullible as children; they themselves knew that the rumour was nonsense, that it had been started by a notorious chatterbox and 'buffoon' – the convict Kvasov, whom everyone had long ago stopped believing and who did nothing but tell lies – and yet all the men had seized on his tidings, discussing them and weighing them up, enjoying themselves and finally growing angry with themselves, ashamed of ever having listened to Kvasov.

'Who's ever going to sack him!' one man cried. 'His neck's far too thick, he'll just shake them off.'

'Yes, but he's got superiors, you know!' retorted another, a strong-headed, intelligent man who had seen a few things in his time, but was one of life's born arguers.

'Crow don't peck crow's eyes out,' observed a third, grey-headed man morosely, as if to himself, as he finished his soup alone in a corner.

'You don't suppose his superiors are going to come and ask you if they should sack him or not, do you?' added a fourth man indifferently, picking out a few desultory notes on his balalaika.

'And why not?' retorted the second man furiously. 'All us poor beggars could ask for it, see, we could all give evidence if they started questioning us. Instead we waste our time blabbering, and when it comes to the crunch we don't do a thing.'

'What do you expect?' said the balalaika player. 'That's what prison's all about.'

'What about what happened the other day?' the argumentative man continued feverishly, not listening to him. 'There was a bit of flour left over. We collected all the scrapings, the very last morsels of the stuff they were, see; we were going to have them taken away and sold. But oh no, he found out what we were up to; somebody informed on us; they confiscated the flour – "interests of economy", they called it. Can that be right, I ask you?'

'So who are you going to complain to?'

'Who do you think? To the inspector who's coming, of course.'

'Which inspector's that?'

'It's true, lads, there's an inspector coming,' said a lively young man who had been a clerk and could read and write – he was reading *The Duchess Lavallière*, or something of that sort. He was always high-spirited and entertaining, but the men also respected him for a certain knowledge and experience of worldly matters. Not paying any attention to the universal curiosity he had aroused with regard to the impending visit of the inspector, he went straight up to the 'cookmaid' and asked him for some liver. Our cooks often did a bit of business on the side like this. They might, for example, buy a large piece of liver with their own money, cook it and sell it to the convicts in small portions.

'Half a copeck or a copeck?' asked the coc

'Give me a copeck's worth – I'll make them all jealous!' replied the convict. 'It's a general, lads, a general from St Petersburg that's coming; he's going to inspect the whole of Siberia. It's a fact. They were talking about it up at the governor's house.'

The news caused an unusual stir among the men. The questions kept up for a good quarter of an hour: who was this, what kind of a general was he, what was his rank, and was he more senior than the generals in our town? Convicts are on the whole very fond of discussing ranks, officials – which are more senior than others, which can be overruled and which can do the overruling. They will even argue the merits of one general over another so heatedly that they almost come to blows. It might be wondered what the point of all this is; but the fact remains that a detailed knowledge of the generals and of the powers that be is the measuring-stick by which the degree of a man's knowledge, good taste and previous standing in society is gauged. The subject of the higher authorities is widely considered by the convicts to be the most elegant and important topic of conversation in the prison.

'So you see, it is true, they are going to sack the Major after all,' said Kvasov. He was a small, red-faced man, emotional and extremely muddle-headed. It was he that had been the first to announce the news about the Major.

'He'll bribe his way out of it,' the sullen-looking, grey-haired convict, who had now finished his soup, retorted abruptly.

'And what a bribe it'll be!' said another. 'He's raked in a fair bit of money with all those raids of his. He was in charge of a battalion before he came to us. Only the other day he was trying to get himself married to the priest's daughter.'

'Yes, but he didn't make it, did he? They showed him the door; that means he's poor. What kind of a husband would he make? All he's got is the clothes he's standing up in. He lost everything he owned at cards back at Easter. Fedka told me.'

'No, the man's not extravagant, he's just a sieve.'

'Ah, my friend, I was married too, once: it's no good a poor man getting married: if he does, the night'll always be too short for him,' observed Skuratov, choosing this moment to enter the conversation.

'Well what do you know? You're the one we're talking about,' said the free-and-easy clerk. 'I'm telling you, Kvasov, you're a real idiot. Do you think the Major would ever be able to bribe a general like that, do you think a general like that would come specially all the way from St Petersburg just to inspect the Major? You're soft on top, my boy, that's what I'd say.'

'What, you mean because he's a general he won't take the bribe?' asked someone in the crowd, sceptically.

'Course he won't; if he does, it'll have to be a whopper.'

'Yes, he'll take a whopper, as befits his rank.'

'Generals always accept bribes,' observed Kvasov, firmly.

'You've had experience of giving them, I suppose?' said Baklushin, who had suddenly come in, with contempt. 'I bet you've never even seen a general in all your born days!'

'Course I have.'

'Liar.'

'Liar yourself.'

'Here, lads, if it's true he's seen a general, let's hear him tell us all what general it is he knows. Come on, tell us, because I know all the generals.'

'I've seen General Zibert,' answered Kvasov, somewhat uncertainly.

'Zibert? There's no such general. He must have looked you in the rear, this Zibert, when he was still just a lieutenant-colonel, and you were so scared you thought he was a general.'

'No, you listen to me,' howled Skuratov, 'because I'm a married man. There really was a General Zibert in Moscow, he was from one of those German families, but he was a Russian. He used to say confession to a Russian priest every year at Assumption time, and he was that fond of drinking water, lads, he was like a duck. Every day he drank forty glasses of Moscow river-water. They used to say he took it as a cure for some complaint or other, his manservant told me so.'

'And I suppose he kept carp in all that water in his belly, did he?' asked the convict with the balalaika.

'That's enough out of you! We're talking about a serious matter, but you ... Who's this inspector, then, lads?' a restless old convict asked, thoughtfully; this was Martynov – he had served in the army as a hussar.

'It's all a load of rubbish!' observed one of the sceptics. 'What will they think of next? Rubbish, the lot if it!'

'It's not rubbish,' said Kulikov dogmatically. Until now he had preserved a majestic silence. He was a man of some authority, aged about fifty. He had an extremely handsome face and a manner that was somehow contemptuously majestic. Of this he was aware, and was proud of it. He was part gipsy, had earned his living as a horse doctor, and was now one of the prison vodka sellers. He was a clever man and had seen a lot of the world. He let his words fall as if they were silver rubles he was giving away.

'It's true, boys,' he continued quietly. 'I heard about it last week; there's a general coming, one of the really high-up ones, he's going to do an inspection tour of the whole of Siberia. Of course, they'll all try to bribe him, all of them, that is, except old Eight-Eyes: he won't dare to go near him. Generals are all different, you know, boys. They come in all shapes and sizes. All I can tell you is that no matter what happens, our Major will stay right where he is now. That's certain. We've all had our tongues cut out, and none of the higher-ups are going to tell on their own kind. The inspector'll take a look at the prison, then he'll go away and report that he found everything working fine ...'

'That's as may be, lads, but the Major's got the wind up: he's drunk first thing every morning.'

'He drives a different cart in the evenings. Fedka told me.'

'You can't wash a black dog white. It's not anything new, him being drunk, is it?'

'Here, what sort of a do is that, if not even the general lifts a finger! It's high time folk stopped pandering to their stupid honours!' the convicts said among themselves, getting excited.

The news of the inspector's visit passed round the prison in a flash. Men wandered about the yard, impatiently reiterating the tidings to one another. Others said nothing on purpose, preserving an air of indifference and thereby apparently trying to give themselves more importance. Yet others really were and remained indifferent. Convicts with balalaikas sat on the steps leading up to each barrack. Some of them chatted and talked. Others sang, but in general all the men were in a state of extreme excitement that evening.

At about ten o'clock we were all counted, herded into our different barracks and locked up for the night. The nights were short: we were woken at around five o'clock in the morning, yet we never all got to sleep before eleven at night. Until eleven there was constant bustle and conversation and sometimes, as in winter, there were *maydans* as well. The night brought intolerable heat and airlessness. Though waves of cold night air did come in through the open window, the convicts tossed and turned on the plank bed all night, as if in delirium. There were teeming myriads of fleas. We had them in winter as well, in fairly large numbers, but from the beginning of spring onwards they multiplied in such quantities that, although I had heard about this phenomenon, I had not been able to believe it until I had experienced it for myself. And the nearer summer came, the meaner and more vicious the fleas became. It is true that one may get used to fleas; I myself found that this was so; but none the less they are a sore trial of a man's endurance. They used to torment you to the point where you lay at last in a kind of fever, with no sense of sleeping at all, only of delirium. When finally, just before morning, the fleas subsided, as if the life had gone out of them, and just when you seemed to fall into a delicious sleep in the chill morning air, the pitiless tattoo of the drum would suddenly start up outside the prison gate, and reveille would begin. Cursing, huddled in your sheepskin coat, you would listen to the loud, clear sounds as though you were counting them, while through your sleep would break the intolerable thought that this was how it was going to be tomorrow, and the day after that, and so on for several years on end, right up to the very day you got your freedom. You would ask yourself when it would come, that freedom, where it was. But now you had to wake up; the everyday jostling and coming and going had started ... Men were getting dressed, hurrying to work. It was true that you could sleep again for an hour at midday.

The story about the inspector turned out to be true. The rumours grew stronger and stronger each day, and at last everyone knew for a certainty that a high-up general was coming to do an inspection tour of the whole of Siberia, that he had in fact already arrived and was in Tobolsk. Fresh rumours arrived in the prison every day. There was news from the town, too: it was said that everybody had got the wind up, that there was a great commotion as they all tried to present the best possible appearance. The higher administration was apparently organizing receptions, balls and other grand occasions. The convicts were sent out in droves to level the streets in the fortress, pull up tussocks of grass, paint the fences and the fence-posts, do re-plastering, greasing – in short, they were trying in one fell swoop to put right everything that would be the object of inspection. The men knew very well what was afoot and they discussed it with ever-increasing fervour and good humour. The scope of their imaginings reached colossal dimensions. They were even getting ready to present a *complaint* if the general were to ask them whether they were satisfied with their living conditions. And all the while they quarrelled and shouted abuse at one another. The Major was in a great state of excitement. His visits to the prison grew more frequent, he shouted at the men more often, struck them, had individual convicts taken to the guardhouse and showed a revived interest in cleanliness and proper behaviour. As luck would have it, at about this time a small incident took place in the prison, one which did not at all upset the Major in the way it might have been expected to, but which on the contrary seemed to please him. In the course of a fight one convict stabbed another in the chest, just below the heart.

The convict who committed this crime was called Lomov; the wounded man was known to everybody as Gavrilka; he was a hardened vagrant. I do not recall if he had a second name – we always called him Gavrilka.

Lomov came of a prosperous peasant family from T. province in the K. district. The Lomov family lived together in one place: there were the old father, the three sons and the father's brother.

They were wealthy muzhiks. People all over the province said of them that their capital amounted to as much as three hundred thousand rubles in paper money. They ploughed the land, dressed hides, traded, but occupied themselves primarily with moneylending, the concealment of stolen property and other similarly shady business. Half the peasants in the district were in debt to them, working for them as bonded slaves. The Lomovs had the reputations of being clever, wily muzhiks, but in the end they had started to get too big for their boots, especially when a certain very important local bigwig took to making stops at their house whenever he was *en route* somewhere, grew personally acquainted with old man Lomov and got to like him for his sharp insight and resourcefulness. The Lomovs suddenly took it into their heads that there was nothing they could not do, and they began to run ever greater risks in illegal enterprises of various kinds. Everyone grumbled about them; everyone wished the earth would open and swallow them up; but they just strutted around more and more conceitedly. District police officers and assessors were nothing to them. In the end they went off the rails and lost everything, not, however, because of their delinquency or any of the secret crimes they had committed, but because of a completely nonsensical, trumped-up charge. They owned a large farm situated some ten versts from the village, the kind of property that is known in Siberia as a 'holding'. One autumn they had six Kirghiz farmhands living there, men who had worked for them as bonded slaves for as long as anyone could remember. In the course of a single night all these Kirghiz farmhands were murdered. An investigation was begun, one that dragged on for a long time. During the investigation a lot of other unpleasant things were brought to light. The Lomovs were accused of killing their farmhands. They themselves told the story, and the whole prison knew it; it was suspected that they owed the farmhands an enormous sum of money in wages, and that in spite of their great wealth they were mean and greedy, and had murdered the Kirghiz farmhands in order to get out of paying their debt. In the course of the legal proceedings and the trial the whole of their wealth was liquidated. The old man died. His sons were sent to various places of exile. The father's brother and one of the sons

ended up in our prison doing sentences of twelve years each. And
for what? They were both completely innocent of the deaths of the
Kirghiz farmhands. Some time later Gavrilka, too, made his appearance in our prison; he was a notorious chiseller and vagrant,
a cheerful, and aggressive character who had taken the blame for
all the murders. Although I never heard him admit to having done
them, everybody in the prison was quite convinced that the Kirghiz
farmhands had been his victims. Gavrilka's dealings with the
Lomovs dated from the time when he had still been a vagrant. He
had arrived in the prison to do a short sentence for desertion from
the army and for vagrancy. He had murdered the Kirghiz farmhands with the assistance of three other vagrants; they had thought
they might get rich quickly by plundering the holding.

The Lomovs were not liked in our prison, of that I am certain.
One of them, the nephew, was an excellent fellow, intelligent and
easy to get along with; but his uncle, the man who had stabbed
Gavrilka with the awl, was a slow-witted, cantankerous muzhik. He
had quarrelled with many of the convicts before, and they had
never failed to give him a good beating. Everyone liked Gavrilka
because of his cheerful, harmonious temperament. Even though the
Lomovs knew that it was he who was responsible for the murders
and that they had been sent to prison for what he had done, they
did not quarrel with him; and he for his part never paid them the
slightest attention. Then quite suddenly a quarrel started between
Gavrilka and the uncle; it was about a whore. Gavrilka had begun
to boast of her favours; the muzhik had grown jealous, and one fine
noon had stabbed him with an awl.

Although the trial had ruined the Lomovs, in the prison they
lived like kings. It seemed they had money. They kept a samovar,
drank tea. Our Major was aware of this and nursed a violent hatred
towards both the Lomovs. He made no bones about finding fault
with them in front of everyone, and in general did his best to make
their lives a misery. The Lomovs' explanation for this was that the
Major was trying to extort a bribe from them. But they never gave
him anything.

Of course, if Lomov had only stuck the awl in a bit further he
would have killed Gavrilka. But the affair had ended in no more

than a few scratches. The Major was informed. I remember the way he came tearing in, out of breath and obviously pleased. He treated Gavrilka in a remarkably affectionate manner, just as if he were his own son.

'Now then, my lad, do you think you can manage to walk to the hospital or not? No, we'd better take you there by carriage. Get a horse ready for him!' he shouted to the duty sergeant, making a show of great haste.

'But really, your honour, I can't feel a thing. He barely grazed me, your honour.'

'You never know, you never know, my dear young fellow; we must wait and see ... It's a dangerous place for a wound; it all depends on the place; right under the heart, the bandit! And as for you,' he roared at Lomov, 'I'll give you what for ... To the guard-house with you!'

And he really did give him what for. Lomov was brought to trial, and though the wound was the very merest scratch, the intention was clear. The offender had the length of his sentence increased, and was given a thousand lashes. The Major was quite content ...

Finally the inspector arrived.

He came to visit our prison on his second day in the town. This happened to be a holiday. Several days previously everything in the prison had been washed, polished and licked into shape. The convicts had all had their heads freshly shaven. They wore white, clean clothing. In summer all the men wore the regulation white linen jackets and trousers. On the back of each man's jacket a black circle, some four inches in diameter, was sewn. For a whole hour the convicts were instructed in how to answer if by chance the exalted visitor should greet them. Rehearsals were held. The Major fussed about like a madman. An hour before the general was due to appear, all the men were standing to attention at their posts like statues. Finally, at one o'clock, the general arrived. He was a high-up general, so high-up that it seemed every administrative heart throughout all Western Siberia must tremble at his approach. His entrance was severe and majestic; behind him reeled a large retinue of local officialdom, including several generals and colonels. There was one civilian, a tall, handsome gentleman in a tail-coat and city

shoes who had also come from St Petersburg and who wore an air
of great ease and independence. The general turned to him often
with great politeness. This the convicts found quite fascinating: the
man was a civilian, yet he was treated with such esteem, and by a
general such as this one, too! Later on they found out the civilian's
surname, and who he was, but before that speculation was rife. Our
Major, attired in a tight-fitting uniform with an orange collar, his
eyes bloodshot, his face purple and covered in pimples, did not
seem to make a particularly favourable impression on the general.
Out of especial regard for the exalted visitor the Major had not put
his glasses on. He stood some distance away, as stiff as a poker, and
his whole being seemed to be feverishly awaiting the moment when
he might be required to fly into action in order to fulfil some request
of His Excellency. He was not, however, required to do anything.
The general made the rounds of the barracks in silence, took a look
in the kitchen, apparently tried the soup. I was pointed out to him:
I had done this and that, and was a nobleman.

'Aha!' replied the general. 'And how is he behaving himself now?'

'Satisfactorily, so far, your excellency,' was the answer.

The general nodded, and some two minutes later he left the
prison. The convicts were of course dazzled and overawed, but they
were also left in a state of some bewilderment. The idea of making
a *complaint* to the general about the Major was now of course quite
out of the question. And indeed, the Major had been quite confident beforehand that this was how it would be.

* 6 *

PRISON ANIMALS

For the convicts, the purchase of the bay horse Gnedko which took
place in the prison soon afterwards was a much more pleasant and
engaging form of entertainment than the general's visit. It was the
custom for there to be a horse in the prison for the carting of water,
refuse and the like. A convict was designated to look after it. He

also drove it, accompanied by a guard, of course. There was more than enough for our horse both morning and evening. The old Gnedko had worked for us for a very long time. He was a willing brute, but worn out. One fine morning, just before St Peter's Day, he fell down as he was bringing in the evening barrel of water, and died a few moments later. The men were very sorry for him, and they all gathered round him, discussing and arguing. The former cavalrymen, gipsies, vets and so on whom we had among us took advantage of this occasion to air a great deal of specialized knowledge about horses, and even started quarrelling with one another on the subject – but they could not bring Gnedko back to life. The horse lay dead, with a swollen belly which everyone seemed to feel obliged to poke with their fingers; the Major was informed of the act of God that had taken place, and he decided that a new horse must be bought forthwith. On the morning of St Peter's Day, when we were all gathered together after mass, some horses that were for sale were brought in. It went without saying that it was the convicts themselves who were responsible for making the purchase. Among us there were some real connoisseurs, and it would have been hard to swindle two hundred and fifty men who in their previous lives had concerned themselves with little else. Kirghiz peasants, horsedealers, gipsies and tradesmen all came forward. The convicts awaited the appearance of each new horse with impatience. They were as happy as young children. Most flattering of all to them was that here they were almost like free men; it was as if they were buying a horse for *themselves* out of their *own* money, with full entitlement to do so. Three horses were brought and led away again, the fourth animal being the one that was selected for purchase. The horsedealers who had come in looked around them with a certain amount of wonder and timidity, and from time to time gave a backward glance at the guards who were accompanying them. The two-hundred-strong band of these men, shaven, branded, in fetters, on their home ground inside their prison retreat, the threshold of which no one from outside ever crosses, demanded its own form of respect. The men used up all their resources of cunning as they tested each new horse that was brought in. They would examine and feel every part of the animal's body with a

businesslike, serious, preoccupied air, as though the very well-being
of the prison depended on it. The Circassians even mounted the
horses and took them for a gallop; their eyes burned, and they
jabbered to one another in their incomprehensible dialect, baring
their white teeth and nodding their swarthy, hook-nosed profiles.
Some of the Russian convicts seemed compeletely riveted by the
arguing of these men; they looked as though they would have liked
to leap forward and embrace them. They could not understand the
words being spoken, but they tried to guess the verdict by the
expression in the Circassians' eyes; would the horse do or not? Such
intensely concentrated attention would have seemed strange to any
casual observer, who might have wondered what it was that
agitated these convicts so, especially men like these who were
normally so humble, so downtrodden, and who did not even dare
to utter a word in the presence of others of their own kind. It was
as if they were buying the horse for themselves, as if it were very far
from being a matter of indifference to them which animal was
bought. Apart from the Circassians, it was the former gipsies and
horsedealers who were most prominent: they were given priority of
place, and their opinions were listened to first. There was even a
kind of well-mannered duel between two of the men: the convict
Kulikov, formerly a gipsy horse thief and horse-trader, and a self-
taught vet, a wily Siberian muzhik who had only recently come to
the prison and who had already managed to take over the whole
of Kulikov's veterinary practice in the town. Before the arrival of
Yolkin (the Siberian muzhik) Kulikov had had no rivals; he had
run a large practice and had of course received financial rewards
for his services. He was up to every gipsy, charlatan trick in the
book and was far less knowledgeable than he pretended to be. As
far as his income was concerned, he was an aristocrat compared to
the rest of us. His experience, intelligence, boldness and determination had long brought him the involuntary respect of all the convicts in the prison. He was listened to and obeyed. But he did not
talk much: when he did say anything, it was as if he were parting
with a silver ruble, and he only opened his mouth when something
really important was at stake. He was a real dandy, but he did have
a great deal of genuine, authentic energy. He was already getting

on in years, but he was very handsome and very intelligent. For us noblemen he reserved a certain refined courtesy, blended with an extraordinary sense of personal dignity. I think that if he had been dressed up and brought along as Count Someone-or-the-other to some club in the capital, he would have found his feet at once, would have played whist, talked brilliantly – not a great deal, but with authority – and no one throughout the whole evening would probably ever have guessed that he was not a count but a vagrant. I am quite serious about this: so clever, keen-witted and quick on the uptake was he. What was more, his manners were excellent, foppish even. He must have seen something of the world in his time. But his past was shrouded in a mist of uncertainty. He was in the special category. However, with the arrival of Yolkin who, although he was a muzhik was a most wily specimen of the breed, about fifty years of age and a religious dissenter, Kulikov's veterinary glory began to fade. Within the space of some two months, Yolkin had succeeded in taking over almost all of Kulikov's town practice.

Yolkin was successful in treating with very little difficulty cases which Kulikov had refused to have anything to do with. Yolkin even cured horses which the town's regular vets had not wanted to treat, considering them incurable. This muzhik had been sent to our prison together with some other men for petty counterfeiting. What could have led him to get mixed up in such things at his age? Laughingly he used to tell us how they had needed three gold coins in order to make one counterfeit one. Kulikov was rather miffed by Yolkin's success as a vet, and indeed his renown was beginning to fade among the convicts. He kept a mistress in the suburbs, went around in a long-waisted velveteen coat, wore a silver ring on his finger and another on his ear, and had boots of his own with fancy edgings: now, suddenly, for lack of income, he had been compelled to become a 'barman', and for this reason everyone expected that the two enemies would very likely have a go at one another over the purchase of the new Gnedko. The men were awaiting this event with curiosity. Kulikov and Yolkin each had their supporters. The leaders of both these teams were already starting to get worked up and to hurl abuse at each other. Yolkin was already on the point of twisting his wily face into its most sarcastic smile. But it was not to be like this: Kulikov did not turn nasty, but acted in a masterly fashion, without the slightest unpleasantness. He began by conceding a few points, even listening with respect to his rival's criticisms; but seizing on one of the latter's assertions, pointed out to him modestly and firmly that he was mistaken; and, before Yolkin could gather his wits together and talk his way out of it, Kulikov proved that he was mistaken in precisely this respect and that. In short, all the wind was taken out of Yolkin's sails in the most unexpected and skilful manner, and although he still emerged as the winner, Kulikov's supporters were content.

'No, boys, he's not so easily put off, he stands up for himself, you bet he does!' some of the men said.

'Yolkin knows more,' others observed, in a rather conciliatory tone, however. Both teams suddenly started to make up to each other.

'It isn't that he knows more, it's just that he has a lighter touch. And where cattle are concerned, Kulikov can handle anything.'

'He can handle anything, that lad.'

'Anything at all . . .'

The new Gnedko was at last chosen and bought. He was a magnificent beast, young, fine-looking and strong, with the most affectionate and frisky manner. He was of course beyond reproach in every other respect, too. The men began to bargain: the owner wanted thirty rubles; the men were only prepared to pay twenty-five. The haggling was intense and lasted a long time, as the price was gradually reduced, and the owner gave way. In the end the men started to find the whole business ridiculous.

'Going to pay for it out of your own pocket, are you?' some of the men asked. 'What's the point of bargaining like this?'

'Are you trying to save the government a bit of money, then?'

'Come on, lads, it's still money, you know. It belongs to the artel . . .'

'The artel! Well, there's one born every minute . . .'

The bargaining finally ceased with the price fixed at twenty-eight rubles. The Major was told, and the purchase confirmed. Bread and salt were of course produced, and the new Gnedko was led into the prison in proper fashion. I do not think there was a single convict who on this occasion did not pat Gnedko on his neck or stroke his muzzle. That very same day Gnedko was set to the task of carting our water, and everyone watched with curiosity as the new Gnedko brought the barrel in. Roman, our water-carrier, eyed the new horse with extreme satisfaction. He was a muzhik of about fifty, imperturbable and taciturn by disposition. It is a fact that nearly all Russian coachmen are of an imperturbable and taciturn disposition, as if it really were true that the constant handling of horses gives a man an especially stoical and dignified temperament. Roman was quiet, kindly disposed towards everyone, and tight-lipped. He took snuff from a snuffhorn, and had driven the prison's Gnedkos for as long as anyone could remember. The horse that had just been bought was the third Gnedko the prison had had. All the men were agreed that a bay (*gnedoy*) horse was the right colour for a prison, that it somehow 'matched our home environment'. Roman was also of this opinion. Not for anything in the world would the men have bought a skewbald horse, for example. The job of water-carrier was reserved in perpetuity for Roman as if by right, and none of us would ever have dreamt of questioning that right. When the old Gnedko had fallen down and died, no one, not even the Major, had thought of blaming Roman for it: it was the will of God, quite simply, and Roman was a good coachman. The new Gnedko soon became the darling of the prison. Although the convicts were a grim bunch of men, they would often go up to the horse and stroke it. Sometimes when Roman came back from the river he would get down from his cart in order to close the gate which the duty sergeant had opened for him, and Gnedko, now inside the prison, would stand with the barrel, waiting for him, giving him a sidelong look. 'Go on your own!' Roman would shout to the animal, and Gnedko would immediately start drawing the cart alone, would take it as far as the kitchen and then stop, waiting for the cooks and the *parashniks* with their buckets for the water. 'He did it on his own! He always does what he's told.'

'I don't know: he's just a poor animal, but he understands.'

'Good boy, Gnedko!'

Gnedko would shake his head and snort, as if he really did

understand and was pleased with the praise he received. And someone would be sure to take a piece of bread and salt out to him right
there and then. Gnedko would eat it and toss his head again, as if
to say: 'I know you, indeed I do! I'm a nice horse and you're a good
man.'

I was also fond of taking Gnedko's bread out to him. I enjoyed looking at his handsome muzzle and feeling his soft, warm
teeth in the palm of my hand as he nimbly polished off what I gave
him.

Our convicts would on the whole have been kind to animals, had
they been allowed to keep them; they would have liked nothing
better than to raise a great number of domestic animals and birds
in the prison grounds. What better way could there have been, one
might suppose, of mitigating and improving the grim, ferocious
character of such men, than a pastime such as this? But it was not
permitted. Neither our routine nor the nature of the place made it
possible.

Nevertheless, during my time there the prison did have one or
two animals in it. Apart from Gnedko, we had dogs, geese, the goat
Vaska, and – for a time – an eagle.

As I mentioned earlier, the prison had a dog called Sharik, an
intelligent, affectionate creature with which I was friendly. Dogs
are, however, regarded by the common people as unclean animals,
undeserving of attention, and so Sharik was ignored by most of the
men. The dog got by somehow, slept in the yard, ate scraps from
the kitchen, and was of no especial interest to anyone; but it knew
everyone, and considered everyone its master. When the convicts
were returning from work, Sharik would run to the gate at the
shouted command 'Corporals!' which came from the guardhouse,
and greet the members of each work party affectionately, wagging
his tail and giving each man a friendly look as he came in, hoping
to be patted or stroked. But for many years he had not been patted
or stroked by anyone except myself, and for this reason he liked me
better than any of the other convicts. I cannot remember now how
it came to be that another dog, Belka, appeared in the prison. I was
responsible for introducing a third dog, Kultyapka; I had brought
him back, still a puppy, from the place I had been working in. Belka

was a strange creature. Someone had once run him over with a cart,
and his spine was dented; when he ran it looked from afar as though
one were seeing two white animals that had grown together. He was
covered in some sort of mange, and his eyes were festering; his tail
was bare and scruffy, almost hairless, and it was forever between
his legs. Thus smitten by the outrages of fortune, he had apparently
decided to resign himself. He never barked or growled at anyone;
it was as though he did not dare to. For most of the time he hung
about behind the barracks, since it was there that he was mostly
likely to find things to eat; if he caught sight of any of us, he would
roll over onto his back when we were still some yards away, as a
sign of submission, as if to say: 'Do with me what you like, I won't
protest.' And every convict in front of whom he rolled over in this
way would give him a jab with his boot, as if he considered himself
under an obligation to do so. 'Filthy brute,' the convicts would say.
But Belka did not even dare to yelp, and if he really did feel the pain
he would just moan softly and plaintively. He would go through the
same performance of rolling over on his back whenever he encountered Sharik or any of the dogs he met on his forays outside the
prison. He would roll over and lie still submissively whenever any
big, lop-eared dog rushed at him, snarling and barking. But dogs
like submissiveness and obedience in one another, and the ferocious
dog would immediately quieten down, pausing with a certain
reflectiveness above the obedient dog that lay before it with its legs
in the air, and would begin to sniff it slowly all over. What thoughts
passed through Belka's head as he lay there, trembling from head
to foot? 'Is he going to maul me, the bandit?' was probably one of
them. But once he had sniffed Belka all over, the dog would leave
him alone, finding him to be of no special interest. Belka would
immediately leap up again, and hobble off after the long procession
of dogs that were following some Zhuchka or other. And although
he knew for a certainty that he would never be on intimate terms
with the bitch, this hobbling after her in the distance was none the
less a consolation in his misfortunes. He had obviously given up
thinking about such things as honour. Having lost all his prospects
for the future, he now lived for nothing but food and quite freely
admitted this to himself. I once attempted to give him a pat; this

was such a novel and unexpected experience for him that all of a
sudden he sank down on all fours, trembling all over, and began
to whine loudly with tender emotion. I used to pat him often, as
I felt sorry for him. For his part, he could not meet me without
whining. He would see me from afar and whine, whine piteously
and ailingly. In the end he was torn to pieces by other dogs on the
rampart outside the prison.

Kultyapka was quite a different sort of dog in temperament. Why
I brought him from the workshop to the prison when he was still
a blind puppy, I do not really know. I enjoyed feeding him and
rearing him. Sharik quickly took Kultyapka under his wing and
slept in the same place with him. When Kultyapka began to get a
bit bigger, Sharik let him bite his ears and pull at his coat, and
played with him in the way that grown dogs normally play with
puppies. It was an odd fact that Kultyapka hardly grew upwards
at all, but only lengthways and in breadth. He had a shaggy coat
of a sort of light, mousy colour; one of his ears flopped down, while
the other was erect. He had a volatile, enthusiastic temperament,
like every puppy who, overjoyed to see his master, whines, barks,
tries to lick his master's face, and is ready to display all his other
feelings as well: 'Just let me show you how enthusiastic I am, and
to hell with proper manners!' Wherever I was, at the call of
'Kultyapka' he would suddenly appear from some corner or other,
as if from beneath the earth, and would fly towards me, whining
with enthusiasm, rolling along like a ball, and making somersaults
in the air. I grew inordinately fond of this little monster. It seemed
that fate had prepared nothing but joy and contentment for him.
But one fine day the convict Neustroyev, who made women's shoes
and dressed hides, started paying him particular attention. Something had suddenly occurred to him. He called Kultyapka to him,
felt his coat and pushed him gently over onto his back. Kultyapka,
not suspecting anything, whined with contentment. But next
morning he had disappeared. I spent a long time looking for him;
it was as if he had vanished into thin air. Only after a few weeks
did all become clear: Neustroyev had been very taken with
Kultyapka's coat. He had skinned the dog, dressed the hide and
used it to line the velvet winter boots which the auditor's wife had

ordered from him. He showed me the boots when they were finished. The 'fur' looked beautiful. Poor Kultyapka!

Many of the convicts dressed hides, and they often brought into the prison dogs which had good coats and which disappeared almost instantly. Some of these dogs were stolen; others were bought. I remember seeing two convicts busily discussing something behind the kitchens one day. One of them was holding on a leash the most magnificent black dog, which obviously belonged to some expensive breed. Some good-for-nothing flunkey had abducted it from its master and sold it to our shoemakers for thirty silver copecks. These convicts were making preparations to hang it. That was done very easily; they would then skin the animal, and throw its carcase into the large, deep cesspit which was located in the rearmost corner of the prison grounds, and which stank to high heaven during the summer heatwaves. From time to time it was cleaned out. The poor dog appeared to understand the fate that lay in store for it. Searchingly it looked in turn at the three of us, only occasionally daring to wag its lowered, bushy tail, as if it desired to mollify us by this sign of its trust in us. I left as quickly as I could, and have no doubt that they concluded their business satisfactorily.

It was also by chance that we came to have geese in the prison. Who had bred them and who their rightful owners were I have no idea, but for a time they really kept the convicts amused, and even came to be talked about in the town. The goslings had been hatched out in the prison and were kept in the kitchen. When the brood had grown into young geese, the whole gaggle of them was in the habit of accompanying the convicts on their way to work. As soon as the drum was beaten and the work parties began to move towards the gate, our geese would run cackling after us, flapping their wings. One after the other they would flutter over the high bar of the gate and unfailingly waddle off towards the right flank, where they too would line up, awaiting the end of the drill. They always attached themselves to the largest party and would graze somewhere close by while the men were working. As soon as the party began to drift back to the prison again, they too would begin to move. The town was filled with talk about the geese that went to work with the convicts. 'Look at that, there's the convicts with their geese!'

passers-by would say. 'However did you manage to train them?' 'That's for your geese,' someone might add, giving us alms. However, in spite of all the devotion of those geese, every one of them was slaughtered for some feast day.

No one would ever have dreamed of slaughtering our goat, Vaska, but for a certain peculiar circumstance that arose. Again, I have no idea where he came from or who brought him in, but suddenly a pretty little white goat turned up in the prison. Within a few days he had succeeded in endearing himself to all of us, and he became a general source of entertainment, of consolation, even. The men thought up an excuse for keeping him: since there was a prison stable, there had to be a prison goat for it. However, the goat did not live in the stable, but began by being kept in the kitchen, and later roamed freely around the whole of the prison. He was a very graceful, frolicsome creature. He would come running at the call of his name, jumped up on benches and tables, butted the convicts and was always skittish and frisky. One evening – this was when Vaska's horns had begun to grow – the Lezghin Babay, who was sitting on the barrack steps with a crowd of other convicts, took it into his head to engage the goat in a butting match. They had been knocking their heads together for quite a time – this game with Vaska was a favourite pastime of the men – when Vaska suddenly bounded onto the topmost step of the entrance, and as soon as Babay turned away, pranced up in a flash, tucked in his front hooves and butted Babay in the back of the head with all his might, so that Babay was sent flying head over heels down the steps, much to the delight of all who were present, not least Babay himself. In short, everyone was very fond of Vaska. When he reached a certain age the men held a serious consultation, as a result of which a certain operation was performed on him that one of our vets was very good at. 'If he doesn't have it, he'll smell of goat,' the convicts said. After this operation, Vaska began to grow enormously fat. Indeed, it was as though he were being fattened for the kill. At last he grew into a fine goat, with very long horns. He was extraordinarily stout, and walked with a waddle. He also was in the habit of accompanying us to work, much to the general amusement of the convicts and of the passers-by we encountered. Everybody

knew Vaska, the prison goat. Sometimes, if they were working on
the river bank, for example, the convicts would gather supple
willow fronds and leaves from other plants and trees, together with
flowers from the rampart, and would deck Vaska out with them:
they would twine his horns round with sprays and flowers and
cover his entire body with garlands. Vaska always used to come
back to the prison ahead of the convicts, decked out and garlanded,
and they would follow him with something that bordered on pride
if any passers-by were watching. The goat's popularity reached
such heights that some of the men even conceived the idea, like
children, of coating its horns with gold leaf. They only talked of
doing this, however, and it was never actually done. I remember,
though, that I asked Akim Akimych, the best gilder we had after
Isay Fomich, whether it was really possible to gild the horns of a
goat. He started by having a good look at Vaska, gave the matter
serious consideration and then replied that it probably could be
done, 'but it would soon rub off and there really wouldn't be any
point in it'. That was the end of the matter. And Vaska might have
gone on living in the prison for a long time and died of shortness
of breath; but one day, as he was leading the convicts back from
work covered in his flowers and garlands, he ran into the Major,
who was driving along in his droshky. 'Stop!' the Major roared.
'Who does this goat belong to?' The matter was explained to him.
'What? A goat in the prison, and without my authorization?
Sergeant!' The sergeant appeared and the Major ordered him to
have the goat slaughtered instantly. It was to be flayed and its hide
sold at the bazaar, the money received from the sale to be paid into
the convicts' prison fund and the goat-meat added to their soup.
There was a lot of talk in the prison; a good deal of sorrow was
expressed, but no one dared disobey the Major's orders. Vaska was
slaughtered down by the cesspit. One of the convicts bought all the
meat, thus adding one and a half rubles to the prison fund.
Kalatches were bought with this money, and the man who had
bought Vaska sold the meat in portions for roasting. The meat was
really extraordinarily tasty.

We also had an eagle living in the prison with us for a time. It
was one of the breed known as *karakus*, the small eagle of the

steppes. Someone had brought it to the prison wounded and exhausted. All the convicts gathered round it in a circle; it was unable
to fly: its right wing trailed along on the ground, and one of its legs
was out of joint. I remember how fiercely it looked around it as it
eyed the inquisitive crowd of convicts, opening its humpbacked
beak as it prepared to put up a fight for its life. When the men had
had a good look at it and had started to go their separate ways, it
hobbled off, limping and flopping along on one leg, beating its
good wing in the air, to the very furthermost part of the prison
grounds, where it hid in a corner, pressing itself close against the
palings of the fence. It stayed there for about three months, never
once coming out from its corner. At first the men used to go to see
it frequently, and would set the dog on it. Sharik would fly at it
furiously, but seemed afraid to go right up to it; the convicts
thought this was very funny. 'Wild brute!' they would say. 'He'll
not give in!' Later on, Sharik began to torment the eagle viciously;
his fear vanished, and when he was let loose at the bird he always
contrived to grab it by its injured wing. The eagle would defend
itself, beak and claw, with all its might, and like some wounded
king, skulking in its corner, it would view the inquisitive beings that
had come to look at it with savage pride. At last all the men grew
bored with it; they turned their backs on it and forgot about it.
None the less, every day some scraps of fresh meat and a crock of
water appeared beside it. Someone was looking after it. At first it
would eat nothing, and went without food, but it would never take
it from anyone's hand, or if there were any people about. I observed
it from a distance on several occasions. If it did not see anyone
about and believed itself to be alone, it would sometimes venture
a little way out of its corner and hobble along beside the fence, some
twelve paces from its home, and then hobble back again, as if it were
taking physical exercise. If it caught sight of me, it would immediately scurry back to its corner as fast as it could, limping and
flopping; throwing back its head, it would open its beak, and its
feathers would ruffle up in instant readiness for combat. No
stroking or petting could mollify it: it would peck and struggle,
refuse to take the meat I offered it, and all the time I stood over
it it would look me fixedly in the eye with a gaze that was hard and

penetrating. Full of solitary malice it was waiting for death, trusting and forgiving no one. At last the convicts began to remember about it again, and although nobody had shown any concern for it or even mentioned it for some two months, all the men suddenly appeared to be sympathetic to it. Some said it ought to be taken out of the prison. 'Let it die if it's got to, but not in prison,' they said.

'It's a wild bird, you know, it needs its freedom, you'll never teach it to live in a prison,' others agreed.

'It's not like us, then,' somebody added.

'Don't be stupid: it's a bird, and we're human beings, aren't we?'

'The eagle, my friends, is the king of the forest ...' began Skuratov; but on this occasion no one listened to him. One day after dinner when the work drum had been sounded the men took the eagle – one of them holding its beak shut, as it had begun to struggle fiercely – and carried it out of the prison. They went as far as the ramparts. The twelve men who made up this party waited with curiosity to see where the eagle would go. It was strange: they were all somehow contented, as if in some way they too had been set free.

'Look at the sonofabitch: you try to help it and all it does is bite you!' said the man who was holding it, looking at the savage bird almost lovingly.

'Let it go, Mikitka!'

'There's no point in trying to put him in a cage out here. Give him his freedom, give him the genuine article!'

And Mikita hurled the eagle off the ramparts and into the steppe. It was far into autumn, a cold, dark day. The wind was whistling over the bare steppe, hissing in the dry, yellow tussocks of grass. The eagle set off on an even trajectory, beating its great wings as though in a hurry to get away from us, anywhere at all. The convicts watched with curiosity as its head flickered through the grass.

'Just look at him,' said one man, thoughtfully.

'And he doesn't look round!' added another. 'He hasn't looked round once, lads, he just keeps on going.'

'What did you expect, did you think he was going to come back to say thank you?' asked a third.

'Freedom, that's what it is. He can smell his freedom.'

'He's out in the big world, now.'

'You can't see him any more, lads ...'

'What are you standing around here for? Get marching!' the guards started to shout, and everyone trailed silently off to work.

* 7 *

THE COMPLAINT

The publisher of these notes by the late Aleksandr Petrovich Goryanchikov considers it his duty to begin this chapter by making the following announcement to readers:

In the first chapter of *Notes from the House of the Dead* there is a brief reference to a parricide, a member of the nobility. He was presented, among other things, as an example of the lack of feeling with which convicts will sometimes talk about the crimes they have committed. It was also said that this murderer had not admitted his guilt in court, but that, to judge from the stories of those who knew all the details of his case, the facts were so clear that there could be no doubt about the matter. These same people told the author of the *Notes* that the criminal was a man of utterly dissolute behaviour, who had fallen into debt and had killed his father out of greed for his inheritance. Moreover, everyone in the town where this parricide had worked told the same story. The publisher of the *Notes* is in possession of fairly reliable information concerning this latter circumstance. Finally, the *Notes* say that the murderer was constantly in the most excellent and cheerful frame of mind while he was in the prison; that he was an unstable, flippant man, unreasoning in the extreme, though by no means unintelligent, and that the author of the *Notes* never observed any particular sign of cruelty in him. This sentence is added: 'It goes without saying that I did not believe he had committed this crime.'

The other day the publisher of *Notes from the House of the Dead* received notification from Siberia that this criminal really had been in the right all along, and had suffered ten years of penal servitude for no reason. His innocence had been established officially, according to the processes of the law. The true perpetrators of the crime had apparently been found and had confessed, and the unfortunate man had been released from prison. The publisher has no reason to doubt the authenticity of this information ...

There is no need to add any more. No need to expatiate on the tragic profundity of this case, on the young life ruined by such a dreadful accusation. The facts of the case are all too clear, all too striking.

We are of the opinion, too, that if a case such as this is possible, this very possibility adds a new and glaring facet to the overall picture of the House of the Dead.

But let us continue.

I have already said that I did finally adapt myself to my situation in the prison. But this adaptation was attained with much pain and constraint, and only very gradually. In essence, it took me almost a year to reach this stage, and it was the most difficult year of my life. That is why it has remained in my memory in its entirety. I think I can remember every hour of that year in the sequence in which it occurred. But as I have also said, there were other convicts who could not 'adjust' to this life. I often remember thinking to myself during that first year things like 'What are they really feeling? Have they really adjusted? Are they really as calm as they look?' And these questions preoccupied me greatly. I have already mentioned that the convicts lived here not as if this were their home, but as in some wayside inn, *en route* somewhere. Even the men who had been condemned to spend their whole lives here were fidgety and anxious, and each of them dreamed of that which was almost impossible. This habitual restlessness, which was displayed silently but obviously, this strange, impatient fervour of involuntarily expressed hopes which were at times so divorced from reality that they resembled a kind of delirium and which, perhaps most strikingly of all, persisted in men of the most hard-headed intelligence – all this created an extraordinary atmosphere in the place, so much so that these oddities were possibly its most characteristic feature. One somehow felt at once, almost at first glance, that there was nothing like this outside the prison. Here everyone was a dreamer, and this was immediately obvious. The place had a morbid feel to it, stemming from the fact that this daydreaming made most of the convicts look sullen and morose, and somehow unhealthy. By far the greater number of them were silent and malicious to the point of hatred and did not like to display their hopes openly. Forthrightness and frankness were held in contempt. The more unrealizable were the hopes of these men, and the stronger their own sense of their unrealizability, the more stubbornly and chastely they would keep them to themselves, unable, however, to renounce them. It was quite possible that some of them were privately ashamed of these hopes. There is in the Russian character so much down-to-earth sobriety, so much inner mockery primarily directed at the self ... It may be that it was this perpetual state of secret discontent with themselves that caused these men to be so impatient in their day-to-day dealings with one another, to be so implacable and jeeringly malicious in one another's regard. And if, for example, one more forthright and impatient than the others suddenly stood up in their midst and said out loud what was on all their minds, he would be snubbed, cut off short and laughed to scorn. It always seemed to me, however, that the most zealous persecutors were precisely the ones who had gone further than anyone else in their building of dreams and hopes. Forthright and uncomplicated men were, as I have already said, generally regarded as the crassest idiots, and were treated with contempt. Each man was so morose, so self-absorbed that he despised anyone who was good-natured and lacking in self-absorption. With the exception of these straightforward, uncomplicated chatterers, all the other men – the ones who kept silent, that is – were sharply subdivided according to whether they were good-natured or malicious, cheerful or sullen. The malicious, sullen ones were very much in the majority; the few who were talkative by nature were restless gossipers and envious troublemakers. They poked their noses into everyone's business, but never showed anyone what they themselves might really be like as people, or what went on inside them. To do so was not *à la mode*, it was not accepted. The good-natured convicts – a tiny bunch – kept quiet, nursed their hopes to themselves, and were, needless to say, more inclined than the morose ones to believe in the possibility of their realization. But it seemed to me that there was yet another category of convicts: the ones who had given up all hope. Such, for example, was the old man from the Starodubye settlements; cases like this were very rare, however. The old man (I have mentioned him before) looked calm enough, but several tell-tale signs led me to believe that his inner state of mind was an atrocious one. He did, however, have one salvation, one escape: this was prayer, and the idea of martyrdom. The convict who went mad, the one who used to read the Bible and went for the Major with a brick, was probably another of those who had given up every last hope; but since life without hope is impossible, he had found a way out for himself through a voluntary, almost artificial martyrdom. He declared that he had gone for the Major quite without malice, solely out of a desire to take suffering upon himself. Who knows what psychological process must have been taking place in his soul at that time? No man can live without some goal to aspire towards. If he loses his goal, his hope, the resultant anguish will frequently turn him into a monster ... The goal of all the convicts was freedom and release from prison.

But now I see that I am trying to classify all the prisoners into categories; that, however, is not really possible. Reality is infinitely various when compared to the deductions of abstract thought, even those that are most cunning, and it will not tolerate rigid, hard-and-fast distinctions. Reality strives for diversification. We too had our own special form of life; even if it did not amount to much, it was ours none the less, and it was not merely some official existence but our own, inner, private life.

As I have already inferred, however, I found at the beginning of my time in the prison that I was unable to penetrate the inner fabric of this life, and was indeed incapable of doing so; at the time, therefore, all its external manifestations tormented me with an inexpressible anguish. I sometimes found myself hating these fellow-sufferers of mine. I would even envy them and curse destiny. I envied them because they were among their own kind, were companions to one another and understood one another, even though in actual fact they were all just as sickened and revolted as I was by this companionship of the lash and the stick, and all kept their eyes averted from the others. Once again I repeat that this envy, which visited me in moments of resentment, had a legitimate foundation in reality. Those who say that noblemen and the educated have no worse a time in our prisons and penal institutions than ordinary peasants really do not know what they are talking about. I am familiar with this proposition, have heard it bandied about of late, have read about it. The foundation of this idea is a sound and humane one. It is that all are people, all are human. But as an idea it is far too abstract. Too many practical considerations are left out of account in its formulation, circumstances that can only be understood if they are experienced in reality. I say this not because I think that the nobleman and the man of education are more sensitive, that they feel pain more acutely or are more highly developed. It is difficult to gauge the soul and its development by the application of fixed criteria. Not even education is a reliable indicator in this regard. I would be the first to testify that I have encountered signs of the most advanced spiritual development among the sufferers of this oppressed and unenlightened *milieu*. In prison it sometimes happened that you might be familiar with a man for several years thinking he was a wild animal, and you would regard him with contempt. And then suddenly a moment would arrive when some uncontrollable impulse would lay his soul bare, and you would behold in it such riches, such sensitivity and warmth, such a vivid awareness of its own suffering and the suffering of others, that the scales would fall from your eyes and at first you would hardly be able to believe what you had seen and heard. The reverse also happens: education sometimes cohabits with such barbarity, such cynicism that you are filled with disgust, and no matter how good-natured or favourably prejudiced you are, you can find in your heart neither justification nor excuse.

This is to say nothing of such things as the change in one's routine, one's way of life, food, and so on, which cannot but be more difficult for a man from the upper stratum of society than it is for a muzhik who has often gone hungry while he was free and who in prison can at least eat his fill. About this I do not propose to argue. We should assume that for a man with any strength of will at all, this is a small inconvenience compared to the other discomforts he experiences; though a change of routine is really no trivial matter, and may even have a considerable effect on a man. But there are discomforts in the face of which all this pales into insignificance, to a point where one ceases to notice the filthiness of one's living conditions, the iron grip of one's captors and the meagre, ill-prepared food. The smoothest city slicker, the most pampered milksop will, after working in the sweat of his brow, working as he never did in freedom, be glad to eat black bread and soup with cockroaches floating in it. It is possible to get used to this, too, as the comic prison song about the fine gentleman who became a convict relates:

> They give me cabbage leaves and water –
> I wolf them down for all I'm worth.

No; much more important than all this is that within some two hours of his arrival in the prison, each ordinary newcomer grows to be just like all the other convicts; he is *at home*, a householder in the prison artel, with the same rights as any other. He is understood by everyone, and he understands them, is familiar to them all, and is considered by them as one of *their own*. This is not the case with the *nobleman*, the gentleman. No matter how fair-minded, good-natured and intelligent he is, the other convicts will continue to hate and despise him for years on end; they will never understand him and, most importantly of all, they will not trust him. He will never be their friend and companion, and although with the passage of years he may finally reach a point where they no longer insult him, he will never be one of them, and will forever be painfully conscious of the fact that he is an outsider, and alone. This ostracism is sometimes practised by the convicts quite without malice, unconsciously. The gentleman is not one of them, and that is that. There is nothing so terrible as to live in a social environment that is alien to one. A muzhik who has been deported from Taganrog to the port of Petropavlovsk finds there Russian muzhiks exactly like the ones he has left behind; he at once comes to terms with them, fits in with them, and within a couple of hours is living quite peaceably in the same hut with them. Not so the gentleman. They are separated from the common people by the most profound abyss. This is only *fully* to be observed when the *gentleman*, deprived of his previous rights by the force of external circumstances, suddenly turns into a common peasant. Not even if you associate with the common people all your life, consort with them every day for forty years on end, whether in the formal, administrative context of government service, for example, or even in the simple, friendly role of benefactor and surrogate father, will you ever get really to know them. Whatever you see will be a kind of optical illusion, and nothing more. I am aware that everyone without exception reading this remark will say I exaggerate. But I am convinced that it is true. My conviction comes not from books, or from speculation, but from lived experience, and I have had a great sufficiency of time in which to put my conviction to the test. Possibly one day everyone will realize the extent to which it is justified ...

As if according to some plan, events confirmed my observations from the outset, and they had a nerve-racking, morbid effect on me. During that first summer I would wander about the prison almost entirely on my own. I have already related how I could not even pick out and appreciate those convicts who might have been friendly towards me, and who were indeed friendly towards me later on, though never on an equal footing with me. I also had companions who were noblemen like myself, but their companionship did not lift the burden from my soul. It was as if there was nothing I could face in my surroundings, and yet there was no escape from them. And then one of those events occurred which right from the start made me aware just how much of an outsider, a special case I was in the prison. One clear, hot working day that summer, it must have been getting on for August, at around one o'clock in the afternoon, when everyone usually took a rest before the afternoon's work, all the convicts suddenly got to their feet as one man and began to form themselves into ranks in the prison yard. I had known nothing about it until that moment. At that time I was so immersed in myself that I hardly noticed what went on around me. Yet the prison had been in a state of obscure agitation for some three days past. It was possible that this agitation had begun much earlier, as I reflected subsequently, calling to mind some of the convict talk I had overheard, and also the general quarrelsomeness, sullenness and, in particular, the resentment I had observed in them of late. I had ascribed this to the crushing physical labour they had to do, to the long, tedious summer days, to their helpless dreams of forests and freedom, and to the short nights, during which it was very hard to get enough sleep. Perhaps the effects of all this had now combined to produce a single outburst. The ostensible pretext for it, however, proved to be the prison food. For several days of late there had been loud complaints and expressions of indignation in the barracks, particularly when the men came together in the kitchen for dinner and supper. They were angry with the cooks and even tried to have one of them sacked and replaced by another man. The new cook had, however, been immediately told to quit and the old one recalled in his stead. In short, the convicts were in a restless mood.

'It's hard work, but all they give us to eat is tripe,' someone in the kitchen would growl.

'If you don't like it why don't you order blancmange?' another would rejoin.

'I'm very fond of soup with tripe, friends,' a third would chip in. 'It's good.'

'But if all you get is tripe, does it taste good then?'

'After all, it is the season for eating meat now,' said a fourth. 'We slave away in the brickworks, and after he's done his day's work a man feels like having a bite to eat. And what kind of food is tripe?'

'If it's not tripe, it's hard.'*

'Tripe and hard, that's all we ever get given. What kind of food is that? Eh?'

'Yeah, it's rubbish.'

'He's filling his pockets again, I do believe.'

'It's none of your business.'

'Whose business is it then? My stomach belongs to me. If we all made a complaint, we'd get some action.'

'A complaint?'

'That's right.'

---

* i.e. heart. The convicts used to say 'hard' as a kind of sarcastic joke. (*Note by F. M. Dostoyevsky*.)

'Seems they didn't beat the complaint you made last time out of you properly.'

'He's right, you know,' added another man, peevishly; until now he had not said a word. 'Talking's easy enough. What are you going to say in this complaint of yours, you tell us that first, fathead.'

'All right, I'll tell you. If everybody'll come along with me, I'll speak out along with them. The poor cons, that is. There's some of us as has their own food to eat, and others as has to make do with the prison muck.'

'Look at him, he's green with envy! His eyes are all lit up goggling at what belongs to other people.'

'A man should look after his own, not to go gaping after what others have got.'

'Should he, indeed? I'll argue about that with you till I've got grey hair. So you're well-off, are you, since you're going to sit there with your arms folded?'

'Yeroshka's well-off, he's got a dog and a cat.'

'But let's face it, lads, what are we sitting here for? It's high time we stopped pandering to their stupid honours. They're flaying the hide off us. Why shouldn't we complain?'

'Why shouldn't we complain? You just want to be fed with a silver spoon. It's prison, see – that's why!'

'When the people fall out, the governor grows stout.'

'That's right. Eight-Eyes is as fat as a barrel. He's bought himself a pair of greys.'

'And he likes a drink, too.'

'The other day him and the vet were fighting over a card-game.'

'They were playing all night. He spent two hours bashing away at the vet. Fedka told me.'

'That's why we get soup and hard.'

'You're a lot of idiots, you are. It's not for us to go sticking our necks out.'

'But if we all come forward, then at least we'll see what kind of an excuse he'll give. It's worth being firm.'

'Excuse! All you'll get is a kick in the teeth, if I know him.'

'And a trial . . .'

In short, everyone was in a state of excitement. At this time the prison food really was bad. What was more, one thing kept piling up on top of the other. Worst of all was the universal mood of depression, the suffering concealed as a matter of habit. By their very nature, convicts are quarrelsome and rebellious; but they seldom all rebel together or in large numbers. The reason for this is at they are constantly at loggerheads with one another. Every one of them felt this: that is why there was far more bad language than there was action among us. On this occasion, however, the excitement did not simply fade away without any result. The men began to gather in groups throughout the barracks, discussing the matter with one another. They cursed as they bitterly recalled the Major's administration of the prison; they wormed out of each other all their most secret resentments. Some of the men were particularly excited. On occasions like this, instigators and ringleaders always emerge. The ringleaders in cases of complaint are usually men of outstanding character, and they are found not only in prison but in all artels, labour gangs and the like. They constitute a special category of human being, and are the same wherever they are encountered. They are quick-tempered men with a passion for fair play; they are most forthrightly, sincerely convinced that fair play is certainly, indisputably and – most important of all – imminently possible. Such men are by no means more stupid than the others, some of them are even quite intelligent, but they are too hot-headed to be sly or calculating. In such cases there are also to be found men who are skilful in the art of directing the mass of their fellows and in winning their cause; these represent another type of popular leader, one that is extremely rare in Russia. Those of whom I speak now, the instigators and ringleaders in cases of complaint, nearly always fail in their mission and end up being sent to prison and penal servitude. They fail because of their hotheadedness, but their fervour gives them an influence on the mass of their companions, who will follow them willingly. Their real and honest indignation has an effect on everyone, and even the most undecided men end by attaching themselves to them. Their blind certainty of success tempts even the most inveterate sceptics, even though it is a certainty with such shaky, puerile foundations that an onlooker might wonder how anyone could ever bring himself to follow them

at all. The main thing is, however, that they are the first to come
forward, and they do so entirely without fear. They rush forward
like bulls with their heads lowered, often without any knowledge
of the cause they are defending, and with none of the caution, the
practical Jesuitism with which even the most debased and squalid
individual will sometimes win his battle, reach his goal and come
away unscathed. They nearly always damage themselves in some
way. In ordinary life such men are bitter, peevish, irritable and
intolerant. Most often they are extremely blinkered, but this, in
part, constitutes their strength. The most annoying thing about
them is that instead of having any clearly defined aim, they
frequently rush off at a tangent into some trivial matter that has
nothing to do with the cause in question. This is their undoing. But
the mass of their fellows understands them; in this they are strong
... But now I must give a brief explanation of what a *complaint*
is ...

In our prison there were several men who had been gaoled for
making complaints. They were the ones who were most excited
now. There was one man in particular named Martynov, who had
previously served with the hussars, a hot-tempered, restless, suspicious individual, though he was honest and truthful. Another was
Vasily Antonov, a man with a sort of cool irritability, an insolent
stare and a haughty, sarcastic smile, but who was also honest and
truthful. I cannot describe them all here; there were too many of
them. Petrov, incidentally, fairly shuttled to and fro, lending an ear
to what was said in every little group, and saying little; he was
obviously excited, and was the first to rush out of the barrack when
the men began to form into lines in the yard.

Our duty sergeant, who performed the role of a sergeant major,
appeared at once in a cold sweat. When they had finished lining up,
the men asked him politely to tell the Major that the convicts would
like to have a word with him and ask him personally about one or
two matters. All the veterans had followed the duty sergeant out
and had lined up on the other side of the yard, facing the convicts.
The request the duty sergeant had received from the men was most
unusual, and had filled him with horror. But he did not dare delay
in reporting the matter to the Major immediately. For one thing,

if the convicts had taken things into their own hands like this, then it was perfectly possible that something even worse might happen. All the prison officers were terrified of the convicts in their charge. For another, even if nothing were to happen, even if all the men straightway thought better of it and dispersed, the duty sergeant was still bound to report all that had taken place to the authorities. Pale and shaking with fear, the duty sergeant set off at the double for the Major's house, not even making any attempt to question the convicts or to remonstrate with them. He had realized that they would not talk to him now.

Knowing nothing of what was taking place, I too went out to line up with the men. I only learned all the details of the incident later on. Now I thought some sort of roll-call was being held; but when I did not see the sentries whose task it was to conduct such checks I was surprised and began to look about me. The faces of the men were excited and irritable. Some were pale. All the convicts were silent and preoccupied as they waited to say to the Major what it was they had to say to him. I noticed that many of them were looking at me in great astonishment, but that they turned away without saying anything. They evidently found it strange that I should wish to line up with them, clearly not believing that I had any complaint to make. Soon, however, nearly all those who were standing next to me began to take notice of me again. They all looked at me questioningly.

'What are thou doing here?' Vasily Antonov asked me in a loud, surly voice. He was standing a little farther away from me than the others. Until now he had always used the 'you' form of address when speaking to me, and had talked to me politely. I stared at him in bewilderment, still trying to fathom the meaning of this, already surmising that something unusual was taking place.

'Yes, indeed, what business have you got standing here? Go back into the barrack,' said one young prisoner, a military convict with whom until now I had been quite unacquainted, a quiet and good-natured man. 'This hasn't got anything to do with you.'

'But everybody's lining up,' I replied. 'I thought it was a roll-call.'

'Ugh, look what's crawled out of the woodwork,' shouted one man.

'Iron nose,' said another.

'Fly-swatter,' said a third with unspeakable contempt. This novel term of abuse drew a burst of laughter from the men.

'He's only allowed in the kitchen as a favour,' someone added.

'They're well-off wherever they go. Here they are doing penal servitude, and they've got kalatches to eat and money to buy sucking-pigs. You've got your own grub; what are you doing out here?'

'This is no place for you,' said Kulikov, approaching me casually. He took me by the arm and escorted me from the ranks.

Kulikov was pale, his black eyes were glittering and he had been biting his lower lip. The Major's arrival was not something he was awaiting with indifference. I should observe that I was very fond of watching Kulikov during all incidents of this kind, on all occasions, that is, when he had to stand up for himself. He gave himself all kinds of airs, but he did what was asked of him. I think he would even have gone to the scaffold with a certain outward stylishness. Now, when everyone was using the familiar mode of address to me and hurling abuse at me, he made a point of re-doubling his politeness towards me; at the same time, what he said to me was particularly haughty and assertive, and did not admit of any retort.

'Now then, Aleksandr Petrovich, we've our own private business to attend to here, and it doesn't affect you. It'd be best if you'd go off somewhere and wait ... Your folk are all in the kitchen, why don't you join them there?'

'Why don't you go to the devil instead?' someone chipped in.

It was true: through the raised kitchen window I could see the Poles; but there seemed to be a lot of other people there, as well. Puzzled, I went into the kitchen, pursued by laughter, oaths and the 'tyu-tyu' sound the convicts made instead of whistling.

'His lordship's displeased with us! ... *tyu-tyu-tyu!* To hell with him!'

I had never been exposed to this level of insult before, and on this occasion I found it very painful. But I had poked my nose in at the wrong time. In the kitchen I was met by T—wski, an open-hearted young man without much education, and very attached to B. The convicts had made an exception in his case, and were quite fond of him. He was bold, courageous and strong, and this was evident in all his gestures.

'What's this, Goryanchikov!' he shouted to me. 'Come in here!'

'What's going on over there?'

'They're presenting a complaint, didn't you know? They won't get anywhere with it, of course: who's going to believe a bunch of convicts? They'll start looking for the ringleaders and if they find us over there we'll be the first to be charged with fomenting a riot. Remember the reason we were sent here. They'll just get a thrashing, but we'll be made to stand trial. The Major hates the lot of us and there's nothing he'd like better than to ruin us. He'll use us as an excuse.'

'And the convicts will gladly inform on us,' added M—cki, as we went into the kitchen.

'Don't worry, they won't let us off lightly!' said T—wski.

In the kitchen, besides the noblemen, there was also a large number of ordinary convicts. They had all stayed behind here as they did not wish to take part in the making of the complaint – some out of cowardice, others because they were thoroughly convinced of the futility of any complaint. Akim Akimych was here, too, an inveterate natural enemy of all such complaints. In his opinion, these interfered with the smooth running of the prison work and with public morality. He was keeping quiet, waiting for the end of the incident with the greatest of calm, quite unconcerned about its outcome, and totally confident of the inevitable victory of order and the will of the authorities. Isay Fomich was here, too, hanging around looking very bewildered, letting his head droop and listening to our talk with eagerness and trepidation. He was in a paroxysm of fear. All the Polish commoners were here, too – they had joined forces with the Polish nobles. There were also some timid Russians, men who never said anything and had a perpetually downtrodden air. They had not dared to come forward with the rest and were waiting sadly for the incident to conclude. Finally, there were some perpetually gloomy, austere-looking convicts who were not at all timid. They had remained behind out of a stubborn and disgusted conviction that the whole affair was a lot of nonsense and that nothing would come of it except trouble. None the less, it appeared to me that they did not feel entirely at their ease in the present situation, and they did not look very sure of themselves. Although they knew that they were perfectly in the right as far as the complaint was concerned – this was subsequently proved to be the case – they felt like turncoats who had let the artel down: it was as if they had informed to the Major on their own fellow-convicts. Yolkin, too, was here, the Siberian peasant who had been sent here for forging coins and who had taken Kulikov's veterinary practice away from him. The old man from the settlements at Starodubye was also here. The cooks had all stayed behind in the kitchen, too, probably because they considered themselves representatives of the authorities, against whom it would be improper for them to rebel.

'All the same,' I began, turning to M—cki uncertainly, 'apart from the men here, nearly everybody else has joined in.'

'So what?' growled B.

'We'd have been risking a hundred times what they're risking if we'd gone with them; and why should we do that? *Je hais ces brigands.* Do you really suppose for one moment that their complaint will be successful? Who wants to get mixed up in stupid goings-on like that?'

'Nothing'll come of it,' chipped in another of the convicts, a stubborn and resentful old man. Almazov, who was also here, hastened to agree with him.

'Except that half a hundred of 'em'll get a flogging ... otherwise they'll be no better off than they were before.'

'The Major's here!' someone shouted, and all the men rushed eagerly to the windows.

The Major had come flying into the yard in a vicious rage, red in the face, and with his glasses on. Saying nothing, he went up to the foremost line of men. He was always extremely self-possessed on such occasions, and never lost his presence of mind. But he was almost invariably half drunk. At that moment, even his grubby peaked cap with its orange band and his dirty silver epaulettes had something menacing about them. At his heels came the clerk Dyatlov, a very important person in our prison, who was really responsible for running the whole institution and who even exercised a certain influence on the Major – he was a wily fellow, who had all his wits about him, but he was not a bad man. The convicts liked him. He was followed by our duty sergeant, who had quite clearly just received a most severe dressing-down and was visibly expecting to receive another that was ten times worse; after him came three or four guards, and that was all. The convicts, who at the time the Major had been sent for had all apparently taken off their caps, now straightened themselves up and set themselves to rights; each one of them shifted his weight from one leg to the other, and then they all froze on the spot, waiting for the first word, or rather shout, from the prison's supreme authority.

It came soon enough; by his second word, the Major was roaring at the top of his voice, which on this occasion had a kind of falsetto screech in it: he was really violently worked up. From the kitchen windows I could see him running along the foremost line of men, grabbing them by the collars and questioning them. Because we were so far away, however, we could hear neither his questions nor the convicts' replies to them. All we could hear was his falsetto screech, as he shouted:

'Rioters! ... beat the daylights ... troublemakers. You are a troublemaker!' he yelled, as he rushed at a man.

The man's reply could not be heard. But a moment later we saw one of the convicts being singled out and sent off to the guardhouse. A minute later he was followed by a second, and then by a third.

'You'll all be put on trial! I'll teach you! Who are those men in the kitchen?' he screeched, catching sight of us at the open windows. 'I want all you men down here! Get them all down here at the double!'

The clerk, Dyatlov, came up to the kitchen to see us. In the kitchen he was told that the men there had no complaint to make. He immediately went back and reported this to the Major.

'Oh, so they haven't have they?' he said, some two tones lower, clearly gratified. 'Never mind, get them all down here!'

We came out of the kitchen. I had the feeling that we were rather ashamed of doing so. And indeed, all the men hung their heads as they went.

'Ah, Prokofiev! And Yolkin, too, and there you are, Almazov ...

Stand here, stand here, the lot of you,' said our Major, in a soft voice, speaking faster now, looking at us with a benign expression. 'M—cki, you're here, too ... We must write down their names at once. Dyatlov! Take down the names of all those who are satisfied and all those who are dissatisfied, every one of them, and give the list to me. I'll have you all ... put on trial! I'll teach you, you villains!'

The threat of a list produced the required effect.

'I'm satisfied!' came a depressed shout from the ranks of the men who were dissatisfied, but it was somehow lacking in conviction.

'Aha, you're satisfied, are you? Who else is satisfied? Come forward, all those who are.'

'I'm satisfied, I'm satisfied,' chorused several more voices.

'Satisfied, are you? Somebody led you astray, did they? So there were ringleaders, there were troublemakers, were there? So much the worse for them!'

'Merciful Lord, what is all this?' someone shouted from the crowd.

'Who was that? Come forward, that man!' roared the Major, charging off in the direction from which the voice had come. 'Was that you, Rastorguyev, are you the man who shouted? To the guardhouse with you!'

Rastorguyev, a tall, puffy-faced young convict, came forward and slowly ambled off in the direction of the guardhouse. It had not been him who had shouted, but since he had been singled out he offered no resistance.

'You're all spoiled rotten!' the Major howled after him. 'Look at your fat mug, I bet you haven't had a shit for three days! I'll find you all out! Come forward all those who are satisfied!'

'Satisfied, your honour!' came a chorus of several dozen gloomy voices; the rest of the men remained obstinately silent. But this was what the Major had been waiting for.

'Right, so you're *all* satisfied?' he said hurriedly. 'I could see you were, I knew it all along. It's the troublemakers! There are obviously troublemakers among them!' he continued, turning to Dyatlov. 'We must investigate this matter more closely. But now ... now it's time for work. Sound the drum!'

He assisted in person as the convicts were given their various tasks. The convicts went off to their places of work in depressed silence, glad at least to be out of the Major's sight so soon. But after the tasks had been allotted, the Major went straight to the guard-house and dealt with the 'troublemakers' – not too harshly, however. He even hurried the floggings. It was said afterwards that one of the men had begged for mercy and had been let off. The Major was plainly not quite in his element and was even, perhaps, a little scared. A complaint is always a tricky business, and even though the protest the men had made could hardly be called a proper 'complaint', as it had been made not to the prison governor but to the Major, it was still an embarrassing, unpleasant incident. What was particularly upsetting was that nearly all the convicts had joined in the protest. The affair must be snuffed out at all costs. The 'troublemakers' were soon released. Next day the quality of the prison food improved, though this state of affairs did not last long ... In the days that followed, the Major took to visiting the prison more often, and to finding things that were wrong. Our duty sergeant went around with a worried expression on his face, his usual routine upset; he seemed quite dazed with astonishment. As for the convicts, it was a long time before they settled down again; their previous excitement had gone, however, and instead they seemed puzzled and uneasy. Some of them even appeared to be ashamed of themselves. Others aired their views on the incident, peevishly but in few words. Many of the men made fun of themselves openly, as though they were punishing themselves for having attempted to make a complaint.

'Right, lads. We've made our bed, now we must lie on it,' one would say.

'We've had our bit of fun, now we've got to earn it,' another would add.

'Where's the mouse that can bell the cat?' a third might ask.

'It takes a thrashing to make the likes of us see reason, that's a fact. We're lucky he didn't whack the lot of us.'

'You want to think more and talk less in future!' someone would say, bitterly.

'Is this you giving lessons, professor?'

'So what if I am?'

'And who do you think you are, pushing yourself forward?'

'I'm a man, same as you are.'

'You're a dog's arse, you.'

'Dog's arse yourself.'

'Here, here, that's enough of that! What's got into you?' the men all round would shout at the two who were arguing.

That same evening, the evening of the day on which the complaint had been made, as I was returning from work I met Petrov behind the barracks. He had been out looking for me already. As he approached me, he seemed to be muttering something that sounded like two or three muffled exclamations, but when he drew close to me he fell silent and started to walk along mechanically beside me. The whole of the foregoing incident was still weighing heavily on me, and it occurred to me that Petrov might be able to throw some light on certain aspects of it for me.

'Tell me, Petrov,' I asked him, 'are you people angry with us?'

'Who's angry?' he replied, as though coming to his senses.

'The convicts . . . with us noblemen.'

'Why should we be angry with you?'

'Well, because we didn't take part in the complaint.'

'Why should you want to complain?' he asked, as though he were making an effort to understand me. 'You've got your own grub.'

'Oh, for heavens' sake! Some of your lot have their own food, but that didn't stop them from coming forward. We ought to have gone along with you – as your companions.'

'But . . . what kind of companion could you ever be to us?' he asked in bewilderment.

I threw him a quick glance: he really did not understand what I was talking about, could not for the life of him see what I was getting at. I, on the other hand, understood him perfectly at that moment. It was only now that a certain question that had been stirring within me for a long time past, nagging away at me, was finally cleared up, and I suddenly realized the truth of what I had previously only dimly surmised. I realized that I should never be accepted by the men as their companion, not even if I were to remain a convict forever, not even if I were to belong to the special category. Petrov's expression at that moment has stayed in my memory ever since. In his question: 'What kind of companion could you ever be to us?' there had been such unfeigned simplicity, such forthright bafflement. I wondered if his words could possibly contain some shade of irony, bitterness or mockery. Of that there was not a trace: I was simply not his companion, and that was all. 'You go your way, and we'll go ours; you have your business to attend to, and we have ours.'

I had really believed that after the complaint they would start getting at us and making our lives unbearable. Nothing of the kind took place: there was not the slightest reproach, not even the slightest hint of a reproach did we hear. No especial resentment was expressed towards us. They merely went on chivvying us a little on occasion, as they had done before, and that was all. And they showed not the slightest anger towards those convicts who had not wanted to take part in the complaint, and who had stayed in the kitchen, nor towards those who had been the first to shout that they were satisfied. No one ever even mentioned this. I found this latter circumstance particularly hard to understand.

* 8 *

COMPANIONS

I was naturally drawn more towards men of my own class, to the 'noblemen', in other words, particularly in the early days. But of the three former Russian noblemen in the prison (Akim Akimych, the spy A—v and the man who was thought to be a parricide), I spoke and associated only with Akim Akimych. I must admit that I went to Akim Akimych only when I was more or less at my wits' end, and at moments of the most intense tedium when it seemed there was no one else I could turn to. In the previous chapter I made an attempt to classify the prisoners by categories, but now, as I remember Akim Akimych, I reflect that it might be possible to add to the list yet one more category. It is true that he would be the sole representative of this category: it was that of the convicts who were utterly indifferent, men for whom it was all the same whether they lived in prison or at liberty. One would have thought it unlikely that a prison would contain men of this kind – but Akim Akimych was apparently an exception to the rule. He had set himself up in the prison as though he intended to live his entire life there: everything that surrounded him, from his mattress and pillows to his eating utensils, was solidly arranged as though it was meant to last throughout a prolonged stay. There was not a trace of anything makeshift or temporary about it all. He still had many years of his prison term to serve, but I doubt that he ever thought about his release. If he had reconciled himself with reality, however, it was not out of any leaning he might have had in that direction, but out of submissiveness, which for him was the same thing. He was a good-hearted man, and he helped me along at the beginning of my term with advice and practical services; but sometimes, I am afraid, especially at first, he bored me to death and had the effect of making worse my already far from happy state of mind. Yet it was my own unhappiness that impelled me to talk to him. I would sometimes long for a little lively conversation, even if it were bitter, impatient and resentful; we could at least express resentment about our fate together; but he would remain silent as he made his lanterns, or else he would talk about the military review there had been in such and such a year, who the officer in command of the division had been, what his name and patronymic were, whether he had been pleased with the review or not, how the signals for the skirmishes had been changed, and so on. He would tell me all this in a steady, decorous voice that was reminiscent of the dripping of water. He betrayed not the slightest animation as he told me that he had received the 'St Anne's Ribbon' for his part in some campaign or other there had been in the Caucasus. All that was noticeable was that at this point in the conversation his voice became even more solemn and sedate than usual; he lowered it slightly, and even made it sound rather mysterious as he pronounced the words 'St Anne's'; his silence, which lasted for some three minutes afterwards, had a peculiar gravity ... During that first year I had moments of stupidity when I (always quite suddenly) would begin to loathe Akim Akimych for no reason that was apparent, and I would curse

destiny that it had put me head to head with him on the plank bed.
I would usually reproach myself for this an hour later. But this was
only during the first year; later on I settled all my differences with
Akim Akimych, and viewed my previous stupidity with shame. I
remember that I never quarrelled with him openly.

Apart from these three Russians, there were eight other noblemen in the prison while I was there. With some of these Poles[36] I
got along fairly well, and even enjoyed their company, but not with
all of them. The best of them were morbid, exclusive and intolerant
in the highest degree. Later on I stopped talking to two of them
altogether. Only three of them were educated: B—ski, M—cki and
the old man Ż—ski, who had once been a professor of mathematics
somewhere; he was a pleasant, kind-hearted character, a great
eccentric and, in spite of his education, of extremely limited intelligence. M—cki and B—ski were quite different. I got along well with
M—cki from the first; I never quarrelled with him, and I respected
him, though I was never really fond of him. He was a deeply
mistrustful and resentful man, but he had a remarkable capacity for
self-mastery. It was the very extent of his self-control that put me
off him: one somehow felt that he would never open his heart to
anyone. But I may have been mistaken. He was a man of strong
character and excellent breeding. The extreme, almost Jesuitical
skill and caution which he applied in his dealings with others
demonstrated his deep, latent scepticism. Yet his was a soul that
suffered from this very duality, from this conflict between his
scepticism and his deep, unshakeable belief in some of his own
convictions and aspirations. In spite of all his worldly skill, however, he carried on a running battle with B—ski and T—ski. B—ski
was an invalid, somewhat prone to consumption, nervous and
irritable, but basically very kind-hearted and even generous. His
irritability sometimes reached into extreme intolerance and the
most capricious behaviour. I could not cope with these histrionics,
and later stopped seeing B—ski, though I never lost the fondness
I had for him; with M—cki, on the other hand, I never once
quarrelled – but I had no fondness for him. When I stopped seeing
B—ski I found that I also had to stop seeing T—ski, the young man
I mentioned in the previous chapter in connection with the com-

plaint. I was very sorry about this. The fact was, however, that he was so attached to B—ski and had such a deep reverence for him that anyone who crossed his path even slightly at once became T—ski's enemy, more or less. I think that he also fell out with M—cki over B—ski, though he held out for a long time. But all these men suffered from a kind of moral and mental sickness; they were bitter, irritable, mistrustful. This was understandable: they had a very hard time in the prison and their situation was far worse than ours. They were far from their own country. Some of them had been sent here for long terms – ten or twelve years – and what made things most difficult for them was that they viewed everyone around them with deep prejudice, seeing in the convicts nothing but brutality. They could not and would not see in them a single redeeming feature, a single trace of humanity, and this, too, was perfectly understandable: they had been compelled to take this point of view by force of circumstance, by fate. It was quite obvious that they were utterly miserable in prison. Towards the Circassians, the Tartars and Isay Fomich they were friendly and affable, but they avoided all the other convicts with detestation. Only the Old Believer from the Starodubye settlements earned their complete respect. It was, however, noteworthy that during all the time I was in the prison, not one of the convicts ever reproached them because of their origins, their religion or their mode of thinking, in the way that is sometimes, though admittedly not very often, the case among our common people with regard to foreigners, particularly Germans. Perhaps, however, it is only the Germans they laugh at: a German represents something extremely comical for the Russian peasant. The convicts treated our Poles with far more respect than they ever gave us Russians, and they never *got at* them. But I doubt whether the Poles ever noticed this; they probably did not care to, and were unwilling to give it any consideration. Apropos of T—ski: he it was who, when this group of men had been in transit from the place of their initial exile to our prison, had carried B—ski in his arms practically all the rest of the way after B—ski, being of debilitated health and constitution, had grown exhausted somewhere about half way along the road. The men had previously been sent to U—gorsk.[37] They said they had liked it there, much better than our fortress. But they had carried on some kind of correspondence, a perfectly innocent one, with some exiles in another town, and because of this it had been considered necessary for the three of them to be transferred to our fortress, closer to the scrutiny of the higher authorities. The third man was Ż—ski. Before they arrived, M—cki had been the only Polish nobleman in the prison. He must have been truly miserable during the first year of his deportation.

This Ż—ski was the old man I have already mentioned, the one who was forever saying his prayers. All the political prisoners were young men, some of them very young indeed; Ż—ski was the only one who was over fifty. He was, it is true, a decent man, but he was also rather strange. His companions B—ski and T—ski thoroughly disliked him and said of him that he was foolish and stubborn. I do not know to what extent they were justified in their opinion of him. In prison, as in every other place where human beings are herded together by force, against their will, I think it is true to say that men fall out with one another and even grow to detest one another more readily than they do in freedom. There are many contributing factors. But Ż—ski really was a rather stupid and unpleasant individual. None of his companions seemed to get along with him, either. Although I never quarrelled with him, I never spent much time in his company. I think he had a good knowledge of his subject, mathematics, and I recall that he was forever trying to explain to me in his semi-Russian some peculiar astronomical system he had devised. They told me that he had once had an exposition of this system published, but that the scientific world had poured nothing but ridicule on it. I think he was slightly soft in the head. He used to say his prayers for days on end, something which earned him the convicts' universal and lasting respect, right up until his death. But he had won the respect of the convicts from the very start, after his adventure with our Major. The Poles had not been shaven on their way from U—gorsk to our fortress, and they had grown beards. When they were brought before the Major he flew into a rage of indignation at such a breach of the regulations, one for which they, however, were not responsible.

'Look at them!' he roared. 'They're vagrants, brigands!'

Ż—ski, who at this time understood very little Russian and
thought they were being asked whether they were vagrants or
brigands, replied:

'We're not brigands, we're political offenders.'

'Wha–a–t? Do you dare to be insolent? Insolence!' roared the
Major. 'To the guardhouse with you! A hundred strokes of the
birch, right now, this very instant!'

The old man was flogged. He lay down without protest, bit his
hand and took his punishment without the slightest cry or groan,
never moving a muscle. B—ski and T—ski, meanwhile, had gone
into the prison, where M—cki was waiting at the entrance for them.
He rushed straight up to them and embraced them, though he had
never seen them in his life before. In a state of great agitation over
the way they had been received by the Major, they told him all
about Ż—ski. I remember M—cki telling me about this: 'I was
beside myself,' he said, 'I didn't understand what was happening
to me, and I was shaking as though I had a fever. I waited for Ż—ski
at the gate. He would have to come straight from the guardhouse
where he was being flogged.' The gate was opened: Ż—ski, averting
his eyes from everyone, his face pale and his bloodless lips quivering, passed between the convicts who had gathered in the prison
yard, having learned that a nobleman was being flogged; he walked
into the barrack, went straight to the place assigned to him on the
plank bed, and without saying a word got down on his knees and
began to say his prayers. The convicts were both struck and moved
by this. 'When I saw that old man,' said M—cki, 'with his grey hair,
his wife and children left behind far away in his own country, when
I saw him after that shameful punishment, down on his knees,
saying his prayers, I rushed behind the barracks and stayed there
for two hours completely out of my mind; I was in a frenzy . . .' The
convicts had a very high regard for Ż—ski from that time onwards,
and they were always respectful to him. They were particularly
appreciative of the fact that he had not cried out under the birch.

It is, however, important that the whole truth be told: this
example can in no way be taken to show how the prison authorities
in Siberia treated deportees of the nobility, whether Russians or
Poles. This example merely illustrates that from time to time one

may encounter an unpleasant character, and that if the unpleasant character also happens to be a senior commanding officer with a certain degree of autonomy, a deportee to whom he takes an active dislike may expect a rough ride. It is impossible to ignore the fact, however, that the men at the very highest levels of the Siberian prison administration, the men on whom the tone and attitude of all the other commanders depends, are very scrupulous with regard to deported noblemen, and in some cases even contrive to make life easier for them than for the convicts of the lower classes. The reasons for this are plain: for one thing, these high-up officials are themselves noblemen; for another, it has been known for certain noblemen to refuse to lie down under the birch, and to assault their punishers, a circumstance which has in the past led to terrible atrocities being committed; and lastly, there is what seems to me the most important point, and that is that some thirty-five years ago a large number of deported noblemen appeared in Siberia; over the thirty years that followed, these same noblemen managed to make a place for themselves, and got themselves recognized all over Siberia to such an extent that in my time, according to an already long-established tradition, the authorities were treating the upper-class offenders of a certain category differently from other deportees. The commanding officers lower down the scale also adopted this view, and obediently adjusted their general attitude in accordance with it. But many of these lower-ranking officers were of limited intelligence, and were privately critical of the orders they had received from on high; they would have been very, very glad to have been able to run things in their own way without anyone interfering. This, however, they were not really allowed to do. I have firm grounds for believing this to be so, and for the following reason: life in the second category of penal servitude, to which I belonged and which was made up of convicts who were being held in the prison under military supervision, was infinitely harder than it was in the other two categories, the first, which involved work in the mines, and the second, which involved work in the factories. It was harder not only for the noblemen but for all the other convicts as well, for the simple reason that it was run along military lines, very much like the convict battalions of European Russia.

The military supervision was stricter, the routine was harsher, the convicts were kept in fetters the whole time, were constantly under guard and under lock and key; this was not nearly so much the case in the other two categories. That was at least what all the convicts in our prison said, and there were some connoisseurs among them. They would all have gladly belonged to the first category, officially considered the strictest one, and spent a great deal of time dreaming about this. (All the men who had been in them spoke about the convict battalions of European Russia with horror; they maintained that these were the toughest penal institutions in the whole of Russia, and that life in Siberia was paradise compared with what went on over there.) Consequently, given the harshness of the routine in our prison, given its military command, presided over by the governor-general himself, and given the occasional readiness of certain officious outsiders to report on the sly to the right quarters, whether out of resentment or from jealousy, that disloyal officers in such-and-such a category were being soft on political offenders – if, I say, in such a place as this the upper-class criminals were viewed slightly differently from the rest, how much easier things must have been for them in the first and third categories. From my experience of our prison, I believe it is possible for me to generalize about this aspect of penal servitude as it is manifested all over Siberia. All the rumours and tales on this subject which reached me from deportees in the first and third categories confirmed my deductions. The authorities really did treat us noblemen with a greater degree of care and attention. Certainly, as regards the work we had to do and in the matter of our living conditions, we were not let off at all lightly: we had to do the same work as all the rest of the convicts, wear the same fetters, submit to the same locking-up procedures – in short, we had to put up with what all the men suffered. And indeed, there was nothing that could have been done to alleviate this state of affairs. I knew that *in the recent past* there had been so many informers, so many intrigues, so many traps laid in the town that the authorities were really afraid that someone might inform on them. And what more terrible news could an informer pass on than that in a certain category some of the convicts were being let off lightly? Thus they were all frightened, and we were treated like all the other convicts; a certain exception was, however, made with regard to corporal punishment. It is true that if we had deserved it, we would have been well and truly flogged – if, that is to say, we had committed some breach of the regulations. That much was demanded by the requirements of duty and equality. But we were never flogged without reason, frivolously; such frivolous treatment was, however, given to the lower-class convicts, particularly by some lower-ranking officers and commanders who liked to take advantage of every possible occasion to wield the big stick. We knew for a fact that when he had got to hear about what had happened to the old man Ż—ski, the prison governor had been very angry with the Major and had told him to exercise more restraint in future. This story was told me by all the men. We also knew that the governor-general, who had trusted our Major and even looked up to him as a practical man of some ability, had himself given the Major a good talking-to when he had found out about the matter. And our Major had taken heed. How, for example, he would have loved to get his hands on M—cki, whom he loathed because of the things A—v reported about him; but he could not flog him, even though he sought every pretext for doing so, made M—cki's life a misery, and watched him constantly. The whole town soon knew about the incident with Ż—ski, and public opinion was not on the Major's side; a lot of people spoke out against him, and some even said unpleasant things about him. I can still remember my first encounter with the Major. While we had still been in Tobolsk, we – myself, that is, and another deported nobleman together with whom I had gone into penal servitude – had been told scare stories about the unpleasant character of this man. Some upper-class deportees who had been in Tobolsk for twenty-five years had received us with great sympathy and had stayed in touch with us all the time we had been in the transit prison, had warned us about our future commander and had promised to do everything they could, through their contacts with acquaintances, to shield us from his persecution. The governor-general's three daughters, who had come over from European Russia and were staying with their father at that time, received letters from them and apparently spoke up for us. But what could their father

do? He simply told the Major to be more careful in future. At about
three o'clock that afternoon, I and my companion arrived in the
town and the guards took us straight to our commander. We stood
around in the vestibule, waiting for him. Meanwhile the prison
duty sergeant was sent for. No sooner had he appeared than the
Major, too, came in. His crimson, pimply and aggressively unpleasant face made us both feel decidedly unwell: he was like some
malignant spider darting out at a poor fly that had been caught in
its web.

'What's your name?' the Major asked my companion. The Major
spoke rapidly, abruptly and jerkily, and was obviously trying to
make an impression on us.

My companion gave his name.

'And yours?' he continued, turning to me, staring at me fixedly
through his glasses.

I, too, gave my name.

'Sergeant! Take them to the prison immediately, see that they have
their heads shaved, civilian style, half the head only; get fetters on
them tomorrow. What are these overcoats you're wearing? Where
did you get them?' he asked suddenly, transferring his attention to
our grey prison coats, with which we had been issued in Tobolsk,
which had yellow circles sewn on their backs, and in which we now
stood before his penetrating gaze. 'This is a new uniform! It must be
some new uniform ... it's still being designed ... in St Petersburg ...'
he said, turning us round, one after the other. 'They've brought
nothing with them?' he suddenly asked the guard who had led us in.

'They've their own clothes, your honour,' replied the guard,
stiffening to attention momentarily with a slight quiver. Everyone
knew about the Major, had heard stories about him: he had
terrorized the lot of them.

'All their clothes are to be confiscated. No, let them keep their
underwear, the white stuff, that is, if there's any coloured stuff
confiscate it. Have it all auctioned. Money to go into the prison
fund. Convicts don't own property,' he continued, looking at us
severely. 'Mind now, you'd better behave yourselves! I don't even
want to know you exist! Or else ... it's cor–poral pu–nishment! Put
one foot wrong and its the r–r–rods! ...'

After this reception I felt positively unwell all evening. These sensations were made worse by what I saw in the prison; but I have already described my entry into it.

I said a moment ago that those put in charge of us did not – did not dare – make any exception for us or give us a lighter workload than that given the other convicts. There was, however, one time when they did attempt to do this: for three whole months B—ski and I were allowed to work as clerks in the engineers' office. But this was done in the greatest of secrecy, and it was the engineering authorities who were responsible. In other words, all the other people in authority knew what was going on, but pretended they did not. This occurred while G—v was still in command. Lieutenant-Colonel G—v was a real godsend to us, though he only stayed with us a short time – no more than six months, if I am not mistaken, and it was possibly even less – before he left for European Russia. He made a deep and lasting impression on the convicts. The convicts did not simply like him, they adored him, if such a word may be used in the present context. How he managed to do it, I have no idea, but he won them over right from the start. 'He's our father, we don't need our own!' the convicts used to say time and time again during the entire period he was in command of the engineering section. I believe he was a thoroughly debauched individual. He was a short man, with an insolent, self-confident look in his eyes. But he was kind to the convicts, kind almost to the point of tenderness, and he really did love them as a father. Why he loved them so much, I cannot say, but he could not see a convict without saying something kind and cheerful to him, without laughing and joking with him. More importantly, there was in his behaviour no trace of authority, nothing even slightly indicative of an unequal, merely official kindness. He was a companion to the men, and very much one of themselves. But in spite of his democratic instinct, the convicts never once made the mistake of treating him with familiarity or lack of respect. Quite the contrary: a convict's face would light up on meeting the commander, and he would take off his cap and smile when he saw him approaching. The commander's every word was cherished as though it were treasure. Such popular men really do exist. He was a man of magnificent bearing, and always

walked gallantly and erectly. 'He's an eagle,' the convicts used to
say of him. There was, of course, nothing he could do to make things
easier for them; he was merely the person in charge of the engineering work, which continued as it had done under all its previous
commanders, following its customary procedures which had been
established long ago once and for all. The most he might do was,
if he came across a working party and saw that the job was finished,
to detain the men for less than the whole of the work period and
to let them go back to barracks before the drum was beaten. But
what the convicts liked was his trust in them, the absence of
nitpicking and irritability in his behaviour, and his total avoidance
of the use of certain abusive forms in his official dealings with them.
I think that if he had lost a thousand rubles, even the most hardened
robber in the prison would, upon finding them, have given them
back to him again. Indeed, I am certain that this would have been
so. With what great fellow-feeling the convicts learned that their
'eagle' commander had had a deadly quarrel with our hated Major.
This had happened during the first month of the commander's time
in the prison. He and the Major had once been in the same regiment
together. They had met like old friends, after not having seen one
another for a long time, and had gone on drinking bouts together.
But suddenly a break had occurred between them. They had
quarrelled, and G—v had become the Major's deadly enemy. It was
even rumoured that on this occasion they had fought, something
that was always perfectly possible where our Major was involved:
he frequently became embroiled in fights. When the convicts got to
hear about this, their joy knew no bounds. 'How could Eight-Eyes
ever cope with a man like him! The commander's an eagle, and
Eight-Eyes is a ...'; and here a word unfit for print was used. The
men were terribly curious to know which of the two had won the
fight. If the rumour about the fight had proved to be untrue (which
possibly was the case), our convicts would have been extremely
annoyed. 'No, of course the commander won,' they said, 'he isn't
big, but he's able to look after himself, and the Major probably
crawled under the bed to get away from him.' But soon G—v left
the prison, and the convicts fell once more into despondency. It is
a fact that all the engineering commanders we had were good men:

three or four of them occupied the post while I was in the prison. 'We'll never get another like him, say what you like,' the convicts would say; 'he was an eagle, an eagle and a friend.' This same G—v was very well disposed towards us noblemen, and near the end of his tenure he sometimes used to have B—ski and myself come and work in the office. After he left, arrangements there were re-established on a more regular basis. Among the engineers there were those (one man, in particular) who viewed us sympathetically. We used to go there and copy documents; our handwriting had even begun to show signs of improvement when suddenly there came a directive from on high, ordering us back to our previous work immediately: someone had informed on us! But it was really just as well: we had both started to grow tired of the office. After this, and for the next two years, B—ski and I hardly ever parted company: we did the same tasks, most often in the workshop. He and I used to spend a lot of time talking together; we would talk about our aspirations, our convictions. B—ski was a fine man, though he had some very strange, even eccentric ideas. There is a certain category of very intelligent human beings that is sometimes prone to become set in thoroughly paradoxical notions. They have suffered so greatly for these in the course of their lives, have acquired them at such a high price, that it is too painful, is indeed impossible for them to give them up. B—ski would wince painfully at every objection I would make, and his replies would be full of sarcasm. It is possible that in many respects he was closer to the truth than I was – I really cannot say. But in the end we parted company, and I found that very hard: we had already shared too much together.

Meanwhile, as the years went by, M—cki seemed to grow more and more gloomy and melancholy. Dejection and anguish were eating him up. Previously, when I had first come to the prison, he had been more sociable and had displayed his true feelings more frequently. When I arrived in prison he had already been there for two years. At first, he showed an interest in much of what had taken place in the outside world during those two years; these were things of which he had had no idea, being cooped up in prison as he was; he would ask me questions, listen, grow excited. But finally, as the years went by, all of this somehow began to concentrate within him, and went to his heart. The coals were being covered by ash. Resentment grew stronger and stronger within him. '*Je hais ces brigands,*' he used to say to me frequently, observing the convicts with loathing. By that time I had become better acquainted with the convicts, but none of my arguments in their favour had any effect on him. He could not understand what I was talking about. Sometimes, however, he would agree with me, almost absent-mindedly; but the following day he would say again, over and over: '*Je hais ces brigands.*' I should note in passing that we often used to talk together in French; because of this, one of the works supervisors, an engineer by the name of Dranishnikov, invented for us the name 'medics', I don't know why. M—cki only showed any signs of animation when he remembered his mother. 'She is old, she is ill,' he would say to me, 'she loves me more than anything else in the world, yet I am here and don't know whether she is still alive or not. It was enough for her to know that I'd been made to run the gauntlet ...' M—cki was not a nobleman and had been subjected to corporal punishment before being deported. As he recalled this, he would grit his teeth and attempt to avert his gaze. Of late he had begun increasingly to go around on his own. One morning at twelve he had been summoned to see the governor. The governor had come out to greet him with a cheerful smile.

'Well, M—cki, and what did you dream about last night?' he had asked.

'I fairly shook all over,' M—cki said, as he told us. 'It was as though someone had stuck a dagger into my heart.'

'I dreamed I got a letter from my mother,' he had replied.

'It's better than that, much better,' the governor had said. 'You're free! Your mother filed a petition ... The petition was granted. Here's a letter from her, and here's the order for your release. You can leave the prison immediately.'

He turned to us, his face pale. He had not really taken the news in. We congratulated him. When we shook hands on it, his hands were cold and trembling. Many of the other convicts also congratulated him, delighted with his good luck.

M—cki became a settler and remained in our town. Soon he was given a job. At first he often used to visit the prison; whenever he was able to, he would tell us various bits of news. Political news was what interested him most.

Besides M—cki, T—ski, B—ski and Ż—ski, there were two other very young men who had been sent here to do short sentences; they were not well educated, but they were honest, straightforward and forthright. A third, A—czykowski, was really just a simpleton, and there was nothing particularly remarkable about him, but a fourth man, B—m, who was already getting on in years, made a thoroughly nasty impression on all of us. I have no idea how he had managed to end up among political offenders such as ourselves; indeed, he did not consider himself one of us. He was a vulgar, petty bourgeois character with the habits and morals of a small shop-keeper grown rich on the petty swindling of his customers. He had no education whatsoever and was quite uninterested in anything apart from his trade. He was a house-painter, an exceptionally good one, marvellous. The prison authorities soon got to hear about his talents, and everyone in the town was soon asking B—m to paint their wall and ceilings for them. Over a period of two years he had painted and decorated nearly all the government apartments. The occupants of the apartments had paid him out of their own pockets, and he had made quite a decent living. But what was best of all was that his companions started being sent out to work with him, too. Two of the three men who invariably accompanied him learned his trade, and one of them, T—rzeweski, began painting as well as B—m himself. Our Major, who also lived in a government house, asked for B—m in his turn and told him to paint all the walls and ceilings. B—m really excelled himself on this occasion – not even the house of the governor-general was so well decorated. The house was wooden, single-storeyed, rather dilapi-dated and very shabby on the outside; inside, however, it was decorated like a palace, and the Major was delighted ... He rubbed his hands and said that now he must certainly get married. 'With a house like this I can't possibly not be married,' he added, earn-estly. He grew more and more pleased with B—m, and also with the other men who worked along with him. The work continued for a whole month. In the course of this month the Major com-

pletely revised his views on political offenders and began to show
them special favours. It got to the point where he eventually
summoned Ż—ski from the prison.

'Ż—ski!' he said. 'I humiliated you. I had you flogged for no
reason, I know that. I'm sorry. Do you understand? I, I'm – sorry!'

Ż—ski replied that he understood.

'Do you understand that I, I, your superior officer, have summoned you in order to beg you for forgiveness? Do you realize what
that means? What are you compared to me? A worm! Less than a
worm – you're a convict. While I, by the grace of God,* am a
Major. A Major? Do you understand that?'

Ż—ski that he understood that, as well.

'Right, then, so I'm making my peace with you. Do you realize
the full extent of what that means? Are you capable of understanding that, of realizing it? Just think about it; I, I'm a Major ...' –
and so it continued.

Ż—ski described this scene to me himself. Apparently that
drunken, cantankerous and disreputable Major did after all possess
some human feelings. Indeed, if one takes into account the nature
of his opinions and his total lack of education, such a deed might
almost have been considered a generous one. But it is quite possible
that the fact that he was drunk had a lot to do with it.

The Major's dream was never realized: he did not get married,
although he had fully determined that he would as soon as his house
had been decorated. Instead of getting married, he had to stand
trial and was ordered to hand in his resignation. During his trial
all his previous sins were dragged out into the open. One must
remember that he had once been the town's governor ... The blow
fell on him unexpectedly. The convicts were wildly delighted with
the news. This was a festival, a celebration! The Major was said to
have wailed like an old woman, and the tears had flooded down his
cheeks. But there was nothing he could do about it: he handed in
his resignation, sold his pair of greys together with all the rest of
his property and sank gradually into destitution. Later on we used

* This, quite literally, was the expression used in my time not only by the Major, but
also by many other commanders of lesser importance, especially those who had risen
from the lower ranks. (*Note by F. M. Dostoyevsky.*)

to encounter him in his old, threadbare civilian frock-coat and his cap that had a cockade on it. He would glare at us convicts resentfully. But all his charisma had vanished along with his uniform: in his uniform he had been an object of terror, a god, but in his frock-coat he suddenly became a complete nonentity, resembling nothing so much as a flunkey. It is remarkable to what a degree the authority of such men is derived from their uniform.

* 9 *

AN ESCAPE

Soon after our Major's forced resignation, some far-reaching changes took place in the prison. Its function as an institution for penal servitude was abolished, and instead a military-style convict battalion was formed, modelled on the convict battalions of European Russia. This meant that deported convicts belonging to the second category were no longer brought to our prison. From now on it began to be populated exclusively by military convicts, by men, that is, who had not been deprived of their statutory rights, men who were soldiers like any other soldiers, except that they had been flogged and sent here to do short sentences (six years maximum), and who when they left the prison went back to their battalions to serve in the ranks, as they had done before. Those who returned to the prison because of a second offence, however, were given a twenty-year sentence, as previously. Even before this change was instituted we had a military category in the prison; but these military convicts had lived among us only because there was nowhere else for them. Now the whole prison had been turned into a military category. Of course, the former penal convicts, the genuine civilian prisoners who had been deprived of all their rights, had been branded and had half their heads shaven, remained in the prison until their sentences were up; no new convicts arrived, and those who remained gradually served out their sentences and left, so that after ten years there was not a single penal convict in our prison. The special category was also retained, and serious military

offenders were still sent there from time to time, pending the
opening in Siberia of projects involving the heaviest forced labour.
And so life for us continued more or less as before: the same
conditions, the same work and almost the same rules and regulations, with the sole exception that the administration altered and
became more complex. A field officer was appointed, a divisional
commander, and also four commissioned officers who did spells of
duty at the prison on a rota basis. The veterans were also abolished;
in their place there were appointed twelve duty sergeants and a
capitaine d'armes. The convicts were divided into units of ten men
each, and corporals were elected from each unit – on a nominal
basis, of course. Needless to say, Akim Akimych was immediately
made a corporal. All this new apparatus, together with the whole
prison with its administrative ranks and its convicts, remained at
the disposal of the governor, who was the highest authority. That
was all that happened. The convicts were naturally very excited
at first; they discussed their new superiors and tried to guess what
they were like. However, when they saw that everything was
basically just the same as it had been before, they immediately
calmed down, and the life of the prison continued in its usual way.
The main thing was that we had all been delivered from the Major;
it was as if everyone could breathe freely again and recover their
lost morale. The convicts lost their intimidated look; each man now
knew that in case of need he could have a word with the person in
charge, that only if some mistake had been made would the innocent ever be made to suffer instead of the guilty. And vodka
continued to be sold in the prison, just as it had been in the past,
and on the same basis, and this in spite of the fact that in place
of the veterans we now had duty sergeants. These duty sergeants
were mostly decent, intelligent men who understood the nature of
their situation. However, some of them initially displayed a feeble
tendency to show off and, because of their inexperience, to treat the
convicts as though they were soldiers. But soon even these came to
understand what was what. Those who took too long in arriving
at such an understanding had the essence of the matter pointed out
to them by the convicts themselves. There were a few rather sharp
skirmishes: for example, the men might bribe a duty sergeant with

liquor, get him drunk, and then inform him in their own way that he had been drinking with them, and that consequently ... The upshot of this was that the duty sergeants looked on indifferently, or rather tried not to see the bladders being brought in and the vodka sold. That was not all: just as the veterans had done, the duty sergeants went down to the bazaar and bought the convicts kalatches, beef and the rest – anything that did not raise too many eyebrows. Why all these changes were made and why convict battalions were introduced, I do not know. It all happened in the final years of my imprisonment. However, I still had two years to live in these new circumstances ...

Am I to describe the whole of that life, all of my years in prison? I think not. If I were to write down in ordered sequence everything that happened, everything I saw and experienced during those years, I would of course end up writing three or four times the number of chapters I have already written. In the end, such a description would become monstrous. All the events could come out sounding the same. This would be particularly so if the reader had already managed, from the chapters I have written so far, to form an even slightly realistic impression of what life was like in the second category of penal servitude. I have tried to depict the whole of our prison and everything I experienced during my years in it as one vivid, graphic picture. I do not know whether I have attained that goal. And indeed, it is not really for me to judge. I am, however, convinced that it is possible for me to conclude my narrative at this point. Moreover, as I write down these memories I am occasionally stricken with depression. In any case, it is hardly possible for me to remember everything. The years that followed have somehow been erased from my memory. I am convinced that I have forgotten many of the things that happened. All that I remember is that all those years, each in essence so similar to the other, passed drearily and sluggishly. I remember those long, tedious days as being monotonous as the dripping of water from the roof after rain. I remember that it was only a passionate desire for resurrection, for renewal, for a new life that strengthened my will to wait and hope. And in the end I did grow stronger: I waited, I counted off each day and, even though there were still a thousand of them left, I

marked them one by one with satisfaction, escorted each, buried it
and at the beginning of each new day felt glad that there remained
not a thousand days, but only nine hundred and ninety-nine. I
remember that during all this time, in spite of having hundreds of
companions, I experienced the most terrible isolation, and in the
end I came to cherish that isolation. Inwardly alone, I reviewed the
whole of my past life, turned everything over in my mind, right
down to the last detail, weighed up my past, imposed an inexorable
and severe judgement on myself, and sometimes even blessed fate
for having sent me such isolation, without which neither this self-
judgement nor this stern review of my past life would have been
possible. What hopes did not beat within my heart in those days!
I thought, I determined, I swore to myself that in my future life
there would be none of those previous mistakes and lapses. I drew
up a mental plan of the future and pledged myself to stick to it.
Once again there rose within me a blind faith that I would fulfil this
plan, that I was capable of doing so ... I eagerly awaited my
freedom, I called upon it to come quickly; I desired to put myself
to the test again in a new struggle. At times I was seized by
convulsions of impatience ... But it is too painful for me to remember now my state of mind at that time. All this affects no one except
myself, of course ... But the reason I have written all this down is
that I believe it will be understood by anyone who serves a prison
sentence in the flower of his years and strength, for the same things
are bound to happen to him.

But why dwell on this? ... I will do better to recount something
else, so as not to make my conclusion too abrupt.

It has occurred to me that someone may ask whether it was really
impossible for anyone to escape from the prison, and whether no
one ever escaped during all those years. I have already said that a
convict who has been in prison for two or three years begins to
attach a certain value to those years, and is forced to the conclusion that it is better to serve out the rest of his term without
making trouble or taking risks, and to leave the prison when his
sentence is over and become a settler in the officially approved
manner. But such a conclusion is only arrived at in the mind of a
convict who has not been sentenced to a long term of imprisonment.

Those with long sentences may be prepared to risk a great deal ...
In our prison there was very little of this kind of thing, however.
I am not sure whether this was because the men there were particularly intimidated, because the supervision was particularly strict
and military, or because the location of our town (exposed and in
the steppe) did not favour such attempts – it is hard to say. I think
perhaps a blend of all these factors played its part. It really was
rather difficult to escape from our prison. Yet one such case did
occur while I was there: two men made an escape attempt, and they
were two of the most serious criminals in the place ...

After the Major's removal from office, A—v (the man who had
been his spy in the prison) had been left completely isolated and
without protection. He was still a very young man, but his character
had grown stronger and more pronounced with the years. He was
on the whole an insolent, decisive man, and of great intelligence.
If he had been given his freedom he would have continued to spy
and to get involved in various underhand dealings, although he
would not have let himself be caught as stupidly and improvidently
as he had the last time, when he had paid for his stupidity with
deportation. Among other things, he practised making forged passports while he was in our prison, though I cannot confirm this with
absolute certainty. I heard from other convicts that this was the
case. They said that he had done work of this kind even during the
period when he had made his visits to the Major's kitchen, and that
he had made quite a reasonable profit out of it. In short, he seemed
to be capable of doing anything that would 'change his fortune'.
I had occasion to experience something of what he was like: his
cynicism reached the most outrageous degree of insolence, the most
cold-blooded mockery, and it aroused an over-mastering revulsion
in me. I think that if he had had a strong desire for a glass of vodka,
and if the only way to obtain a glass of vodka had been to murder
somebody, he would have murdered, as long as he could have done
it on the quiet, without anyone finding out. In the prison he had
learned circumspection. It was to this man that Kulikov, a convict
in the special category, turned his attention.

I have already mentioned Kulikov. He was no longer young, but
he was impetuous, lively and strong, with considerable and various

abilities. There was strength in him, and he still had a desire for life; such men live to a great age. If I had ever started to wonder why nobody ever tried to escape, Kulikov would have been the first person to occur to me in such a connection. Who had the greater influence on whom, A—v on Kulikov or Kulikov on A—v, I do not know, but they were a match for each other and just the right kind of men for such an exploit. They grew friendly. I think that Kulikov was relying on A—v to forge passports for them both. A—v was of noble birth, and had moved in good society: that held a promise of adventures somewhat out of the ordinary, if only they could get to European Russia. Heaven knows what they agreed and what hopes they had; but one thing is certain, and that is that their hopes went well beyond the normal routine of Siberian vagrancy. Prison must have been claustrophobic for men like these. They agreed to escape.

But it was impossible to escape without the connivance of a guard. It was necessary to get a guard to go along with them. In one of the battalions stationed in the fortress there was a Pole, an energetic fellow who perhaps deserved a better fate; he was getting on in years, but he had a great deal of pluck and stamina, and was a serious person. As a young man, when he had only just come to serve in Siberia, he had deserted because of homesickness for his native country. He had been caught, flogged and given two years in the convict battalions. When he had been drafted back into the army again, he had thought the better of his ways and had begun to perform his military service with great zeal, to the best of his ability. He was made a corporal for distinguished service. An ambitious, self-confident man, he knew his own worth. He both looked and spoke like one who knew his own worth. During those years I encountered him several times among our guards. In addition, the Poles told me a few things about him. It seemed to me that his previous depression had become a latent, speechless and obsessive hatred. This man was capable of anything, and Kulikov had not erred in choosing him as a companion. His name was Koller. The two men agreed on a day for their escape. It was June, the hot season. The climate of our town was fairly equable; in summer the weather was settled and hot: just right for vagrants. There was no question of their being able to set off straight from the fortress: th whole town stood in an exposed location, open on all sides. There was no forest for quite some distance around it. They would have to change into civilian clothes, and to do this they would first have to get as far as the suburbs, where there was a hideout Kulikov had known for years. Whether his suburban friends were fully cognizant of what was going on I do not know. One must suppose that they were, though this was not quite cleared up later on, at the trial. In a corner of the suburbs that year a certain young and very prepossessing lady had recently begun her career; her name was Vanka-Tanka, and she held great promise for the future, some of which was later on fulfilled. She was also known as 'The Fire'. She too apparently played a part in the escape. Kulikov had spent the whole year at the point of financial ruin because of her. One morning our bold fellows went out to have their tasks assigned to them as usual and cleverly arranged to be sent out with the convict Shilkin, a stove-maker and plasterer, to plaster the empty barracks of a battalion the soldiers of which had been transferred to a camp some time ago. A—v and Kulikov went along with him as bearers. Koller turned up to act as one of the guards, and since two guards were needed in order to supervise three men, Koller, as corporal and senior army man, was readily given the task of training a young recruit in the duties and responsibilities of being a guard. Our gaol-breakers must have had a very strong pull on Koller, and he must have had a great deal of faith in them to follow them, being as he was an intelligent, down-to-earth, circumspect man who had seen long years of service, of late successful ones.

They arrived at the barracks. It was about six o'clock in the morning. They were the only people around. After they had been working for an hour, Kulikov and A—v told Shilkin that they were going to the workshop to see someone and also to get some imple-ment they appeared to be lacking. They had to deal cunningly with Shilkin, as naturally as possible, in other words. Shilkin was a Muscovite, a stove-maker by trade. He was from a family of Moscow tradesmen, and was crafty, pushing, intelligent and taci-turn. He was frail and emaciated-looking. Ideally he ought to have spent his whole life dressed in a waistcoat and dressing gown,

Moscow-fashion, but fate had decreed otherwise, and after lengthy
wanderings he had settled down in the special category of our
prison, the one that contained the most fearsome military criminals.
What he had done to deserve such a career, I do not know; but he
never seemed particularly discontented; he conducted himself
calmly and meekly; only occasionally he would get as drunk as a
lord, but even then he would behave himself properly. Needless to
say, he was not an accomplice in the escape conspiracy, and his eyes
were keen. Kulikov winked at him and told him they were going
to fetch some vodka which had been hidden in the workshop the
day before. This immediately drew Shilkin's sympathy; he nodded
to them without the slightest suspicion and stayed behind with the
recruit. Kulikov, A—v and Koller set off for the suburbs.

Half an hour went by; the men did not return, and suddenly,
thinking back, Shilkin began to reflect. He had seen a few things
in his time. He began to figure out what had happened: Kulikov
had been in an odd state of mind; A—v had seemed to be whispering to him on two occasions. At any rate, Kulikov had winked at
him a couple of times, he had seen that; now it was all coming back
to him. There had also been something fishy about Koller: at least,
as he had been getting ready to go with the others, he had started
to lecture the recruit on how he should behave himself while they
were gone, and this had not seemed quite natural, not coming from
Koller, at least. In short, the more of such figuring Shilkin did, the
more suspicious he became. Meanwhile time was passing, the three
did not return, and his disquiet grew beyond all bounds. He knew
very well how much he stood to lose by this venture: the suspicions
of the authorities might very well be directed at him. It might be
thought that he had knowingly let his companions leave as part of
a mutual agreement, and if he were to delay reporting the disap-
pearance of the two men these suspicions would acquire an even
greater degree of probability. There was no time to lose. At this
point he remembered that Kulikov and A—v had seemed particularly close of late; they had whispered together frequently, had
often taken walks behind the barracks together, out of sight of
everyone. He remembered that even then he had had certain ideas
about them ... He looked searchingly at his guard: the young

recruit was leaning his elbows on his rifle, yawning and picking his nose with a most innocent air, so that Shilkin did not bother to tell him his thoughts, but simply told him to follow him to the engineering workshop. They must ask if the three men had been there. But it turned out that no one there had seen them. All Shilkin's doubts vanished. If all they had done was to go drinking and having a good time in the suburbs, which was something Kulikov liked doing, Shilkin reflected ... but it could not even be that that had happened now. They would have told him of what they intended to do, as there would have been no point in concealing it. Shilkin stopped work, and not bothering to look in at the barracks, went straight to the prison.

It was almost nine o'clock when he reported to the sergeant major and told him what was up. The sergeant major looked aghast and did not want to believe it at first. Of course, Shilkin presented the whole matter only in the form of a guess, a suspicion. The sergeant major rushed straight off to see the Major. The Major immediately went to see the prison governor. A quarter of an hour later all the necessary measures had been taken. The matter was reported to the governor-general himself. These were serious criminals, and St Petersburg might kick up a big row because they had escaped. Rightly or wrongly, A—v was classified as a political offender; Kulikov belonged to the special category – that is to say he was an arch-criminal, and a military one at that. This was the first case there had ever been of men escaping from the special category. It was recalled among other things that, according to the regulations, each special category convict was supposed to work under the supervision of two guards – at the very least, there was supposed to be one guard for each convict. This regulation had not been observed. The matter looked as though it might have unpleasant consequences. Special couriers were sent around all the rural districts and all the surrounding villages to make proclamations concerning the escaped convicts and to issue descriptions of them. Cossacks were sent out to run them down and capture them; letters were written to the heads of neighbouring districts and provinces ... In short, everyone was in a great flap.

Meanwhile, another sort of excitement began to stir in our

prison. As they came in from work, the convicts immediately
learned what was up. The news quickly got round to all the men.
Everyone heard it with great, concealed joy. Every heart trembled
... Apart from the fact this incident interrupted the monotonous
life of the prison and churned up the ant-hill, this escape, and such
an escape at that, somehow struck a familiar chord in each man's
soul and brushed strings that had long lain forgotten; something
that was akin to hope, courage and the possibility of 'changing
one's fortune' stirred in every heart. 'Those men escaped; so why
... ?' And with this thought each man recovered his lost morale and
looked at the others with a challenging glance. At the very least,
everyone felt suddenly proud and began to look down on the duty
sergeants. Of course, the authorities immediately rushed to the
prison. Even the governor arrived. Our men took heart and looked
bold, even slightly contemptuous, with a kind of stern, silent
gravity, as if to say: 'We know a thing or two.' It goes without
saying that all the convicts had known in advance that the authorities would come to the prison *en masse*. They had also been aware
that there were bound to be searches, and everything had been
hidden away beforehand. They knew that in such cases the authorities were always wise after the event. So it was: there was a great
to-do; everything was searched and rummaged – and nothing was
found, of course. The convicts were sent off to do their afternoon
work under a reinforced guard. By evening the sentries were visiting
the prison every minute; the men were counted an extra time and
twice the usual number of mistakes was made in the process. This
in its turn caused a hullaballoo: everyone was told to go out into
the yard, and the count was made over again. Then we were
counted yet again, this time by barracks ... In short, there was a
great furore.

But the convicts did not turn a hair. They all looked quite
detached and, as always during such incidents, they conducted
themselves with uncommon propriety throughout the whole of that
evening, as if to say 'You won't find fault with us.' The authorities
naturally suspected that the escaped convicts had accomplices
among the prisoners, and gave orders that the men were to be kept
under observation and their conversations monitored. But the

convicts merely laughed. 'No one would ever leave accomplices behind on a job like that!' 'You do a job like that on the quiet or not at all.' 'Would men like Kulikov and A—v leave loose ends lying around on that kind of a business? They've got it all sewn up. Those lads have seen a few things in their time: they can get through locked doors!' In short, Kulikov's and A—v's fame grew far and wide; everyone was proud of them. It was felt that the exploit would be remembered by the most distant generations of convicts, that it would outlive the prison itself.

'Those lads are masters!' some of the convicts said.

'There they were thinking none of us would ever escape. But we escaped!' added others.

'Escaped!' said a third, looking around him with a certain degree of authority. 'Who escaped? ... It wasn't you, was it?'

At any other time, the convict to whom these words had been addressed would have made a challenging reply and defended his honour. But now he was meekly silent. 'Not everyone can be like Kulikov and A—v, that's a fact; deeds before words ...'

'And what are we all doing here anyway, lads?' said a fourth man, breaking the silence. He was sitting unobtrusively by the kitchen window, his cheek propped in his hands. His voice was slightly singsong, slack with a kind of self-satisfied emotion. 'What are we doing here? We're neither alive nor dead. *E–ekh!*'

'Prison's not a shoe. You can't shake it off just like that. What's the *e–ekh* for?'

'But look at Kulikov...' one of the hotheaded convicts, a young, inexperienced lad, broke in.

'Kulikov!' Another took up the refrain at once, looking askance at the greenhorn. 'Kulikov! ...'

This meant: 'There aren't many Kulikovs in the world!'

'And what about A—v, lads, there's a cunning one for you!'

'You bet! He could even turn Kulikov round his finger. He's a slippery customer.'

'I wonder if they've gone far, lads? It'd be good to know ...'

And immediately there began a discussion as to whether they had gone far, in what direction they had gone, where it would be best for them to go and which district was closer. There turned out to be men who knew the surrounding countryside. They talked about the inhabitants of the neighbouring villages and decided they were not the right sort of people. They lived too near the town, they were up to all the tricks. They wouldn't play along with convicts, they'd catch them and give them up to the authorities.

'Those muzhiks round here are an evil breed, lads. Some muzhiks, they are.'

'They're a fickle lot.'

'They're too fond of their stomachs. Don't get caught by them, they'll kill you.'

'Well, but our lads . . .'

'You know whose side they're going to be on. But our lads are not like that.'

'Well, we'll find out, if we don't kick the bucket first.'

'What do you mean? Do you think they'll be caught?'

'They'll never catch them, that's my opinion!' another of the hot-headed convicts chimed in, banging his fist on the table.

'Hm. Well, that's as may be.'

'You know what I think, lads?' Skuratov broke in. 'If I was a vagrant, they'd never catch me!'

'Oh, you!'

Laughter broke out, and the other men pretended not to listen. But Skuratov was losing his self-control.

'They'd never catch me!' he repeated, forcefully. 'I've often thought about it, lads, and I'm surprised at myself: I'd just squeeze through a crack in the wall, and they'd never catch me.'

'What about when you got hungry? You'd end up going to the muzhiks to ask for bread.'

There was general laughter.

'Ask them for bread? No, I wouldn't.'

'You want to watch your tongue. You and your uncle Vasya murdered the cow curse,* that's why you were sent here.'

The laughter grew louder. The serious convicts looked on with even greater indignation.

---

* That is to say, they killed a muzhik or old peasant woman suspecting that he or she had cast an evil spell which made their cattle die. There was among us one such murderer. (*Note by F. M. Dostoyevsky.*)

'That's a lie!' shouted Skuratov. 'It's Mikitka who invented that story about me, and it's not about me, anyway, it's about Vaska, I just got dragged into it at the same time. I'm a Muscovite and I've been used to being a vagrant since I was a kid. When the deacon was teaching me to read and write he used to pull me by the ear and tell me to say: "Support me, O God, by thy great peace, in thy mercy ..." and so on, and I used to say after him: "Report me, O God, to the police, in thy mercy," and that's the kind of thing I've done ever since I was a child.'

Everyone roared with laughter again. That was what Skuratov wanted, however. He could not get along without playing the fool. The men soon left him alone and started a serious discussion once more. Those who did most of the talking were the old men and the gaol-breakers. The younger and quieter men made do with enjoying the spectacle, and they craned their necks forward as they listened. Rather a large crowd had assembled in the kitchen; needless to say, no duty sergeants were present. No one would have dared to say a word if they had been there. Among the men who were enjoying watching the discussion the most I noticed Mametka, one of the Tartars, a short man with high cheekbones, a thoroughly comical individual. He hardly knew a word of Russian, and could understand practically nothing of what the men were saying, but he was craning his neck forward because of the crowd, and listening with pleasure.

'What do you say, then, Mametka, *yakshi* (bad)?' said Skuratov, turning to him for want of anything better to do; he had been abandoned by all the others.

'*Yakshi! Ukh, yakshi!*' muttered Mametka, getting very excited and nodding his comical head at Skuratov – '*yakshi!*'

'They'll not catch them, *yok* (no)?'

'*Yok, yok!*' – and Mametka began to mutter again, this time waving his arms about in the air.

'You mean it's all a lot of hot air, eh?'

'Yes, yes, *yakshi!*' replied Mametka, nodding his head.

'Well, *yakshi* it is, then.'

And Skuratov, giving the Tartar's cap a flip and pulling it over his eyes, went out of the kitchen in the most cheerful frame of mind, leaving Mametka somewhat bewildered.

The intensification of security inside the prison and the increase in the number of raids and searches made in the surrounding countryside continued for a whole week. I do not know how it was, but the convicts always managed to get immediate and precise information about the manoeuvres of the authorities outside the prison. In the first few days the news was all in favour of the escaped convicts: there was not a trace of them, they had simply vanished into thin air. The men laughed. All their concern about the fate of their escaped companions had disappeared. 'They'll not find a thing, they're not going to catch anybody!' they said, pleased with themselves.

'Not a sign of them. Like bullets from a gun, they are.'

'Farewell, don't yearn; I'll soon return!'

It was known among us that all the peasants in the surrounding countryside had been put on the alert, and that every suspicious location, every wood and ravine, was being watched.

'They're crazy,' the convicts said, laughing. 'Our lads are sure to have found somebody to take them in and hide them by now.'

'Of course they have,' said others. 'Those lads aren't daft; they'll have had it all set up beforehand.'

The men went even further in their hypotheses: it was said that the fugitives might still be in the suburbs somewhere, hiding out in a cellar until the 'aggro' was over and the hair had grown back on their heads. They would stay there for six months, a year, and then they would go ...

In short, everyone was in a rather romantic mood. Then suddenly, some eight days after the escape, it was rumoured that the men's trail had been found. This absurd rumour was of course immediately put down with scorn. But that same evening it was confirmed. The convicts began to get uneasy. The following morning people in the town were saying that the escapers had been caught and that they were being brought back to the prison. By afternoon, more details had become available: the men had been caught in a village some seventy versts away. Finally, some precise information came in. (The sergeant major, returning from a visit to the Major, announced as an established fact that the men were to be brought to ·   ·   ʒ and sent straight to the guardhouse.) There was no more room for doubt. It is difficult to convey the effect this news had on the convicts. At first they all seemed to get angry, but then they fell into a kind of melancholy. Later on a feeble attempt at jeering and gibing manifested itself. The convicts began to laugh, not at the capturers but at the captured. At first it was only a few of the men who laughed like this; later on almost everyone joined in, except for a few of the serious, steadfast convicts who were of an independent cast of mind and were not to be put off their mark by a bit of jeering. They observed the frivolity of the mass of their companions with contempt, and said nothing.

In short, to the extent that the convicts had previously sung the praises of Kulikov and A—v, they now reviled them, and even took pleasure in doing so. It was as if they had somehow offended everyone. It was said contemptuously that the fugitives had grown very hungry, that they had not been able to last out and had gone into the village and asked the muzhiks for bread. For a vagrant, this was the last stage of degradation. These stories were, however, untrue. The fugitives had been tracked down; they had tried to hide in some woods; the woods had been surrounded. When the men had seen there was no hope of escaping, they had given themselves up. There had been nothing else left for them to do.

But when that evening the fugitives were actually brought to the prison, bound hand and foot and escorted by gendarmes, all the convicts poured over to the fence to see what was to be done with them. Of course, they could see nothing but the carriages of the Major and the prison governor standing outside the guardhouse. The fugitives were put into a secret cell, fettered, and brought to trial the following day. The jeering and contempt of the convicts soon evaporated. People got to know more details of what had happened, it was realized that there had been no alternative for the men but to give themselves up, and everyone began to follow the judicial proceedings with great sympathy.

'They'll hang a thousand on them,' some said.

'Never mind a thousand,' said others. 'They'll kill them. A—v might get a thousand, lad, but they'll kill the other two, because they're special category.'

Their guesses were incorrect, however. A—v was only given five hundred strokes; his previous good behaviour and the fact that this was his first offence were taken into account. Kulikov was, I believe, given fifteen hundred strokes. The floggings were conducted quite leniently. Being sensible men, the three implicated no one else at their trial, answering clearly and accurately, and saying they had merely escaped from the fortress and had not hidden out anywhere. Koller was the one I felt sorriest for: he had lost everything, every last hope; his sentence was heavier than the others, two thousand, I think it was, and he was sent away from our prison to do his penal servitude elsewhere. A—v was flogged lightly, on compassionate grounds; the doctors saw to this. Afterwards, however, A—v strutted about the hospital, saying that now he was game for anything and that he would do rather better next time. Kulikov conducted himself as he always did – sedately and with decorum, and when he came back to the prison after his flogging, he looked as though he had never been away from it. But the convicts looked at him with different eyes: in spite of the fact that Kulikov always knew how to stand up for himself, in any situation, the convicts somehow lost their respect for him and began to treat him more casually. In short, Kulikov's reputation suffered badly as a result of this escape. Success means so much to human beings ...

* 10 *

LEAVING PRISON

All this took place during the last year of my imprisonment. That last year is almost as memorable to me as my first one; the very last period of my sentence particularly so. But I do not propose to go into all the details. I will mention only that during this year, in spite of all my impatience to be through with my sentence, I found life easier than I had done during all the previous years of my deportation. For one thing, I had many friends and companions among the convicts, who seemed to have finally decided that I was a decent fellow after all. Many of them were devoted to me and sincerely fond of me. 'The pioneer' was almost in tears as he conducted my companion and myself out of the prison; later, after our release, we stayed for another whole month in a government house in the town, and he used to come to see us practically every day, just in order to have a look at us. There were, however, some men who remained sour and forbidding right up to the end, and who evidently found it hard to bring themselves to say a word to me – heaven knows why. It was as if there were an invisible wall between us.

During this last period I received more privileges than at any other time during the whole of my sentence. I discovered some old schoolfriends of mine among the military men in the town. With these I renewed my acquaintance. Through them, I was able to get more money, to write letters home and even to obtain books. I had not read a single book for several years, and it is hard to describe the strange excitement I felt as I read my first book in prison. I remember that I began to read it one evening, after lock-up, and I went on reading all night, until daybreak. It was an issue of some journal or other. I felt as though tidings from another world were hurtling towards me; my previous life rose brightly and vividly before me, and I tried to guess from what I read to what extent I had fallen behind, and what the topics were that occupied men's minds nowadays. I seized on every word, tried to read between the lines, tried to find hidden allusions to the life I had known; I searched for traces of what had stirred informed opinion in my day, and how sad I felt when I realized now the degree to which I was a stranger in this new life, a disjointed member. I would have to get used to this new world, make myself acquainted with this new generation. I read with particularly avid attention those articles that were signed by persons I knew and had previously been close to me ... But there were so many new names: new men had emerged, and I was in a hurry to get to know them; I found it vexing that I had so few books at my disposal and that it was so hard to get hold of them. Previously, during the Major's term of office, bringing books into the prison had been a risky undertaking. If one was searched, there were bound to be questions asked: 'Where did you get these books? Do you have contacts, then? ...' And what could I have replied? So, living without books, I had perforce become immersed in myself; I had set myself questions to answer, had tried to solve them, had at times been tormented by them ... But I shall certainly never be able to describe all that! ...

I had entered the prison in winter, and so it was in winter that I was to leave it, on the same date as that on which I had arrived. With what impatience I awaited the coming of winter, with what satisfaction I observed the end of summer, the fading of the leaves on the trees and the withering of the grass on the steppe. Then summer was over, and the autumn wind began to howl; the first snowflakes began to fall ... At last this winter, so long awaited, had arrived! Sometimes my heart would begin to pound violently as I sensed the great advent of freedom. But it was a strange thing: the more time passed and the nearer the end of my sentence approached, the more and more patient I became. During the last few days I astonished even myself, and I reproached myself: I seemed to have become utterly cold-blooded and indifferent. Many of the convicts who encountered me in the yard during the work break used to congratulate me, saying:

'Well, well, Aleksandr Petrovich, you'll soon be a free man. You'll be leaving us poor sods here.'

'Come now, Martynov, aren't you due for release soon, too?' I would reply.

'Me? No fear. I've got another seven years to slog my way through first.'

And he would heave a sigh, stand still with an absent-minded expression, as though he were gazing into the future ... Indeed, many of the men congratulated me with sincere joy. It seemed to me that all the men had started to be more friendly towards me. I had evidently ceased to be one of them; they were already saying goodbye to me. K—czyński, a Polish nobleman, a quiet, unassuming young fellow, shared my fondness for taking long walks in the yard during the work break. He believed that fresh air and exercise would keep him healthy, and make up for all the harm done by the suffocating nights spent in the barrack. 'I just can't wait for you to be released,' he told me with a smile, when he met me one day out walking. 'When you leave, I'll know that there's exactly one year left until I'm released, too.'

I will observe here in passing that all our daydreaming about it and our lack of habitual contact with it made freedom seem to us in some way freer than freedom itself, the freedom that is to be found in the real world, that is. The convicts had an exaggerated notion of real freedom, and this is a characteristic that is understandably to be found in every prisoner. The down-at-heel personal attendant of some officer or other appeared to us as very nearly a king, because his head was not shaven and he did not wear fetters and walk in the company of a guard.

On the evening of my last day, I took a walk at twilight around the entire length of the prison fence *for the last time*. How many thousands of times I had walked round that fence during those years! Here in the first year of my imprisonment I had wandered alone, friendless and broken in spirit. I remember then how I would count the thousands of days I still had to serve. Lord, how long ago that was! Here, in this corner, our eagle had lived in captivity; this was where I had used often to meet Petrov. Even now he had not left my side. He came running up to me and, as if guessing at my thoughts, walked beside me silently in a kind of private wonderment. Mentally I took my leave of our barracks' blackened, timbered frames. How inhospitable those barracks had seemed to me *then*, at the start of my sentence. Even they must have grown older – but I could see no difference. How much youth had been buried in vain within these walls; how much power and strength had perished here for nothing! For the whole truth must be told: all these men were quite remarkable. These were perhaps the most gifted, the strongest of all our people. But mighty powers had perished in vain, perished abnormally, unlawfully, irrevocably. Yet who is to blame?

That was the question: who was to blame?

Early next morning, before the men went out to work, as it was just beginning to get light, I made the rounds of all the barracks in order to say goodbye to all the convicts. Many a sturdy, calloused hand was extended towards me in friendly greeting. Some of the men shook hands with me in a thoroughly comradely manner, but they were few. Others knew very well that I was soon to become someone very different from themselves. They knew that I had friends in the town, that when I left here I would go straight to *the masters* and would sit down with those masters as an equal. They understood this, and although their farewells were friendly and good-natured, they made them not as to one of their companions but as they would to a 'gentleman'. Some turned away from me and sourly refused to return my farewells. Some even looked at me with a kind of hatred.

The drum was sounded, and all the men set off for work; I, however, remained behind. That morning Sushilov had been practically the first man to get up, and he had exerted all his energies to make tea for me. Poor Sushilov! He wept as I gave him my prison clothes, my shirts, my underfetters and some money. 'That's not it, that's not what I want,' he said, barely managing to keep his lips from trembling. 'How will I ever manage without you, Aleksandr Petrovich? Who'll be left for me when you've gone?' I also said my last goodbyes to Akim Akimych.

'You'll be out soon, too!' I said to him.

'Oh, I shall be here for a very long time yet, sir,' he muttered, as he pressed my hand. I embraced him, and we kissed.

Some ten minutes later the convicts left for work. We, too, left the prison, never to return to it – I, that is, and the companion with whom I had come here. We had to go straight to the smithy to have our fetters removed. But no guard accompanied us with his rifle: instead, we went with a duty sergeant. Some of our convicts removed our fetters in the engineering workshop. I waited as my companion had his fetters taken off, and then went up to the anvil myself. The smiths made me turn round with my back towards them, lifted my leg from behind and placed it on the anvil ... They made a great fuss, trying to do the job as neatly and as efficiently as possible.

'The rivet, turn the rivet first ...' ordered the senior smith. 'Hold it steady, that's right. Now hit it with the hammer ...'

The fetters fell to the ground. I picked them up. I wanted to hold them in my hand, to have a last look at them. Already I could hardly believe they had ever been on my legs at all.

'Well, God go with you!' said the convicts in voices that were curt, gruff, but somehow also pleased.

Yes, God go with you! Freedom, a new life, resurrection from the dead ... What a glorious moment!

NOTES

1 (p. 22) *a settler*: The Russian word is *poselenets*, the designation for someone who had finished his term of penal servitude and had gone to live in one of the Siberian convict settlements. Return to European Russia was not permitted, although Dostoyevsky himself received special permission to do so.

2 (p. 22) *the little town of K.*: Kuznetsk.

3 (p. 32) *kalatches*: White bread rolls.

4 (p. 33) *so now we have to walk the green street*: 'Walking the green street' meant running the gauntlet in convict parlance.

5 (p. 36) *the famous system of solitary confinement*: Tsar Nicholas I had proposed the introduction of one-man cells in Russian prisons similar to those found in London penal institutions. In 1845 a special commission had been set up to develop and implement such a project.

6 (p. 42) *take a copeck in the name of Christ*: This autobiographical episode is repeated by Dostoyevsky in his novel *Crime and Punishment* (Part II, Chapter 2).

7 (p. 49) *Bender pox*: This was the popular name for the plague epidemic which raged in Moldavia, Wallachia and Bessarabia from 1765 until 1772, and which eventually spread to Kiev and Moscow, causing considerable public disorder.

8 (p. 52) *The chieftain of one of the neighbouring peaceful tribes*: During the war for the annexation of the Caucasus, the mountain tribesmen were referred to as 'peaceful' (*mirnyye*) and 'hostile' (*nemirnyye*).

9 (p. 53) *Kantonist*: A soldier's son, who on the day of his birth became a member of the military and was subsequently educated in a military academy. This reservist category existed until 1856.

10 (p. 61) *an Old Believer, an old man who had come to us from the settlements of former Vetka schismatics at Starodubye*: An Old Believer is a Russian Orthodox believer who does not accept the liturgical reforms introduced by Patriarch Nikon in the mid

seventeenth century. Starodubye, a country district of Chernigov province, was a centre for Old Believers, who settled there at the time of the liturgical dispute. In the face of religious persecution the schismatics fled Starodubye, settling on the island of Vetka on the river Sozh. In 1764, on the ordering of Catherine II, they were driven from Vetka and returned to Starodubye.

11 (p. 61) *a Yedinover church*: The Yedinovers were a sect of Old Believers who made a partial union with the established Russian Orthodox Church and submitted to the Synod in 1800. The Yedinovers agreed to accept established Orthodox priests on condition that they be allowed to retain certain rituals, together with the pre-Nikonite service books.

12 (p. 62) *it seems to me that it is possible to tell a man by his laugh*: Dostoyevsky develops this idea in his novel *A Raw Youth* (Part III, Chapter 1).

13 (p. 80) *on the evening before he was due to be beaten*, etc.: Dostoyevsky alludes to this same episode in his tale *Uncle's Dream* (Chapter XV).

14 (p. 84) *Such an outfit was known as a* maydan: *Maydan* is a form of the Turkish *meydan* = a village market place. In Russian thieves' slang *maydan* meant 'a gambling den' or simply 'a game of cards'.

15 (p. 93) *the Jew Yankel in Gogol's* Taras Bulba: Yankel appears in Chapters X–XI of *Taras Bulba*. In his youth Dostoyevsky had written a play called *The Jew Yankel*.

16 (p. 104) *Meshchansky Streets*: St Petersburg had three Meshchansky Streets – Bolshaya (Great), Srednyaya (Middle) and Malaya (Little). They were notorious for their gambling dens and drinking saloons.

17 (p. 105) *almost as good as Bryullov*: K. P. Bryullov (1799–1852), the famous Russian portrait painter.

18 (p. 133) *Napoleon*: Reference is to Napoleon III (1808–73), President of the Second Republic of France, who in 1852 proclaimed himself Emperor. He was Napoleon I's nephew.

19 (p. 134) *Countess Lavallière*: The Duchess Lavallière was a favourite of Louis XIV. She is mentioned by Dumas *père* in his novel *Le Vicomte de Bragelonne*.

20 (p. 139) *They are not men of words*, etc.: Compare this with a similar passage in *Notes from Underground* (Part I, Chapter 3).

21 (p. 142) *Ch—v, K—v*: The towns are evidently Chernigov and Kiev.

22 (p. 164) *the Tsar's emblem*: This was the *zertsalo*, a trihedral prism displaying the ukases of Peter the Great concerning observation of the law: it was employed in Russian legal institutions as an emblem of justice.

23 (p. 165) *there were only three such days in the year*: The other two days were at Easter.

24 (p. 168) *For some unknown reason hay was always spread on the barrack floors at Christmas*: The hay-spreading was to signify Christ's birth in the manger, and is an old Russian tradition.

25 (p. 185) Filatka and Miroshka, *or* The Rivals: *Filatka and Miroshka the Rivals, or Four Grooms and One Bride* was a popular vaudeville by the St Petersburg actor P. G. Grigoriev (1807–54). It is mentioned in Gogol's *Nevsky Prospekt*.

26 (p. 186) Kedril the Glutton: 'Kedril' is a corruption of 'Pedril' or 'Pedrillo'. A 'Fragment of the Comedy of Don Juan and Don Pedro' is found in the anthology *Russian Dramatic Works of 1672–1725*, compiled by N. S. Tikhonravov (St Petersburg, 1874), and it is on this fragment that *Kedril the Glutton* must have been based.

27 (p. 200) *The orchestra struck up the Kamarinskaya*: The Kamarinskaya is an orchestral composition by the Russian composer M. I. Glinka (1804–57).

28 (p. 200) *The 'pantomime with music'*: The plot of this pantomime was well-known, and resembles an episode in Gogol's *Christmas Eve*.

29 (p. 203) *'The Sun is Going Down' rang out*: This was a song by S. Mitrofanov.

30 (p. 210) *T—k*: Evidently Tobolsk.

31 (p. 232) *a booming laugh like that of Gogol's Nozdryov*: Nozdryov is a character in Gogol's *Dead Souls*.

32 (p. 232) *those days of which 'the legend's fresh, but scarce to*

be believed': A quotation from the play *Woe from Wit* by A. S. Griboyedov (Act II, scene 2).

33 (p. 238) *a touch of Manilov-like sentimentality*: Manilov is a character in Gogol's *Dead Souls*.

34 (p. 262) torban: A stringed instrument related to the bandore.

35 (p. 275) *receive me, O Lord, even as the robber*: Cf. the Prayer of St Basil the Great, which contains the passage: 'Receive me, then, O Lord and lover of mankind, even as the harlot, as the robber, as the publican, as the prodigal ...' (*The Orthodox Liturgy*, SPCK, 1982).

36 (p. 323) *some of these Poles*: These were Polish revolutionaries. Their names were Szymon Tokarzewski (the author of *Siedem lat katorgi*, a memoir of seven years' penal servitude in the Omsk prison, published in 1907), Aleksander Mirecki (who first appears in the *Notes* in the course of Part I, chapter 2), Józef Bogusławski, Józef Żochowski, Karol Bem, Józef Anczykowski, Ludwik Korczyński and Jan Musiałowicz.

37 (p. 324) *U—gorsk*: The town of Ust-Kamenogorsk.

READ MORE IN PENGUIN

In every corner of the world, on every subject under the sun, Penguin represents quality and variety – the very best in publishing today.

For complete information about books available from Penguin – including Puffins, Penguin Classics and Arkana – and how to order them, write to us at the appropriate address below. Please note that for copyright reasons the selection of books varies from country to country.

In the United Kingdom: Please write to *Dept. EP, Penguin Books Ltd, Bath Road, Harmondsworth, West Drayton, Middlesex UB7 ODA*

In the United States: Please write to *Consumer Sales, Penguin USA, P.O. Box 999, Dept. 17109, Bergenfield, New Jersey 07621-0120*. VISA and MasterCard holders call 1-800-253-6476 to order Penguin titles

In Canada: Please write to *Penguin Books Canada Ltd, 10 Alcorn Avenue, Suite 300, Toronto, Ontario M4V 3B2*

In Australia: Please write to *Penguin Books Australia Ltd, P.O. Box 257, Ringwood, Victoria 3134*

In New Zealand: Please write to *Penguin Books (NZ) Ltd, Private Bag 102902, North Shore Mail Centre, Auckland 10*

In India: Please write to *Penguin Books India Pvt Ltd, 706 Eros Apartments, 56 Nehru Place, New Delhi 110 019*

In the Netherlands: Please write to *Penguin Books Netherlands bv, Postbus 3507, NL-1001 AH Amsterdam*

In Germany: Please write to *Penguin Books Deutschland GmbH, Metzlerstrasse 26, 60594 Frankfurt am Main*

In Spain: Please write to *Penguin Books S. A., Bravo Murillo 19, 1° B, 28015 Madrid*

In Italy: Please write to *Penguin Italia s.r.l., Via Felice Casati 20, I–20124 Milano*

In France: Please write to *Penguin France S. A., 17 rue Lejeune, F–31000 Toulouse*

In Japan: Please write to *Penguin Books Japan, Ishikiribashi Building, 2–5–4, Suido, Bunkyo-ku, Tokyo 112*

In Greece: Please write to *Penguin Hellas Ltd, Dimocritou 3, GR–106 71 Athens*

In South Africa: Please write to *Longman Penguin Southern Africa (Pty) Ltd, Private Bag X08, Bertsham 2013*

PENGUIN AUDIOBOOKS

A Quality of Writing that Speaks for Itself

Penguin Books has always led the field in quality publishing. Now you can listen at leisure to your favourite books, read to you by familiar voices from radio, stage and screen. Penguin Audiobooks are ideal as gifts, for when you are travelling or simply to enjoy at home. They are produced to an excellent standard, and abridgements are always faithful to the original texts. From thrillers to classic literature, biography to humour, with a wealth of titles in between, Penguin Audiobooks offer you quality, entertainment and the chance to rediscover the pleasure of listening.

You can order Penguin Audiobooks through Penguin Direct by telephoning (0181) 899 4036. The lines are open 24 hours every day. Ask for Penguin Direct, quoting your credit card details.

Published or forthcoming:

Emma by Jane Austen, read by Fiona Shaw

Persuasion by Jane Austen, read by Joanna David

Pride and Prejudice by Jane Austen, read by Geraldine McEwan

The Tenant of Wildfell Hall by Anne Brontë, read by Juliet Stevenson

Jane Eyre by Charlotte Brontë, read by Juliet Stevenson

Villette by Charlotte Brontë, read by Juliet Stevenson

Wuthering Heights by Emily Brontë, read by Juliet Stevenson

The Woman in White by Wilkie Collins, read by Nigel Anthony and Susan Jameson

Heart of Darkness by Joseph Conrad, read by David Threlfall

Tales from the One Thousand and One Nights, read by Souad Faress and Raad Rawi

Moll Flanders by Daniel Defoe, read by Frances Barber

Great Expectations by Charles Dickens, read by Hugh Laurie

Hard Times by Charles Dickens, read by Michael Pennington

Martin Chuzzlewit by Charles Dickens, read by John Wells

The Old Curiosity Shop by Charles Dickens, read by Alec McCowen

PENGUIN AUDIOBOOKS

Crime and Punishment by Fyodor Dostoyevsky, read by Alex Jennings

Middlemarch by George Eliot, read by Harriet Walter

Silas Marner by George Eliot, read by Tim Pigott-Smith

The Great Gatsby by F. Scott Fitzgerald, read by Marcus D'Amico

Madame Bovary by Gustave Flaubert, read by Claire Bloom

Jude the Obscure by Thomas Hardy, read by Samuel West

The Return of the Native by Thomas Hardy, read by Steven Pacey

Tess of the D'Urbervilles by Thomas Hardy, read by Eleanor Bron

The Iliad by Homer, read by Derek Jacobi

Dubliners by James Joyce, read by Gerard McSorley

The Dead and Other Stories by James Joyce, read by Gerard McSorley

On the Road by Jack Kerouac, read by David Carradine

Sons and Lovers by D. H. Lawrence, read by Paul Copley

The Fall of the House of Usher by Edgar Allan Poe, read by Andrew Sachs

Wide Sargasso Sea by Jean Rhys, read by Jane Lapotaire and Michael Kitchen

The Little Prince by Antoine de Saint-Exupéry, read by Michael Maloney

Frankenstein by Mary Shelley, read by Richard Pasco

Of Mice and Men by John Steinbeck, read by Gary Sinise

Travels with Charley by John Steinbeck, read by Gary Sinise

The Pearl by John Steinbeck, read by Hector Elizondo

Dr Jekyll and Mr Hyde by Robert Louis Stevenson, read by Jonathan Hyde

Kidnapped by Robert Louis Stevenson, read by Robbie Coltrane

The Age of Innocence by Edith Wharton, read by Kerry Shale

The Buccaneers by Edith Wharton, read by Dana Ivey

Mrs Dalloway by Virginia Woolf, read by Eileen Atkins

READ MORE IN PENGUIN

A CHOICE OF CLASSICS

Anton Chekhov	**The Duel and Other Stories**
	The Kiss and Other Stories
	Lady with Lapdog and Other Stories
	The Party and Other Stories
	Plays (The Cherry Orchard/Ivanov/The Seagull/Uncle Vanya/The Bear/The Proposal/A Jubilee/Three Sisters)
Fyodor Dostoyevsky	**The Brothers Karamazov**
	Crime and Punishment
	The Devils
	The Gambler/Bobok/A Nasty Story
	The House of the Dead
	The Idiot
	Notes from Underground and **The Double**
Nikolai Gogol	**Dead Souls**
	Diary of a Madman and Other Stories
Mikhail Lermontov	**A Hero of Our Time**
Karl Marx	**Capital** (in three volumes)
	Early Writings
Alexander Pushkin	**Eugene Onegin**
Leo Tolstoy	**Anna Karenin**
	Childhood/Boyhood/Youth
	The Cossacks/The Death of Ivan Ilyich/Happy Ever After
	The Kreutzer Sonata and Other Stories
	Master and Man and Other Stories
	Resurrection
	The Sebastopol Sketches
	War and Peace
Ivan Turgenev	**Fathers and Sons**
	First Love
	A Month in the Country
	On the Eve
	Rudin